THE
SCORPION
AND THE
NIGHT
BLOSSOM

月落花如血

BOOKS BY AMÉLIE WEN ZHAO

THE SONG OF THE LAST KINGDOM DUOLOGY
Song of Silver, Flame Like Night
Dark Star Burning, Ash Falls White

THE BLOOD HEIR SERIES
Blood Heir
Red Tigress
Crimson Reign

AMÉLIE WEN ZHAO

THE SCORPION AND THE NIGHT BLOSSOM

月落花如血

HARPER

Voyager

Harper*Voyager*
An imprint of HarperCollins*Publishers* Ltd
1 London Bridge Street
London SE1 9GF

www.harpercollins.co.uk

HarperCollins*Publishers*
Macken House,
39/40 Mayor Street Upper,
Dublin 1
D01 C9W8
Ireland

First published by HarperCollins*Publishers* Ltd 2025
1

This one's for the C-drama girlies.

1

The nights have been longer and more beautiful since their world began to bleed into ours. It also gives them more time to hunt. But tonight, I will not be prey.

Through the silk-spun mist, moonlight catches on the wicked curves of my crescent blades, two snug against my palms and six more tucked up my sleeves and bodice for quick access. My thumbs rest against the grooves of the unique talismans engraved on the hilts by my father. The magic of these talismans, activated with a touch of spirit energy, amplifies the power of my blades and makes them lethal weapons against demons.

I move quietly through the fog, each step carefully stitched between silvergrasses and pines, weaving in a manner that renders me ghostly on a mountaintop dulled to shadows and smoke. My senses are weaker than theirs—it's hard hearing past my own breathing—so I don't know if any are waiting for me out here in the dark. If they are, I'm prepared. I've spent years learning how to fight them.

Not by choice, of course. I once had a normal life as the daughter of a seamstress in our village. My sister and I grew up surrounded by fine needles and soft silks, in patterns both beautiful and ordinary, that we delivered all across the Central Province. But then the Kingdom of Night broke the Heavenly Order across the realms, destroyed the border wards that kept our realms separate, and demons—mó—began to invade the Kingdom of Rivers, the mortal world. Soon our emperor and his armies fell to the powerful demon queen, then province after province collapsed, and the immortals in the Kingdom of Sky raised the wards on their realm and left us on our own.

I was ten years old the night the ministry of my province dissolved. I swapped needles for knives, silks for talisman spells, and lost my father in a lesson I will never forget.

Nine years later, I am still alive.

And tonight, I will not be prey.

When the sound of rushing water threads through the trees and the ground begins to flatten, relief lightens my chest. I've survived another trip to the moon spring at the summit of the westernmost mountain range of our kingdom. I will harvest light lotuses: flowers that drink in the magic of stars and are rich with the life energy that fuels our mortal souls. I will return to my village of Xī'lín and grind the petals and seeds into an elixir.

And my mother will live for a few months more.

Waves lap at the root of a great willow, swallowing the grass and muddy banks at my feet. I push past the curtains of wisteria that grow thickly around the spring—and freeze.

Beneath the moonlight filtering through the fog, the water is red.

My senses sharpen. Too late, I catch the sweetly putrid

stench in the breeze. Too late, I notice the shadow in the middle of the spring. As fear tightens my chest, I feel the press of its gaze upon me.

Demon.

Mó take on a human appearance; beneath their beauty are their true monstrous forms, yet on the surface, there isn't much to differentiate them from mortals. This one has taken the form of a young man. Through the branches of the willow, I see the powerful muscles of his shoulders, the spill of his hair in the moonlight. He carries a fresh, half-eaten corpse in his arms, blood spattering his chest. I am relieved to see it. Only the young, lesser mó will consume mortal flesh. The Higher Ones are less inclined toward the taste of our flesh; they prefer our souls.

The young male holds his hand out toward me.

"*Come.*" His voice is song. The air heats with the signature dark energy of their kind, and I feel the power of his magic in that command. It's a spell that mortals are powerless to resist.

Most mortals.

Unbeknownst to the mó, I'm holding Shield, the first of my father's crescent blades that I learned to use. Shield has a talisman that blocks attacks—including magical ones.

I tap my thumb to the blade's hilt and push a small spark of spirit energy against the engraved talisman. I sense it activate, its power flowing through me to resist the dark magic of the mó's command.

I will my body to relax. As much as I hate it, I have to play the part of prey. In fighting the mó, I have only two advantages: that of surprise and that of being underestimated. I can't let this demon know that I am armed against his magic . . . or that I have magic of my own.

Though all mortals are born with life energy flowing red in our veins, few of us are able to channel spirit energy: the life force and magic of immortals and, some say, the gods. Those of us with the ability to do so are named practitioners: warrior-magicians who dedicate our lives to learning the martial arts and cultivating our magic.

Most died in the war against the Kingdom of Night.

I brush aside the willow branches and step into the water.

Moonlight bathes me, almost too brightly. My reflection is silver in the bloody water, and as the mó's gaze snaps onto me, I know what he sees. I'm dressed in the breezy gauzes and pretty silks of a village maiden. My hair is in a long, loose braid woven through with a chaste white ribbon, a few strands curling over my cheeks, the soft nape of my neck. My crescent blades are hidden away in sheaths sewn into my wide sleeves, courtesy of my sister's clever design. Most important, a protective jade pendant hangs against my collarbone, safely tucked beneath the collar of my dress.

The mó watches with interest, and I return his gaze. This part isn't hard. Like all beings of his kind, he is beautiful, the perfectly honed edge of a silver blade: black hair that falls like a living shadow down his back. Skin that looks sculpted, unmarred by scars or any of the traces that illness leaves on us mortals. It is a cruel design of nature that takes advantage of our most primitive instincts: create something so impossibly, perfectly beautiful to lure prey in, and give it unmatched power.

It is no wonder mortals are dying out.

The mó drops the corpse he's been feasting on. I try not to glance at the flash of entrails and hair at the edges of my vision as his victim falls into the water with a splash. I only hope it does not ruin the lotuses that I need for my mother.

I keep my smile, hoping the mó does not hear my quickening heartbeat as he draws closer. It is unsettling, not knowing if my hunter will eat me or ravish my body or drink my soul. Or perhaps all three.

The mó rises from the water and approaches me. This one is naked, confirming my theory that he is young: more animalistic in nature, not yet having learned human customs. Water sluices off his powerful muscles as he stops before me. His tongue darts out, and his eyes roam over me with unabashed hunger.

Disturbing as it is that the mó mirror our bodies, I find it worse that they also mirror our physical needs: hunger, thirst, lust, exhaustion. The only difference is that they feast on *our* flesh and drink *our* souls.

The worst? They don't even *need* them to survive. To them, our flesh and souls simply taste like honey. Like sunlight. Like sweet morning dew. I know this because one of them told me as she drank my father's soul. I will never forget her smile and the way she licked her lips, the casual cruelty of her laughter while I watched.

I force myself to stand very still as the mó closes the distance between us. His smile is almost lazy as he lifts a hand and runs it down my cheek. I suppress a shiver at how warm his skin is, how human he appears despite being a creature of yīn, of darkness and night and moon.

The mó catches my shudder and inhales, mistaking it for desire. His eyes—deep red like those of all beings from the Kingdom of Night—darken with want.

Two can play at this game. My maiden's outfit has tricked him into lowering his defenses. He thinks me a powerless mortal girl—not a trained practitioner who is capable of putting up a fight.

As the mó lowers his mouth to my throat, I strike.

There are three key differences between mó and mortals. One slash to the major artery on his neck reveals the first: instead of blood, out pours a substance resembling black smoke. Mó's ichor is poisonous to mortals, known to cause paralysis and pain. I pivot away, and my second crescent blade—Poison, named for its talisman—bites deep into his neck.

The mó lets out a snarl, an inhuman sound reminding me of just exactly what he—it—really is. As he jerks away, my lips curl in grim satisfaction. It's too late: poison has begun to spread through his veins.

The third crescent blade I select, which I've named Striker, is reinforced with a talisman that gives it extra power as I drive it into the demon's chest—into the soft spot between the ribs. The second difference: in the place of a mortal's heart, the mó have cores of dark magic.

The demon's scream sounds uncannily human, but I grit my teeth and follow him like we are in a twisted dance as he stumbles back, trying to extricate himself from my blade.

My blade has cut through his core. I will my gaze to never stray from his face as his flesh cracks like porcelain, melting away into the smoke and shadows that make up these creatures. I savor the fear in his eyes, the ichor dripping down my blade, and for a moment, I'm ten years old again, crouched in the kitchen with my mother's prone body in my arms, shielding my baby sister from the sight of the woman who was not a woman drinking my father's soul. For a moment, the events of that night unwind, but I shake them off and know that I am not a helpless child anymore. I am powerful, and I am the hunter.

I twist Striker one more time, and the blade finishes its work. With a guttural scream, the demon's body dissolves in a swirl of shadows, a melting face, a pair of glowing red eyes, twisting horns and pointed ears—its true form beneath its beautiful mortal skin, and echoes of the dark energy that once made up its core. In a last gasp, it rushes toward me.

I force myself to remain still. When I blink again, there is only wind in my face, the faint rustle of the willow leaves and wisteria at my back.

The final difference: mortals have souls, but demons don't. Few of our souls make it to reincarnation, but the mó simply dissolve, leaving nothing of what they once were in this world.

I exhale sharply and examine my hands. My fingers tremble as I clean my blades in the water, careful not to touch the ichor steaming from their steel.

One day, I will be strong enough to no longer be afraid.

A flick of my wrists and Poison, Striker, and Shield are back in my sleeves. The water runs red, soaking me up to my waist and staining my dress, but I can't help thinking there is a twisted beauty to the sight of the light lotuses drifting white against the crimson. My stomach tightens, though, at the sight of how meager their numbers have become.

I wade through the bloody water and harvest them, counting each one: six precious flowers, six months of my mother's life. I will brew them tonight and store them—one vial for one month. Harvest them too early or store them for too long, and they lose their effectiveness.

This should be enough to last Mā for the next season.

These trips have come to define my life, as though my existence is meted out one season at a time, one vial of elixir for each cycle of the moon. Just one lotus can replenish the life energy of an injured practitioner, even bring someone back from the brink of death. They are rare. And with the ever-darkening night, they are dying out.

That's why this is my last trip for the next few months. I can no longer depend on light lotuses to sustain my mother's life. I need something stronger, something that will mend a half-devoured soul. Something that exists in the fabled realm of immortals, across the border in the Kingdom of Sky.

I cradle the lotuses against my chest. Tonight, though, this is enough.

I tuck them carefully into the concealed pockets in my bodice. Then I turn away from the blood-soaked spring and the dead human body and wade back up to the bank.

My sister will be so upset that I've ruined the dress she made me.

It's nearing dawn when I return home. Unlike most other villages, Xī'lín did not fortify its walls in the war against the Kingdom of Night. Instead, my father and the other village practitioners set up magical wards all around the periphery to keep out anything non-mortal.

Nine years later, our village still stands, one of the last in the Central Province. The mó attacked our province first, breaking the wards between realms so they could take down our emperor and his army in the Imperial City. The devastation quickly spread throughout the province as the demon armies fed on us and our soldiers. But I've heard rumors that life remains somewhat normal in the Northern, Southern, Eastern, and Western Provinces, especially far out toward the borders of the mortal realm and the Four Seas of the dragon realms. As the months turned to years and the mó remained in the Imperial City, folks in the Central Province began to migrate to the outskirts of the kingdom.

I enter our village through the pái'fāng, feeling the faint swirl of spirit energy as the wards' magic brushes against my skin. Inside the gate, the rows of clay houses with their gray-tiled roofs and curving eaves sit silent on either side of the dusty road. Once, hawkers would have been setting up their tarps along the streets, ready to receive traders from the Silk Trail that wound through the Kingdom of Rivers.

Now the Trail is gone, as are most of the Xī'lín villagers. I don't know why Bà didn't just pack our bags and migrate south toward the sea in the early days. But I'm still here. I tell myself it's because I'm not strong enough to take my mother and my little sister beyond the protected borders of Xī'lín on a journey through the mó-infested province. Yet there's another reason, one that I've kept to myself. Leaving feels like abandoning the last traces of Bà that remain in this world. Leaving feels like giving up.

My house sits on a corner, with an old plum blossom tree bent over it. My father loved this tree; he named both me and my sister after it. And it saved my life when I was born.

When I step through the rickety bamboo door, everything is as I left it. The lanterns are unlit, the shutters tightly closed, though a pale predawn light seeps through the cracks, revealing the silhouette of my mother. She is curled up on the birchwood bed that doubles as her seat during the daytime.

"Mā, I'm back," I say softly, striding over and placing a kiss on her forehead. She is perfectly tucked beneath our finest blankets, and I brush a hand over the little chrysanthemum flowers Méi'zi sewed for her. I can see in the semidarkness that my mother's eyes are open.

I turn away. "Did you sleep well?"

Silence.

"I had a good trip," I continue, moving to unload my pack. "The flowers are still in bloom: peonies and orchids, osmanthus and cherry blossoms. You'd love them, Mā—and so would Bà. And I saw a giant carp. You used to tell me stories of how they were descended from the dragons of the Four Seas, do you remember?"

No response.

Gingerly, I take out the light lotuses. They're still glowing softly, as if I hold stars in my palms. I set a kettle of water to boil, then rinse the flowers in the water bucket.

"I came across one." My words are no longer light and cajoling. "A young male, newly formed." A flash of his beautiful face, the body with the entrails showing. "I took him down in two strokes, Mā. Poison first, to slow him and distract him—then Striker to his core. Bà would be proud, right?"

Nothing.

I grasp the pestle and mortar and begin to crush the light lotuses. They are meant to be sacred, containing the life energy of stars, and it always feels as though I am committing a sin, taking them and grinding them up.

I no longer care. I would commit a thousand lifetimes of sin if that meant I could protect my family.

I'm careful to scrape every last piece into the kettle to stew. Once the flowers are brewing, I take the bucket of water and sit by my mother.

"Come, let's get you up," I murmur. She's nothing but skin and bones, and I am afraid my coarse hands will snap her as I bring her into a sitting position. Méi'zi usually does this. She is much better at it—at being gentle, at taking care of things— but I wanted to do it today, since this is my last day here.

I dip the towel into the water bucket and turn to Mā. The sun is nearly out, and light filters through our wooden shutters onto my mother's face. My breath hitches for a moment.

Her eyes are wide open, and they are staring at me. There is no flicker of recognition in them. Wisps of her hair—now completely white—fall into her face, and she makes no motion to brush them aside. Her mouth is slack; a line of drool winds down her chin.

Every so often, there are moments that nearly break me. This is one of them.

It is one thing to die. I miss my father more than life, but that is an old pain, a scar that has grown over even if it will never truly heal.

My mother is a wound in my chest that tears itself open sunrise after sunrise. To see her alive yet not, existing with a half-devoured soul, is a reminder of everything I have lost and everything I might still save.

Of all that has befallen us, it is the cruelty of hope that hurts the most.

I lower my gaze to her swollen hands, reminding myself of how those fingers taught me to sew. My eyes heat, and for a moment, I wish I were back in the spring with that demon.

I swallow hard, pick up my mother's arm, and begin washing her.

Throughout nine years of searching, I have never come across anything similar to what's become of my mother. I've seen the shriveled corpses mó leave in the wake of their feasting, but I always thought drinking a mortal's soul meant killing us outright—that is, until my father threw himself at the demon drinking my mother's soul before the mó had completely finished. Sometimes, I look up at the doorway and still expect to see my father lying there, clutched in the demon's grasp and bleeding out, his hands clawing the floor as she covered his mouth with hers and drank his life from him.

Most of all, I remember that demon's face. I remember how she stood gracefully afterward and conversed with me, my father's blood still staining her teeth. I remember the flash of garnet winking in the sunlight, the hoops of her hair done in imperial fashion, and the rustle of her clothes, spun of the finest samite. I remember the cruel, impossible beauty of her face. And I wonder, for the thousandth time, why she did this. Why she killed only my father, then left me, my sister, and a half-dead mother to live in the debris of her destruction.

She is the reason I am leaving my family today to journey to the Temple of Dawn, the fabled practitioning school in the immortal realm.

"Yīng'ying?"

I look up. As my sister bounds into the living room, the memories I hold in the dark of my mind fall away and it is as if the sun shines again.

When my father named us, he might as well have prophesied our lives. My name, Àn'yīng, is an uncommon one, meaning "cherry blossom in the dark." I was born during the thickest blizzard of the winter. My father said he had been lost in the snow, half-frozen and unable to find his way home, when he saw a flash of red in the dark: miraculously, a single blossom on our tree was in bloom. It was then that he heard my cries, which he said had guided him safely home.

When my sister was born, it was the warmest day of spring. She was named Chūn'méi, after the flowering plum in our yard.

Bà made a mistake in naming me, though. The tree outside our home is a plum blossom, not a cherry blossom. Strange, for Bà never made mistakes. He only made puzzles, and secrets to those puzzles. Secrets that he took to his grave.

"You tricked me *again!*" Méi'zi exclaims, her mouth puckered as she glares at me. "You promised you wouldn't leave for the mountains without telling me." Her gaze travels to the towel in my hands and the bucket at my feet. "And that's *my* job."

Méi'zi's and my appearances seem to reflect our names, too. Where she takes after Mā, with her large brown eyes, open face, and soft features, I am cut to be more angled, my face narrower and my eyes as black as Bà's were. Méi'zi was always the one beloved and favored by the villagers; I, much less so.

I catch my sister's wrist as she swipes for the towel. Her hands are soft, fine, and delicate, made for threading silk through needles and spinning fabrics into dresses. Over the years, she's grown calluses from the rough work we've had to do to survive, but nothing like my own—and I intend to keep it that way, just as I promised our father. Méi'zi was five when the war against the Kingdom of Night broke out, and she does not remember much of the life we lived before nor of the parents we lost.

"I want to do this today," I tell her, pushing her hand back and returning to scrub at a sore on my mother's back. "Why don't you make breakfast?"

Something in my tone makes her look up, her eyes catching the first rays of sunlight like honey. Her hair, long and wavy unlike my own straight locks, falls in her face, which is no longer smiling.

"You're leaving," Méi'zi whispers. "You're leaving today, aren't you? That's why you went to the spring last night."

I study her face and wonder who will brush her hair for her when I am gone. "There's a convoy passing by the border in two days' time," I say. "It's full of mortal recruits heading to the immortal realm. It's my safest option—"

"Nothing about a mortal going to an immortal training temple across these lands is *safe*," Méi'zi seethes. Not for the first time, I wonder if my father was wrong in thinking that I was the one who inherited his fighter's spirit. "You promised me you'd reconsider. You've been lying to my face!"

I have, but only so we won't fight. Nothing will change Méi'zi's mind about stopping me from going to the Temple of Dawn, and nothing will change my mind about going.

"It's our only option, Méi'zi," I shoot back. "The wards Bà and the other village practitioners set up around Xī'lín are old. They're growing weaker by the day, and sooner or later, a mó is going to break through them. That Higher One from nine years ago—"

I bite my tongue, but it's too late. We each draw a sharp breath. Speaking of that day is a knife through both our chests.

Méi'zi's lips thin and her chin juts in an expression that is a jarring reminder of my mother's when she was still herself. "Bà wanted us to live well," my sister says, and I don't miss the tremor in her voice.

"Bà wouldn't just want me to sit on my hands and do nothing," I counter. "All our village practitioners are dead." She flinches, but I refuse to soften the blow. "I need advanced training in the practitioning arts so I can protect us."

"You could keep training on Bà's books," Méi'zi argues. "It's worked well enough so far."

"It's not enough—"

"It's enough to get by! It's a dangerous journey to the immortal realm—you could *die!*"

"With just Bà's books from mortal practitioners, I'll never find the cure for Mā." I press my point home. "That's not something a regular practitioner can teach me, Méi'zi. The pill of immortality, the one that can heal Mā's soul? That's old magic, from the gods and the immortals."

Méi'zi falls silent, and I know I've won. But it certainly doesn't feel that way when she finally whispers, "I've already lost Bà and Mā. I can't lose you, too, jiě'jie."

It's the way she calls me "older sister" that nearly shatters my resolve. "You won't," I say, gentler now. "I'll be back every few months." It's a week's journey to the fabled temple that sits just beyond the borders of the immortal realm, but I don't say that. I'll make it work. I have to.

I'm glad the water boils in this moment. It pulls our attention, and I don't miss the hungry, hopeful look in my sister's eyes as I walk over and smother the flames in the clay stove.

Méi'zi watches as I take out six vials and pour just enough

of the elixir into each one. I stopper each vial, and carefully, so carefully, I store five in the birchwood coolbox that rests in the secret space between our floorboards.

Méi'zi follows me as I take the last vial and approach our mother, who's sitting in the exact same position I left her, eyes wide and staring into space, jaw hanging slack. I sit by her side, smoothing out her lank, stray hair. "Come on, Mā," I say softly. "It's not quite your favorite ginseng chicken soup, but it'll have to do."

Méi'zi is silent, tensed up by my side. She does not remember enough of Mā, of the way our mother's laugh used to brighten a room like the sun, of the way her eyes used to sparkle with mischief when she teased our father.

Now our mother gapes into nothingness. I grasp her chin in my hand. As I lift the vial of elixir to her lips, she blinks. Her eyes fly to me. They bulge, and her mouth widens until I see her gums.

My mother screams. I catch her hand as it flies up to strike me, then fend off the other with my elbow. The vial shakes, but I have mastered this—I hold it steady. I cannot spill a single drop. By my side, Méi'zi latches onto one of Mā's arms, trying to pin it down.

"*Mó,*" my mother shrieks. "*HELP ME! MÓ!*"

"Mā." I squeeze the words out in a gasp. "Please, it's me, Àn'yīng—"

"*MÓ! HELP ME! Ā'ZHÀN . . . Ā'ZHÀN!*"

I grit my teeth against her cries for my father and shove the vial into her mouth. I grasp her jaw and tilt her head back so she has no choice but to swallow.

As soon as I am out of her sight, she softens, sucking on the vial like a babe. Her nails loosen from my flesh, and her hands fall slack. When she has drunk the last drop, I set her head against the wall, dabbing her mouth with my sleeve and propping a pillow against her back. There is color in her cheeks now, some flush returning to her papery skin, but I can't be sure if it's the elixir already making its way through her or the result of her earlier exertion.

She's staring at me now. Somehow, her eyes are more alive, and as I tuck her blankets around her shoulders, I pause, meeting them.

My mother's lips part. "Y- . . . Y-Yi . . . ," she rasps.

Hope roars through me. "Mā?" I whisper, my voice shaking. "Mā—"

But the moment's gone; the spark in her eyes is fading. Her head lolls back against the wall, gaze blank again.

I draw a deep, long breath. Exhale, my whole body trembling.

Then I finish tucking her in, fluffing the pillow one last time before I turn away.

"Yīng'ying, your arms." Méi'zi's voice is barely a whisper. She's sprung back now that our mother has calmed down and stands by our kitchen table, her arms wrapped around herself. She looks so small and forlorn, younger than her fourteen years of age.

I look down and notice the blood pooling along my elbows. My mother has gouged gashes in my forearms with her nails this time.

"I'm fine." I force a smile as I take my sister in my arms. She snuggles in quickly, and I feel her tension disappear as I stroke her hair. We stay like this for a while, each drawing strength from the other.

"I'm going to clean up," I whisper, pressing a kiss into her hair. She smells like flowers, like bedsheets, just as I always remember her.

She nods against me and pulls back, then sets to cleaning up after me.

I stalk over to the bedroom my mother used to share with my father, which Méi'zi and I have taken over. I slide the old bamboo doors shut and cross to the farthest corner of the room. There, I sit, draw my knees to my chest, and hold myself tight, waiting for tears that have long run dry.

2

I doze off at some point, and I dream of her. In my dream, it is night: she stands outside my window beneath the old plum blossom tree, skin pale as milk, hair the black of a raven's wing, lips red as blood. She does nothing. Only watches me. When I turn to look at her, she's gone, and all that's left is a swirl of crimson petals, silvered by the moon. It's the same nightmare, the one that jerks me awake in the dark, wondering about the shadow outside my window shutters. The one that I no longer know how to distinguish from reality.

I wake with my heart thumping, mouth dry, drenched in sweat. Méi'zi is curled up next to me in a pool of sunlight. For a moment we're ten and five years old again, sleeping in the daytime, huddled together on the floor of our living room. We were terrified of the dark and took to sleeping only when the sun rose and its light warmed us. There is no sense to that—mó have no preference as to whether they hunt us during night or day—but it was one of those foolish childhood beliefs that helped us survive the first years: get through one more night and the sun would be up, and we'd live.

Méi'zi and I got through it all together.

I don't move but hold her tightly against me, breathing in her scent and soaking in the warmth of the sun. After our province fell, several in our town chose to end their own lives. Our world was barren, bloodied, and dying, and they found no reason to live any longer.

But I know my reasons to live. I count them to myself every night, like a litany in the darkness. Three, to be exact.

To protect Méi'zi.

To save Mā.

And to hunt down that Higher One who took my father's life and my mother's soul.

All this I can achieve at the Temple of Dawn, the fabled practitioning temple the immortals in the Kingdom of Sky once set up with the mortals of the Kingdom of Rivers to train us in the arts of practitioning. It's said that the temple is more beautiful than any mortal palace, with burnished golden roofs wrought from molten phoenix feathers, pillars built from the pearls of the Four Seas, and jade floors gifted by the gods themselves. The temple has produced the most powerful mortal practitioners in history, some so great the legends say the gods took favor upon them and granted them immortality.

With tales like that, it's no wonder thousands of mortals used to kill themselves trying to get there and get in each year. Hope, as I've said, is the cruelest affliction.

And I'm no exception to its lure.

I know from Bà's notes that the tales are real but that reality is not nearly as romantic as the stories. Each year, the

Temple of Dawn accepts mortal disciples and begins their training. At the end of the discipleship, the temple holds a set of trials. The mortals who pass these trials—the best of the best—are granted a pill of immortality to strengthen the spirit energy in their cores. As a result, some grow so powerful that they live to be hundreds of years old . . . or even become immortal. Those who choose to accept the pill are offered a place in the Kingdom of Sky, a chance to cultivate the eternal life of glory and power the immortals hold.

But my jade pendant told me something my father's notes did not: a pill of immortality can also mend a broken soul. A mortal's soul is made of life energy that is slowly drained throughout the course of our limited years. But spirit energy, the makeup of an immortal's blood and soul, is eternal, and even one drop can replenish a mortal's soul and save it from the brink of death.

That's what the pill of immortality contains.

Without disturbing Méi'zi, sleeping against my chest, I reach to my neck and pull out my jade pendant. It glimmers in the sunlight as I brush a thumb against it, my heartbeat calming at the familiar sight. It is a broken circle of jade, plain and jagged at the edges where the missing half should be, but it is the reason I have found the courage to go on all these years.

This pendant is another riddle of my father's that I may never solve. He gifted it to me along with my blades when the Kingdom of Rivers first fell. *Keep this with you at all times*, he said. *Inside is a magical guardian who will always watch over you, even if I am not there. All you need to do is speak to it.*

I thought he was just telling a story at the time—for how could a piece of jade watch over me, and why would I need it when I had my own father and my family? I wore the pendant to humor my father, though I misliked how it slapped against my chest when I ran and how its jagged edges sometimes pricked my skin.

But on the night my father died and my mother's soul was half-eaten, I spoke to the pendant out of desperation. I was curled up in this very spot, doors locked, my mother lying prone on the bed outside, my baby sister in my arms. I was looking for something—anything—to hold on to when I thought of the little pendant. I took it out, and it winked at me in the moonlight.

Help me, I whispered. *Please. Someone.*

There was nothing at first. Then the jade pendant warmed in my hands. A glow appeared within it, shifting like molten gold into characters.

I am here was all it showed, but those three words held together my world.

I spoke to the pendant that night. Then the next. *Who are you?* I asked it.

There was a pause. *I cannot say.*

I frowned then, wondering if this was simply a trick enchantment my father had left me.

Yet the words kept coming. *But I am as real as you,* it continued. *Just far away.*

I knew nothing else about its identity, and so I tried not to rely on it too much for fear that it would abandon me eventually, as my parents had. Yet slowly, I began asking it questions. They started small, innocent. How to sow seeds, how to smoke meats and preserve vegetables for the winter. Then the pendant told me of light lotuses as a way to replenish a mortal's life energy and keep my mother alive. It taught me the craftsmanship behind each talisman I used and where I was going wrong, how to channel my spirit energy for the most effective kick.

I remember sitting and staring at the blank surface of the pendant, frustrated that all I had was a few characters at a time. I spent hours imagining who might sit at the other end.

Do you ever feel lonely? I asked it one day.

Another pause, and I could feel my guardian in the jade hesitating; I imagined them on the other end, inkbrush raised, other hand holding their sleeve, as they crafted their response.

It had been a simple one.

Yes.

Several months ago, on my nineteenth birthday, my guardian in the jade told me about the Temple of Dawn . . . and the trials where, if I won a spot, I would be granted a pill of immortality that would replenish Mā's soul.

That quiet, reassuring hand writing those words to me had saved my life countless times throughout the years. I often wonder if it is possible to love someone you've never met, someone you aren't even sure exists. The pendant now rests upon my breast, the guardian a companion to my heart.

Pulling myself from memories, I narrow my eyes, tracking the angle of the sunlight seeping through our shutters. I'd planned to leave in the morning with the full sun behind my back. Night is always when I am at a disadvantage: with weakened visibility, and with the Kingdom of Night continuing to seep into our realm, the moon and stars, too, are fading in the ever-lengthening dark.

But I would take on another mó just to spend five more minutes here, in the sunlight, with my little sister. Just five minutes.

So I do, stroking Méi'zi's soft hair and breathing in her familiar scent as I count down each heartbeat.

When my five minutes end, I stir slightly. "Méi'zi." My voice is a whisper, and I gently pat her shoulders.

She mumbles in her sleep, and I catch the unmistakable words: "Jiě'jie."

I swallow and swipe a thumb across my face, making sure no wetness remains. "Time for chores," I say softly.

She's awake in an instant. The sleep vanishes from her warm brown eyes. She knows what I am really saying: that this is the last time in a long time we will be doing chores together.

Don't cry, I silently implore her. *I need you to be strong for me. For us.*

Méi'zi blinks rapidly, and the vulnerability in her gaze dries up.

"All right," she says firmly. "Chores."

Méi'zi fusses over my ruined silk dress and insists on cleaning it for me before I set out. I know she wants to do this, so I don't object. Instead, I go to our room to finish packing.

There isn't much I'll take with me. A bedroll, a set of spare clothes, a gourd for water, and some plain steamed buns. The items I treasure most, I always keep on me: the battle-ready dress Méi'zi designed, my eight crescent blades, and my jade pendant.

While I wait for Méi'zi to finish, I check the drawers and cabinets one more time. They are filled with my father's tomes on practitioning: hundreds of scrolls I've memorized, shelf upon shelf of practitioning art and magic I have taught myself over the years, starting from the basics at the very bottom.

A ghost of a smile flits across my face as I pull out the very first tome. This was the tome: the only one my father taught me before he died. I remember those days as one would a hazy, golden afternoon out of a dream. They were days filled with uncertainty, but my family was alive and whole. We thought there would be an end to all this, that the mortal armies would rise again under our emperor, that the immortals in the Kingdom of Sky would ally with us to reestablish the Heavenly Order across the realms.

I haven't touched this tome since my father died. Now I crack it open.

In the swirl of dust, I find something tucked within the pages that wasn't there before.

It is a half-sewn silk handkerchief. I recognize the design: pale osmanthus flowers drifting over a sparkling blue sea. Beneath the waves are hints of shimmery scales and a serpentine body—a dragon.

I stare at this handkerchief, trying to remember how I ever could have created such a thing. When I was young, I was fascinated by the stories my mother told me of the realms of this world: besides the mortal and immortal realms, there was the Kingdom of Green Hills, ruled by nine-tailed fox gods; the land of flower spirits; the fiery clouds ruled by the clan of phoenixes; and my favorite, the realm of dragons in the Four Seas.

Though I'd never seen the ocean, I had fervently imagined it: long, rolling currents that the various blues of my silk threads could never capture. My mother promised me we would travel the kingdom as seamstresses, for how could one hope to capture the beauty of our realm in fabric without having seen it? How could I hope to detail the blush of a fragrant jasmine without ever having seen the way the morning dew clung to its petals?

The memories feel as if they belong to a stranger. It is difficult to believe that I was once a girl who loved flowers and wished to sew oceans. The same night my father handed me my crescent blades, he took my needles and silks and shut them in a cabinet.

Life as we know it is about to end, he told me, eyes black as ink, reflecting mine. *Will you give up your dreams to protect our family?*

Now I cannot recall my dreams, cannot fathom ever having had any. I know they must have existed, that I must have wanted more than this life. But that was before everything crumbled to dust, dreams became ashes, and the world turned into a living nightmare.

I don't know how my handkerchief got tucked into this tome, but it doesn't matter. I left that part of me behind when I made that vow to my father.

I'm about to tuck it back when a piece of parchment falls out. It flutters to the floor like a butterfly's wings.

A note. I pick it up and hold it to the light.

My dark blossom,
 I leave this for you in case I am no longer with you someday soon. I chose to train you for a reason. The truth to everything is at the Temple of Dawn. Find the One of the Vast Sea.

It is written in my father's hand, the characters falling vertically in that beautiful, scholar-trained way of his. *Dark blossom*—that's me, Àn'yīng. How many times did he tell us the story of my name, the tree blossoming in the dark?

I frown at the note. My father had many secrets, but I have always assumed that he selected *me* to train in the practitioning arts because I was the eldest, because Méi'zi was barely old enough to run without falling, and that the purpose of my training was solely to protect our family. Yet as I stare at the note that has remained hidden from me for all these years, everything that I believed begins to shift.

I chose to train you for a reason.

My father never spoke of the Temple of Dawn, much less any intention for me to go there. And yet . . . *the truth to everything is at the Temple of Dawn.* Was it his plan all along to have me go there? If so, why? What truth will I find there, and who is the One of the Vast Sea?

Questions swirl into my head with a dizzying rush. My father never told many stories of his time in the immortal realm. All I know is that he passed the Temple of Dawn's trials, but he did not take the pill of immortality and chose to return to the Kingdom of Rivers in pursuit of a mortal life. I do not know why.

I reread his words several times but cannot glean any more meaning from them. The note is intentionally cryptic . . . as though he was afraid this information might fall into the wrong hands. But who could he have been guarding against?

I hear Méi'zi calling my name from the next room.

I crumple the handkerchief and note in my fist. No time to think about my father's riddles. Whatever his reasons, I am going to the Kingdom of Sky.

When Méi'zi comes in with my dress freshly cleaned, I slip it over my thin shift. It is easy for me to tuck the handkerchief and note into one of my long, billowing sleeves.

Then I strap on my crescent blades, one by one.

I walk the perimeter of the house, checking the protection talismans I've freshly drawn in my own blood on the clay and bricks. In the past months, I've gone around the periphery of the village, replenishing the old, fading wards from our dead village practitioners. I know mine are nowhere near strong enough to hold off a Higher One, but I can at least keep the lesser demons away until I am back again.

When my work is done, I lean against the trunk of the old plum blossom tree. The sun blazes from behind clouds, igniting the sky in shades of fire. I take in the familiar curves of my town, how the houses wind over hills, the gray tiles of their roofs like a dragon's scales. There used to be willows threading between the buildings, red lanterns hanging from them, and everywhere the cacophony of children's laughter and street hawkers.

Now the trees are bone-dry and all is eerily silent but for the whistle of wind.

"Àn'yīng."

I turn to see my neighbor, Fú Róng, coming up the path. My father's senior, she lost her husband to the initial war against the Kingdom of Night, when all able-bodied people were drafted into the imperial army. Fú Róng was pregnant at the time, which is why she stayed behind; as a capable martial artist, she would have made a good fighter.

My father was the one who brought back the ashes of her husband from the war.

She miscarried her unborn child shortly after.

"Fú'yí." I use the shortened version of her last name and *aunt*.

My father led an army comprising soldiers from our province during the initial resistance effort by the Kingdom of Rivers. Yet when he saw the trajectory of the war and how quickly our forces were falling to the Kingdom of Night, he made the critical decision to withdraw our people and focus on fortifying Xī'lín's wards. Now many of the villagers owe their lives and the lives of their families to my father. That is the small comfort I have in leaving: knowing that my mother and sister will not go hungry, that someone will bring the rice harvests to them and help patch the roof over their heads if needed.

After my father's death, I chose to take Fú'yí under my wing. I am not sure why, for she was frail and a widow and had nothing to offer me. Yet I found myself leaving small packs of meat from my hunting trips at her doorstep; I made sure her firewood and coal were stocked in the winter.

And she, too, was there for me, in the ways my mother could not be. She showed me how to strap the cotton padding onto my inner garments when I had my first bleeding. She helped me bind my breasts when they filled. She watched over Mā and Méi'zi in the early days when I sought out the light lotuses and my sister was not yet old enough even to take care of herself.

"You are going today," Fú'yí says softly. Her hair is streaked with gray now. Faded, like most of the rest of our realm. Like always, she smells like a mix of bitter herbal medicine and the faint scent of chrysanthemums that she keeps in her husband's memory.

I cannot think of what to say, so I nod. I have never let myself grow close to Fú'yí. Letting more people into my heart means giving myself more ways to get hurt. If there is one thing I have learned, it is that most of the people you love eventually leave you.

But Méi'zi has no qualms about giving her heart to many. She must have discussed my journey with Fú'yí.

"Not many of us are left, but we will hold the fort until you return," Fú'yí continues, a hint of steel coloring her tone. "Don't you worry about Méi'zi or your mother. These old bones have some martial arts skills in them yet."

I blink. Though I know I am respected for my practitioning skills and my father's legacy, I had not expected any sort of acknowledgment from the remaining villagers—those who have stayed behind because they are old, because they cannot survive the journey out of the Central Province, or perhaps because they have grown roots in our little village and want their ashes laid to rest here. All these years, I have assumed that we've survived on codependency and mutual need; I am unprepared for the emotion in Fú'yí's voice.

"Thank you," I manage.

The woman nods. Something in her face shifts as she reaches out and grasps my hand tightly. "You let those bastards in the Kingdom of Sky know," she says fiercely. "You let them know we are still here. You let them know we are still alive. You show them how strong you are. And when you have learned the arts, just as your father did, you come back and win this war against the Kingdom of Night."

My breath catches. There it is: the sickness of hope. It lights Fú'yí's faint gaze. It lends strength to her fingers.

I have never let myself think that far. For the first few months after the war began, I hoped. We all did. We thought there would be an end to all this.

But then my father died, my mother became a walking corpse, and nine years later, I know better than to think of anything grander than my three promises to myself.

I swallow and briefly squeeze Fú'yí's hand before extricating mine. "You take care, Fú'yí."

She gives me a long look. "All these years and we still don't know why those mó bastards did this," she murmurs, turning to the red sun in the sky. "But you know what I think?"

I sigh. "What?"

"I think there's a reason the mó haven't taken over the entire kingdom yet. I've heard rumors from the Imperial City that the mó cannot sit on our mortal throne or expand beyond the Central Province." Pride lifts Fú'yí's gaze, and her smile is one I will remember for years to come. "It is because there is old magic in the bones of our land—magic as old as the Heavenly Order itself. It safeguards this kingdom for mortals. And it remembers who the true rulers of this realm are."

I know this story: that the dragons—gods of the rivers and seas—created the mortal realm, and a queen among them, the Azure Dragon, laid down her bones across our land. Where she slept, waters gushed, forming the Long River that gave birth to our civilization and gave our land its name: the Kingdom of Rivers.

"But the emperor's line is dead, Fú'yí," I say gently.

"The magic buried deep within this earth is alive, Àn'yīng, and it waits for us," Fú'yí says with the patience of one teaching a five-year-old. "When the gods created the realms, the drag-ons gave the first mortal emperor a drop of their blood. That power runs within us still, centuries later."

I know that tale, one as old as time and told to children before they sleep. I cannot rely on bedtime stories to save my family.

"The signs are there, Àn'yīng," Fú'yí finishes. "The truth waits for those who know where to look."

Then she turns and ambles off to her lonely cottage down the road.

Her words echo something in the note my father left me: *The truth to everything is at the Temple of Dawn.*

Fú'yí's right. Nine years and we still don't know why the Kingdom of Night did this. Why they suddenly broke the Heavenly Order that has governed all realms since the begin-ning of time, shattered the wards between our realms so that the mortal lands began to sink into theirs.

Now our emperor and his heir are dead, the mortal throne is empty, and we live in a dying world where the nights grow longer and darker.

Leaves crunch behind me. I don't need to turn to know that my sister has come outside.

"Was that Fú'yí?" Méi'zi asks, squinting. She catches my worried look and grins. "Don't worry. I'll take care of her when you're gone."

Since when did my baby sister grow up? I wrap an arm over her shoulder, she slips hers around my waist, and we stand together, just watching the clouds move across the sky like molten flame.

Eventually, though, my thoughts turn to the journey ahead of me: two days to get to the pass between the Gods' Fingers, the mountain range that marks the midway point between the mortal and immortal realms. There I'll catch the convoy that will cross the most dangerous lands: mountains and forests haunted by not only spirits and monsters of the mortal realm . . . but the hellbeasts from the Kingdom of Night seeking to break through the wards protecting the immortal realm.

My thoughts must spill through to my sister, for Méi'zi pulls back slightly and glances at our house.

"Mā's asleep," she says softly.

"I know." Perhaps it is better this way. Whether or not I say goodbye to my mother, the woman inside will not know. Still, I can't help but glance at the open bamboo door. In the darkness within, I think I see my mother's silhouette, her tufts of white hair.

I think of the five vials of elixir stored in our coolbox. Five months for me to survive the journey to the immortal realm, hone my skills so I become strong enough to pass the trials and win a pill of immortality. Then I will be free to return to the mortal realm and give the pill to Mā.

I turn away. I shoulder my pack, checking again for my crescent blades, my silken handkerchief, and the jade pendant at my neck.

Méi'zi grabs my hand. "I'll go with you to the gate," she says.

It's a short walk. All too soon, the pái'fāng appears, with the gold-inked characters *Xī'lín Village* now faded and covered in dust. We stop just before it.

Méi'zi turns to me and throws her arms around me. Her grip is like steel. "I'll miss you," my baby sister whispers, and the tremor in her voice breaks my heart open all over again.

I hold her tightly. I can't speak, but I think she understands.

She draws back, and though tears run down her face, she smiles. "But I'll be just fine," she says. "Me and Mā. I'll count down the days to the snows. That's when you'll be back, right?"

"Yes." I reach into my sleeve. "I have something for you."

Her eyes go wide when I retrieve Shield. She darts a glance up at me, and the delight on her face is real. "Truly?" she gasps. "But . . . she's your favorite!"

Of the eight crescent blades my father gifted me, Shield was the first he taught me to use, because it can serve as both a blade and, with just a spark of spirit energy, a shield.

"She is," I say, and press Shield into my sister's palm. "Protect her well. I'd better not see a single scratch on her when I come back for her next season."

Méi'zi beams at me. "I'll keep her safe, don't worry."

"I'll find a way to write," I promise. Then I swallow. "Méi'zi, if I don't return . . ."

Méi'zi's hand flies to cover my mouth. "Don't say that, jiě'jie. It's bad luck."

Gently, I remove her hand. "If I don't return . . ." I steady my voice. I have to speak the hard truths. "Go south. Or west. Anywhere but the Central Province. Promise me."

Méi'zi's eyes shine. "You heard Fú'yí," she whispers. "There is an old magic guarding our land, our people. Even if you don't, jiě'jie, I'll believe in that magic. I'll believe in you."

I cup her chin with my palm. My sister might still trust in magic, but I know better than to trust anything other than my own two hands and my crescent blades.

"The first snows," I tell her. Then I turn and march out through the pái'fāng. I leave my baby sister standing alone beneath the gate, cradling my blade like a favorite doll.

I don't look back.

3

The convoy is late.

It is sunset on the second day of my journey, and I do not wish to spend another night alone in the mountains. Journeying eastward through the Central Province to thick pine forests that wind through a narrow, uninhabited part of the Eastern Province, I have reached Gods' Fingers, the famous mountain range that marks the final frontier of safety in the mortal realm. It is here that the convoy will meet to traverse the most dangerous part of the journey: the last stretch of mortal lands before the immortal realm borders. Named the Way of Ghosts, it is said to be filled with hellbeasts from the Kingdom of Night, prowling in search of a way through the immortals' wards. For the nine years since they invaded our realm, the mó and their beasts have been seeking a way into the Kingdom of Sky—and have yet to succeed.

I pace, fingering the jade pendant at my throat and wondering for the umpteenth time if I read its latest message wrong. The messages are rare and disappear as quickly as they come, with the heat of magic.

Now the pendant remains blank.

The bamboo shadows are lengthening into claws, and the setting sun turns the sky a blood red. I have yet to stumble into any mó, but my luck may soon run out. With the added danger of hellbeasts roaming the Way of Ghosts beyond here, I know I am not strong enough to make it to the Kingdom of Sky alone.

I need this convoy.

I decide to continue east a little in case the convoy has somehow bypassed me and gone farther on.

The rising wind rustles the long silvergrasses, drowning out my harried footsteps as I pick up my pace to a light run. Too soon, I catch something dark smudged against a stalk of bamboo.

Blood, still wet. Fresh.

Alarm tightens my muscles, sharpens my focus to a point. There is a clearing up ahead, and in the dying light, I make out shapes crumpled on the ground.

The convoy.

I select the fourth of my eight crescent blades. The talisman on Shadow activates with a pulse of my spirit energy, shrouding me so that I am nearly invisible to the mortal eye and less detectable to whatever else lurks in these mountains.

My steps fall in near silence as I advance. Between the thinning bamboo, I make out something that raises gooseflesh on my skin: a lone silhouette in the clearing, drenched in the bloody light of the setting sun. A ripple of wind stirs the figure's crimson cloak, illuminating the pattern of golden swirls on it.

I freeze. The color of the exquisite raiment conjures a familiar image in my mind: the red-lipped demon's garnet hairpin glinting as she looked up at me from my father's dead body. The oldest, most powerful of the mó, the Higher Ones, are the royalty of the Kingdom of Night. It is they who led the mó armies into our realm and planned the war strategies. I have heard stories of them: how they are sharper, more beautiful, and more sophisticated than any mortal emperor or empress in history. How they are utterly lethal.

The wind shifts the trees and shadows again, and this time, I catch a clearer look at my quarry. It's not my father's killer. This one is too tall, shoulders wide and muscular—a male.

Higher Ones are exceedingly rare; the only one I have ever seen is the red-lipped woman. If this being in the clearing before me is a Higher One, I have no chance of putting up a fight, even less so of escaping. I am dead either way.

And I would rather go down fighting, with my blades in my hands and on my own two feet.

I palm blade number five, Fleet. The forest around me blurs as I charge, spurred on by the temporary burst of speed Fleet grants me and masked by Shadow.

The mó half turns at the last second. The movement is graceful, and because every ounce of my focus is trained on him, I see him shift as though time has slowed, rendering him like a painting in the dying dusk. His hair, billowing like swirls of ink; his eyes, flashing golden like embers in the sun; the strong, sharp cut to his jaw and the ghost of a smile on his lips. As the wind whips the jade-green leaves into a flurry and lifts his red cloak into a silken dance, his gaze rises to meet mine.

He is *beautiful*.

In that moment, I wish I could carve out my foolish mortal

heart. I know mó are dangerous. I know we exist for them as prey. Still, I can't help but stare.

And then we collide. He grunts as we slam to the ground, my body on top of his, my legs hooked against his for grip, my blades already at work. I aim at his neck with Shadow—

—and he catches my hand.

I'm thrown off guard by this. Shadow is meant to conceal my movements, and the blade itself is impossible to track with the naked eye, even for some mó.

Higher One, my senses scream.

So be it.

I grit my teeth and push, but then I catch sight of something that unsettles me once more.

His expression. He's *surprised.*

I have never seen any mó display such a mortal countenance; I do not think they feel emotions as we do. I hesitate— just for a fraction of a heartbeat, but it is too long. When I aim Fleet at the soft part of his neck, his other hand flies up to snag my forearm, throwing off my strike. Fleet barely nicks the curve of his throat.

His eyes narrow, and a grin drags open his lips, baring his teeth. Faster than I can blink, he flips me over. My head rams into the ground so hard that I see stars and my teeth rattle. I blink furiously, and when my vision clears, I find that I can no longer move. He's holding both my wrists against the ground over my head and pinning me with his body. I can feel the hard planes of his inner armor pressing against me, crushing me under his weight.

He cocks his head, his gaze raking my face. "Do I know you?" His voice is as deep and smooth as the night.

I attempt a kick, but he catches the movement with his

hip, locking my leg with his. He watches me struggle with a small, lazy tilt to his lips, as though he has all the time in the world to play with his food.

"Interesting," he says. "A scorpion dressed as a chaste young maiden. Are there more stingers beneath that beguiling white dress?"

I hate him fiercely in that moment. I'm trapped beneath a mó, my arms too weak, my blades useless between my fingers. He will probably use my body first, then feast on my flesh as he drinks up my soul. I think of my father twitching on the ground, of my mother's blank stare. I think of Méi'zi, small and alone beneath our town pái'fāng, holding on to my blade and the promise I made her.

My throat locks. I think of crying. I think of begging.

But no. *I will not be prey.*

If I am going to die tonight, then I'm going to do my damnedest to take him with me.

I do the only thing I can in this moment: I lunge up and bite his neck, clamping my teeth hard enough to break skin. I know mó have physical sensations, just as we do, and pain is one of them.

The mó shouts a curse and jerks back, but I go with him. I bite down harder, sinking my teeth in with all the hatred for his kind that I have. For all the deaths, all the half-eaten bodies and devoured souls and burned villages. For my father. For my mother. For the childhood stolen from Méi'zi.

I hold on, waiting for his ichor to sear my tongue, for its slow poison to seep into my body.

His skin is warm against my lips. He tastes of sweat, salt, and wind . . . and slowly, trickling into my mouth, is a familiar-tasting, hot coppery liquid.

I blink. It can't be.

Demons don't bleed. They don't have blood.

Which means—

I release him, coughing as his blood swirls on my tongue. My captor groans out another curse, and when my head falls back against the grass, I see my teeth marks on the side of his neck . . . and the fresh red blood dripping from the wound.

My captor shifts so that he is gripping both my wrists with a single hand. He swipes the other at the blood on his neck and stares at his palm for a moment. Then he looks at me in disbelief. "You *bit* me."

"You're not a mó," I gasp.

He swears under his breath again, then leaps up with a fluid lightness to his movements that I have seen in my father . . . and in other practitioners.

Skies. Did I just assault and . . . *bite* a practitioner?

"Observant of you, considering I'm not the one going around taking chunks of flesh out of people," he says, but the disbelief in his eyes is replaced by an edge of laughter as he flicks his gaze to me again. "Ten hells, that *hurt*."

My cheeks heat, but I don't have time for embarrassment and I'm not in the mood to apologize. I scramble to my feet much less gracefully than he did, then spit out the rest of his blood and wipe my mouth.

"What happened here?" I look around, my stomach roiling at the sight of the bodies strewn so carelessly. There are many monsters, ghouls, and spirits that roam the mountains and untamed lands of the mortal realm, but few known to kill us like this. No, the wounds on the victims are singular and clean, resembling the single slice of a blade.

Whatever did this didn't do it to feast.

I count eight dead, and my heart sinks. Eight practitioners from the Kingdom of Rivers slain before the sun has set. Eight mortal lives taken from our ever-diminishing numbers.

My former captor folds his arms. "First you assault me, then you *bite* me, and now you accuse me of murder. Manners, little scorpion."

I shift my blades in my palms, uncertain how to respond. I don't remember the last time I made a joke. And I certainly don't know anyone who would remain so cavalier when surrounded by death or facing the possibility of an imminent death.

"Why are you here?" I ask. If he was looking for the convoy as well, then dragons curse me, for he could have made a good ally. Until I accidentally tried to kill him.

He gives a deep chuckle. "Oh, for the fun of it. What more is there to life than wandering a bloody forest at night, surrounded by demons and getting stabbed and bitten by ill-mannered young maidens?"

I almost want to stab him again, but I settle for a frown. "You're not dressed to travel," I say, my eyes flicking to his crimson cloak, bright against the night that has begun to drape its shadows over us and the bamboo forest.

"Neither are you." His gaze skims my throat, my chest, down to the waist, and snaps back up to my face. "Clever. Dress as a chaste maiden in silks to lower their defenses and lure them in, then cut out their hearts before they know it."

I know he is mortal and I know he is a practitioner, but I still tense as he takes a step closer, then another. My village has largely remained safe from the aftermath of the invasion, but I've heard tales of how desperation brought out the ugliest, cruelest parts of humans.

"Demons don't have hearts." I raise my blades just slightly and bare my teeth. When he stops his approach, a pleasant twinge of power courses through my veins.

"Oh, I wouldn't be so certain."

"I've killed enough to know."

His smile widens. "My outfit is a disguise, much like yours," he continues, answering my earlier question. His hands are slightly raised, as though to signal peace. "The brightest and most beautiful flowers are the most poisonous. Most would think twice about attacking me." He raises an eyebrow and fixes me with a pointed look. *"Most."*

The brightest and most beautiful flowers are the most poisonous. That strikes a chord in me, deeper than he'd know.

I turn away, studying the closest body. The victim is a young woman around my age. Her eyes are still open, blank and unseeing, but the fear in her expression is unmistakable.

I lean down and close her eyes. The proper funeral rite for our realm would be cremation, releasing anything left of their life energies to the realm of death beyond the Nine Fountains in hopes of reincarnation. Unlike immortals, the vast majority of mortals don't reincarnate; our souls are too fragile for that. We are made for one lifetime.

I'm aware of the practitioner watching me. "Why do that?" he asks. "She's gone."

I look away. I don't tell him that every time I see a body, I'm imagining my father's blank eyes and gashed chest. That if I were in the shoes of the dead girl's parents, I would wish for someone to do the same for me.

That, for all the sins I have already sown and the deaths

I have seen, I hope these small gestures will continue to remind me of what it means to be human.

"She lived, once" is all I say as I straighten. We've wasted
enough time dancing around the topic, so I cut straight to the
point. "Are you looking for the convoy?"

"Convoy." His tone is between a statement and a question.

"The convoy to the Kingdom of Sky."

"*Ah.*" The corners of his eyes curve in a look I cannot decipher. "Yet another mortal seeking immortality," he says
softly. "Why is it in our natures to want that which we cannot
have?"

My lips part, but that's when I catch sight of something
over his shoulder. A shift of a shadow between the trees, a
glint of metal—

I'm moving already, acting on instinct as I reach into my
sleeve and sweep my arm out. My sixth crescent blade, Arrow,
flies from my hand. There is a sharp *plink* and the sound of
metal against metal, but my aim was a fraction off, my throw
too weak, and it wasn't enough to fully deflect the dagger
soaring from the trees, toward the red-cloaked practitioner's
head.

I can't even make sense of what happens next. One moment I'm watching the dagger fly toward him. The next, Red
has shifted and the dagger is nowhere to be seen. All I catch
between one blink and another is a billow of his crimson cloak
in a phantom wind, as if I've missed a few moments of time.

Red spares me a glance over his shoulder, and I swear he
smiles before turning his attention back to the part of the
bamboo forest where the attack came from.

I raise Fleet and Shadow just as the assailant steps out
from the darkness.

He's huge, dressed in black practitioner's robes and holding a long, thick saber that looks as heavy as me . . . one that is covered in drying blood.

Around him, figures are emerging from the forest: practitioners, judging from the sophistication of their weapons and practiced fighting stances, all young and dressed in dark, travel-suited shifts and boots. I'm certain, from the fullness of their frames and the crispness of their clothes, that they must be from the other provinces, perhaps nearer to the borders of our kingdom, where the mó have not reached.

I count six of them, each armed with different weapon types: bows and arrows, serrated-metal whips, throwing stars, spears, and swords. They're all aimed at me and Red.

They must be the convoy . . . or what's left of it.

The largest of them—the one who attacked us—takes a step toward me, and to my surprise, so does Red. They're equal in height, but the newcomer is built like a brute, with a neck as thick as a tree trunk and hands that look as though they could crush my head. Metal sings through the air as he draws his saber.

Red stands calmly, arms folded. Smiling. Somehow, that sends a chill down my spine.

"Believe this belongs to you," he says, and when he holds out his hand, the brute's dagger flashes in his palm.

The brute snarls and lunges. Quicker than a blink, Red tosses the dagger at his face, forcing him to pivot so he doesn't get stabbed by his own weapon.

The newcomer just manages to swipe his weapon from the air. He looks *pissed*. I would be terrified to be on the receiving end of that look, but Red doesn't balk. Instead, he smirks at me. "I think we're better off without the convoy if it's going to be them, don't you?" he asks me.

"Bastard," the brute sneers. "All these bodies you see? *I* killed them. The rest obey *me*."

The world cracks on those words. As I stare at his widening grin, everything suddenly comes together into a horrifying, gruesome picture. The dead practitioners, their flesh unconsumed and their chests sliced open.

"Why?" The question slips from my lips before I can help it. My head feels oddly light. This is all wrong. This convoy was meant to unite us in the face of our common enemy, the mó.

The murderer turns to me, and his grin splits his face. "Why?" he repeats. "Don't you know how the temple at the Kingdom of Sky works? They don't let in all the riffraff. You have to survive their selection tournament to qualify. Only the best mortals can make it out alive; out of those, only a handful are selected to become immortal." His eyes glow maniacally. "And if I eliminate the strongest of the convoy, I eliminate competition."

Red snorts, and every eye in the clearing turns to him. He's covered his mouth with the back of his hand, as if he's trying to smother his laughter. "Excuse my manners," he says, and with what appears to be incredible restraint, he schools his features into a semblance of seriousness. "See, I don't think that's how it works. Even if you kill every single eligible practitioner out here, you still won't be chosen if you're—let me put this delicately—shit."

The brute turns an ugly shade of plum. I hear one of his lackeys call out to him, "Yán'lù, want us to finish them off for you?"

I tense, but Red laughs again. "Can't even do your own dirty work?"

The brute—Yán'lù—spits in the grass. "Stand down," he bellows at the lackey, and turns to Red. There's something assessing in his gaze, something I don't understand as he growls, "I didn't want to fight you."

"Worry not," Red says breezily. "It won't be a fight."

Yán'lù snarls a curse. Faster than I anticipated, he pounces, his saber swinging with the force to take down a tree.

Red easily sidesteps the blow—and the next, and the next. There is an exquisite grace to the way he moves, as if each step is effortless for him. He hasn't even drawn his sword; a smile dangles at the edges of his lips as though this is all a child's game for him. His crimson cloak and the bursts of spirit energies between him and Yán'lù whip up fallen petals and dust around them, and in the elegance of his steps, he is impossibly *beautiful*.

As though he hears my thoughts, his eyes flick to me and he cocks his head, flashing me a lazy grin. My cheeks heat, and I'm suddenly furious at myself and my traitorous, fluttering heart. *The most beautiful things are the most dangerous.* I have known this since I opened the door to the lovely red-lipped woman that sunlit morning nine years ago. It is carved into my heart, along with the death of my father and the loss of my mother.

Now my idiocy costs me again.

I notice, a half beat too late, that Yán'lù has turned to *me*. He is panting, his expression beyond furious, and I know he is looking for an easy target to kill and save face in front of his lackeys as he swings my way.

My crescent blades are up, but I no longer have Shield, and

I'm not powerful enough to block against a proper weapon. No one has ever taught me to spar with a real sword.

The first blow throws me off balance. I feel Yán'lù's strength rattle my teeth as I stumble back.

I lift my head, panting. Panic grips my chest. I know that when the next swing comes, I'm dead.

Except it doesn't.

Instead, there is a flash of crimson before my eyes. I hear a screech of metal against metal. An incredible gust of power ripples through the clearing, rustling the grass and bamboo all around us.

Red stands before me, his cloak settling with the falling leaves and dust. He holds a sword, long and straight. In the darkness of night, it catches the dusty moonlight filtering through the clouds, glinting as if it is made of molten silver.

Molten silver, with a streak of fresh blood at its edge.

Yán'lù has leapt back to the edges of the clearing. When he swipes his hand at his midriff, I see dark red glistening against his fingers.

"Touch her and I'll show you how it feels to actually have aim."

Red's tone has completely changed. It is cold, with an edge of cruelty, stripped of any earlier nonchalance or playfulness.

Yán'lù spits, but he knows defeat when he sees it. He raises his saber and points at both of us. "Even if you reach the Kingdom of Sky, you're *dead,* both of you," he growls. "The Temple of Dawn tournament starts now, as soon as we step beyond Gods' Fingers into the Way of Ghosts. And I'll be watching your every move." He gestures at his group of lackeys. "Let's go."

They back into the trees and vanish into the shadows.

Red turns to me, sheathing his sword in one smooth stroke. He looks unbothered, his hair slightly mussed from the fight in a way that strangely suits him.

"Why did you do that?" I demand. I can't make out his expression beneath the shifting clouds, but I do not lower my own blades. "Why did you save my life?"

"Out of the kindness of my heart." He approaches me, stopping two steps away, as though he knows the measure of my discomfort. "Would that be so hard to believe?"

"Yes."

He laughs without abandon. Then he holds out his hand and unfurls his fingers. In his palm is Arrow, the crescent blade I used to deflect Yán'lù's first attack.

"For whatever reasons the Heavens or fates have conspired, our paths crossed," he says. "You saved my life, and I mislike owing debts. In the churn of lives and destinies, all things happen for a reason, don't you think?" He holds the blade out to me. An offering, but not without my yielding a step.

"Our paths crossed because I thought you were a mó and tried to kill you," I say flatly. "I hardly think that deserving of any grand notions of fate or destiny."

He regards me with amusement. "Even the unlikeliest circumstances are a matter of fate. Today, the stars and skies preordained me the gift of a charming maiden who tries to stab me and bite off my neck. Skies, I must have upset you greatly in a past life."

"Mortals don't reincarnate."

"Mm. All the better that you met me before those brutes found you, then, no?"

I narrow my eyes, thinking back to the tremendous undercurrent of power I felt when he showed his spirit energy to block the brute's swing. If he decides to kill me, it won't be a matter of a step or two.

So I take the steps and close the distance between us. His palm is smooth and warm when I pick up Arrow. I slip the blade into my sleeve, feeling whole once more.

"Thank you," I say. His lips curl, and I think I see something genuine behind that smirk. "What did he mean when he said the tournament starts now?"

"Rumor has it that the trials begin as soon as we set foot beyond these mountains. The first challenge is to get through the Way of Ghosts and cross the border of the Kingdom of Sky. What better way to test for strength than to see who survives a death trap of monsters and demons from the Kingdom of Night?"

I struggle to reconcile this turn of events with the recollections from my father's journal entries. "I thought they would train us before the trials."

"Train us? I highly doubt that." Red's eyes glint. "As far as I know, we're on our own."

I am beginning to realize how underprepared I am to survive this tournament. Not when my competition is the likes of this man and Yán'lù.

"Keep that stinger of yours sharp, because no one will see it coming." Red touches his neck again, where the blood from the wound I gave him glistens dark beneath the moonlight. He makes a quick gesture; the air shifts with spirit energy as a talisman forms, dissipating the blood. "Well, I can't say it's been a pleasure, but it *has* been fun. I hope to see you on the other side, little scorpion."

Before I can summon a response, the jade pendant against my clavicle heats.

A message has come through.

My heart lurches into my throat as I fish it from my collar and hold it up. In the moonlight, I make out a single character:

RUN.

4

Wingbeats in the skies.

I don't have time to ponder the message from my pendant and how it knows, how it spoke to me when I didn't ask it for help this time. I do the only thing I can think of in that moment.

With Fleet in my hands, I leap at Red's retreating back.

He's so quick, he almost reacts in time. I see him turn, the moonlight casting his eyes like coins that reflect the color of his cloak. He reaches for me, but I crash into him first and we slam into the long grass.

He flips me easily and pins me against the ground, his legs twining against mine to hold them down as I kick. I bring up Fleet, but he knocks it from me before I even realize his hand has moved. Then his fingers are at my throat, his body crushing the air from my lungs.

I can't speak, can't breathe. Stars pop in my vision.

Ironic, that I was trying to save him—and now he is going to kill me.

His face is so calm, nearly *bored,* and still undeniably beautiful as he lowers it to mine. "Fool me once, I let you go. Fool me twice . . ." His fingers tighten.

I choke, but that's when a shadow falls over us. We're beneath a great cathaya tree, its branches fracturing the skies and the moon—and I see it the moment the slivers of light wink out.

The practitioner darts a glance over his shoulder just as the creature comes into view. Its wings are so massive, the air stirs the silvergrasses all around me and the ground jolts as it lands in the clearing where we confronted Yán'lù, where the rest of the convoy was slain.

Red swears softly, and his fingers lift from my windpipe. Even with my vision clearing, there is no mistaking the beast that stands in the clearing less than twelve paces from us.

From here, it resembles a winged tiger the size of my house—but as it turns and stalks into the moonlight, I see that it is nothing but a mass of shadows on a gnarled skeleton. Bones jut from its ribs and wings, as sharp as razors and undoubtedly capable of slicing me in half. Its hollow eyes flash with the blood red of beings from the Kingdom of Night: enhanced vision to allow them to see in a land of eternal darkness.

I've read of this hellbeast in the studies put together by mortal practitioners. It has a name: Qióng'qí. One of the great Four Perils of the Kingdom of Night, which once stalked the mortal lands . . . before the Heavenly Order. And now that the Kingdom of Rivers is sinking into the Kingdom of Night, their creatures are coming through the broken wards to haunt our lands. My father's wards and my careful maintenance of them have kept my village safe . . . yet I can't help but think what will happen once those fragile spells fade away.

Red shifts his head to me. Slowly, he presses a finger to his mouth.

Obviously. I roll my eyes, and he smiles. Like he thinks I'm funny.

Hilarious that both of us might be torn to shreds and devoured in seconds.

I flick my wrist, and Shadow slides into my palm. I slice open the skin on my index finger and jam it against the hilt. As the talisman ripples into effect, the night grows a bit darker, more muted, and I know we're protected.

Red inhales sharply—just as Qióng'qí turns its dripping maw toward me.

"It smells blood." Red's mouth is by my ear, his breath tickling my cheek. I hear what he doesn't say: *You've just exposed us.*

"Got a better idea?" I hiss.

He draws back, flicks a glance at the forest ahead of us. "Stay here," he says, and then with that too-light movement typical of a well-trained practitioner, he leaps up away from me . . . and takes off.

I roll to my elbows, heart pounding as I search the darkness between the cathayas. He's gone.

And I'm left, alone and defenseless, against one of the four foulest mythological beasts to ever grace the Kingdom of Night.

As a snarl rumbles like thunder behind me, I think of an old joke my father told me. *It is night, and a group of merchants is traveling deep in the mountains. Suddenly, they happen upon a tiger. They are not fast enough to outrun it, not strong enough to fight it. What do they do?*

You don't need to outrun the tiger, I said, *so long as you can outrun the slowest merchant.*

Méi'zi was horrified at my answer, but my father roared with laughter.

I don't need to outrun Qióng'qí. I just need to outrun the slowest practitioner in these mountains.

I think of Yán'lù, of where he and his cronies disappeared. They can't have gotten far. And I may not be as strong as him or as powerful as that bastard Red, but I'm fast.

I'm on my feet in an instant, Fleet in my hand. This time, in my other, I palm my strangest and least used seventh blade, Heart.

Heart bears a talisman that my father invented: a spell of true aim according to the fiercest desire of the wielder's heart. Over the years, I've used it to lead me to the light lotuses and to guide my hand where my skill was lacking. But Bà warned me that the talisman can be unreliable: sometimes the mind doesn't know what the heart wants.

I know what I want in this moment. I want to see that brute Yán'lù torn to shreds by Qióng'qí.

I'm running already, my senses in overdrive. Fleet powers each of my steps so that my strides are longer, faster—but it's still not enough to shake the beast. I hear it crashing through the trees just steps behind me, feel the ground shake beneath each of its great paws.

I jam my bleeding thumb into Heart.

Irritatingly, Red's face pops into my mind first, impossibly beautiful and sharply elegant. I focus my thoughts to Yán'lù's twisted smile, the practitioners he killed, and how I want him to pay for what he did.

I feel a slight pull at my blade as it begins to direct me— into the darkness between trees, into the unknown. Gusts of wind from the beast's great wings slam into my back, knocking my knees together. Desperately, I blink the sweat from my eyes, but the forest around me blurs into a mass of shadows and echoes of the beast's vicious snarls.

This could be my last few seconds in this realm, in this life, and all I feel is anger and burning shame that I couldn't do better, that I've failed and that my failure means sentencing my mother and my sister to death.

Something tugs sharply at my foot, and the world veers off balance. I blink and I'm on the forest floor, supporting myself on my hands and knees, my left ankle twisted at an unnatural angle. As pain sears up my leg, I have strength enough to lift my head and meet my death.

That skeletal tiger's face greets me, hollow red eyes burning. It opens its maw, each tooth longer than my crescent blades, dripping with saliva.

In the shadow of my death, I glimpse her again: the Higher One of nine years past. She appears as a red silhouette beneath the darkness of the pines, watching me calmly as she always does in my hallucinations. Drifting, as always, just out of sight. Reminding me that, in spite of all the years of training I have done, I am still powerless.

She's gone in a blink. Above me, Qióng'qí's tongue unfurls, a spiked thing said to scrape the flesh from victims' bodies.

Then, it pauses. Lifts its head, attention pulled by something out in the forest.

I flip my blade in my palms and am about to aim a strike when the unimaginable happens.

Qióng'qí straightens and, like a scolded dog, backs several steps away.

The wind shifts, followed by the sound of near-undetectable footsteps approaching me. A hand slides across my back. I feel a ripple of a talisman warm my chest, soothing my frantic heartbeat.

"Think of the one wish you hold in your heart," comes a voice, deep and melodic and strangely familiar. "The one thing you'd wish for before you leave this world."

It is a bizarre thing to ask in the face of death, but I obey. My fear abates slightly as I speak. "I want my mother and Méi'zi to be safe."

My vision is settling. A face emerges from the darkness, one of heartbreaking beauty, like the legendary heroes in our childhood stories. "What else?" he murmurs. "Something that *you* want, for you."

"I want to see the ocean." The confession unravels from my lips. My throat rasps, and my words are nearly lost, but I think of the girl who sewed the handkerchief. Yes, I was once a girl who wished to see the realm—all of it. Long, rolling deserts like burning gold. Rivers that bleed from tears of dragons. The ocean, which one tome claimed was as vast as the sky itself and undulated like a living, breathing thing. There must have been beauty here, once. "I want to see the world."

When I blink again, the shadows have lifted slightly, and the hellbeast is nowhere to be seen. Leaning over me is the red-cloaked practitioner. He's no longer smiling. "I told you to stay," he says, his hands on my elbows as he pulls me to my feet.

I twist away but stumble as pain shoots up my left ankle. Those hands find me and hold me steady.

"And I was supposed to follow your instructions and do nothing while a legendary demonic beast figures out how it wants to eat me." I spit out this reply with the last of my dignity.

I feel as though I have been undressed, my barest and most vulnerable parts exposed to him. Weak, slow, and now wounded. I'd wanted—*needed*—him as an ally, but he will never agree at this point. Who would take a deadweight in a situation where physical prowess is necessary?

He presses a finger to his lips and, in a fluid motion, he kneels. His hand slides to my left ankle. I jump at the shock of his palm against my bare skin. Spirit energy stirs, and as warmth spreads through my injury, the pain dulls.

He is healing my ankle.

"Where is it?" I hate how my voice shakes. "Where's the hellbeast?"

"Gone." Red gazes up at me, eyes clear and calm. Kneeling at my feet, his hand warm against my skin, there is a gentleness to his touch that twists my stomach.

"What did you do?" I whisper.

"Qióng'qí feeds on fear. I helped you take the fear away."

Logically, it makes sense—and I curse myself for not having thought of that earlier. But I'm thinking of the moment *before* that. Before he arrived, when the beast had caught sight of something . . . and backed away.

A distant scream curdles the air. A familiar, snarling bark follows, cutting it off abruptly.

I dig my nails into my palms. This is wrong. Yán'lù and his cronies are *practitioners*. We are all mortal, meant to be fighting together against a common enemy.

The Temple of Dawn has made that impossible with its twisted tournament.

Like it or not, I am already in the game.

"Ally with me," I say. Like this, him kneeling before me, we are close, close enough for me to feel the heat of his breath as he lifts his face to meet my gaze. His hand is still at my ankle, where pulses of his spirit energy flow into me like waves . . . and the pain of my injury has faded.

"Ally with you," he repeats, and in a fluid move, he stands. He doesn't break our gaze as an indolent smile curves his lips. "And why would I do that? What can you offer *me*, little scorpion?"

I do not miss the way his eyes flick to my lips, tracing up the edge of my jaw and cheeks slowly, deliberately, almost like a physical caress. I hold very still. The village elders who grew up at a time when customs were still upheld would shudder at his insinuation. But those customs—along with most societal norms—have long eroded. I have heard stories of women who traded their bodies in exchange for protective talismans. Fathers who gave their blood for a scrap of food to feed their children.

I am not above any of that. I will do what is practical.

My crescent blade Heart is still in my hand. I lift the knife to the practitioner's cheek and touch it, just lightly enough so it does not cut. "I have saved your life twice. You stated you do not like owing debts."

"Debts that are now repaid." He watches me over the edge of my blade, dark eyes never leaving my face.

"The road ahead is long. Better to have someone watch your back while you sleep."

"Or a knife in my heart before the morning to eliminate your strongest competition."

I'm not above that, either. Eventually, that will come to pass, because if it comes down to a tournament, I will eliminate anyone and anything in the way of my getting that pill for my mother.

"Not before we get to safety," I say. "Until then, you have my undying loyalty." His lips quirk at the word *undying*. "I'm quick and I'm smart." *I have a jade pendant that watches over me.* "I'm good with my blades. And . . ." I swallow and take a small step forward. We are now chest to chest, knee to knee, so that I feel the rise and fall of his body with each breath and the brush of his cloak against my dress. "I could be good at other things, too."

He gives me a dull look I cannot read, then matches me with a step backward, creating distance between us again. "*Safety* is a long way off, little scorpion," he says. "That half-wit Yán'lù spoke truth. The first test of the tournament starts beyond these mountains. The area between Gods' Fingers and the Kingdom of Sky is filled with monsters the Kingdom of Night has sent in an attempt to wear down the immortals' wards."

The Kingdom of Night has wanted to overtake the Kingdom of Sky's power, favor, and authority under the Heavenly Order for years. It's impossible, though, for demons to slip through the immortals' wards, which are built to accept only those who bleed red. A first, that our fleshly mortal bodies should serve to our advantage.

I cross my arms. "In that case, perhaps you should pray that I'm here to help."

"I don't pray."

"You were caught off guard twice. Thrice, if you count my attack. If I hadn't saved you—"

"I meant to ask. Why *did* you attack me?" He's grinning now, leaning closer and gazing up at me from under those long, dark lashes.

"I—" I'm caught off-guard as his question brings to my

mind the moment in that clearing. The wind, catching in his hair and cloak, the leaves, framing him like a painting. "You were standing all alone in the midst of a dozen dead practitioners. What was I supposed to think?"

He blinks slowly, and I find my heart quickening and my face beginning to heat beneath his gaze. "It wasn't because you found me handsome enough to be a mó?"

I lash out, and Fleet finds his throat before either of us can draw another breath. My face is burning, but I glare up at him. "You might've died twice had I not been there," I say levelly. "I have secrets that will see me through alive, that warn me of danger before it manifests. How do you think I caught wind of Qióng'qí before it appeared?" I'm bluffing, but he doesn't have to know that. "I'm not as strong or as well trained as you, but I have much to offer. Ally with me."

"Hmm," he says, and I feel the hum of his voice reverberate down my crescent blade. "If we're going to be allies, you'll have to work at pointing those stingers somewhere else, little scorpion."

"Stop calling me—"

He moves so fast, I don't even catch it. All I know is that there was a blur of red, pressure on my hand, and then Fleet and Heart are both in his hands. My breath catches in my throat. He is even more dangerous than I imagined.

"Interesting." He's studying the talismans engraved in the hilts. "Well, then, what will it take to begin this alliance?"

I understand the message he is sending me, accepting my offer with my crescent blades in *his* palms.

"Your name," I reply.

He flips his palms and extends both blades toward me,

hilt-first. His attention is back on me, and I cannot say I dislike it. "Yù'chén."

Yù'chén—a homonym that sounds like *meet the dawn*. It's a lovely name. No surname, but I won't ask.

I take Fleet and Heart back. I'm careful not to touch his fingers. "Àn'yīng." No surname, and I won't offer.

His lips quirk. "A lovely name."

Embers of anger spark inside me. "Do not," I say in a low voice, "mock my name."

He blinks. "I wasn't. I wouldn't." He arranges his features into a more cordial smile, his gaze softening in a semblance of warmth. "I find it lovely. The songs and poems all laud the beauty of nature in daylight, beneath the warmth of the sun. Rare are those who appreciate the beauty in darkness."

I frown, uncertain how to react to his words. But I remember how quickly his face changed, and I tell myself not to forget. Masks, too, can be weapons.

Yù'chén must sense my unease, for he gives me a smile radiant enough to melt hearts. With a flourish, he proffers something to me on his palm. It's a flower as red as his cloak, its petals round and tapering to razor-sharp edges. I recognize it: a scorpion lily, known for slicing the skin of those who try to pick it. It is frequently depicted in paintings of the realm of death beyond the Nine Fountains and symbolizes predestined tragedy.

"A beautiful flower for a beautiful maiden." Yù'chén's smile is startlingly sincere, but I catch hints of mirth at the edges of his eyes.

I make a sound between my teeth and shove his arm away from me. "A flower foretelling a tragic fate? You can keep it."

He waves his hand and the scorpion lily vanishes like a trick of the light.

In the forest of cathayas extending into the Way of Ghosts, another drawn-out wail pierces the darkness, followed by that nightmare of a growl.

Yù'chén nods in the direction of the trees. "You thought Qióng'qí was bad? That was only the warm-up."

As though on cue, a seam opens in the sky, and there is a flash of white light. Two sparks of fire drift down toward us, the flames slowly dying out to form curling, golden pieces of parchment.

I stretch out my palm, and the parchment comes to rest on it, delicate as the wings of a butterfly. By my side, Yù'chén has an identical parchment.

I hold mine up and read the characters written in swirly golden ink:

> *The Temple of Dawn*
> *cordially invites you*
> *to participate in*
> *the Immortality Trials.*

5

It is when the sunset lights the clouds and treetops aflame that I think of home, of Méi'zi and Mā.

The Immortality Trials began with the invitation we received two days ago. The First Trial listed on it is deceptively simple: arrive at the Temple of Dawn by sundown on the third day.

Thanks to Yù'chén's healing talismans, my ankle has mended. The Way of the Ghosts has been eerily peaceful. The cathaya forest seems to extend endlessly, yet I know that, far off to the northeast, our realm ends and the immortal one begins. The legends say the border is marked by a great waterfall that pours into the Four Seas, and overhead, beyond a wall of clouds, is the Kingdom of Sky . . . and the Temple of Dawn.

The red-cloaked practitioner—Yù'chén—and I have formed a routine. We travel by day and sleep by night, alternating watch shifts. Sometimes I hear screams pierce the night or wake certain that a red-lipped shadow watches me from the darkness between the trees. But we have yet to run into danger. It is as if the forest holds its breath. The calm before the storm.

Sunsets are the only time I have to myself. As I slip away from Yù'chén to bathe, the tension falls from my body in the certainty that he won't follow me. The practitioner is disarmingly charming, and more and more, I find myself lowering my guard around him against my better judgment.

I slip out of my silk dress and carefully set it, along with my crescent blades, on the outcropping of rocks on the banks. I'm still in my shift as I lower myself into the burbling stream. I mislike being completely naked and defenseless, so I do not go far. My blades have never been more than an arm's length away since my father handed them to me.

I close my eyes as the rush of water envelops me, and I think of home. Méi'zi must be cooking at this hour—she'll be making congee, her best dish, with a neat sprinkle of scallions. It is as though I am there with them: I see her stirring the pot over the clay stove, hear the clatter of wooden spoon and bowls. She'll sit next to Mā and feed her. Mā has always taken better to Méi'zi, like an animal sensing gentleness and innate goodness.

An ache grips my chest so hard that my throat locks and I cannot breathe. I am glad to sink beneath the water, where my tears leave no trace.

When I surface, I know something is wrong. The chatter of golden pheasants and brown-tailed sparrows has fallen silent. Between the cathaya trees, where the sun's golden beams had been filtering through, a shadow grows.

Something within it moves.

I measure the distance. I'm about twenty paces from

whatever is materializing, and I'm well hidden behind the rocks on the banks. Any sounds I make are swallowed by the rush of the stream. There is a chance I can wait this thing out—but if not . . .

I need my blades.

I slice through the water, careful not to make a sound, slow enough that my movements won't be seen. When I reach the rocks and the cranny where I've hidden my things, I peer over.

Out of the darkness steps a thing that sends fear ratcheting through my body like lightning. This beast is massive: hair draping its bulky human body with distorted, abnormally long arms; an unhinged, gaping maw dangling from the gleaming-white bone of an ox's skull with four great horns.

Like every practitioner back in the day, my father had owned a copy of the *Classic of Mountains and Seas*: a record of all mythical beings and legendary monsters known to exist across the realms. I'd flipped through it as a child, in turns fascinated and frightened by the illustrations of beasts both beautiful and terrifying. After Bà died, I'd studied the book because my life depended on it.

I recognize the beast that fits this description: Áo'yīn, an ancient being that the mortal practitioners classified as one of the Ten Fearsome Beasts from the Kingdom of Night. It loves the flesh of mortals more than anything.

The hellbeast huffs as it scents the air. It turns its head toward me, its eyes mere pricks of demonic red in those hollow sockets, and I flatten myself behind the outcropping of rock and pray the water carries my scent away.

Slowly, I reach for my crescent blades, taking one in each hand. I watch the creature's great shadow darken the rocks, its reflection appearing in the stream, dappled by the water, the currents breaking around its body.

It lets out a low, chittering sound, and I ready my blades. Just as I'm prepared to lash out, a clump of bushes several paces away rattles.

A large huff of air as the beast shifts its head in the direction of the sound. The putrid smell of rotting flesh hits me and I resist the urge to gag. Then its shadow and its scent vanish.

I draw a swift, silent breath.

Thank the skies.

That's when I hear the whimper. It locks me in place, crawls down my chest, and twists my heart, rooting out a memory I have buried deep. Méi'zi, shaking and eyes wide, nails digging into my arms as she listens to the sounds of the Higher One drinking my father's life from him, then tearing his heart from his body.

Trying to steady my breathing and the tremor in my hands, I peer around my hiding place.

Áo'yīn has lumbered over to a crop of cathayas. Where it goes, an unnatural darkness follows, as though the Kingdom of Night itself spills from its essence.

Mere steps from the beast, crouched in a bush of camellias, is a girl. She is small—shorter than me, her frame made scrawnier by the oversized white shift she wears. Her hair is done up in two buns, and from what I can see, her face is childlike in proportion, wide-set eyes fearful even as she bares her teeth at the beast.

What is a child doing in the Way of Ghosts?

Áo'yīn's teeth flash. Faster than I can fathom, it pounces at her, a skeletal claw seizing her legs.

The girl gives another muffled cry. She scrambles forward and trips, her ankle held by the beast. As she turns onto her back, her skin *shifts*. It seems to morph with her dress, the silk and skin fusing into white fur, her feet and hands replaced by claws. By the time the beast drags her back to it, she's no longer a girl but a small white fox.

Realization clicks in. Not a girl, not a fox . . . but a *yāo'jīng*. The term comes to me from the tales of old: malicious spirits and monsters that roam the mortal lands, haunting human villages and stealing newborns. Some will lure mortals into traps, creating halfling offspring who inherit a mix of human and monstrous characteristics, yet fall into the same classification as their yāo'jīng parents. They are rejected by human society and, if not killed, are left to prowl the wilds with the monsters.

This girl must be a halfling child of a human and a fox spirit.

Disgust coils in my stomach. A thing like that has no place in our realm. It's said that the gods laid down a set of rules across all the realms before the beginning of time: the Heavenly Order, which governs the fates of humans and demons and immortals and all mythical beings. To separate the weak from the strong, the prey from the predator, the gods forbade love between mortals and mythical beings—even the monsters and spirits residing in our realm.

Still, halflings exist within the mortal realm. These creatures wander the fringes of this world, abominations under the Heavenly Order.

As I watch the creature struggle, however, I am unable to block out how its snarls turn into soft, desperate cries. Its fox form has fallen away, its body reverting to that of the willowy girl, terror widening her eyes as she fights for her life. And I find that I can't stop thinking of Méi'zi. Of how they are similar in size and build. Of how, in spite of whatever else it is, the creature is half-human. Blood wells up from the gashes Áo'yīn's claws pierce in the halfling girl: red and glistening, just like mine.

If I let this yāo'jīng die . . . I can't help but feel I am letting go of what makes me human.

I know it in my heart before I register that I am moving. I hoist myself onto the bank, my bare feet on the silvergrasses, my crescent blades in my palms.

I whistle at the hellbeast.

Áo'yīn stops what it is doing. Those red pinpricks in its empty eye sockets come to focus on me. With another strange, chittering sound, it discards the yāo'jīng like an unwanted doll and turns to face me.

Bile rises in my throat, but I force my mind to steady. I've studied the notes of mortal practitioners—the handful of accounts from rare survivors of encounters with Áo'yīn near the borders of the demonic realm. Qióng'qí prefers to devour victims smelling of fear, which is why Yù'chén found a way to ease my fear.

What is Áo'yīn's weakness?

There was a practitioner's account of a boy who, in the face of certain death, chose to sing. He explained that he had sung of all the joys in his life, for those were the memories he had wished to carry with him beyond the Nine Fountains into the realm of death.

He lived to tell the tale.

Joy. Áo'yīn is repelled by joy.

I do not think I have sung since my father died. As Áo'yīn

lumbers toward me, I think of my mother, of the way she hummed when she sewed. I hold on to a memory: a summer morning, sunlight pooling like honey through the fretwork shutters, spilling on Mā so that she appears like spun gold. She has a silk scarf in her hands, her needle flashing like a silver fish darting through iridescent blue waves, but to me, she might as well have been making magic.

I think that is the moment I fell in love with sewing— because, with nothing but my fingers and needles and thread, I could weave the world around me.

I blink and I'm holding knives instead of needles; my hands are coarse and callused, my palms a tapestry of mud and blood. Shadows wrap around me like living, breathing things; I feel hot puffs of breath in my face that smell like rotting flesh.

But when I look up, Áo'yīn has stopped. It towers over me, arms as thick as tree trunks and capable of snapping my spine like a twig. Its jaw, all glistening bone and saliva, hangs open as it gapes at me. Strips of flesh dangle from those rows of teeth, and they clack together in that bizarre chittering sound as the beast lowers its face to mine—almost inquisitively.

It inhales deeply.

I conjure the thought of me defeating this hellbeast, of winning a spot in the trials and Mā taking the pill of immortality. Of that honey-sunshine afternoon, sitting by my mother's lap and listening to her sing again.

Then I plunge Striker upward into Áo'yīn's maw.

I do not even know if mortal steel is capable of slaying mythological creatures from the Kingdom of Night—but if my crescent blades can defeat mó, then I reason they can at least maim a legendary hellbeast enough to slow it.

What happens next, I cannot explain.

Striker begins to glow. The glow comes from within the blade, growing sharper and brighter, as if it has drunk all the light of the stars in the skies and forged it into molten steel. As I watch, that light shoots into Áo'yīn's open jaw. Spirit energy sizzles in the air like lightning as the light begins fissuring Áo'yīn's form, as if it is cracking open from the inside out.

The beast's scream of anguish rattles my teeth, reverberates in my skull. I cannot hear myself think, cannot feel anything but its pain in those moments—that and the crescent blade's hilt, which has begun to burn in my hands. And when I look down . . .

Light shimmers beneath my skin, pouring from my flesh and veins into the blade. Striker is still aglow, but I cannot pinpoint the source of the light. I only know that the blade and I are connected, golden light fracturing from the cracks that have spread through Áo'yīn.

Áo'yīn howls as its form collapses, turning to smoke and ichor like the mó I have slain. Within heartbeats, the shadows are gone, and I am kneeling in the cathaya forest with my crescent blades in my palms and the ichor of a hellbeast on my fingers.

My head is spinning. I lift my hands, but they are normal now. The light writhing beneath my skin . . . I must have imagined that. When I lift Striker, there is no trace of light on the flat steel blade; I see only a sliver of my own reflection, eyes wide with fear, hair slicking the sides of my face.

The ichor on my skin is beginning to sting. Quickly, I wipe it off in the grass around me, but a burning sensation spreads through my fingers.

Movement in my peripheral vision pulls my attention. I tense, Striker out and Fleet in my other hand.

It's the yāo'jīng. She's back in her full human form, watching me from where Áo'yīn had her in its clutches. She's panting slightly, crouched in unnatural stillness reminiscent of a small animal—a little fox, perhaps. A deep gash on her cheek bleeds.

I've never seen a halfling child before; so rare and despised are they that even the stories and paintings don't acknowledge their existence. The depictions of yāo'jīng I have come across are all twisted, vicious monsters, eerie in their human-like appearances.

There is an ethereal, nearly inhuman beauty to the girl's face: the sharp angle of her jaw, the perfect smoothness of her skin, the distance between her angled eyes. It is only when she blinks that I realize her eyes are a deep amber.

She blinks again, then does the strangest thing.

She inclines her head to me.

Then she's gone. I am alone in the cathaya forest that spans the Way of Ghosts. The sun has set, its last rays of fire receding from the sky, yielding to the deep blue hues of twilight and true night. Wind threads through the branches, bringing the coo of a bird . . . and the crunch of leaves.

I spin, lashing out with Striker before I catch a blur of red. The curve of my blade comes to rest against the exposed crook of a throat, steel to skin. And I lift my gaze to meet a familiar one.

Yù'chén's breathing hard, one hand raised in a placating motion. Slowly, he uncurls his other from the hilt of his sword and raises it, palm out to me. Completely weaponless.

"I heard the screams," he says calmly. His throat moves against the edge of my blade.

I swallow, but I cannot bring myself to lower my blades despite the ache flaming up my wrists from Áo'yīn's ichor.

"It's all right now." His eyes narrow, taking in our surroundings before coming back to focus on me. He's speaking to me in a low voice, as though I am a wild animal to be scared off at any moment. And I realize how tightly I am wound, how quickly my heart races. "It's all right now, little scorpion."

It's that infernal nickname that brings me back.

I loose a breath and shift my crescent blade away from his throat. My hands are beginning to spasm with pain, the skin turning red. I know ichor is poisonous to mortals, and I've never been this careless as to get it on myself before—but I've also never fought off a legendary hellbeast.

The hilts of my crescent blades burn against my palms. I can't help it; I let my blades drop.

"Let me see," Yù'chén says, and after a pause, I hold out my hands.

Yù'chén lifts his gaze to mine. "Does it hurt?" he asks.

I look away. I don't want to say yes. I don't want to admit to weakness. And I don't want him to see the tears welling in my eyes.

What happens next is something I would never have expected.

Slowly, Yù'chén lowers his mouth to my knuckles. I suppress a shiver at the warmth of his breath as he presses two fingers to my hand and writes out a talisman. He blows on it, golden life energy streaming like sunlight from his lips to my skin.

I can only stare at him as the pain dulls. I'm not used to kindness in this dying world, where I've been surviving on my own for so long. That must be why his gentle touch inspires another emotion in me, fluttering in my chest like a trapped butterfly. Something akin to the fear and the thrill of when one starts to fall.

"I saw you defeat Áo'yīn," he says quietly, moving to perform the talisman on my other hand. "What did you do to it?"

"I stabbed it." Skies, my voice sounds so horribly thin. I suddenly feel exhausted, as if I could sink onto the silvergrass and sleep for days.

"You *stabbed* Áo'yīn?" Yù'chén echoes. He straightens and his hands on mine tighten momentarily. "How?"

I have no idea how to describe to him the light, the glow, the rush of power I felt as I carved the blade up. Even if I could, I don't know that I want to. So instead, I mimic angling my blade up and make a stabbing sound with my teeth.

Yù'chén chuckles, which sends a strange warmth shooting through my stomach. The healing talismans glow with his life energy across my knuckles, working on their own now, though he doesn't let go of my hands. And I don't pull them away. "Do you have any idea how lethal that beast was?"

I shake my head. "Do you?"

"I've studied all facets of practitioning extensively. Áo'yīn is one of the ten most feared beasts from the demonic realm. And you just fought it . . . and lived."

I don't know what to make of everything that just happened, so I say nothing.

Yù'chén is watching me closely. His voice is different when he says, "You saved the yāo'jīng."

I close my eyes. With the pain receding now, my exhaustion

begins to kick in. The world sways slightly, and I fear I will pass out.

Hands at my elbows, warm and steady. When I open my eyes again, my red-cloaked ally fills my vision. "Why?" he asks.

I don't understand why it matters to him. Most mortals view yāo'jīng with disgust. They are like us but not; they are unwanted by whichever other realm created them, and so we do not want them, either. They are not extraordinarily powerful, but they are different . . . and I think that terrifies us.

Yet, looking at the yāo'jīng's face, at her utter terror and helplessness, I was reminded of Méi'zi. Of myself, on that sunny afternoon, kneeling on my kitchen floor and watching my father die.

"She was a life," I find myself whispering. My thoughts tumble in the darkness of night; the combination of fatigue and fading adrenaline fogs my mind. "She, too, had a beating heart."

I realize how much of a fool I sound. There is no place for sympathy at the Temple of Dawn—in this nightmare of a world we now live in. I could have been hurt, or worse, I could have *died*. Then how would Mā regain her soul? Who would take care of Méi'zi—kind, gentle Méi'zi, whose hands are soft from her silks and needles?

I am suddenly so angry with myself. In a moment's sympathy, a moment's *weakness,* I jeopardized my family's lives.

Yù'chén is so close to me, I feel the heat radiating from his body. He is watching me with a look I cannot read, one that is different from the amusement with which he typically beholds the world. No—in this moment his gaze is intimate, *searing,* as though he sees right through the cracks in my armor.

His lips part, and his gaze trails down my body. Suddenly, I see what he sees: my skin through the wet silk, the way my dripping hair curls over my breasts, how my shift barely covers my thighs. I think of the words he spoke to me when we made our alliance: *What can you offer me, little scorpion?*

I'm shivering, my blades glimmering on the grass at my feet—out of reach. Bile rises in my throat. I have no disillusions that I will find a great, epic love like those the ancient poems sing of. But yielding my body to a stranger for survival is a line I have not crossed.

Yù'chén releases my elbows. Before I know what he's doing, he bends and sweeps up my crescent blades from the ground. Carefully, he places Striker and Fleet back into my palms. Then there is a swirl of red, a flutter of cloth, and his cloak settles over my shoulders, draping me in warmth, his warmth. His fingers barely scrape my collarbone as he fastens the knot. Gently, so gently, he smooths out the wrinkles in the fabric and tucks the collar under my chin.

The gesture reminds me so much of the way my mother used to dress me when I was a child.

I have not been touched like this in over nine years.

I look into Yù'chén's eyes. He holds my gaze. Slowly, he pushes a lock of wet hair out of my face, his fingers grazing my cheek.

I know fear well: living as the prey in a world dominated by my hunters has taught me the feeling. Your pulse races, your breathing turns shallow, and there is a tightness in your chest and a dizziness in your head. But I have learned to live with it. I have sharpened it into a weapon, let it make me steadier, faster, crueler.

Now I feel all those sensations. My heart tumbling. My breaths quickening. My head spinning. As though I stand at the edge of a cliff, and with one wrong step, I will fall.

Only this is different, somehow.

Yù'chén breaks the moment first. He takes a light step back, dragging his hand through his hair. "We're nearing the edge of the forest. If the accounts are correct, we will arrive at Heavens' Gates before nightfall tomorrow."

I am glad we are talking again, of concrete plans, of actions. He's right: the Heavens' Gates mountain range is the seam between the mortal and immortal realms. If we reach it, we will have survived the Way of Ghosts . . . and arrived at the border of the Kingdom of Sky.

"We'll take it at a run," Yù'chén continues. His face is tipped eastward, his brows furrowed as he considers this plan. His hair is wind-whipped and wild, but it suits him. He pauses to look at me.

"I'll be fine," I say shortly.

"I know," he says. His lips curve in a smirk, but I do not find it insulting. "I would not question the Slayer of Áo'yīn."

No, I find that I like it.

"Back to camp," Yù'chén says, gesturing in its direction with his head. "Though I did nothing as impressive as killing a mythological monster, I did shoot a pheasant for dinner. This way."

I realize I am smiling. Quickly, I turn and retrieve my dress and remaining blades from where I left them by the river, then hurry to catch up with him. "Your cloak," I call. "You can have it back."

He is in a tight shift and pants, all black, fitted to his sculpted muscles. He throws me a glance over his shoulder and says drolly, "I'd rather you return it to me when you are decent."

My face heats. I can't think of a clever response to that.

"You needn't show your stingers at all times, little scorpion," he continues. "Learn to rely on other people. It can be nice."

I watch his retreating back blend into the darkness of the trees.

6

I sleep well for the first time since I left home. When I wake, it is to the sound of birdsong, the kiss of a breeze on my cheeks, and the movement of sunlight across my eyelids. Fabric scratches at my chin.

I open my eyes. I'm curled up on my bedroll on the forest floor, the early morning light dripping through a canopy of golden larches overhead. My pack serves as my pillow, and I'm draped in a cloak. *His* cloak.

I study the gold stitching on its collar, the threads reminiscent of those spun by desert silkworms of the Western Province. The red is an unusual shade, the weave as fine as those Mā used to make for the nobility of the Imperial City. Curious, I bring it to my nose and inhale the crisp scent of pine, soap, and something I can't place. Something that reminds me of a cool night breeze.

I sit up, only to find the owner of the cloak watching me.

The practitioner, Yù'chén, is perched against a bush of silvergrass, arms tucked behind his head, his black tunic dappled with sunlight and shadows of leaves. He's chewing on a stick of sugarcane, but his gaze stirs heat beneath my skin. I can't help but think of the way he blew on my hands to heal them yesterday, of how gentle his fingers were as he wrapped his cloak around me.

A wicked gleam enters his eyes. He shoots me a toothy grin. "See something you like?"

I draw his cloak tighter over my chest and bristle, the memories bursting like bubbles. "Your shirt's torn in a few different places, and your cloak could use some patching," I snap.

"Mm. Should I simply go without them?"

I grit my teeth and fling his cloak at him. He catches it with the tip of his boot.

I threw out the retort on a whim, but as I turn my attention to myself, my heart sinks. Áo'yīn's claws have shredded gashes in my dress, tearing through Méi'zi's careful stitches. I didn't notice last night in the cover of darkness as I hurriedly slipped it on, but in the daylight, they are glaringly obvious. My throat tightens as I run my hands over the tears. It's silly, fussing over a dress, but this was the only gift from Méi'zi I brought with me.

"Might I hazard a guess at your profession?" The practitioner's watching me with that lazy smile of his.

"You may not." I snatch back my finger from where I've been picking at the torn stitches.

"A seamstress," he says, and at my silence, his grin widens. "Did I guess true?"

I study the ruined fabric. "No," I say quietly. "I just like to sew." I blink, and correct myself. "I used to, that is."

As we pack up and set off, my thoughts return to my strange encounters with the two hellbeasts from the Kingdom of Night. I still can't make sense of the way Qióng'qí seemed to back away from me just moments before Yù'chén arrived, nor can I explain how I slew Áo'yīn. I might have fought mó with my crescent blades, but hellbeasts are legendary creatures said to be under the command of the demon queen herself.

I chose to train you for a reason, my father wrote.

Again, I have the feeling that my father has woven secrets through my life, secrets that I have yet to unravel, beginning to manifest in signs here and there. A glowing blade that slew a legendary hellbeast, for one.

"Have you fought a hellbeast?" I ask. I'm aware of just how jarring my voice sounds, cutting through the silence and our steady footfalls. The forest has grown still as we near Heavens' Gates, the white cottontail rabbits and golden-tailed pheasants and chittering sparrows acutely absent amidst the mist-twined firs.

Yù'chén casts me an amused look. "Is this how you were taught to make small talk?"

"*Have* you?"

He turns his face from me. The sun shifts against his face, spinning gold into his hair. "I know a lot about the mó and their beasts. I've been to the Imperial City."

"You've been to the Imperial City?" I've heard stories of the fallen palace, lost to the demon realm—how it's mired in an eternal night, how red-eyed beasts and hungry demons prowl the grounds in the darkness. "What's it like?"

"Dark. Cold. Filled with mó and hellbeasts. The wards are so broken that sometimes you don't know if you're walking in the mortal realm or the demon one."

His expression has closed off. I'm about to ask him more—

why was he there, what was he doing?—when he nods at something ahead.

"We're almost at Heavens' Gates. Blades ready. There could be other candidates here."

The cathayas and larches are beginning to thin out, and before us rises what looks like a wall of jutting rock. It is only when I look up through the canopy that I realize two things: First, that this is no wall. And second, how the Heavens' Gates received their name.

We stand beneath a nearly vertical set of cliffs. They soar into the skies, disappearing into dense fog. Pines and lichens dot the surface, growing from fissures that might serve as hand- and footholds . . . but apart from that, a single slip is a fall to the death.

It seems we weren't the only ones who survived the Way of Ghosts. Up high, against the flat wall of rock, I spot a figure zigzagging upward. From trees to outcroppings of rock, the candidate moves with fluid ease. It isn't long before the mist curling over the mountain swallows them.

I'm decent at climbing mountains, but not *cliffs*. I know that the practitioners of old trained with an art called qīng'gōng, which rendered them capable of inhuman feats: walking on water, scaling vertical walls, jumping impossible distances. I saw my father in action, his steps lighter and nimbler than those of ordinary mortals, imbued with an unearthly grace. And I've recognized that same grace in Yù'chén's movements.

I glance at him now. I have no doubt he can climb these cliffs without issue. Without me. And an alliance is only useful so long as both sides provide value.

My fingers tighten on the hilts of my blades.

Yù'chén sheds his cloak and folds it into his silk storage

pouch, then stretches in his formfitting black tunic and pants. He catches me looking at him and flicks me a lazy smile that sends little tingles to my toes. "Shall we race?" he says, leaning against a boulder and crossing his arms. His muscles stretch the fabric of his shirt taut—as if I need another reminder of how thin and weak my own arms are.

I dart a glance upward—the clifftop is so high, it disappears into the clouds—and wet my lips, deciding what to do.

Tell him I have no qīng'gōng skills and ask for help, and he'll likely ditch me.

Don't tell him, and I *will* fall to my death.

"I . . ."

"Don't tell me you're afraid."

"I'm not," I snap, but his grin has widened. I spin away from him, and in a gust of stubbornness, I whip out Fleet and Arrow and make for the mountain in a running leap.

My blades lodge in the fissures easily enough, and my feet find purchase against two cracks in the surface. I heave myself up, searching for the next fissure to stab my blades into.

I don't make it twenty feet before I slip.

When I land, it's not on the ground.

I swallow a shout as I roll away from the body tucked into the long silvergrass. It was obscured by the tall bush and trees where I stood earlier, but now I clearly see it: a practitioner, his body bent and broken from a deadly fall. The furs and thick brocades of his cloak indicate a northern origin, as do his sheepskin boots. His sword lies a few paces from him, and his rucksack's split open, its contents oddly strewn out toward a copse of trees.

I follow this strange trail toward a particularly large bush.

It takes my mind a moment to discern what I'm looking at—and what's looking *back at me.*

A boy rises from the bushes. At first, I think he's unclothed, but that isn't possible, because his skin is *green* and scaled—and it's shifting colors to match the foliage around him as he straightens and cocks his head at me.

His long hair is white, and his eyes gleam like jade. He grins at me, revealing too many white teeth and a forked tongue that darts between them.

Before I can do anything, he leaps for the mountain. His skin shifts to match the rock's dun color, and in the blink of an eye, I've lost him between the craggy rocks and the trees.

"Yāo'jīng," Yù'chén says, stepping out behind me.

"How can yāo'jīng get into the Kingdom of Sky?" I ask. "The trials aren't for them."

"The trials are for anyone mortal enough," Yù'chén replies. "As someone said, they, too, have beating hearts. They also bleed red. Those are the two litmus tests to pass through the wards into the immortal realm."

I think of the little white fox yāo'jīng I encountered yesterday as my gaze drifts back to the dead practitioner. His eyes are still open.

I step forward and swiftly shut his eyes, willing my breathing to settle as I force the memory of my father's face back into that dark corner of my mind. When I turn around, Yù'chén is watching me. The teasing has vanished from his expression, the quarrel from mine, as though it took a dead body for us both to remember what's at stake here. What the outcome of all this might be.

At least for me.

He flicks his gaze up at where the shapeshifter vanished. "There are more candidates here than I thought there would be. I'll need you to keep your stingers out, little scorpion." He begins to unwind the long silk sash that belts his waist as he approaches me.

I take a step back. "What are you doing?"

He arches a brow. "Anchoring us together."

My lips part in a breath. "Why?"

He steps forward, tipping his head and granting me a charming smile. "To keep you close."

My hand is already on his chest, Arrow pointed at his throat. "You should know by now that that won't do you any favors."

"Mm. Well, on second thought, it's the most practical way for you to use your hands if you need to fight. I can't very well carry you in my arms, and you can't use your blades if you're busy holding on to me. If we're anchored together, side by side, we can both climb and leverage each other's strengths should an attack come." He holds up the end of his belt. "May I?"

When I don't object, he reaches for my waist and draws me toward him until we are hip to hip. His hands are large and warm, more careful than I imagined as he begins to wind his sash around my abdomen. I try not to breathe as his fingers graze my ribs through the thin silk of my dress.

When he is done, he does not step away. Instead, he gives the sash a satisfied tug and holds his hands out to me, palms forward. "A warm-up on qīng'gōng," he prompts.

I slide my blades back into my sleeves and splay my fingers against his. My pulse quickens at the touch, at how smooth his skin feels against my callused palms. Dimly, I wonder at how he has no calluses of his own.

"Focus on the flow of spirit energy within you," he says. I nod; I have taught this to myself. "Now focus on the flow around you. In the air, on the ground, in the trees, and in the grass."

I close my eyes. I try, but it is akin to attempting to focus on every current in an ocean.

"It's too much, isn't it?"

I nod.

"When using qīng'gōng, you have to home in on a specific point of focus. Use the energy there as your basis for action. Decide what you're trying to do: Are you trying to hold on to the rooftop, or jump off of it, or pivot, or a mixture of all those? That will determine how you channel your spirit energy. Now I want you to focus on me."

I open my eyes. It is hard *not* to focus on him: Yù'chén simply commands attention. Every part of him—from his night-dark eyes to his strong, elegant jaw and soft, full lips—simply demands to be looked at. This close, I feel his energy as an irresistible pull, and I willingly comply.

"Do you feel my spirit energy?" His voice has dropped to a meditative murmur. It thrums in his chest, in the thin silks that separate us.

I nod.

"I'm going to shift my energy. I want you to respond."

There: a shift in his palm, flowing from his arm and rooted in his chest, culminating in a spark that leaps from his fingers.

I push against that spark. The air ripples, and we both sway back as our spirit energies deflect our palms from each other. And finally, I *understand*. It is one thing to read the theories, to practice by yourself against inanimate objects; it is entirely another to *feel* it from someone else.

I realize I'm smiling. Quickly, I school my features. "Again," I demand.

He complies. His palms press to mine. I push, and this time, I can't hide my grin.

"Good," Yù'chén says, his lips curling as he raises his hands. There's a challenge to his gaze, and the spark of it catches fire in my chest as he commands, "Again."

This time, when our palms meet, he pulls. I feel it, an insistent tug against my energy. A flutter in my chest.

I dare myself to pull, too.

Yù'chén exhales sharply as, suddenly, whatever small gap existed between us is gone. We collide in a whirl of spirit energy, fingers interlocked, breaths tangling, the planes of his body hard against me. Startled, I place my palm against his chest to steady myself—and I feel the strong pulse of his heartbeat.

Yù'chén's hands find my hips, settling there gently. The seconds trickle away as we look at each other. "Very good," he says.

A distant yell shatters the moment. Yù'chén glances up, and I quickly disentangle myself from him.

From the mist above and several dozen paces to our right, a candidate plunges down like a rock. He crashes into the trees and disappears from sight. His scream falls abruptly silent.

"Well," Yù'chén says. "This will be fun."

★   ★   ★

He is impossibly fast and steady. As I stab my blades into fissure after fissure, I know without a doubt that I'm slowing him down—and that he doesn't need me. More than a few times, I slip, and my stomach jolts with swooping terror of a fall. But then the sash between us stretches taut, and I'm left hanging against the mountain, looking for purchase.

When we're far up enough that the treetops blur into a patch of green, the mist thickens. Soon, everything around us—the outcroppings of rock, the pines growing from them—turns into shadows.

Yù'chén is tiring; I can sense it. Catching me and anchoring each of my falls has drained him; I hear his breathing growing labored, feel his movements slowing. Up here, the rocks are damp and slippery from the fog.

How much farther?

In the haze of my exhaustion, I catch movement to my right. An old, gnarled pine grows from the side of the mountain . . . and between its leaves, I make out a pair of eyes. Familiar, amber eyes.

It's the little white fox yāo'jīng. She's crouched in the branches, watching me. Without a word, she lifts a hand and points somewhere beyond me to my left. Then she vanishes into the mist.

My heart pounds as I turn to follow her warning. It's impossible to see anything in this fog. Yù'chén is on my left, and we have about an arm's length of sash between us. There is no easy way for me to cross over him to defend the open space on his side.

I shift closer to him. "Yù'chén," I whisper.

He glances down at me, and it is this moment that costs him.

A slice of metal in the air; Arrow's already out of my

palm and flying toward the missile. I hear a *plink* as my blade
intercepts the other. I hold out my hand, waiting for Arrow
to return—the talisman on it ensures that it always comes
back—and that's when the second knife comes.

Yù'chén shifts sharply, but there is little space to maneu-
ver. He grunts as the blade cuts his side.

He slips.

I bite down a scream and focus on anchoring myself to
the rock, but he catches himself, right next to me. The mist
whirls from our movement, and blood sprays the mountain
red.

Yù'chén's blood.

I hear Arrow whistle through the air and hold out my
palm. My fingers close around its familiar hilt as I turn to face
our attacker.

The assailant leaps out of nowhere. I catch the flash of a
dagger as he aims at Yù'chén; at the same time, I send Arrow
back at him.

He lands on the cliff wall above us and parries my attack
with a violent slash downward. There is a *clink* as Arrow's
trajectory is broken and its momentum cut off.

It tumbles in the air and plummets. My stomach twists as
it disappears into the mist below.

Yù'chén is holding on to the rockface by my side, scram-
bling to find purchase after his slip. Blood drips from his
wound, and as the assailant aims for him again, I know he is
not ready to defend himself.

I reach over Yù'chén. My foot finds a crack in the mountain. With my right hand, I whip out Striker and plunge it into
a crack in the cliff face. With my left, I raise Fleet and parry.

I catch a glimpse of our assailant's face—and recognize him as one of Yán'lù's cronies.

I cry out as his blow smashes my arm into the mountain. He might have broken something in my hand, and I can barely hold on to Fleet. I think of Arrow plunging into the mist below.

I will not lose another blade.

Bile rises to my throat. He knows Yù'chén is the strong one—that if he just kills Yù'chén, both of us are done for.

This must be why, when he aims his dagger at Yù'chén again, I move to shield my ally's body with my own.

White-hot pain explodes in my side. I cry out and try to twist away, but Yán'lù's crony is still holding on tightly to his dagger, which is lodged in my midriff.

I kick him in the chest, hard. Through my tears, I see the assailant reaching for something—anything—to latch onto.

I kick again, and this time, the pain nearly takes me out as his dagger rips from my side and he falls.

The problem is, I fall with him.

The world tumbles around me, and my consciousness slips for a moment. When I come to, I'm dangling against the mountain. Above me: the sash tying me to Yù'chén. Below me: a thousand-foot plunge. Blood from my open wound seeps through my dress, droplets disappearing into the endless mist below.

In my haze, I hear Yù'chén say my name. "Àn'yīng. *Àn'yīng, look at me.*"

My eyes flutter, but I obey. He's holding on to a jutting rock just above me, just out of reach. His muscles are stretched taut against his tunic. The sash digs into both our waists.

Just one cut, I think. It would be so easy for him to be rid of me. Just one cut with his sword.

"I can't reach you." He sounds strained. "I need you to haul yourself up. Just one pull."

Just one cut. The pain tugs at me, and as I nearly go under again, I hear his voice piercing the fog in my mind.

"Àn'yīng, I need you to pull yourself up."

My arms comply. I grip the sash and pull. Once. Twice.

A strong hand wraps around my waist, and then we're ascending, so fast it feels like flying—or perhaps I'm so close to unconsciousness, I can't tell what's real anymore. My cheek is pressed to a warm neck, and each breath brings me the familiar scent of that red cloak. Somehow, I know that I won't fall.

Between one leap and another, the wall of rock angles out, then stretches into flat terrain.

Yù'chén gives one last heave, and we're there. With a groan, he sprawls backward onto the clifftop, and I go with him. We fall still, and I surrender to this moment of peace. Yù'chén's chest rises and falls beneath me. We are a tangle of limbs and breaths, but my cheek rests against him and I hear the steady, strong *thud-thud-thud* of his heart.

He sighs and utters a shaky laugh, then his other arm falls against the small of my back. "Fuck," he says.

I let him hold me for a few more heartbeats. I know I shouldn't, but it feels good to be held instead of to hold.

When I feel strong enough to lift myself, I push up against him so I can look into his face. Lying against the rock with his hair fanning out in loose locks, framing his face, he blinks and watches me. His hand is on my waist, pressing on my wound to staunch the bleeding; his spirit energy warms me, weaving itself into a healing talisman. Even in his state of exhaustion, even wounded . . . he is helping me. As the clouds shift and the sun caresses the sharp edges of his jaw, I feel again that flutter in my heart.

"Why did you risk your life to save me?" I croak.

He snorts, a sharp shift of his chest. "Why did you risk your life to save *me*?"

I close my eyes and speak the truth. "Because if that candidate killed you, I'd be dead, too."

Yù'chén doesn't reply for a few moments. When I open my eyes, I find him still looking at me with that expression I find so hard to read. He lifts a hand and brushes my hair from my eyes. His fingers graze the side of my face.

"Because you are a life," he says. "You, too, have a beating heart."

The exact words I gave him when he asked why I saved the yāo'jīng.

"You're frowning," he observes, and I'm keenly aware of the tip of his thumb still tracing down my jaw, keeping the wind from stirring my hair. "Are my words so hard to believe?"

"Yes." None of it answers my question of why—why did he ally with me when he knew I was weaker, why did he save me—because I'm convinced there must be a reason. In the world I've come to know, people don't help others without selfish purpose.

Yù'chén is watching me with that searing gaze of his, but if he sees the disquiet in my thoughts, he says nothing of it. "Can you stand?" he asks.

I push myself to my feet, trying not to sway. He's healed my wound, but the blood loss makes my head feel light. "Yes."

"Good." He tilts his face up to something behind me and narrows his eyes. "Because this trial isn't over yet."

7

I turn.

We are at the clifftop. The expanse of rock is broken by lush, flat-topped pines. The mist has evaporated. The sun caresses my face and illuminates a radiantly beautiful sight.

Clouds roll beneath us in every direction, pouring over mountaintops. The morning light filters through, dusting treetops a dusky gold. In the distance, high in the skies and as faint as a mirage, I see it: nestled between the hazy shapes of mountains that seem to drift above the rolling clouds, flashes of gold from the eaves of curving rooftops, and white stone pillars blending into the mists.

The immortal realm.

And I stand at its threshold.

I realize I'm gripping Yù'chén's forearm, my other hand curled around the jade pendant at my chest. "We made it," I whisper. Possibilities bloom before me, as warm and tangible as the sunlight on my face. Mā, brown eyes sparkling and mouth curved in a smile as she bends over her sewing.

Méi'zi by her side, silver needle flashing in perfect harmony with Mā's.

Everything is right here, before my eyes.

"We just have to make it through the Sea of Clouds," Yù'chén says. He points. "See those outcrops of rock? We need to cross those. You can jump, can't you?"

I follow his finger. There, beginning at the edge of this mountaintop and dotting a path through the clouds, are what appear to be floating slabs of rock. No, not floating slabs of rock. Mountains, whittled to pillars by wind and water over time. I've studied them—the Immortals' Steps, spoken of as half-mythical in our mortal realm. So few have survived the treacherous Way of Ghosts and Heavens' Gates to see them, the stories have become mixed with legend.

The steps have another name: the Dragons' Pass, for—as the stories say—far, far below us, hidden beneath the Sea of Clouds, is the actual ocean . . . and the beginning of the realm of dragons. I breathe in deeply and notice a briny scent on the breeze.

"The ocean!" I exclaim. I turn to Yù'chén. "It's below us, isn't it?"

His expression softens as he looks at me. "Yes. We are at the seam between the realms."

I watch him unwind the sash around our waists until there's only one loop tied around each of us.

"We'll be anchored," he explains. The sash trails between us, long enough to bridge the distance between the pillars of the Immortals' Steps, so that we're still tethered. "I'll go first."

I follow him forward. It's a clear day, and I don't spot any other candidates . . . yet. The clouds seem to race beneath us, and my toes tingle as I look down. I have no idea how far the fall is; I can't even hear the sound of waves below, only the whistle of the wind stirring wisps of mist. But according to the tales, prowling those seas are vicious, flesh-eating sea monsters and ocean spirits who thirst for mortal blood.

Yù'chén studies the first of the Immortals' Steps. "Don't let me fall," he says, and without another word, he leaps.

I dig my feet into the edge of the cliff, but my worry is unfounded. Yù'chén slices through the azure sky with the grace of a dancer, the sun catching the sharp edges of his features and tangling in his wild black hair. I find myself wanting to hold on to this image forever in my memory—a reminder that there is yet beauty in this world.

Yù'chén lands perfectly in the center of the first step. He twists toward me and gives a little bow.

I roll my eyes. It's about a twenty-pace jump, which I know I can manage.

I lower my stance, coiling my body tightly.

That's when I feel it: a coldness behind me, a caress of something I can only describe as darkness against my back. Bile rises in my throat as something tugs at my core . . . an old memory, as if my body and soul recognize this.

I know what I will see when I turn—the same thing that has always haunted me from the corners of my eyes, the edges of my imagination and sanity. A flash of red, the curve of a smile, the wink of a garnet. Gone in a blink.

Yet this time, the vision is different.

As I turn, I glimpse a swathe of darkness that swallows the blue sky and morning sun at the other end of the mountaintop. I have the impression of a crescent moon hanging in a black sky like a bone-pale scythe . . . and beneath, like the centerpiece, is the familiar flash of red.

The image is gone in the next blink, and I'm standing there with a pounding heart, staring at the shadows between the pines. Clouds race over the skies, shifting pockets of light; and though I know it wasn't real, my body reacts anyway, my mind filling in the spaces with the red of her silks and the white of her smile and the raven black of her hair as though a part of me *wants* it to be real, *wants* to hold on to her.

My knees go weak. There is a roaring blankness in my head as time fractures, and I am back in my kitchen in that moment my father died and my mother's soul was nearly devoured, frozen and helpless, my life rapidly spinning out of my control.

Somewhere in the white fear of my mind, I hear a voice. It pulls me back, back until the mountaintop and the pines and the sunlight materialize again.

"Àn'yīng!"

It's Yù'chén.

I know I need to go to him, but I can't. I can't tear myself away from my own mind, from the image of the woman with the red lips. Time has flowed backward; the Àn'yīng with her crescent blades is gone, and I am once again ten years old and terrified.

"Àn'yīng!" Yù'chén shouts. A gale has whipped up around us, carrying his voice to me. I hear something like fear in his tone . . . and then it shifts completely. The panic vanishes. It pitches low and sensual, echoing in a hauntingly musical way: *"Àn'yīng, I command you to come to me."*

The tender caress of his words renders my mind blank, relaxes my muscles. I cannot remember why I was so frightened. I cannot remember anything more important than following that command.

I turn to Yù'chén, the wind screaming in my face. My foot takes a step toward the edge of the cliff—but that is when something deep inside me stirs, whispering of danger. I pause and look up.

Yù'chén stands across from me, on the first of the Immortals' Steps in the rolling Sea of Clouds. The sun gilds him, worships him in a halo of light, and I remember the first time I saw him, rendered like a painting in that crimson cloak of his. Now his dark eyes are wide, his lips are parted, and his hand is reaching for me—

The brightest and most beautiful flowers are the most poisonous.

As I stare at him, the strange haze over my mind begins to clear, overtaken by a realization that grows terrifyingly clear. I think back to every small memory, every unanswered question or unexplained occurrence. The way Qióng'qí backed away from me that first night, as though by someone's command. How eerily quiet our journey has been in a forest supposedly teeming with monsters from the Kingdom of Night. And earlier, as we scaled Heavens' Gates, how he spoke and commanded my body to pull itself up toward him.

I have felt the pull of this type of magic before, and I know the type of creature that can wield it.

Mó.

Impossible. I have seen Yù'chén bleed. I have heard the beat of his heart.

"Àn'yīng," he calls again, and his voice is a song, a spell that reaches for my soul. "*Come to me.*"

My muscles burn as I resist the pull of his magic, the power of his command wrapped around my heart and tugging me forward. I gasp as my leg shifts toward the edge of the cliff.

Gritting my teeth, I wrench my mind from the lure of his

voice. My hands are at my waist, swiping out Fleet and Striker by instinct even as my mind swirls.

Demons have no hearts and cannot bleed.

But mortals cannot perform enchantments with dark magic.

Movement in the bushes to my left. I pivot, thoughts scattering, just as a blurred figure shoots out and lunges at me.

I raise my hands to parry my attacker's blade. But it's not aimed at me.

Snip.

As though time has slowed, I see my attacker's sword cut through the sash that ties me to Yù'chén. I hear Yù'chén yell as though from a distance, and I understand now—too late— what he was trying to save me from.

"I told you I'd be waiting for you," Yán'lù snarls and slams his heel into my chest. I stumble backward. One, two steps. On the third, my foot treads on empty air.

This time, I fall.

8

It takes me a long time to fall. The wind screams in my ears, and the world around me is a blur of gray clouds. Shapes within them haunt me, forms appearing and disappearing in the gray. But in the moments before I die, I do not see the ones I love.

I see the ones I need to kill.

I see Yán'lù's despicable sneer. I see the red-lipped Higher One, smiling at me from the shadows outside my window. I see Yù'chén in all his impossible beauty, turning to me in the forest glade the first time I met him.

No, I think numbly, fumbling for my blades. No, I cannot die yet. I cannot leave this life with people like them here, in the same world as Méi'zi and Mā.

My crescent blades are still strapped to me. I palm my eighth blade, Healer.

Come on, I think desperately, jamming my palm into the hilt and sending a spark of spirit energy into the talisman. It activates and I hold on to it against the shriek of wind in my ears, the nauseating tumble of free fall that I am in.

But even Healer cannot prevent the certain death rising up to meet me.

The clouds end abruptly, the skies yielding to an expanse of deep blue water glittering like diamonds.

I slam into the sea, and I'm struck with the acute pain of every single bone in my body breaking.

When I was eleven, I nearly drowned. It was my first time seeking out the light lotuses for Mā by a pond in the bamboo forest north of our village. It was a winter's night, the forest floor a maze of glittering ice, yet I could not risk bringing a lantern for fear of attracting mó.

I slipped and fell into the half-frozen pond.

I remember my chest constricting, my muscles ceasing to move as the cold slid like daggers into my bones. The darkness and pressure were overwhelming as I sank into certain death.

A voice, and the water itself, saved me that day.

There is a light in the darkness. A glow, softly pulsing, flickering like the embers of a fire. It winks above me like the beat of a heart. Growing stronger, lighting up the ocean currents around me like strokes of golden ink.

I am here.

There is a voice in the silence. Faint at first, but growing clearer. *Àn'yīng*, it calls, gentle, firm. Familiar. *Àn'yīng, wake up.*

Something in the periphery of my vision flashes. At first, I think it is one of my mother's silver needles. In the shifting waters, I imagine her warm brown eyes, the smile she used to wear so easily, which Méi'zi inherited. Their wavy hair, the way they brimmed with music and sunlight.

I hear their voices now, echoing from somewhere distant.

I am here, they tell me.

I am no longer sinking. Currents wrap around me like the arms of a lover, cocooning me. That flashing, weaving silver comes closer, curling and twisting like a ribbon. Something twines around my body, long and serpentine and gentle, and I feel myself drawn upward . . . toward a pair of large, liquid brown eyes, like those of a snow-pelted deer. Antlers, teeth that flash silver . . . and scales like moonlight.

Dragon, the currents around me whisper.

But there is pressure on my shoulders as though someone is grasping me, and in the spots crowding my vision in the delirium of drowning, I see a face: a young man in a cloak of white, as beautiful as a sea god, long hair sweeping gracefully in the waves. He carries with him the light of the sun, radiant and warm. His expression is gentle, his curved lips mouthing my name as he holds me to him.

Strange that I should dream of someone I don't know.

The vision swirls away as darkness closes in.

I dream of flying on the back of a milk-colored horse with a mane like seawater. I hear that voice saying to me, *I am here,* as clear as crystal above the rush of tides. Yet in my dream, I still search for the ocean my mother so often spoke of in her stories—an ocean I cannot see.

I am here. The roar of wind and water, fading. Warmth and light and something solid beneath me. *Àn'yīng, wake up.*

Wake up.

My eyes fly open.

I'm lying on a flat outcropping of rock. From beneath me comes the sound of crashing waves, yet this high up, all I can see are gray clouds . . . and a trail of rocks jutting into the sky like stepping stones.

The Immortals' Steps.

In the distance, between rolling clouds, are curved golden rooftops and jade pillars, a marble staircase that sweeps up to a grand palace of white stone. The walls are flecked with crystals and inlaid with pearl dust, and when the sun comes out and gilds everything with its rosy, fiery light, I realize that all the depictions of the Kingdom of Sky and the immortal realm were wrong.

It is ten thousand times more splendid than any painting or poem could capture.

I sit, shivering in my drenched silks. My dress has survived, and my crescent blades are still strapped to my sleeves and bodice. I have sustained no injuries or bruises. And somehow, though I remember my body shattering and my lungs filling with water and burning as I drowned . . . I am alive. Breathing.

Healer lies innocuously by my side, as though something—or someone—placed her there. I slip her back into her sheath, sifting through the pounding in my head for memories of that face in the deep, the voice between the currents. Anything that might tell me how I ended up here, on the first of the Immortals' Steps, when my body should be at the bottom of the ocean.

The sun has swung to the west and is sinking beneath

the clouds. The golden haze of the late afternoon has slowly turned to the fiery corals of dusk.

Impossible. It was just midmorning when I crested Heavens' Gates.

A warning bell rings in the back of my head. "Sundown by the third day," I whisper to myself, thinking of the golden invitation tucked away in my bodice. "The First Trial!"

Somewhere in the direction of the palace in the clouds, a gong sounds.

My heartbeat roars in my ears. There will be twelve gongs, I know, each a countdown to the moment the sun sets. Twelve gongs before I must reach the Temple of Dawn.

The Immortals' Steps zigzag through the skies before me. I count ten more steps—and then I have to get up the marble staircase, through the open-air hallways, and into the Temple of Dawn.

I'm not going to make it.

I'm already moving, positioning myself at the farthest edge of this step. I take off at a run, Fleet and Healer cutting through wind as my arms pump. Three steps to the ledge, and with a burst of spirit energy at my heels, I leap through the air.

I land on the next step as the second gong sounds. The sun sets fire to the skies as it sinks, and my heart pounds each beat against my chest as I take the next leap.

Gong . . . gong . . .

Five, six gongs. The clouds are beginning to clear, revealing crystalline skies below and a plunge to the death with a single misstep.

Eight, nine gongs. I can see the temple clearly now, drifting between clouds, hundreds of marble stairs glittering in the sunset, leading up to golden doors.

I'm sweating as I land on the tenth step, the highest and last one. My legs shake as I suck in breaths, blinking to gauge the distance to those marble stairs before me.

I back up to the far end of the rock. As the tenth gong sounds, I take off.

I know I've misjudged the distance as soon as I jump. My spirit energy flickers and sputters out like a flame, and then I'm falling, the marble stairs just an arm's length away. . . .

I scream and plunge my crescent blades forward. They bite into the edge of the marble stairs as I'm dragged down by the momentum of my fall—and by some miracle, Healer catches onto a groove in the stair. I'm dangling off the first marble stair, my arms trembling. One slip and I'm gone, and Mā will die a hollow shell of a person, and Méi'zi will be alone until the Kingdom of Night swallows our realm.

Gong . . .

Sweat and tears roll down my face as, with the last of my strength, I pull myself up.

The final gong sounds just as I haul myself onto the first marble stair. My muscles burn from overexertion, but I'm off, taking the steps three at a time even as the echoes of the last gong fade into silence and the sun slips beneath the horizon. I barrel through the tallest pái'fāngs I have ever seen; knifing into the skies, they are made of glittering marble and bear signs of lacquered wood and lapis lazuli that announce in swirling characters: *Temple of Dawn.*

The gilded temple doors appear before me, cast in the slanting light of dusk. *Hall of Radiant Sun,* announces the gleaming plaque overhead. From within, I hear voices.

I burst into a great hall of pale stone and gold accents. Silk paintings depicting mountains and rivers and rolling clouds flutter between pillars from which incense burners smoke. Guards in white-and-gold lamellar line the hallway, swords gleaming from their hips. My sight is blurring, my heart is pulsing in my ears, and I think I'm about to throw up. I barely notice the crowd gathered at a rosewood dais; I barely see the figures lined up at the very end.

". . . Wèi'fán of the Eastern Province and Zhōu'kāng of the Western Province," a clear tenor voice announces, echoing beneath a yawning fretwork ceiling that gleams with jeweled paintings of phoenixes, dragons, deer, and carp amidst magnificent blooms. "Congratulations on completing the first of the Immortality Trials. The Temple of Dawn welcomes you and invites you to continue your participation."

Claps and cheers sound out from the gathered crowd. I'm moving forward at a limp, dripping water all over the pristine marble floors and the vermilion silk carpet that unfurls through the hall.

"That concludes our roll call for the day—"

"Wait!"

There is a whirl of motion as heads turn, and I feel the immediate gaze of every single pair of eyes in that hall upon me.

"And me," I croak, raising my hand even as the gem-encrusted ceilings begin to spin. "Àn'yīng of the Central Province."

9

I register the shock on the sea of faces, but I'm more focused on the figures on the golden dais. They resemble humans, yet somehow, they are *more:* from the way they glow like the morning sun to how their long robes ripple like celestial rivers. As if they are too light to be tethered to the ground of this realm. Of course, I know what they are.

Immortals.

They look ethereal, their faces holding a gentle flush, exuding life. There is a perfection to their appearance that no mortal body can achieve: their skin is smoothed over as though made of pearl dust; their hair shines with the luster of polished black onyx; their features are distinct, with eyes small or large, faces square or round, noses soft or sharp, yet all coming together to form a portrait of radiant and impossible beauty. They are flowers at the brightest bloom—but while flowers fade and mortals' youth turns to ash, immortals' brilliance is eternal.

There are eight of them, each distinctively dressed in silks and gauzes adorned with flora and fauna, robes crafted so well they ripple with life.

The Eight Immortals. I have read of them briefly in my father's notes—but more so in all the legends of the realms. Long, long ago, they were mortals who crossed the Endless Sea to the realm in the skies beyond ours. The Jade Emperor, ruler of the immortal realm, was moved by their courage. He drew eight drops of his own golden blood, condensing them into pills that would infuse spirit energy into their mortal souls and grant them eternal life. *Find me the best warriors of the mortal realm, and offer them a chance at glory, power, and eternity,* he'd commanded them.

Thus began the Immortality Trials.

I study the Eight Immortals now, seeking a trace of their past in their faces, but they wear their immortality like stone polished smooth by timeless waters. I wonder if eternity would make me forget my humanity, too.

The immortal announcing arrivals pauses and arches a brow. His outfit blazes red and gold, almost imperial in appearance. "Oh?" he says in a lofty, melodious voice, and the bejeweled bamboo scepter in his hands gleams as he leans forward to peer at me. "But the twelfth gong has sounded."

"No need to argue with a mortal who is due for the Nine Fountains, Jǐng'xiù," says an immortal holding a large fan made of what resemble the finest ostrich feathers across the realms. His robes hang loose on him, baring much of his chest. His gaze slides over me as though I am a part of the floor. "I shall call the guards to throw her out."

Sunlight lances off the white-gold armor of the dozens of guards lining the hall.

"No," I gasp, my gaze returning to the immortals seated

on the dais. "I arrived before sundown. I was at the temple threshold by the twelfth gong. I qualify."

There's a sharp intake of breath all around me as the candidates whisper among themselves.

Someone laughs; I trace the sound to an immortal on the far left. They wear a pure blue robe and carry a woven basket of plants: sprigs of heavenly bamboo, sun-yellow chrysanthemums, and jade-green pines, stalks of magic fungi and flowering plums. "She argues!" they exclaim and gift me a wide smile, the corners of their eyes creasing. "I like her. Shall we let her pass?"

"The rules are the rules, Cǎi'hé!" snaps the immortal on the far right. He's holding a white-flowered gourd in his arms. Plumes of golden smoke waft from its spout, curling into the air.

Cǎi'hé tilts their head. "Well, *technically* . . . she *did* arrive at the Temple of Dawn by the twelfth gong. . . ."

The world is no longer spinning. Instead, I feel something hot and powerful course through my veins and fist in my heart.

I am suddenly *furious*. I have crossed the mortal lands and survived all the monsters and demons lurking there; I have fought and bled and sacrificed to reach this place—this place that holds the only key to saving my mother's life. I have lived, picking at scraps and screaming through nightmares of my father's blank, unseeing eyes and harvesting lotuses for my soulless mother in our dying mortal kingdom for all these years . . . and they are arguing over my entry as though it *entertains* them.

Before I know it, I'm shoving through the crowd of candidates. They part before me as though I am something they do not wish to touch. I come to stand before the dais, holding Fleet and Healer in my hands.

"The invitation I received stated that the First Trial was to arrive here by sundown today," I say. I point Fleet at the open doors, where the setting sun colors the skies and the clouds in shades of coral. "It is sundown. I am here. Therefore, I qualify for the Second Trial."

Toward the center of the dais, an immortal leans forward. Her face was in the shadows earlier, but as the light strikes it, I see that her features are softer than the others', her beauty subdued and pure. She holds a lotus; over its blush petals, her eyes rove up the crescent blades in my hands to my soaked white dress and come to meet mine. In the moment that they do, they light up my entire world.

Then her gaze passes easily over me, and I realize that, to these immortals, I am a drop of water in an ocean, a speck of sand in an unending desert.

"I agree with the mortal," she says to the immortal next to her, at the center of the group. He is the tallest and most imposing; he wears a high gray scholar's hat and matching somber robes of heavy brocade. At his hip is a red-tasseled sword. "Honorable Immortal Dòng'bīn?"

"Always the mortal sympathizer, eh, Shī'yǎ?" The immortal with the feathered fan smirks.

"Silence." The immortal at the very center of the group—Dòng'bīn—has spoken. The rest obey, their attention focused on him in a way that tells me he is the highest-ranking. Power crackles from him, electrifying each sweep of his hand, each shift of his body.

That's when I realize: I can argue all I want. I can burn alive with my anger. But in the face of these immortals who guard the gates to the Kingdom of Sky, there is nothing I can do. After all this time, I am still powerless.

"These trials seek those with not only strength of the body but also strength of the mind," Dòng'bīn says. "Persistence against all odds is the spirit of the heart that first tided us through the Endless Sea into this realm." At this, a few of the immortals have the grace to look humbled. Dòng'bīn's gaze, like the center of a storm—cold, ancient, and powerful—shifts to me as he declares, "She may pass to the Second Trial."

My knees knock together; I nearly drop my blades. There's a roaring in my ears as my adrenaline finally leaves me and exhaustion catches up to my aching limbs. The last thought I have before my mind goes blank is that I am going to collapse before an entire hall of immortals and candidates out for my blood.

Except I don't.

Hands catch me, light and warm against my back and my shoulders. Someone whispers in my ear, in my *mind*, telling me to walk, and somehow, I do. I make my way through the crowd of candidates toward the back.

Arms encircle my waist. I'm pressed against someone's chest, hard and firm, my head leaning against a shoulder. My vision settles: high bejeweled ceilings, fluttering silk paintings, white stone inlaid with gold and lapis.

"It's all right now, little scorpion," comes a deep, familiar voice.

Every nerve in me stretches taut to the point of breaking.

It's him.

Yù'chén.

I try to jerk my hand away, but I can barely summon the energy to stand, let alone fight off someone as strong as he is.

Yù'chén pins me in place, twisting my wrists slightly to angle my blades away from him.

I lean back, and he tilts his head with a smile that does not reach his eyes. "Are you really going to stick me in the middle of their pristine palace?" His lips are so close to my ear, I feel the low thrum of his words against my skin. "Right after you were almost disqualified?"

There's a ripple of excitement throughout the hall. On the dais, the immortal with the bamboo scepter shifts, and a glint of gold catches my eye.

I look, and I forget to breathe.

There, nestled like a pearl in the immortal's palm, is a perfect golden pill. It catches the fading sunlight like liquid gold.

"The pill of immortality," Jǐng'xiù booms, his voice amplified by that scepter. "Upon the conclusion of the Immortality Trials, each judge will select one candidate they deem most worthy of taking under their discipleship. They will grant the candidate a pill of immortality created from a drop of their own golden blood and spirit energy and invite the candidate to the Kingdom of Sky to cultivate their power as an immortal.

"You will be judged by a variety of factors: characteristics that each of the Eight Immortals value uniquely, tested in each trial."

I can practically hear each candidate doing the math. By my count, there are over forty of us, and only eight judges. Eight spots.

I have to beat thirty-some other candidates—many of whom are trained practitioners from richer provinces—to win the pill of immortality for Mā.

Jǐng'xiù closes his palm, and the pill vanishes. Around me, candidates blink as though released from a spell.

I feel stronger and more clearheaded than earlier. Yù'chén's hands press against my waist and the small of my back, holding me steady. A tingling warmth I now recognize as spirit energy pours from him into me.

Why? I think, the unanswered question since the first day we met. Why is he healing me and still helping me when I am clearly weak and wounded . . . and most important, when I have seen him use dark magic that only mó can wield?

As though hearing my thoughts, his eyes dip to mine.

I tighten my grip on my dagger. Instantly, Yù'chén's hands snap back around my wrists. The motion is swift, subtle, but his grip is like iron.

"Don't," he murmurs. Slowly, he bends my arms to wrap around his waist, drawing me forward so I have no choice but to lean close to his chest. At the front of the hall, Jǐng'xiù is now giving instructions about our rooms, our schedules, our meals, and the rules of the temple. "You don't want to give them any reason to disqualify you."

I hiss at Yù'chén, "I think they'd appreciate it if I tell them that you—"

"That I what?" He lifts an eyebrow.

I open and close my mouth several times. "Enchanted me," I say at last.

He looks pleased. "Did I?"

"You—" I clench my teeth as several of the candidates nearby glance our way in annoyance.

I angle my dagger at his ribs, and his grip tightens on my wrist as his smile widens. In this bizarre silent struggle, we turn to listen to Jǐng'xiù's instructions.

". . . welcome to attend the Trial Banquet tonight. You will find your Candidates' Courtyard room assignments on your invitations," the immortal says cheerfully.

"Are we free to come and go as we please?" hollers one candidate at the front. "I've got a sweetheart out in the Southern Province!"

This earns him some laughter, and even a few smiles from the Eight Immortals themselves.

Jǐng'xiù chuckles along with the group. "No," he says pleasantly. The candidate with the sweetheart stops grinning. "The wards protecting the Kingdom of Sky are impenetrable. You were granted entry through our wards today by measure of your mortal blood and mortal hearts, but by the twelfth gong, the wards once again sealed off our realm. No one may enter, and no one may leave. And might I remind you that anyone caught cheating, stealing, or exhibiting any other unsavory behavior under the principles of the Heavenly Order . . . will regret having *ever* crossed into this realm."

His words are met by silence. No one is smiling anymore.

Jǐng'xiù throws back his head and laughs. "Oh, you all look so *serious* for a group of mortals who have just passed the First Trial!" He spreads his arms. "Congratulations, candidates. Welcome to the Temple of Dawn."

Yù'chén releases me just as the speech ends. A ruckus arises in the hall as the air ripples with spirit energy. When I look down, my invitation scroll has morphed into a glowing, molten-gold bracelet that twines over my left wrist. At its center is an inlaid mother-of-pearl engraving of a tiny sun over a swirling white cloud—the symbol of the Kingdom of Sky—and a number. It is one that does nothing to improve my mood.

Forty-four. A cursed number: four is the homonym for death.

Yù'chén is studying his own wrist. The number on his gold bracelet flashes: two.

These are not arbitrary numbers; they're the order in which we arrived. I, dead last, the forty-fourth candidate of these trials.

And Yù'chén, second—only because I slowed him down.

A knot hardens in my throat as I remember the Immortal Steps, him reaching for me, eyes wide and lips parted as though in genuine fear.

"You," I grit out, "are a very good liar."

Yù'chén turns to me, not quite meeting my gaze. "If I were, you would not have suspected me," he replies.

It's an admission of what happened out on Heavens' Gates, by the Immortals' Steps. Of the dark magic he used.

I flash my blades at him. "Follow" is all I say as I whip around and begin walking down the hall, merging into the rest of the crowd as they stream toward the Candidates' Courtyard. I'm keenly aware of the Eight Immortals' eyes on me, of the guards watching me as I pass them.

Yù'chén gives a low chuckle as he falls into step behind me.

The Hall of Radiant Sun opens to a veranda of billowing gauze drapes and high marble pillars that catch the rays of the setting sun. On either side, glittering waterways fall into mist and nothingness below. All around us, as far as the eye can see, are rolling clouds painted in the last rosy corals of sunset.

Méi'zi would have loved it.

The voices and footsteps have faded. The candidates have gone far ahead, mere silhouettes between the translucent gauze drapes.

I slow to a stop and glance behind me. Yù'chén stands several paces away, making no move to approach. An errant breeze sets the drapes around us aflutter. I glimpse his crimson cloak, his untamed black hair, and a corner of his soft lips and strong jaw.

I don't know how he did it, but I do know that there is something terribly wrong with him. Mortals shouldn't be able to command other mortals as mó do. In the context of this trial, it gives him a horrifying advantage over the rest of us.

"How did you do it?" I ask quietly.

He only stares at me, saying nothing. This close, in this perfect, radiant realm of white stone and pale clouds and fiery skies, he looks ethereal in a way that shouldn't be possible.

I raise my blades. "Speak, unless you want me to report this to the Eight Immortals."

"I was trying to save your life," he says. "You were frozen, and I couldn't think of any other way—"

"*How?*" I demand again. "I've studied practitioning for nine years. I've never come across any talisman or form of magic granting a mortal the power of command over another's mind. That's dark magic, unheard of even in the yāo'jīng. So don't you dare lie to me." The more I speak, the more convinced I am that the man standing before me is a creature wicked and dangerous—one that shouldn't be here. And when he remains silent, each heartbeat between us compounding his guilt, I say softly, "What kind of a monster are you?"

At this, he flinches and turns his face from me. I catch the sharp hitch to his breath, the movement of his throat as he swallows and, at last, speaks. "Halfling," he says quietly. "I'm a halfling. Half-demon, half-mortal."

My thoughts stutter. "That's impossible," I whisper. "There are no mó halflings." The wards between our realms have been sealed for eternity since the gods created the world under the Heavenly Order. Mó ichor is poisonous to mortals; it is said the dark force that runs in their bodies counteracts the life force of mortals, making it impossible for a living creature to bear both.

"There is," Yù'chén says. "One."

I stare at him. Slowly, everything clicks into place. How impossibly powerful he is. How he was able to wield spirit energy, the energy only immortals and mortal practitioners can use. How he was able to call off Qióng'qí, and perhaps so many other beasts of the Kingdom of Night along the way, yet still present to me the evidence that made me trust him. Blood and heart—and dark magic.

And . . . the way he looked at me after I saved that halfling from Áo'yīn. The gentle way his fingers touched me, smoothing my clothes and straightening my collar.

I shake off the memory and stagger away from him. He's half-mó. Half a demon, half of something that should never have set foot in this realm. Half of the creature that destroyed my world and tore apart my family and drank my mother's soul—

I turn to run, but his hands close over my wrists, dragging me back to him. "Wait," he's saying, desperate. "Àn'yīng—"

"Don't touch me," I gasp, and to my surprise he obeys. He steps back from me and lifts his hands in a placating gesture. His chest rises and falls sharply, and my attention snags on the soft spot between his ribs.

I need to kill him. I'll put a blade in his heart now, push his body off the edge of this corridor into the skies—

"Give me a chance." His voice is low, deep and intoxicating with a power I should have realized was demonic from the very first day. He holds a hand out to me, palm-up. "Cut it open."

I hesitate only for a fraction of a second before I plunge my blade straight through his palm.

Yù'chén gasps in pain, but I'm focused on where the steel of Fleet connects with his flesh. Blood, red and warm, wells up and drips down the sides of his hand, his wrist, his forearm. It splatters the perfect white marble, gleaming like rubies under the dying sunlight.

I remember why I decided to trust him in the first place. *Demons don't bleed.*

I look up at him to find his eyes on me. His jaw is clenched, his mouth in a sullen curve. But he does not pull away. Without breaking his gaze from mine, he wraps his long fingers around my hand, curling them over the hilt of the blade wedged in his flesh to reach me. Blood drips down his arm as he draws my hand to him and presses it against his chest.

I start, but he holds me firmly—and that's when I feel it: the pulse beneath my palms. A memory surfaces, of him pulling me onto Heavens' Gate, his body warm and firm beneath mine. My cheek against his chest, listening to the strong *thud-thud-thud.*

Demons don't have hearts.

"Half-mortal," Yù'chén says. Our fingers are intertwined over the steady beat of his heart. "You heard the Eight Immortals: 'By measure of your mortal blood and mortal hearts.'"

"You are no mortal," I growl.

"The wards admitted me. I qualify, too."

I narrow my eyes. "The immortals," I say slowly, "have

spent the last nine years building their *wards* against the mó. They should know that one has managed to slip through."

Yù'chén's mouth twists into a humorless smile. "Little scorpion," he says, "if you report me, what do you think they'll do to you? The entire hall saw me helping you earlier. They saw us leave together. They'll think us either allies or lovers—"

"*Don't,*" I snarl, "debase my name by suggesting I am involved with the likes of *you.*"

His smile slips. "You know it's true. Whatever they do to me, they'll do to you for being involved with . . . the likes of me."

I stare at him, furious. As much as it kills me to admit it, he's right. If I'm the one who reports him to the immortals, they might decide I have something to do with the mó. I recall their impassive expressions and distant gazes. They barely admitted me into the trials earlier. Something tells me they won't bother listening a second time.

I have fought too hard to get here. And I have too much to lose.

My blade is angled against his chest, the soft spot between his ribs where his heart beats. All it would take is one push.

Yù'chén senses my hesitation. "Àn'yīng, please," he says. "You see it, too."

I shake my head. "The only thing I see," I say, "is that you're a *monster.*"

"I was born in the Kingdom of Rivers, just like you—"

"*You are nothing like me!*"

I twist my blade in his hand, and he makes a choked sound, his knees buckling at the pain. I bend over him, my other blade swiftly finding his throat. He goes still, breathing hard. A malicious thrill swoops through me. This time, *I* have the power.

"Why are you here?" I demand.

His lashes flutter. "The same reason as you."

"Liar."

"Can't I want what you want?" he rasps. "A better life, in a better place? Or am I not human enough to desire that?"

The tip of my blade digs into the curve of his neck, drawing a line of red. As I stare at it, I find that I cannot move.

"I mean you no harm, Àn'yīng." The way he speaks my real name sends shivers down my spine, for all the wrong reasons. "I am a life. I, too, have a beating heart."

And just like that, with those words, the moment's gone. I know that, despite every vow I've made myself regarding the mó, I cannot kill this man right now.

With a hiss, I pull my blade from his palm.

He curses and doubles over, cradling his wounded hand. Red puddles on the pristine white floor. I study his blood under the faint light of dusk, searching for abnormalities. But it's the same red as mine.

By the time I look up, his bleeding has already slowed; his flesh is already beginning to knit together.

My hands fist. "You'll live to see the next trial," I say coldly, and turn to leave.

"Wait," he says, pushing himself to his feet. His fingers wrap around my wrist, spinning me so I'm forced to look at him.

"Àn'yīng," Yù'chén says. He tries to smile. "Ally with me."

The sincerity in his voice is so damn real.

"Don't *touch* me," I snap again.

His smile falters, but he lets go. He stands there with his

hands by his sides, one blood-soaked. "Ally with me," he repeats.

I level a blank look at Yù'chén. "I don't think you understand," I say. "From now on, I want nothing to do with you."

His lips part as he searches my face. His gaze ensnares me.

I hold it and carve my words to hurt. "You *disgust* me."

Then I twist away and leave him there, caught in the shadows of twilight with the question I didn't ask.

Why? Why does he still want me to ally with him when I have made clear my revulsion for him? When I have nothing to offer in terms of skill or physical prowess?

After all that . . . why?

It no longer matters. In the end, if the trials do not kill him, I will.

10

With every passing second, I wonder if I've made the wrong choice.

The back of the temple opens to a terrace garden of white stone: *Clear Skies Pavilion,* announces a marble sign. Wisteria in soft hues of purple, blue, and pink whisper gently in the breeze; magnolia trees line the path to a rounded moongate in the wall to the right. *Candidates' Courtyard,* reads the plaque above the circular opening. To the left is another moongate that leads to a river reflecting the rosy skies like the finest blown glass; directly ahead, the veranda appears to end in a stirring sea of clouds.

I turn and follow the path into the Candidates' Courtyard.

Beyond the moongate are the dormitories. Joined into one long structure that wraps around a courtyard, they are accented with gray-tiled roofs and rosewood and pale walls, perhaps to mimic the style of the mortal realm. Night has fallen, but a series of lanterns light the long, open-air veranda that winds outside our chambers. At the center of the courtyard is a curving pond, flecked with lotuses and the glow of fireflies. Willows dip their branches into the water, and orchids and flowering plum trees lean over to gaze at their reflections.

For a moment, I stand taking this all in: the cool breeze on my face, the lantern light hitting the water at angles that make me think of the glittering threads Mā used to sew with. I think I catch the flash of a carp tail and the shimmer of scales as it darts beneath the surface.

There is a peace here that I haven't known in nine years.

I make my way down the veranda. Elegant rosewood doors are marked with numbers; mine, the forty-fourth, is at the very end.

I slide open the doors and step inside. It takes me a moment to believe what I'm seeing.

Smooth wood floors polished to a gleam, warmed by the lambent light of lanterns. A bed wider than I could ever have imagined, laid with silks as soft as dreams. Gauze drapes fluttering gently before a balcony that overlooks the sea of clouds, silvered in the moonlight. And beyond, the shapes of mountains and rivers and oceans adrift amidst curls of mist. My chambers are larger than our cottage in Xī'lín.

Was this truly where my father trained for years? And why . . . why did he leave this place to return to the mortal realm? He wasn't married to Mā at that point, and he had been raised an orphan with no ties drawing him back to the Kingdom of Rivers.

I peel off my muddied dress and place it by the side of the bathtub, along with my crescent blades. Plumes of steam rise from the water, and I exhale as I sink in and stretch out, my head resting against the curved back. Flower petals drift in the water, their fragrance soothing me. I wish to curl up here and sleep for a hundred years. For the first time in a long time, I am free of the gnawing dread and bone-deep fear that come with survival.

It feels so good, I could weep.

But Mā and Méi'zi are not here. They are a realm away, trapped by that ever-present fear of mó, of death, of agony. The memory of Méi'zi standing at our village gates, hugging my dagger to her chest, sears my heart.

My eyes fly open.

Floating in the water between petals of eastern rose and osmanthus is my jade pendant. I lift it, studying the way it catches the light of the lanterns, the green stone cloudy and veined, the broken edge jagged but not sharp enough to cut. I know every detail of this pendant by heart. If I close my eyes, I can conjure the precise style of calligraphy that appears in golden strokes within the jade. I know the way my guardian speaks, formal and direct and . . . warm.

My guardian has watched over me for nine years and led me here, to the Temple of Dawn. "I'm here," I murmur. I squeeze the pendant, watching a drop of water trickle down its smooth surface. "Thank you."

Of course, the stone remains stubbornly blank.

I retrieve my handkerchief from the bodice of my dress, unfolding the note within. My father was clever enough to cast a talisman over the parchment to protect it from the elements: the note is as smooth and pristine as the day I found it, the ink unmarred by water, mud, or blood.

I read the note as I have done every night since discovering it, the characters ingrained in my mind. " 'The truth to everything,' " I whisper. " 'Find the One of the Vast Sea.' "

I've arrived in the Kingdom of Sky, where my father's secrets have led me to more questions than answers.

I scrub myself with the various scented powders by the edge of the tub, then towel off. My dress is torn and dirty and still wet with ocean water; I'll have to clean it and mend it if I can find a sewing kit. For tonight, I'll need to make do with something else.

From an elegant cabinet filled with outfits in shimmering silks and samites, I choose a deep-blue dress, admiring how the fabric ripples with iridescence in a way that no mortal can weave, and how it slides through my fingers like water. It fits perfectly, slipping over my shoulders to hug the shape of my body. My favorite piece, however, is the pair of new black leather boots in the bottom drawer.

This dress isn't made to fit my blades, so I improvise, selecting four: I strap one to each wrist and one in each boot, fixing my sleeves to ensure they're concealed. I'm twining my hair into a tight braid with my white ribbon when a gong sounds to announce the beginning of the Trial Banquet.

Forty-four candidates. This time, I'm rested, strong, and ready to study my competition.

When I slide open my doors, candidates are already making their way down the courtyard. I follow, fingers tapping against the crescent blades within my sleeves, as I instinctively search the crowd for Yù'chén.

When we file through the moongate to the terrace, I hear gasps.

At the front of the terrace, a marble bridge has appeared over the clouds. The moon hangs at the other end, full and larger than I have ever seen it, as if I could climb onto the bridge railing and press my finger to its surface. The candidates exclaim in delight at the engravings on the bridge: dragons and phoenixes, sun and stars, lotuses and irises that seem to undulate as we cross.

We arrive at a garden bathed in the moon's glow. Illuminated by softly pulsing lights that resemble bottled stars are arrays of white osmanthus, anise magnolias, blush hibiscus, and more, their fragrances twining between jade tables heaped with steaming trays of food. Here and there, pavilions rest along winding streams, situated for gazing into the forest beyond.

"The Celestial Gardens!" I hear one of the candidates exclaim, the inflection to her speech marking her as from the Western Province. "I've read about them in our town library books. They're more beautiful than I imagined."

I make for an empty table behind a tight-knit group of people. That's when I feel someone watching me.

I look up.

Yán'lù's face is twisted in a sneer, his eyes narrowed as they follow me through the shifting crowd. I didn't catch sight of him back at the Hall of Radiant Sun, and he wouldn't have dared to try anything there under the eyes of the immortals . . . but now, in these gardens, there are too many ways he could kill me and make it look like an accident.

I look away from him, determined not to let him cow me. I sense his gaze trailing me; his cronies, too, have stopped talking and watch me hungrily. I slide my blades into my palms as, out of the corners of my eyes, I see Yán'lù turn and break away from the group, making straight for me—

"Hi!"

A girl cuts into my path. It takes me a moment to place the face, the wide-set eyes and delicate lips now curved in a wide, toothy grin, the two buns atop her head. Something in her amber gaze clicks into place.

It's the fox spirit halfling. I remember her eyes watching me from behind the tree on the mountain, her silent warning as one of Yán'lù's cronies attacked me.

"I'm Lì'líng," she says brightly.

I almost recoil, all my preconceptions of yāo'jīng filtering through my mind—but above it all, I recall the announcer's voice, mingling now with Yù'chén's: *By measure of your mortal blood and mortal hearts.*

Whether or not she is a halfling, the immortals' wards admitted her into this realm and into these trials.

"Àn'yīng," I mumble. It's been a while since I've exchanged niceties not at blade point.

"I know! We all saw your entrance earlier." Her eyes warm, and there's a knowing glint to them as she adds, "Thanks for looking out for me. You must be hungry!"

I catch Yán'lù watching me through the crowd as Lì'líng pulls me in the opposite direction. I half listen to her chatting, but my muscles are tensed, my fingers brushing the hilts of the blades concealed in my sleeves.

Lì'líng keeps up a steady, nearly pleasant stream of conversation that is less a conversation than her exclamations over the delicacies on the platters we pass by: ". . . honeyed dates, osmanthus rice cakes . . . and ooh! Lotus-wrapped glutinous rice with *chicken!*" She pauses and waves at the two people standing beneath a great magnolia tree. "Look! I brought us a new friend."

"Was this *friend* forced to listen to you talk about glutinous rice balls?" asks the tall girl. Her arms are folded, and she's dressed in an all-black hàn'fú in thick brocade, a material commonly used in the north. Her skin is as pale as death, and there are deep shadows beneath her eyes, as though she hasn't slept. She looks supremely bored.

"It's not glutinous rice balls, Tán'mù, it's *lotus-wrapped glutinous rice*," sniffs Lì'líng. "How can you aspire to be a rice connoisseur without being able to distinguish between these?"

Tán'mù gives her a flat look. "I *don't* aspire to be a rice connoisseur—"

"Same difference," says their other companion. "All edible." He tosses a lotus-wrapped glutinous rice up in the air and opens his mouth wider than humanly possible—then swallows it whole, leaves and all. His tongue darts out, unnervingly long, as he licks the juices from his chin. There is something so familiar about his jewel-green eyes framed by arched brows and the shock of white hair that spills to his shoulders.

"You!" I exclaim. The last time I saw him, he was green and covered in scales, climbing the cliffs at Heavens' Gates. Now he looks mostly human but for his white hair and green eyes. It's the shapeshifter yāo'jīng.

He shoots me a grin with too many rows of white teeth before unclamping them to shove a whole peach inside.

"That's Fán'xuān," Lì'líng chirps. "He's like our deranged little brother."

"You're the deranged one," Fán'xuān bites back over his chewing, "if you think red beans are the best stuffing for glutinous rice."

Lì'líng fires up. "Red beans *and* salted egg yolk, you fish-brained turtle—"

They get into it then, Fán'xuān arguing for pork-and-mushroom stuffing.

I realize I'm staring and quickly look away. Tán'mù, how-ever, watches me like a hawk. The look on her face is less than friendly. "Where's your lover?" she asks.

It takes me a second to realize she's talking about Yù'chén. "He's not my lover."

She shrugs and turns her attention to a platter of shred-ded pheasant wrapped in milk skin. Her left wrist flashes, and I catch the number fifteen on it. A two-pronged spear is strapped to her back. I wonder if she's one of the candidates who received training at a mortal practitioning school before coming here. I know those still exist, and some have man-aged to escape the Kingdom of Night's invasion—for now.

"I'm only asking because he's Number Two," she says as she chews. "The higher numbers are usually targeted first."

I wonder if my Number Forty-Four has a silver lining after all. "Who's Number One?" I ask.

"She's over there," Lì'líng chimes in, appearing to have won the argument with Fán'xuān. She flicks her gaze to a table toward the center of the terrace, where a tall, sturdily built girl is holding court. She is muscular, her rich yellow shift complementing her tanned skin and suggesting Western Province origins. I've heard that in the Golden Desert, where the sun blazes bright and mó are least likely to wander, mortal practitioning schools thrive between the sand dunes, training powerful practitioners who patrol the desert to guard against the Kingdom of Night. "Her name is Xiù'chūn."

"I saw her get through the First Trial," Fán'xuān offers between bites of braised chicken. "It looked like a game to her." His golden bracelet flashes, and I take note of his ranking: twenty-four. Interesting, since he clearly scaled that mountain before Yù'chén and me, but I get the feeling he somehow doesn't care.

I try to catch Lì'líng's number, but her wrist is turned away from me as she peels another lotus-wrapped glutinous rice and bites off half. "Mm," she sighs. "Dates."

I'm suddenly starving. I pile food onto a plate and eat, the flavors melting against my tongue, richer and better than anything I've tasted before in my life. There's duck stewed with wine and cauliflower, steamed lotus root with shrimp, spiced mutton, pork in thick soy gravy . . . I don't think I've seen this much food in over nine years. Or, ever.

Suddenly, I feel disgusted. Here I am, stuffing my face and enjoying the luxuries, when Mā and Méi'zi are sharing a meager meal. I think of our watery congee, boiled with the rabbit I hunt and the black fungus I harvest.

I set my platter down a bit too hard. "Excuse me," I begin, but that's when a hush goes through the crowd of candidates.

The Eight Immortals are here. They glide more than walk across the bridge, their sleeves and gauzes billowing, their skin seeming to soak in the moonlight so that they glow with it. Behind them, dressed in simpler white shifts and armor, are the immortal guards.

The candidates straighten as the immortals cross the bridge and come to a stop on the terrace. Immediately, I spot the one who vouched for me, Shī'yǎ. Interestingly, she is flanked by a guard—the only one of the Eight Immortals to have an escort.

When my gaze slides to the guard's face, I nearly forget to breathe.

His face. I recognize it—slim and chiseled with those long,

sweeping eyes, a countenance that reminds me of clear river water and sunlight. He wears the white-gold lamellar armor of the immortal realm's soldiers, and his hair is pinned up, but there is no doubt about it.

He is the stranger whose face I dreamt beneath the sea.

"Candidates!" Jǐng'xiù's voice booms across the garden, tearing me from my thoughts. "I hope you are enjoying our Trial Banquet!" There's enthusiastic cheering and clapping. Full bellies mean loyalty. "Over the next days, the Temple of Dawn is yours to explore. We have sparring rooms, weapons, talismans, and everything else you'll need to train yourselves. While the wards have admitted you into the temple, you will not have access to the Kingdom of Sky beyond these grounds." A disappointed murmur rises among the candidates, and Jǐng'xiù's grin widens as he spreads his arms. "For that, you'll have to wait until you've passed all the trials and received our nomination for immortality."

Every nerve in me stretches taut as I recall the golden pill Jǐng'xiù held up earlier, as bright as a small star in his palm. The key to a better life for most of us, to safety and security and glory.

For me, the medicine to save my mother's life.

The atmosphere is suddenly tense, as though the same thought is on every one of the forty-four candidates' minds.

"The Temple of Dawn observes a number of rules per our Precepts, copies of which you'll find in each of your chambers," Jǐng'xiù continues. "So long as you observe our Precepts, you are free to spend your time in the temple as you wish until the Second Trial. Enjoy your stay!" With a flourish of his sleeves, he turns to leave with the other immortals.

"Hold on," calls a candidate. It's Number One, Xiù'chūn.

Her voice is steady, without an ounce of fear or timidness to be addressing the Eight Immortals directly. "Are you going to tell us more about the Second Trial?"

Jǐng'xiù glances over his shoulder. "And why would I? It wouldn't be a trial anymore, would it?"

"We'll at least receive notice of when it starts, right?" Xiù'chūn presses.

Jǐng'xiù's smile is cold. "Oh, you'll know when it begins" is all he says. Wisps of cloud are forming at the Eight Immortals' feet, lifting them into the air. Before any of us can do anything, they drift into the night sky like stars, and then they're gone.

"Wait." I start to feel as if there's something I'm missing. "He didn't tell us about classes or who's going to be training us."

Lì'líng bites her lip. "There are no classes," she says. "I think there used to be—at least, that's what we heard in the—" She's cut off when Tán'mù shoots her a look, and quickly changes tack: "But in recent years, we've heard rumors they're no longer training practitioners since the last few years of the war. Just recruiting the best of us into their kingdom."

My mind reels. This isn't what I read in Bà's journals. I remember his entries about long, detailed courses teaching martial arts, talismans and enchantments, and the techniques to cultivating our spirit energy. He studied at the Temple of Dawn as a candidate for years before going through the trials.

No classes. No training. And a Second Trial that might start at any moment.

I'm so screwed.

I turn, ignoring Lì'líng as she calls after me, because I can't respond, not when it feels like my world and the hope

I clung to for so long is falling apart. If I nearly died trying to reach this place, I have zero chance of surviving the next trials against the likes of Yù'chén and Yán'lù. Zero chance of earning a spot and winning the pill my mother's life depends on.

I hurry back across the marble bridge, the silver luminescence reflecting from its too-beautiful engravings now hurting my eyes. I need to get to my room, need to get a letter out to Méi'zi, think through my options.

I don't notice the shadow behind me until it's too late.

My blades are in my hands, but as I raise them to strike, the air shifts. I taste spirit energy, see it shimmer as the talisman my assailant has drawn takes effect.

Clouds billow in and swallow the bridge so that the night turns into an expanse of shifting gray silhouettes.

A shape lunges out of the fog. Before I can scream, fingers wrap around my neck in a choke hold, and a voice hisses by my ear.

"Did you think I'd forgotten about you?"

I'd recognize Yán'lù's twisted snarl anywhere.

I lash out, but he's locked both of my wrists in his grip. The courtyard is empty and dark, moonlight pooling around pockets of shadows. I can hear sounds of laughter and conversation from the banquet drifting toward us beyond the unnatural fog Yán'lù has cast.

"You should've died back at the Immortals' Steps when I pushed you into the sea. But someone's been helping you all along, eh?" Yán'lù inhales deep, like he's scenting me. "Who is it?"

Black spots erupt in my vision as his hand squeezes tighter over my throat. He's not only trying to kill me; he's turning it into a sport. And he's having *fun*.

"I want to know who it is," he whispers. "And until I find out, I'm going to enjoy hunting you down. I'm going to enjoy watching you *suffer*." His laugh is low. "What are you going to do now, my little flower? There's no one here to help you."

"There is someone here," comes a voice, masculine and pleasant, though tinged with frost.

The pressure on my throat loosens; as I lurch away, Yán'lù shoves me, hard. The world swings off balance, and a crack of pain streaks up my wrists as I slam against the marble floor of the bridge.

I clench my teeth and look up. My vision's blurred, but between the distant lights and the white osmanthus trees at the end of the Celestial Gardens, a figure has emerged, approaching with sharp, steady footfalls.

Clack. Clack. Clack. With each step, tremors of spirit energy roll through the marble bridge.

"We were just having a friendly chat," I hear Yán'lù reply. "Isn't that right, my flower?"

I grit my teeth against the pain in my wrists. "That's right," I say. My voice shakes, but I swallow and try again. "We're fine."

I blink the haze from my eyes. In the moonlight, between the softly shifting flower trees of the gardens in the distance, stands a tall, pale-robed silhouette. He's broad-shouldered, dressed in white silks, his lamellar glinting like gold scales.

Not a candidate—a guard. Through the fog, I can't make out any of his features except for the jut of his chin, the cold, stern line of his mouth. There is a silent air of power to him, like the deep undercurrent of a flowing river.

The guard addresses Yán'lù, ignoring me. "The Temple of Dawn's Precepts state there is to be no slaughter on temple grounds—"

"—outside of the trials," Yán'lù sneers. I'm shocked at his audacity, to interrupt an immortal like that. He seems to sense how this one holds no power over our fates in the tournament. "Trust me, I'm well aware of my rights as a candidate in the Immortality Trials."

The newcomer takes a step toward Yán'lù, and it is as though thunder rolls over our bridge. Spirit energy, stronger than any I have ever felt, reverberates from the immortal's core, stirring a wind and bringing with it the scent of rain.

Yán'lù suddenly looks less smug.

"I care nothing about your status as a candidate of the Immortality Trials." The immortal's tone is cold enough to freeze oceans. "My duty is to the Temple of Dawn. My job is to protect it and its guests according to the values of the Kingdom of Sky and the Heavenly Order."

"As I said, we were having a *friendly chat*," Yán'lù spits, though he backs away slightly. He turns to me, and his eyes glint with the promise of unfinished business. "Sweet dreams, my *flower*." He steps past the immortal, making for the banquet again.

The spirit energy in the air shifts, and the thick fog from Yán'lù's talisman begins to dissipate as the guard approaches me. I tense. He's seen me at my weakest; he could report this to the Eight Immortals, ending my chances of winning the trials.

The immortal's shadow falls over me, mirroring its owner to extend a hand.

I look up, and the world around me seems to fade until I am back in the ocean. Between the silent and vicious currents, between dreams and reality, I'd seen a face so beautiful I'd thought him a god of the sea, expression gentle as he inclined his head to me.

I blink the memory away and I'm back on the bridge, the immortal guard bending toward me with his hand outstretched. It's him—there's no doubt about it—I'm gazing up at the man who saved me in the sea: chiseled face and sharp, angled jaw, long eyes framed by eyebrows like a sweep of ink. His hair is neatly cinched, and not even a single golden thread embroidered on his collar is out of place.

He gazes back at me, eyes clear and steady beneath his lashes. I search them for a flicker of recognition, but there is only a cool detachment to his expression, his face too still and too smooth to read. Almost as if it's a practiced mask.

"You have nothing to fear from me," he says, though his words are no longer bladed. "I promise you I haven't a say in the trials. As I stated, my duty is to the Temple of Dawn. My job is to protect it and its guests."

I hesitate, then at last place my hand in his. A tingle rushes through my fingers, along with the heady realization that I am touching an immortal for the first time in my life. His skin is surprisingly callused, in a way I hadn't imagined immortals' could be. Easily, he lifts me to my feet, placing one hand on my shoulder to steady me. Then he retracts his hands and places them behind his back.

"You . . ." I swallow. *You appeared before me in the ocean today.* I realize how mad I would sound.

He's waiting for me to finish my sentence. The heartbeats stretch out between us.

"Yes?" he prompts, lifting an eyebrow.

I can't look away from him. Skies, I need to get a grip.

I swallow. "Thank you," I say, "for helping me."

His eyes flick to my palms, swift and assessing. "Your hands are bleeding."

"I'm fine," I say quickly, lacing my fingers behind my back. *Don't let anyone see your weakness.*

I try not to squirm under the long, appraising look he gives me. I hold my breath right until he inclines his head and turns. Tendrils of clouds curl over his shoulders as he begins walking away.

"Wait," I blurt out. *Why did I see you in the sea? Why did you save my life?* Those are the questions I want to ask, but instead, I say, "Why did the Honorable Immortal Shī'yǎ vouch for me?"

He tips his head toward me over his shoulder. "You arrived at sundown. Therefore, you qualified."

Trying to glean any information from him is like trying to reach through a wall of ice. So I ask, "How can I thank her?"

"You don't. The rules are the rules. The Honorable Immortal Shī'yǎ was merely respecting them." He begins walking again, and I hear his voice drift over the wind to me: "There is no partiality to the trials. Only those who win and those who die."

The Candidates' Courtyard is utterly silent when I return; everyone is at the banquet, enjoying themselves. I'm glad for this as I pace along the open-air veranda, rounding the pond to my chambers. When I reach my door, I find a small lacquered box sitting just outside the pool of warm lantern light. I check the box for any poison or enchantments before I pick it up and slide the lid open.

It's a sewing kit. As I run a finger over the different needles, the hundreds of threads that glow beneath the lantern, Yán'lù's threats seem to fall away. The world softens, and for a moment, I can imagine the girl who wished to sew oceans. The girl who made the handkerchief.

Caution bleeds into my delight. I don't know who this gift is from, whether friend or foe, or whether it is simply the magic of the immortal realm that heard my wish and conjured it into reality.

I sense a shift in the shadows behind me. But when I look up, the courtyard is still empty. A gentle breeze ripples the waters of the pond, stirring the lotuses and dappling the moonlight. For a second, I think I see a silhouette beneath the great weeping willow across the water, sense a pair of eyes watching me through the darkness. I blink, and there is nothing but swaying branches.

I step through my doors and pull them shut behind me, making sure to latch them. I mark talismans on the doors and windows.

I place the sewing kit by my pillow. Then I grab Méi'zi's dress and hold it tightly to me as I fall onto the bed.

Sleep takes me, and I do not dream.

11

I chose to train you for a reason, my father wrote.

I do my best to remember that as I fail practice after practice after practice.

If I thought the Temple of Dawn beautiful in the dusk, it is even more so during the day. The training halls are all open-air, upheld by columns of marble carved with immortals dancing amidst flowering trees, phoenixes, dragons, and deer. The sun pours in through the gauze drapes, lending a golden shimmer to everything. Outside, beyond the halls and gardens and ponds, white clouds drift into eternal blue skies. Once in a while, I hear the trill of distant laughter, glimpse immortals soaring across the sky, borne on wisps of cloud or the wings of great cranes.

It's perfect. It's everything we don't have in the mortal realm.

For some reason, Fú'yí's wrinkled old face comes to me, her expression fierce. *You let those bastards in the Kingdom of Sky know. You let them know we are still here. You let them know we are still alive.*

The immortals are powerful—perhaps more so than the mó. And clearly, if they're holding this tournament every year, they know there are still mortals out there fighting for survival.

Why haven't they tried to help us?

"Focus, Àn'yīng!"

I blink and find Lì'líng's large amber eyes peering at me. "I am," I say.

"You've sunk into the pond!" she exclaims, pointing.

I look down to see that I'm up to my knees in water.

Lì'líng has decided to adopt me into her group, and I can't say that I'm anything but grateful. We haven't spoken of the incident with Áo'yīn, or how she saved my life on Heavens' Gates, but that cements my trust in her. She could have killed me back when I was weak from fighting Áo'yīn, or when I was about to be attacked by Yán'lù's crony at Heavens' Gates.

But she didn't. Instead, she's spending time training me in qīng'gōng.

I cast an envious glance at where the shapeshifter Fán'xuān, in the form of a giant carp, circles just beneath the surface of the water. I know that most of the candidates here have likely had more training resources than I. The Second Trial could start at any moment, and being able to walk on water could save my life.

But try as I might, something isn't working.

We're in the Celestial Gardens today, practicing by a stream that winds to the very edge of the grounds before plunging off into the skies. Fán'xuān seems to be enjoying himself, swimming downstream and plunging off the edge of the waterfall before resurfacing as an enormous crane. Tán'mù still looks as though she hasn't slept, though her throwing stars meet every single target.

Most of the other candidates give us a wide berth; no one wants to associate with a group of yāo'jīng. I don't blame them; we all grew up on the same stories of how the yāo'jīng steal mortal babies from their cradles and drink their blood.

But I discover that these stories are just that. Lì'líng shows a fondness for chicken dishes, Fán'xuān will pour entire platters of food down his throat, and though I'm not sure what Tán'mù is, the one thing that unites them all . . . is how *human* they are. And how easily I interact with them. So far, they've been careful not to reveal much of their backstories to me, and I'm fine with that. We're not here to become friends, after all.

"Try it again," Lì'líng says encouragingly. In the daytime, she looks bright-eyed and energized, her cheeks round and her lips as red as cherries and prone to laughter. She crouches by a growth of orchids, their yellow petals bright against her white robes. She has twined a flower into her hair, and I can't help but think of how lovely it looks with her amber eyes. "Remember, find the *rhythm* of the water's spirit energy, which will always be moving, and point yours so that it flows in the opposite—" She pauses, her nose twitching in the exact manner of a small fox. "Is that soy chicken?"

I bite down a smile as I look back at the water. The currents flow so fast, it seems *impossible* to pinpoint any form of energy and be able to . . . walk on the surface. There's a reason the practitioners in the storybooks take entire lifetimes to cultivate these types of abilities.

I draw a deep breath, focusing in on the energies flowing in the water. It is complete chaos, attempting to catch any of them; they slip in and out of my grasp, a tumultuous mess.

I summon what I can of my spirit energy, channeling it to the soles of my feet. I take a step forward—and plunge face-first into the water.

I hear snickering around me when I come up for air, coughing and spitting water.

"Walk it off, walk it off," Tán'mù says. She glances at Lì'líng, who looks crestfallen. By her side, the yellow orchids seem to droop their heads. "Maybe we try archery instead."

I catch movement across the clearing. Beneath a copse of golden ginkgos is a familiar figure. Watching me.

Yù'chén covers his mouth with a hand, but I can see the traces of laughter on his face. He's in his crimson cloak, cinched at the waist for easier movement. His sword is strapped to his hip, and on his other shoulder hangs a siyah-horn bow.

He straightens and tips his chin at me, smirking as though to say, *Watch me.*

Effortlessly, he takes off at a run and leaps into the air, too high, too light, and too graceful. His cloak trails bright red, stirring petals into the air. Between one blink and another, his bow is in his hand and his arrow nocked. He takes aim and fires—one, two, three times.

He alights before the wooden target. Three perfect bull's-eyes. The last arrow splits the first.

Yù'chén dips into a bow as the crowd watching breaks into scattered applause. When he rises, he catches my gaze and arches an eyebrow.

I fist Striker and turn away. Out of the corner of my eye, I see a group of girls approach him.

My thoughts have drifted to him more often than I would've liked over the past few days: I'm filled with a gnawing dread that I've made the wrong choice by not reporting him to the immortals. But reporting him could endanger my own standing in the trials.

I can't think of protecting kingdoms when I can't even save my own mother.

At night, though my body is sore and my every last nerve is fried from training, I work on a secret of mine.

I'm sewing a pair of gloves for Méi'zi. It's a way we communicated with each other growing up: leaving little gifts under each other's pillows, from socks to scarves to hats. When our kingdom fell and I gave up my needles for my blades, Méi'zi continued this tradition. Throughout the years, her gifts have become more and more elaborate, her stitches coming in neater and tighter and her patterns blooming in ways I could never have imagined. My sister makes magic when she sews.

But there is something to the sewing kit I was gifted that feels like magic, too. I have studied the threads beneath the lantern light, marveling at the way they seemed to vanish at certain angles. They are finer than any silks I've encountered in the mortal realm, and the way they blend into fabric makes me suspect that they were not made by human hands. In the myths and journals of mortal practitioners, there is a type of cloth woven by the song of the fish-tailed sea spirits in the ocean's depths. The fabric is said to ripple like water, and clothes spun of sea silk are meant to feel like clouds.

The only person in the realms who knows my love for sewing is my guardian in the jade. Though I'd hoped for the sewing kit to be a gift from them—a secret signal of sorts between us—my pendant has remained silent since my arrival.

My gloves are almost complete. My skills are rusty, but I've sewn a golden-roofed palace on clouds and a tiny figurine in a white dress: me. I thought of giving embroidered-me a wide smile to show my victory but decided to go with a scowl. More realistic that way.

Méi'zi will recognize my stitches and the message within: that I've reached the Kingdom of Sky safely.

Now I just need to figure out a way to send it to her. I know a talisman—similar to the one on Heart—that practitioners use on messenger doves to help them reach the intended recipient. The problem is, no matter how skilled a messenger dove, it can't cross realms or wards.

No one may enter, and no one may leave. I've thought through the Eight Immortals' warning, and I wonder if there is a loophole. *No one* does not mean *nothing.* If an animal or inanimate object can cross the wards, can't I conjure a talisman to guide the gloves to Méi'zi?

I decide to test this theory at the end of the week.

I wait until the others are asleep. It's a waning moon, the night perfectly cloaked in clouds when I slip out of my chambers. The courtyard dances with shadows and the rustle of wind that howls mournfully through the mountains beyond this temple.

I make sure the protective talismans I've set on my chambers are undisturbed as I slide the door shut behind me.

A silhouette lunges at me from behind a willow, but I've prepared for this.

I lash out with Poison, feel the satisfying push of resistance as my trusty blade bites into flesh. There's a hiss of pain, and my assailant stumbles, his hand over the gash in his chest.

No slaughter on temple grounds, the Precepts state. That doesn't mean I can't wound.

My assailant looks up and glares at me, blood dribbling

from the corners of his mouth. In the dim moonlight filtering out from behind clouds, I make out his face: one of Yán'lù's cronies.

Alarm bells go off in my head as I turn to another approaching figure and strike with my other hand. Fleet draws blood from the second attacker, but then a third lunges at me from behind, and I don't reach him in time.

My shout is cut off by a meaty hand clamping over my mouth. I spin Poison and Fleet and jab them backward, yet a fourth pair of hands catches them in a firm grip; a fifth person grabs my legs, lifting me bodily from the ground. There's a jab to my wrists, and my crescent blades drop to the ground in two light clinks.

"He said to meet by the waterfall," hisses the assailant holding my arms.

I can't twist out of their grasp, but I don't stop struggling as they carry me through the moongate and past the bridge to the Celestial Gardens. We're heading for the back of the gardens, where the forest grows thick and wild. By now, there's an edge of panic to my anger. They're taking me far from the Clear Skies Pavilion, from the dorms and the training temples, to a place where no one can hear me scream.

Willows and dove trees obscure the sky. Soon, I hear the rush of the waterfall that plunges from the edge of the temple grounds to the abyss and the ocean of another realm far, far below.

My assailants drop me roughly to the ground and pin me there, twisting my wrists just enough to hurt. Someone's palm covers the lower half of my face. From my vantage point, I see only long grasses and the canopy, smell wet loam and the faint fragrance of flowers.

Yán'lù's face appears. I can make out only the glint of his teeth as he smiles in a way that sends cold through my veins.

"Hand off her mouth," he orders. "I want to hear her scream."

The pressure on my face loosens. Then Yán'lù backhands me across my cheek so hard that I see stars, hear a sharp, high-pitched ringing in my ears. When the world settles again, I taste blood on my tongue.

I spit on the grass. "You can't kill me." My voice is barely a croak. "No slaughter on temple grounds. Precepts."

"Oh, I'm well aware," Yán'lù says. His voice is dangerously soft. "But there are so many ways I can hurt you without killing you."

So he's figured out the loophole to this particular precept, too.

My heart hammers, but I force myself to hold very still. If I show fear, I lose. I test my limbs, but there are five of his lackeys pinning me down. The waterfall pounds in my ears; the river is so close to me, I can feel its spray on my skin.

"Unless." Yán'lù crouches by my side. He bends to my ear, and I shiver as I feel his breath against my cheeks. "Unless, my flower, you tell me the secret you hold."

I freeze. What secret could Yán'lù want from me? "I have no idea what you're talking about," I say, but even as I speak, I think of my father, of the note in the handkerchief. *The truth to everything is at the Temple of Dawn.* And I think of Yù'chén, of the dark secret he hides that only I know.

Yán'lù's eyes take on a manic gleam. "In that case, I think we should wash the blood from her lovely, lovely face," he says. "Clean her up a little."

I barely have time to draw a breath as I'm lifted and

dunked backward into the river. It's no use; the currents buffet me relentlessly, and the air immediately burbles from my lips. Water rushes up my nose and fills my mouth, and it is agony. I splutter, my body convulses, my lungs are on fire, and I think I will die—

—and I'm dragged up. I cough out water, my body heaving in great, racking gasps. But as Yán'lù's face appears close to mine again, I lift my chin and meet his gaze. My teeth are chattering so hard that I know he can hear it, but I won't give him the satisfaction of breaking.

I will not be prey.

"Having fun?" he asks. "We can stop, if you beg."

I swallow but keep my lips sealed. *No slaughter on temple grounds. They can't kill me. I'll live.* But my heart and the terror pulsing through my veins scream otherwise.

"No?" Yán'lù says. "Let's clean out your mouth."

Water gags me again, and when I surface, I'm on the verge of begging. My entire body trembles. There's the cold press of a knife against my cheek, and I feel my skin split open, feel warmth down my face.

"Tell me your secret," Yán'lù snarls. "Who's watching over you?"

I think of the immortal guard whose face I dreamt in the ocean that day, who saved me from Yán'lù our first night here. But there is another answer to his question: the reason I'm alive, the one who has watched over me all these years.

My guardian in the jade.

My dearest, oldest secret, passed to me from my father.

I look up at Yán'lù. Then I spit in his face.

For a moment, he's so frozen in his shock and fury that it

might have been funny. But when his hand whips across my cheek, I see white and feel my face slam into the soil.

When feeling returns to me, I'm lying on the grass, head spinning, blood pooling in my mouth. Yán'lù's knife is pressed to my collar. He drags it onto my chest, then down the plane of my stomach. Lower. "I'm going to humiliate you," he snarls, and there is a mad glee to his words. "I'm going to humiliate you until you wish you'd drowned in the ocean that day."

He lifts his knife, and that's when the darkness behind him moves. Between one blink and the next, Yán'lù's dagger spins out of his fingers . . . and simply vanishes.

"Talk to me again about *humiliation*," comes a deep, familiar voice.

There's a sickening *crack,* followed by a shout, and suddenly Yán'lù is sprawled on the ground, his leg twisted at an odd angle.

The figure that steps from the shadows is utterly terrifying and utterly beautiful—a combination I did not know could coexist until I set my gaze upon him in this very moment.

In the moonlight, Yù'chén's deep crimson cloak takes on the color of blood. He hasn't drawn any weapons, but there is something cold and completely lethal to his gaze and his gait, the way he falls very still when his eyes land on the five men pinning me down. The air around him seems to crackle, and I realize it's his spirit energy rolling off him in thunderous waves.

He's *furious.*

"If I were you," he says, "I would let her go."

The biggest and bravest of Yán'lù's cronies opens his mouth to talk back. What comes out instead is a scream.

Something thuds to the grass. I catch sight of fingers and nails, and my stomach turns.

Whimpering, the candidate brings his bloodied stump of an arm to the dim moonlight. "Y-y-you cut off my hand," he stammers, and then his voice rises to a scream. *"You cut off my hand!"*

"Leave any fingerprints on her skin, and it'll be all your hands as well as the softest, smallest parts of your bodies," Yù'chén replies, his tone still low. His sword is at his side, a dark liquid staining its steel. "If I were you, I'd grab your leader and go before that happens."

The others flinch away from me as if I've burned them. They scramble, hauling Yán'lù up by his armpits and dragging him away from us. The one who's lost his hand stumbles after them, keening.

"Wait," Yù'chén says.

They obey, freezing like rabbits.

Yù'chén half turns to them. Half his face is in shadow. "Touch her again—if I even get a *whiff* of you near her—you're all dead. I don't care what the Precepts dictate. I will kill you. And I will make it hurt like *nothing* you've felt before."

Yán'lù's lackeys haul him away, fleeing like dogs with their tails between their legs.

Yù'chén turns to me. He lays his sword down on the grass and, with his hands raised, approaches. I flinch as he crouches by my side. He says nothing, only rakes a gaze down my body. Fury pulses from him in waves.

"You're bleeding." His voice is harsh, but softer now than moments ago. He extends a hand, then hesitates, his fingers curling an inch from my skin. "May I?"

I don't have the energy to resist. In my silence, he touches a finger to my jaw and lifts my face. I see the tightening of his lips as he takes in the cut Yán'lù opened on my cheek.

"I can heal it," he says. "Do you want me to?"

Yes. No. I don't know anymore. Of all the candidates here, he is the most dangerous. I am meant to revile him. But the fight leaves me when his fingers slide across my face and his palm comes to rest against my cheek.

I close my eyes and nod. The warmth of his skin and spirit energy flow into me, and my muscles relax. His other hand is on my shoulder, supporting me, injecting heat into my clothes and my body, drying the water from the river. It feels so good.

"Àn'yīng. Àn'yīng, don't fall asleep." His voice pulls me from the ocean of blackness. I'm slumped against him, my chin tucked against the crook of his neck, my body shielded from the wind by his. "You're in shock."

His thumb traces circles against my cheek; his other hand is warm against the small of my back. I realize it's no longer his spirit energy but his demonic magic that's spreading through my veins, hot and slow and delicious in a way that makes me feel good for all the wrong reasons. My head is foggy, as though I've drunk an entire carafe of plum wine, but between the rising heat in my belly and the strange desire closing my throat, I remember a fact about the mó: how their dark magic is designed to lure mortals to them, to poison our minds like a drug and draw us to them even as they devour us. It's sickening, but in this moment, I can't seem to remember why.

I tip my head back and press my palm to his cheek, turning it to mine.

His eyes glow red with his magic, and a voice in the back of my mind tells me I should be afraid, tells me I should run, but I can only think of the crimson petals of the scorpion lily, the flower foretelling tragedy.

My fingers trail lower, brushing the soft curves of his lips, tracing the hard angles to his jaw. He goes very still at my touch, his lashes casting crescents against his cheeks, breaths warm against my skin.

"Is this your true form?" I barely even know what I'm saying, but the question is one that's been in the back of my mind. Would a half-mó, half-mortal take on the full form of a human? Or does he hide a monstrous thing beneath all this beauty?

Yù'chén's jaw tenses. "Stop," he says, and pulls his face from my grasp.

I feel cold, and I realize he's shut off his dark magic. He continues to hold me, though it's only to stop me from falling.

I blink, then push away from him. Blood rushes to my face. His magic—dark, *demonic* magic—is affecting me in ways that should disgust me.

Yet beneath that is the realization that this man has saved my life once more.

And then it occurs to me: *Who's watching over you?* Yán'lù has asked me, over and over again.

"It's you," I whisper. "You're the one Yán'lù's looking for."

Yù'chén narrows his eyes. "Why would he be looking for me?"

Because you're the one who keeps helping me, I think, and my hands curl into fists. "Why did you help me again?"

He's silent.

"I told you," I continue. "I want nothing to do with you."

Yù'chén angles his face away from me. Still, he says nothing.

I shut my eyes briefly and decide to give him a truth. "I don't want to owe you."

Yù'chén's eyes are fixed on the grass between us, littered with fragments of moonlight like shards of broken porcelain. When he lifts his head again, his expression is casual, the faintest hint of a smile on his lips, as though we were simply having a friendly discussion. "Why were you outside by yourself?"

I hesitate, but I can't think of any reason not to tell him the truth. "I wanted to send my sister something," I reply. "I needed to test whether I could get something through the Kingdom of Sky wards to the mortal realms."

He huffs a laugh, then shakes his head with a sort of helplessness. After a beat, he says, "Let me help you."

I want to say no. I *should* say no.

But I'm feeling a little better, at least strong enough to move around. I'm warm and dry, and honestly, the last thing I want is to return to my chambers and feel Yán'lù's cronies' hands on me in the dark, remember the feeling of drowning.

If there's anything Yán'lù has taught me, it's that there are some mortals capable of greater cruelty than mó.

"All right," I say.

12

My strength returns as I follow Yù'chén through the Celestial Gardens, winding through the forest of flowering trees and willows. It occurs to me that I am doing the exact opposite of what my parents and all mortal stories warned me of when I was a little girl: following a demon through the dark of the woods in the night.

But I am no longer a little girl, and the stories are just stories.

With my blades back in my hands, I feel calmer and in control once again—as much as I can be. Yù'chén weaves and ducks through the dove trees and ginkgos, and I keep my gaze pinned on the red of his cloak, which seems to blur into the shadows.

I begin to wonder if this is all a terrible idea. If getting a message to Méi'zi is worth the risk of being found out and potentially expelled from the trials.

"Where are we going?" I whisper.

"To the wards," Yù'chén says in a low voice. We duck into the shade of the great plum blossom trees that line this part of the gardens: near the front of the grounds but far enough from the Hall of Radiant Sun so we won't be seen. A river runs behind us, curving to the edge of this garden before plunging off the edge in one of those precarious waterfalls.

I frown. "I don't want to get in trouble."

"We'll be in trouble only if we're caught," he replies, and grins as he extends a hand to me.

I dart a glance up at the darkened Hall of Radiant Sun through the branches of the plum blossom tree. Its marble columns and golden roofs rise into the night as if they hold starlight, made ethereal by the way clouds plume around it.

My gaze catches on the glint of a sword, the outlines of the guards between the pillars.

I shake my head. "We're going to be seen."

Yù'chén raises an eyebrow. The usual self-assuredness of his voice hardens, and his eyes flick to me, searching mine. "Can you trust me?"

The world peels away as I stare at his outstretched palm. I think of my little sister, the way her brown eyes will light up when she receives my gloves. The way she might cradle them as she sleeps, instead of the sharp crescent blade I left her.

I have no choice.

I angle my gaze to Yù'chén. "No," I say, and I take his hand.

His fingers wrap around mine and tighten. I suppress a shiver as he draws me forward, in the direction of the winding stream, away from the Hall of Radiant Sun and the guards. Clouds begin to seep into the grass as we near the edge; I hear the roar of a waterfall again, obscured between trees.

Amélie Wen Zhao

We step out, and I inhale sharply.

Ahead of me, plunging from the skies like celestial rivers, are the wards: clear and iridescent and bright, so powerful that I feel the hum of their spirit energies under my skin. I crane my neck, but they shoot into the Heavens like the northern lights at the very edge of our realm. Beyond, the world opens to an expanse of star-strewn night: the mortal realm.

Yù'chén steps into the river. He's dangerously close to the edge where the waterfall courses past the wards, dipping into the mortal realm below, but he stands steady, up to his waist in the water.

He lifts both hands, and his dark magic blooms like a blossom in the night.

Flowers form from the shadows, crimson petals amidst dark-green vines that twine into the immortals' wards. Where they take root, the light of the ward dims. The flowers bloom and bloom, and I recognize them as red scorpion lilies: the type Yù'chén gifted me when we first met. *A flower for a tragic fate.*

When Yù'chén turns to me, the scorpion lilies and vines have braided themselves into an archway, wide enough for one person to slip through. A draft seeps through the opening, bringing with it the briny scent of the sea; the night and the stars within are sharper and brighter. And above him, the light of the wards continues to flow gently, as though nothing has happened.

My heart pounds in my chest. "What is that?" I whisper. "What have you done?"

"A gate," he replies. He's breathing hard, and I catch a red hue to his eyes. "A way through the wards."

I look from him to the gate formed by the scorpion lilies.

The rippling light of the wards gives their petals an almost liquid quality, like blood. *Impossible,* I think.

"I can hold it open long enough for us to get back," Yù'chén continues. He reaches out a hand to me, but I recoil.

"How were you able to create a way through the wards?" My voice is unsteady. "Even the hellbeasts of the Kingdom of Night haven't breached them in nine years."

His face is unreadable. "The immortals' wards are unbreachable from the outside, but less so from within. Plenty of candidates will be seeking a way out despite the immortals' warnings." I think of the candidate with the sweetheart in the mortal realm. When I remain silent, Yù'chén continues: "It's safe, I promise. We'll send your gift to your sister, and then we'll be back as if nothing has happened." His hand is still outstretched.

I gaze out into the infinite night, the tapestry of stars that the gods wove before they made the realms. There, between the clouds, winds the celestial river that the dragons sculpted, glimmering with the pearl dust of their magic. The sky spins, eternal, a reminder of how ephemeral my own life is.

It's beautiful, wild, and utterly free—yet it's terrifying, too.

But there is a part of me that wants to see it.

I step forward, sliding my palm across Yù'chén's and holding his hand firmly. Then I inhale deeply and step into the river.

I'm nearly immediately knocked off balance as the currents sweep me toward the edge with a vengeance. I grab Yù'chén, desperate not to fall into the river again, and he holds me up, snapping at me to ground my spirit energy.

"It's not that deep, Àn'yīng—find the riverbed and plant your feet—"

"Not that deep my ass—*you're* tall enough—"

"Stop and think—you're panicking—" He curses, then in one motion, he grasps my waist and lifts me out of the water. His hands hook me below my knees so I'm anchored to him, my legs wrapped around his waist and my arms around his neck. In the blink of an eye, we're suddenly hip to hip, chest to chest, face to face. The waterfall roars behind me, and my heart is hammering wildly.

Yù'chén's lips part. He's breathing heavily, too, from our scramble and the exertion of the magic he's just performed. Sweat glimmers on his brow; a bead of it trickles down his cheek. "You'll have to try that again," he says, and a hint of mirth curves his mouth.

I can't bring myself to think of a good enough response. I'm very conscious of the waterfall plunging into nothingness just steps behind me, of the heat of his body between my thighs, of the grip of his hands against my skin.

Yù'chén takes a step in the wrong direction, to the ledge of the waterfall. The red glow of the scorpion lilies illuminates the sharp edges of his features. My fingers tighten against his shoulders as my heart goes into overdrive.

"Let me go," I say.

He holds my gaze as his eyes begin to glow crimson. "All right," he says, and with a vicious tug, he tips us off the ledge.

Then he lets me go.

I reach for him. I can't help it; as he spreads his arms, I wrap mine tighter around him and bury my face in his chest. *I'm going to kill you,* I think as the thrum of his laughter vibrates in his throat.

A cluster of clouds swallows us, and everything becomes a dizzying tangle of shadows. I close my eyes. Just as my grip slips, I feel pressure around my waist, the warmth of hands encircling the small of my back.

The feeling of uncontrolled free fall shifts, just as the wind changes. When my stomach settles slightly, I crack open an eye.

The world is no longer spinning. Yù'chén holds me gently, as if we are in an embrace, shielding me from the cold. Currents of magic pulse from him, heating the air—not spirit energy but dark magic. He's manipulating the wind, I realize, calling on it in such a way that it bends its will to him, wrapping around us to steady our descent.

"Àn'yīng." His voice sounds in my ear. "Let go."

I don't know why I do. Immediately, I spin away from him—but he grabs my wrists, then slowly slides his fingers down to twine them around mine.

The clouds have ended. The world opens up beneath us, and in that exact moment, the moon comes out from behind the clouds, larger than is possible in the mortal realm. Its light spills onto the unending expanse of sea below, casting silver into the waves so they seem to spark with stars.

My breath catches.

"You wanted to see the ocean," Yù'chén says. He's watching me, his crimson eyes burning with otherworldly power and magic. A smile curves his mouth, and his face is alight with a joy I have not seen, a look so different from the cynical smirk with which he beholds the world. No, Yù'chén's eyes dance over my face as he looks at me.

"How did you know—" My words falter as I remember, in the haze after Qióng'qí, his voice calming me. *Think of the one wish you hold in your heart.*

I wanted to see the ocean, but I always imagined it as it was in Mā's tapestries: in the daylight, with rays of sun lancing off white-capped waves, filling the waters with every color of blue imaginable.

I never expected my first look of the sea—my first *true* look—to be at night.

And I never expected to love it.

There is something haunting about the darkness that weaves between the waters, but the way the moonlight threads through it in a delicate dance is nothing short of magic. I inhale the briny scent carried by the wind and find that I am smiling.

We slow, and Yù'chén pulls me to him again, wrapping his arms around me. As he lands, the waves seem to swell to catch each of his footsteps. Around us, there is nothing but ocean; in the distance, the columns of rock that are the Immortals' Steps rise into the sky.

I place my feet on the surface of the sea. Immediately, the energies of the waves scatter beneath my toes, and I sink inelegantly into the water.

"Ah." Yù'chén lifts me by my waist, drawing me close so that I'm standing on his feet. By instinct, I wrap my arms around his shoulders. I hear his sharp intake of breath as the fabric of his collar slips and the inside of my wrist brushes against the warmth of his skin. Pressed this close to him, I am afraid he'll feel the frantic beat of my heart.

Yù'chén shoots me a smile that scatters every thought I have. Searching desperately for signs of land beyond us, I dip my head away as my cheeks heat.

"Hmm," Yù'chén muses, casting his gaze around. "The

way I imagined it, my companion in a midnight escapade would have mastered the art of qīng'gōng to walk on water."

I cast him a scathing look. "I am not your companion in a midnight escapade."

That wicked grin again. "No? Then what would you call this?" His eyes narrow as his thumb traces a stroke against my waist. *He is distracting me,* I realize.

"An unfortunate situation," I reply, and stamp hard on his feet. That wipes the smirk off his face. "I need to get to land." I dislike how helpless I sound. I can't do this without him, and we both know it. "I have to find a messenger dove."

"Or," Yù'chén says, "one could summon a messenger spirit in the middle of the ocean."

I stare at him. "Can you?"

He tilts his head and casts me a sly look. "Perhaps. For a price."

I roll my eyes. "What do you want?"

His palms are very warm against my waist, his gaze even more so as it lingers on my face. "What can you offer me, little scorpion?"

I remember when we first met, I wondered how far I would go to get what I want. It has been only one week, but I am a different person. I have seen the deaths of innocents. I have associated with yāo'jīng. I have told myself I am willing to beat out and kill other practitioners to win this tournament if I must.

What shifting line of moral righteousness am I holding myself to?

None, I think, my eyes flicking to his mouth. Nothing matters anymore, not when I have vowed to kill for my own gain.

If there is a price to get a message through to my sister, I will pay it.

I swallow, steadying my heartbeat. "Whatever you ask of me," I say quietly.

Yù'chén's eyes lock on mine. He is no longer smiling. His fingers tighten a fraction against my waist, and as his gaze roams to my lips, I find myself unable to turn away.

"I think I'll save my price for later." His eyes begin to glow again as he reaches out his hand. Ahead of us, the night seems to darken. From that pocket of shadows comes the flutter of wings as something approaches us.

It's a crane. Its snowy feathers flit between darkness and light like an illusion. When it lands beside us with a gust from its wings, I make out the red of its eyes.

It's from the demon realm.

"A shadowcrane," Yù'chén says. "It'll carry the message to your sister."

I study the creature. I thought all beings from the Kingdom of Night were flesh-eating monsters, but the bird only studies me back. It ruffles its feathers and clacks its beak, exceedingly normal in every way but for its flickering form.

"She heeds my word," Yù'chén continues, seeing my hesitation. "She's conjured of shadows and feeds on starlight. I promise she's not like any of those other creatures we encountered."

The shadowcrane watches me with intelligent eyes. Slowly, I reach into my bodice and draw out Méi'zi's gloves. I hold them out to the crane. She blinks and clasps them in her beak with practiced care, then dips her red-crowned head to me.

"Touch her head and think of the destination," Yù'chén tells me. He's watching the exchange with an inscrutable expression, his eyes lingering on the gloves and the clouds and temples of the Kingdom of Sky I've sewn onto them.

I do, picturing Xī'lín, the faded words on the old pái'fāng, the dusty roads that lead to the old plum blossom tree bent over our house. I think of Méi'zi's large brown eyes and easy laughter.

I do not want her to see this creature.

The thought leaps into my mind before I can stop it. The crane draws back. She blinks at me, then dips her head.

"She won't be seen by your sister," Yù'chén says quietly as the shadowcrane takes wing. We watch her rise into the skies, breaking nary a ripple in the ocean. "But she's not a monster, you know."

I tear my gaze from the shadowcrane's flight and find Yù'chén's gaze on me, dark and heady.

"She's a demonic being." My voice sounds uncertain, my words half-hearted even to me.

He's no longer smiling. "Now my price," he says. He is still looking at me, the moonlight bringing out the red of his eyes.

His earlier reference to a midnight escapade takes on a darker meaning as I remember what the mó tend to do to pleasure themselves with mortal bodies. I try to keep my tone light, but I cannot help the fear that colors my words. "Never a favor without something in exchange?"

"I'll let you decide on the charitableness of my nature," he replies. "I want you to walk on water."

My heart stutters as I gape at him, wondering if I heard wrong.

"Go on." He smirks, but there is a touch of frost to his tone now. "For my entertainment this evening, as you haven't much else to contribute."

"Here?" I say. I can't even do it on a still pond, let alone a sea writhing with currents.

"Learning to walk on water is the best way to elevate your qīng'gōng skills, which, if I wasn't clear enough, are terrible. You won't survive the trials without more practice."

"Why do you care?" I say, stung.

"Just try."

I glance at the shifting waves and swallow. They're tumultuous, crisscrossing in every direction possible. "I can't. I know the theory, but with water . . . the currents of energy . . . they're like threads that are all tangled up."

"Threads that are all tangled up," he repeats, then raises an eyebrow. "You're a seamstress. Can you think of it as sewing? Each current of energy is a thread being stitched, and you simply have to stitch the opposite way, in tune."

I look back down at the shifting water, and this time, I latch onto the thought. If I can think of each flow of qì as a thread, perhaps I can learn their magic.

Between one blink and another, the world seems to click into place. I begin to see them all now, the crisscrossing currents of energy, only this time, they're no longer a messy whorl that I can't decipher.

This time, they're *threads*. Living, moving threads I'm trying to pull together. I follow one, then another, and concentrate on one spot.

I lean out with my foot and tap the wave.

It taps back.

"Did you see that?" Excitement bubbles in my chest.

"Honestly, no," Yù'chén says flatly.

But I feel like a child who's discovered the use of my limbs.

I poke my foot out again, and this time, I manage to stand on a wave for one heartbeat.

Yù'chén straightens slightly. "Good. Now move with it. Water is always changing, and so must you. Here." He lets me spin around so my back is pressed to his chest and my heels sit on his toes. His hands fall against my body, one at my hip, the other on my rib cage, holding me steady. When he speaks again, his voice is in my ear: "Read the way the currents flow; you have to always be preparing for the next wave. Try."

I focus on one spot, watching how the waves swell, one after another after another. I strike out with my foot and manage to stand for a breath before my concentration breaks.

Yù'chén's laugh rumbles low in his chest. "Don't strike out like you're spearing fish. Think of yourself as a drifting leaf, riding the wave."

This time, I place one foot on the water, then another, and suddenly I'm balancing on the surface of the ocean as in the paintings of practitioners in all the legends, just as I've read in all my childhood stories. *I am walking on water.*

"I did it!" In my elation, I half turn. "I did—"

My focus slips, and my word becomes a sharp gasp as the water gives way and my foot splashes in. Yù'chén easily lifts me back up, setting me onto his boots. I'm giddy with my success, and he's smiling, too. It lights up his face, softens his mouth, curves his dark eyes. I'm dipping back, his hands on my hips, and he's leaning forward slightly, looking at me in a way that shouldn't be right.

The air between us heats. Yù'chén's smile flickers as he senses it, too. His gaze darkens as he reaches a hand up and brushes a lock of hair from my eyes. His fingers linger on my cheek.

I tense. This is all wrong. No matter how his heart beats, no matter how red his blood runs, he is half a *mó*. Half of one of those monsters that destroyed my family and my realm.

I am certain he can feel the beat of my heart through my chest as he holds me. Watches me, eyes narrowed, mouth tightening as he feels my hands shift into a position where I can easily access my blades.

But I do not reach for them. Instead, I say, "Why are you here, Yù'chén?"

"Here, in the middle of the ocean at night, with you, Àn'yīng?" The way he speaks my name sends a shiver up my spine.

"Here, as in the trials."

"Same reason you and the other forty-two candidates are here."

"But you're"—I suck in a breath, stopping myself sharply as Yù'chén's expression flickers—"different."

Yù'chén draws back slightly, cold air swirling between us. "Because I'm half-mó?" There is frost to his tone once again. "Because I'm not meant to be the same as you? Because I'm incapable of desiring a better life, one away from bloodshed and violence?" His grip is tight on my waist now, in a way that almost hurts.

"I—"

"Say what you mean, Àn'yīng." His eyes are glowing again, and I feel his dark magic stirring. "You think me incapable of wanting what you and other full humans want."

"I don't *know* what you want," I say quietly. "Yù'chén, I've spent half my life fearing the kingdom that is at war with mine, the beings that . . . killed my parents." I swallow, for it is the first time I've confided this to him. "I can't simply undo that just because you've . . . helped me."

"*Helped* you," he repeats, and before I can do anything, he takes my jaw in his hand and angles my face to his, fingers digging into the soft curves of my throat. "Am I too *charitable* to fit your image of mó, Àn'yīng?" His thumb traces the curve to my lower lip. "Should I wish to drink your soul, demand that you use your body to serve me in exchange for my *help?*" His other hand begins to roam up my rib cage as he lowers his mouth to within inches of my neck. His breath is hot against my skin as he whispers, "Should I be the monster you want to see?"

I can't move, can't speak. My heart slams against my chest, and I can't stop the tremor that goes through my body. *I will not be prey,* I think, a desperate prayer, a litany. My blades slide into my palms. *I will not be prey.*

Yù'chén draws back. The red in his eyes is fading, transforming back to an impenetrable black. He looks down at my blades, breathing hard. It's a few moments before he speaks again. "My shadowcrane will inform me when she reaches your sister," he says roughly.

I nod, though I'm trying to stop my teeth from chattering. The hard grooves of my crescent blades dig into my palms, grounding me. "Take me back," I whisper. "Please."

In spite of his anger, he is gentle as he draws me close and calls on his wind again. I hold tightly to him, uncertain whether it is fear or something else that makes my pulse race and my breathing tight.

As soon as we land back in the Celestial Gardens, I push away from him. I hear him call after me, but I don't stop as I make my way toward the Candidates' Courtyard. He follows me in silence, through the moongates and across the open-air hallways, until we approach the steps that lead to my door. The spirit energy of my talismans rush over me as I cross the threshold, and for the first time, my breathing steadies.

"Àn'yīng." Yù'chén's voice is quiet behind me. "I—"

"Yù'chén," I say, spinning around. He's stopped beneath the old willow tree that leans over the pond. Overhead, clouds race over the moon, and I can barely make out his expression. "Don't help me again."

He lifts his gaze to mine, darker than the night. His lips part, but I don't let him speak.

"I don't want to think of you as anything more than a monster," I finish. Then I enter my chamber and slide the doors shut behind me, leaving him standing outside in the shadows.

13

My qīng'gōng skills are so improved the next day that Tán'mù loses her normal sleepy look when she sees me walking on the surface of the pond. It's only for a few seconds, but Lì'líng even abandons a glutinous rice ball (sesame-paste filling) to fling her arms around me and squeal when I manage it. Fán'xuān is chasing dragonflies as a kite-tailed sparrow, then taking dips into the water and surfacing as a freckled carp. I grin when he finally flops onto land in his human form, feet bare and shock of white hair just peeking out above the long grasses. The sun warms the water and the ground; the fragrance of hibiscus, magnolia, and osmanthus sweetens the air, mingling with the laughter and conversation of the other candidates nearby. In daylight, the events of last night seem like a distant dream, gone with the darkness.

Tán'mù folds her arms. "You're taking lessons from someone," she says, picking at a nail. "Is it Number One? Or Yù'chén?"

"No," I reply, but I've never been a good liar.

Tán'mù raises an eyebrow and doesn't pursue the subject further, but my heartbeat quickens at the thought of Yù'chén, of the rule we've broken.

Of the gate in the wards.

I stifle a gasp as the realization jolts through me. Since waking, I've been so focused on driving Yù'chén from my mind that I haven't given thought to that gate. I know nothing about it besides the fact that it's dangerous, a weakness in the wards the immortals have spent years perfecting. And now, I can't recall whether Yù'chén closed it.

I climb out of the water, cursing myself for letting my emotions get in the way of logic last night. We're at the edge of the temple grounds, where one of the celestial rivers winds through mountains and disappears into the sunset. Blossoming cherry trees lean into the waters, their petals and fragrance carried to us by a gentle breeze. In the distance, a phoenix arcs through the clouds like a sunburst.

It's a beautiful day but one I can no longer enjoy—because suddenly, there is nothing more I want to do than make sure Yù'chén has closed that gate.

"I'll be back," I say, and I set off before my friends can ask me where I'm going.

I have no idea where Yù'chén might be at this time of day, but I make for the Celestial Gardens, where most of the candidates train. At this hour it's blissfully empty, with most candidates taking their dinner breaks. Floating lanterns sway beneath osmanthus trees; fireflies dart between camellia and peony bushes, their sparks drifting against a setting sun that casts the clouds in gold.

I find that I can't stop thinking back to the ocean at night, how the haunting darkness of the waves seemed to call to me. And I realize it isn't the ocean I'm thinking of.

You think me incapable of wanting what you and other full humans want.

There was anger in Yù'chén's tone, but I didn't miss what it was masking: pain, and disappointment. I recall how he looked at me after I fought Áo'yīn, the tender way he draped his cloak over my shoulders. And last night, the gentle way he held me, the warmth of his gaze, the heat of his fingers as his breaths brushed my cheeks.

I squeeze my eyes shut to chase away the memory—and that's when I nearly trip over something.

My eyes fly open. At first, I don't see anything. I'm halfway to the gate we left at the wards. Before me runs a river lined with bushes of peonies, orchids, and chrysanthemums. They're so colorful that I almost don't notice the body half obscured between them.

It takes me a moment to recognize the face.

It's Number One. Xiù'chūn. She's lying in the bushes, a near-serene look on her face. She might have been asleep were it not for the bleeding gash in her chest—one that looks like something tore her heart and lungs straight from her flesh.

The world peels away until all I see is the corpse, the blood pooling on the grass and seeping into the mud, as red as garnets. My mind splits, as if half of me is here and the other half is trapped in that scene from nine years ago, watching the red-lipped demon drink my father's soul and slurp his blood and organs from him.

I'm not sure how long I stand there before I come back to my senses. I'm alone between the flowering trees, and it is too silent: the absence of cicadas chirping sends an ominous chill up my spine. The sun slants red near the horizon, fast-disappearing, casting the corpse before me in a bloody light.

Looking at her wounds, at the half-devoured flesh and missing organs, certainty settles within me: there is only one type of being that could have done this.

Demon.

My mind flashes to the gate in the wards leading to the mortal realm.

I'm moving by instinct, Shadow and Fleet in my hands, mind open to the currents of energy around me. The blood is still fresh, gleaming and trickling beneath the fading crimson light. Whoever—*whatever*—did this could still be nearby.

A crackle of footfalls. By the time I pivot, it's too late.

A hand closes around my wrist, the touch cool and unfamiliar. Wind stirs across the clearing, lifting jade-colored willow leaves into the air. The setting sun catches against pale silk with gold threads as the newcomer brushes past me. With a light tug, he draws me into the thicket of trees.

My back bumps against willow bark, and my blades are up, but the newcomer has already let go and stepped back, moving effortlessly as though he is in a dance.

It's him—the immortal whose face I dreamt in the sea. He presses his index finger to his lip, then soundlessly draws his sword and lifts his gaze to the skies. He is masking his spirit energy, yet this close, I sense great waves of it rolling off him, just like last time we met on the bridge.

From somewhere far above, voices sound. Flashes of white cut through the dusk, trailing wisps of cloud as they descend. Immortals.

The guard turns to me and holds out a hand. Without thinking, I take it. I feel a familiar ripple of spirit energy as he lifts his other hand to trace a talisman.

Strange. Immortals don't usually use the techniques that mortals use to channel spirit energy. When you possess that much power, you can weave magic with a flick of your finger, a passing thought.

The talisman masks our movement. I follow him as he hurries through the Celestial Gardens, his movements fluid and powerful. He slows only when the landscape grows familiar and I begin to recognize the patterns of the trees and flowers.

We come to a stop by a small pavilion overlooking a pond. Sprigs of camellias grow by the water, and farther away, I spot a pair of mandarin ducks resting, their brightly colored feathers reflected on the surface. From a distance drifts the sound of conversation and laughter from the other candidates near the Clear Skies Pavilion. Here, though, we are alone and shielded from view.

The immortal releases my hand; his goes to the hilt of his sword. Everything about him is carved with sharp intent, and he looks at me with a practiced blankness. His eyes, though, are swift and assessing, constantly evaluating our surroundings. "It's safe here," he says. His tone is not unkind.

I'm still gripping my blades. I believe him, but I refuse to let go. "Why did you take me away?"

"My priority was to get you out safely."

I watch him carefully. "Why?"

He blinks slowly, his face betraying nothing. "Lady Shī'yǎ vouched for you that day upon your entry to the temple. It is not only your reputation as a candidate at stake should you become entangled in dangerous affairs."

Dangerous affairs. "You saw it, too," I whisper. "Her heart . . ." *Was eaten.*

"Yes, I saw it," he says. "There is something afoot here, but investigating it is my job. Please stay out of it; this has nothing to do with you."

But what if it does? a small voice whispers in my mind, and the confession is on the tip of my tongue: *There is a demon halfling in the Temple of Dawn. We opened a gate in your wards last night.*

If I tell him, I risk losing my place in the trials.

I risk losing Mā.

I try not to falter beneath his piercing gaze, as unyielding as sword metal and as cool as ice. A faint wind stirs his robes; the dusk light gilds his features and weaves molten gold into his hair, and as the willows and camellias dance around us, I feel I have stepped into a fairy tale. This immortal's beauty is as effortless as sunlight dancing on river water.

"Listen to me." He takes a step closer and fixes his gaze on me. Deep, brown eyes, steady as the earth. "From the moment Lady Shī'yǎ spoke for you in the Hall of Radiant Sun, your fate was pulled into the nexus of ours. The politics of immortals is a long, twisted game, and there are many who would wish to oust her for the slightest misstep. If you wish to thank her, then *win*."

At his words, I swallow, the confessions sinking to the pit

of my stomach. Instead, I study his face: the chiseled angles of his jaw, the slim yet strong curves of his cheeks, the symmetry of his lips. Here, this close, the moment in the sea no longer seems like an impossibility.

He is still, studying me, too. The cool austerity of his gaze shifts, and I have the strangest feeling he is searching for something in my eyes. His lips part; he looks as though he means to say more. But then he draws back and begins to turn away. And for some reason, in this clearing lit by the setting sun, beneath the murmuring willows, I feel as though I am dreaming and that I have dreamt this dream before. As though I have more questions I should ask him, but they flit through my mind like dust motes, impossible to catch.

"I'm Àn'yīng," I find myself saying to his retreating back.

From between the willow branches and flowering trees, he glances over his shoulder at me. His eyes soften at the edges. The effect is like watching ice melt over a sunlit river.

"I know," he says. "I'm Hào'yáng."

Hào'yáng. Two characters that could mean *bright sun*, or . . .

I inhale sharply.

Vast sea.

"Wait," I begin, but he's gone already, and I'm alone in a clearing surrounded by water and flowers and the last, warm glow of sunset.

It feels surreal to step into the lantern light of the Candidates' Courtyard and to find Lì'líng, Tán'mù, and Fán'xuān seated at one of the waterside pavilions, enjoying platters of delicacies for dinner. Most candidates have returned from their training, but the sound of conversation around me is a dull roar.

Hào'yáng.

The One of the Vast Sea.

It can't be a coincidence that he's helped me twice now, that he is linked to the judge who vouched for me, that I saw him in the ocean that day. Whether it was real or a dream, Bà sent me here to look for him, and I am at the precipice of unraveling one of my father's secrets.

I fiddle with my jade pendant as I make my way toward where Lì'líng, Tán'mù, and Fán'xuān sit, scanning the faces of the candidates I pass, looking for signs of something off, of anyone missing. With our free schedules, quite a few have not yet returned to our quarters—but it hits me, with the force of a physical blow, who *isn't* here.

Yù'chén.

My insides grow cold.

"Àn'yīng!" Lì'líng calls, leaping up and waving at me with a radiant smile. The sight of her sends a sharp pang of guilt through my stomach. A candidate was murdered, there is danger within these temple grounds—yet I can't speak of it without being implicated in the investigation.

I hesitate, and that's when a loud, reverberating sound fills the night.

Gong . . .

Light streaks across the skies like a shooting star and a messenger appears, carried by wisps of cloud and shimmering in the pale silks and lamellar of the Temple of Dawn. "All candidates are to report to the Hall of Radiant Sun!" he calls.

The refectory is immediately in an uproar. Chairs scrape,

plates clatter, and there's a commotion as candidates scramble to flee to their chambers and grab their weapons before they head to the Hall of Radiant Sun. They think it's the announcement of the Second Trial.

I stand, feeling the solid weight of my blades tucked into my dress.

"Come on!" Lì'líng squeals, grabbing my and Tán'mù's hands. "Come on, Fán'xuān!"

The Hall of Radiant Sun seems to drink in the moon's fluorescence at night. The golden curving eaves and bejeweled pillars gleam in soft lantern light as we file in. Guards in the identical white-and-gold uniforms line every pillar. I search for Hào'yáng—but he is nowhere to be seen.

Shī'yǎ, too, is conspicuously missing. Only four of the Eight Immortals are present. I study their faces as they recline on their thrones, looking for hints of unease or any emotion at all—but it is like trying to gaze into a bowl of clear water.

Though there is one person I've been searching for who is here, and my gaze goes to him like a moth to flame.

Yù'chén leans against a pillar at the very back of the hall, arms folded in an almost indolent manner. As though sensing my gaze, his eyes cut to mine.

I make straight for him, ignoring the way my pulse picks up at the sight of him. He is very still but for the glint of his gaze, his face an indecipherable mask. It isn't until I'm right in front of him that he speaks.

"Come to make a monster of me again?" His voice is low.

I lean forward until we're almost touching. My hand slips to his side—and I dig Poison in against a soft dip in his rib cage. He draws a sharp breath and freezes.

"Move or make a sound, and you're dead," I whisper.

"Mm. Scorpion that you are," he murmurs, but to his credit, he stays where he is.

"The gate. Did you close it last night?"

I can't see his face, can't make out anything in his voice. "I closed it," Yù'chén says, "last night. Feel free to go and check if you're so keen to believe me a liar."

I lean back slightly, studying his eyes. He looks right back at me, cocking a brow. If he isn't lying and the gate is closed so that no hellbeasts or mó could have gotten in . . . that leaves one more possibility.

"Did you kill her?"

I feel the stutter to his breaths, and then warmth against my neck as Yù'chén exhales. "Who?"

"Candidate Number One," I reply. "She's dead. I found her in the Celestial Gardens, with her chest ripped open and her heart devoured."

Yù'chén's jaw tightens. A few of the candidates glance over at us; he wraps a hand around my waist and tugs me sharply forward so I'm pressed against him in a semblance of an embrace. He dips his head, and I shiver as his lips graze my hair. "And you've come to ask me if I killed her, ate her heart, and drank her soul like the wicked demon I am?" he says softly.

I swallow, and his hand tightens against me. I'm the one holding the knife, but he's the one in control.

"Àn'yīng," he says, drawing back slightly. "Even if I feasted on mortal flesh, do you think me so stupid as to leave a half-eaten body in the middle of these temple grounds?" His hand trails up my spine, and a cruel smile curves his lips. "If I were to have devoured anyone's heart, it would have been yours, last night in the middle of the ocean, where no one would have known."

I shove him away. Before I can respond, Jǐng'xiù stands, his bamboo scepter in his hands. The hall goes quiet.

"Candidates." The announcer's voice is grave. "As you're well aware, the Temple of Dawn runs by a set of Precepts made to reflect the ancient Heavenly Order. These Precepts forbid murder on temple grounds." He pauses to sweep a glance over all of us. "A candidate was found dead on temple grounds. The initial investigation concludes she was murdered."

A collective gasp rises from the hall. By my side, Yù'chén tenses.

"This matter is still under investigation. In the meantime, security around the grounds will tighten. Once the culprit is found, they will face not only expulsion from the Immortality Trials but also the harshest of punishment allowed under the Heavenly Order."

My fingers tighten around the hilts of my crescent blades in my sleeves. *Her chest was ripped open*, I think. *Her heart was devoured*. There's a big difference between announcing that a candidate was killed . . . and that she might have died at the hands of a being from the Kingdom of Night.

The crowd is murmuring. Evidently, most of the candidates have figured out who the victim was; Number One was popular, her presence observed with a mixture of awe and jealousy.

Jǐng'xiù taps his bamboo scepter, and the candidates grow quiet again. "While the death of a candidate outside the trials is a grave matter, it poses no challenge to the integrity of our institution. The Temple of Dawn will continue to run on the power of the Eight Immortals and the hundreds of guards dedicated to its protection. The Immortality Trials will continue.

"Which leads me to my second announcement: tonight, we begin the Second Trial."

14

The roar that goes up in the crowd of candidates fades to a high-pitched ringing in my ears. The Second Trial? After all that has happened . . . they're going to proceed with their *tournament*?

"Every year," Jǐng'xiù continues, his voice filtering through to me as though from very far away, "a long-lost island that drifts between all the realms reappears. Mythological beasts of old roam its forests." A hush has fallen over the candidates. "It is in these eternal forests of Péng'lái Island that you will fight to qualify for the Third Trial . . . and earn your way back into the Kingdom of Sky."

Something sparks on my wrist. I look down to see my golden bracelet beginning to glow. It unwinds from my arm, flames catching and transforming it into a burning scroll, as it did when it first came to me at Gods' Fingers.

Welcome to the Second Trial, the parchment reads, and then the fire begins to eat away at it. Sparkling ashes gleam in its wake, and a golden butterfly flutters where there once were flames. I can just make out a number on its wings: 44.

"Find your bracelet to reenter the Kingdom of Sky and pass the Second Trial. You have one hour," Jǐng'xiù booms as my butterfly begins to flit, with astonishing speed, out into the night. "That's it. Those are the rules."

That's it? I want to yell at the Eight. A candidate is *dead*, likely murdered by a demonic beast that is still on the loose. And more of us might be dead by the end of the night.

The immortals don't care. This is all a game to them. And to play their game, to gain immortality, we must leave behind more and more of our humanity.

My hand goes to my jade pendant, nestled beneath my collar. *Is this why you left, Bà?*

In the crowd, another candidate's bracelet has begun to spark. And a third. We're being dispatched in the opposite order of our arrival—perhaps by way of giving the slowest and weakest a way to survive.

"Àn'yīng." Yù'chén's voice jolts me from my thoughts. The light of the butterflies reflects in his eyes, and when he looks up at me, the concern on his face feels too real. "Go," he says in a low voice.

Numbers Forty-Three and Forty-Two are already dashing for the gates. I've missed my head start.

I take a step toward them. I shouldn't be concerned with the safety or politics of the Kingdom of Sky. The immortals have more than enough power and resources to find the culprit for one murder.

I need the pill of immortality to save my mother's soul, and I am the only one who can win it for her.

I hesitate.

"Tonight," I hiss to Yù'chén, "meet me at the Celestial Gardens. I want to see with my own eyes that you closed the gate."

His gaze darkens. "Why don't we survive this trial first, and *then* you can go back to accusing me of the monstrous things you think I do."

I turn and shove through the crowd, already palming my crescent blades. Most candidates step aside to let me pass. Except for one person.

Yán'lù's massive arms are at his hips, one hand curled over the hilt of his broadsword. He's watching me with wide eyes and a crazed smirk. On his wrist is his golden bracelet, which has not yet morphed into the elusive butterfly.

His says 6. There are thirty-eight candidates between us.

I suppress a shudder. I need to get as far away as possible before it's his turn to go.

I dart around him and make for the open gates, finally in sight. My butterfly has already gone out, but I think I spot its golden glow in the night.

Fleet and Poison are in my palms as I reach the marble stairs swirling with clouds. I hurry down them. In front of me, I see the silhouettes of Forty-Three and Forty-Two—and farther ahead, three tiny golden sparks drifting toward the Immortals' Steps. Beyond, somewhere far away in the darkness, is home and Méi'zi and Mā.

I tighten my grip on my blades and touch my collarbone, where my jade pendant rests. A mist has risen from the sea. Brine laces the air, and the crash of waves sounds from far below, a realm away from the Kingdom of Sky and its wards. The wind whips storm clouds across the sky, casting shifting shadows.

I hear footsteps behind me, coming too close and too fast. A glint of metal in the corner of my eyes.

I dodge, swapping Poison for Shadow, as the next candidate's longsword slices down where my head was just a heartbeat ago. She pauses, blinking in confusion as she looks around for me. To her, I have simply vanished in plain sight—but if she were slightly more observant, she'd see a shift in the air, a shadow darker than the rest of the night moving behind her.

She scowls and barrels down the remainder of the stairs toward Forty-Three and Forty-Two. They're not as quick as I am, nor do they have bespelled blades. Their screams are cut short abruptly in the night.

I ignore the way my stomach twists and speed up. I'm careful to duck around where Forty-One is hauling the other two candidates' bodies over the stairs, into the abyss between realms and the yawning black sea below.

When I reach the bottom of the stairway, though, instead of the Immortals' Steps, a marble bridge extends into the night, vanishing ominously into thick clouds. I sense the hum of spirit energies as I near the Kingdom of Sky wards. The immortals must have altered them, for tonight, they allow me to pass without so much as a brush of air against my skin.

And just like that, I've left the Kingdom of Sky. I pause and glance back at the wards, shimmering iridescent and translucent in the night, and I wonder if Yù'chén was telling the truth: that it is much easier to leave than it is to get in.

I glance toward where the clouds swallow the rest of this realm and the next, in the direction I know the Kingdom of Rivers begins. And suddenly, I'm hit with a pang of homesickness so acute that I can't breathe. I don't want to be here, competing in a tournament where I'm surviving by the skin of my teeth. I want to be home in my ramshackle little cottage, laughing with Méi'zi as we dice parsnips for soup, sitting by Mā's knees and listening to her stories, her needle catching the lanternlight as she sews.

But that world no longer exists—hasn't existed in nine years. And this, this is the only chance for me to get it back.

I blink away the stinging in my eyes and take the first step onto the marble bridge. The stone is cool and solid beneath my feet, slightly damp from the clouds all around. Soon, I'm engulfed in a great fog, unable to see anything but a few paces in front of me, unable to hear anything but the sound of my own footfalls and breaths.

Behind me, someone screams. It echoes briefly before being swallowed—as if the silence around me is alive. Cold sweat beads on my skin.

As suddenly as it arose, the fog thins, revealing a dark shape in the night. I make out the flattened tops of trees—parasol trees, lining the rocky steps of an island that has appeared out of nowhere, hanging above the vicious sea.

A tall rock greets me as I step off the marble bridge onto the soft grass of the island in the sky. A puff of wind clears the mist briefly enough for me to read the characters inscribed on the surface of the stone, weather-beaten and scratched as though it has survived the turn of thousands of years: PÉNG'LÁI ISLAND.

The stories surrounding this mystical island are just as Jǐng'xiù said. It drifts across the kingdoms, appearing once a year between the realms . . . and is supposedly haunted by mythological beasts and remnants of old magic that the Kingdom of Sky has purged.

The silence grows stifling as I step beneath the canopy

of trees. The moon is hidden behind rain clouds, and a light drizzle has started, rendering it difficult to make out anything but ghostly shapes and silhouettes. I hold my crescent blades tightly as I move deeper into the forest, intent on getting as far away from the other candidates as I can. I have no idea how big this island is, but within the next hour, it'll be filled with forty other bloodthirsty candidates, all seeking their tickets to the Third Trial.

I think of the look Yán'lù gave me in the Hall of Radiant Sun. Now that we're off temple grounds, the Precepts no longer apply. Which means I need to find my golden bracelet . . . before he finds me.

A sudden howl rises into the night from somewhere nearby, resembling neither man nor beast and sending gooseflesh up my arms. I need to keep moving. The problem is, I've lost track of my golden butterfly in this damned rain.

I keep Shadow and swap Fleet for Heart. The talisman activates with a brief injection of my spirit energy; all I need is to project my greatest desires into the spirit energy flowing from me to the blade to let it lead me.

I close my eyes and focus on the image I have held inside me throughout all these years—the flame of hope that has kept me going when all else failed. Mā and Méi'zi, sitting beneath the old plum blossom tree outside our house, laughing as they water spring onions. The late afternoon sun haloes them, as in a dream, in a haze of gold. It is an outdated memory, one that is over nine years old.

If I can just find my golden bracelet . . . if I can just survive this island . . . if I can just win one of the eight spots in these trials . . . then perhaps I can bring back that hazy, golden afternoon.

Heart shifts in my hand, and I smile—just as another voice surfaces in my memory.

What else? That deep, melodic murmur. *Something that you want, for you.*

I want to see the ocean.

The memory of my mother and sister shifts, and now I'm looking at an ocean under the stars, surrounded by a haunting darkness that frightens me as much as it fascinates me. The heat and pressure of fingers against my waist and rib cage . . . and the face that I hate to dream of at night, eyes aglow in red. Enchanting. Ensnaring.

My eyes fly open. The drizzle has turned into a downpour, and I'm breathing hard in the rain-soaked forest. Heart is pointing forward, and I feel a ripple of spirit energy as the talisman takes effect, my desire determining the direction of the blade.

I just don't know which desire it's pointing to.

I shake my head to clear the heat beneath my skin. No, there is *nothing* across the realms that will unseat my desire for my family's safety.

I hold Heart firmly and take off, following the point of its blade.

The parasol trees and cathayas around me have turned to shadows, branches twisting into claws that tear at me as I run in the heavy rain. It will be impossible for anyone to see their bracelet in these conditions.

Over the sound of the deluge, I hear a distant scream.

How many of us will die here? And what happens to those who don't find their bracelets before time's up?

It's a while before I realize that something's wrong.

I pause in front of a parasol tree, its branches extending

like gnarled fingers. Three ghostly gashes gleam on its trunk: claw marks.

Claw marks I could have sworn I saw just minutes ago.

A sense of unease tightens my stomach. The ancient forest is unyielding, any movement or sound masked by the roar of rain. Twice now, I swear I've seen eyes glinting out at me from the dark, but each time, they vanish before I can take a closer look. More than that is the bone-deep sense of being watched. Of something closing in.

It is a feeling I'm used to, and I know that usually, my instincts are not wrong.

I angle Heart in front of me and continue walking.

It's when I see that tree with the same marks for the third time that I know I've walked into a trap of some ancient magic or talisman.

I spin, Shadow in my other hand as I scan my surroundings. The air in front of me ripples, and between the rain and the darkness, the forest shifts: in the space of a blink, the parasol trees cluster around me tightly to form a cage, each now bearing the three pale claw marks. Overhead, the skies are no longer visible. I'm trapped; I don't know how much time I've lost walking in circles; and worse, I don't know how to get out of it.

A scream sounds from nearby, eerily inhuman, and the hairs on my arms rise. I scan the area, but there's nothing. Only rain, and trees, now all bearing the same three claw marks . . . and now dripping thick red blood.

When I hear the scream again, this time directly behind me, I know I'm being hunted.

I whip around, blades in hands. In the darkness, I see nothing, no one; just the silhouettes of trees.

Gooseflesh breaks out along my body. I wipe my face again. "I will not be prey," I whisper.

As soon as my lips form the words, I feel heat against the skin of my collarbone. My pendant! When I pull it out, it's pulsing gently, warm with magic and aglow in the golden strokes that make up two characters.

"There you are," I whisper, realizing my guardian in the jade must have heard my panic when I'd spoken aloud. The familiar handwriting is a touch of comfort.

Yet when I read the message, I do not feel the steadiness of safety that usually comes to me when my guardian sends word.

I feel a cold twist of fear.

Nightmares, it reads.

As a flash of lightning erupts in the skies, I catch a glimpse of a massive, hulking shape between a tangle of trees a dozen paces from me.

With the second flash, it stands directly before me.

This time, I scream.

15

The thing before me is Méi'zi. It looks like Méi'zi, but it also doesn't—because my little sister's flesh is peeling from her face, her eyes are replaced by dark, bleeding hollows, and her lips are gashed. She's shivering in her favorite nightgown, the plain cloth one I clumsily sewed as a birthday present for her. I recall each stitch of plum blossom, pinks and fuchsias and the green of leaves.

My mind blanks. It's not her—it *can't* be her, my little sister, whom I left safe and sound in our village back home. But as she steps toward me, I see that she's clutching the blade I gave her, Shield, to her chest.

Her gaping hole of a chest, where her heart and lungs and organs should be.

"*Jiě'jie.*" Her voice is a rattle that somehow reaches me through the roar of rain. "*You . . . left me. . . .*"

I bite down on the scream welling up in my throat as my pendant heats again. I grasp at it as if it is a lifeline. My fingers shake so hard I can barely read its words:

Painted skin.

I've read about these creatures. A huà'pí, a painted skin, is a shapeshifting monster that appears in the form of its victim's nightmares. It takes your deepest, darkest fears and turns them corporeal. Unable to stand sunlight, they lurk in the mountains in the mortal realms, hiding in caverns or the thickest forests.

"Help me, jiě'jie," the shape of my little sister begs me, wheezing. She staggers forward, and in spite of all logic, I nearly take a step to catch her.

There's a searing heat against my skin, and I jerk back instinctively.

My jade pendant glows like coal with a command so unlike the gentle, guiding messages it has given me throughout my life:

Destroy it.

The jarring message cuts through the fog of my mind and emotions. I swap Heart for Striker and widen my stance, planting my feet in the mud and grass. The creature stalking toward me in the rain is not my sister. My sister is safe, in Xī'lín, where I have poured my blood and spirit energy into the strongest wards I'm capable of creating to protect her.

I raise Striker as another streak of lightning zigzags across the sky, and that's when I see *her* again: the illusion of my father's murderer that always finds me in my moments of fear. She's just a blur in the rain, a figment of my imagination, yet as always, my mind fills in the details: the red of her lips, of her eyes, of the garnet at her throat and her long flowing dress and billowing sleeves, the utter perfection of a timeless face worn by a Higher One. Reminding me that, after all this time, I am still not good enough, not strong enough, not powerful enough.

The illusion's gone in a blink, but the moment of distraction costs me.

The painted skin slams into me. The world tilts off balance as I'm thrown to the ground. This time, when I look up, Méi'zi's face is full and healed, her brown eyes wide, her pretty cherry lips widen in a horrific, drooling grin as she claws at me.

"*Jiě'jie,*" she shrieks, and her voice turns guttural, like something else is speaking through her. "*Jiě'jie, you left me . . . so let me eat your flesh!*"

This close, I smell the decay of the creature's breath, the stench oozing from its pores. I've read that painted skins are so named because they collect the skins and body parts of their victims and wear them until they rot off.

I lash out with Striker. The creature screams, Méi'zi's face contorting, as my blade splits its forehead and eyes, where I've read such creatures' cores rest. I grit my teeth against the image of my crescent blade plunged into my own sister's face, reminding myself that this isn't Méi'zi but a monster of nightmares.

Still, I hesitate for a heartbeat.

The monster wrenches away from my blade and leaps back, snarling. Its form ripples, dividing into two distinct silhouettes. When I blink again, it's Mā who's gazing back at me. She's lying on the forest floor, and bent over her . . . bent over her . . . is . . .

The Higher One lifts her head, her face as lovely as the day I saw it nine years ago. Unlike in all my visions, I can see her clearly, her teeth bloodstained as she smiles at me.

Terror turns my mind blank. A very distant corner of my mind whispers that this is my own fear turned against me by this monster of nightmares, but I can't think, and all I know is that it's happening again, the event of nine years ago that I was powerless to stop, that took my parents from me and tore my life apart.

"Àn'yīng!" my mother cries feebly. She reaches a hand toward me. "Àn'yīng, help me. . . ."

I'm shaking. My blades feel like foreign objects in my palms. "Mā," I sob, but I can't move. My limbs are frozen, my feet rooted to the ground, ice in my veins.

The Higher One lifts my mother's face to her lips, and that's what finally breaks me.

I'm screaming as I charge, and as I raise my blades and fall upon the Higher One, she looks up at me in a flash of alarm. I plunge my blade into her face, and this time, I do it with all the pent-up fury of nine years. I feel the crunch of bone and sinew give way to fleshy pulp, hear the creature's shriek as its form ripples and it shifts again. It's now my father's body that the Higher One holds: Bà, bleeding, barely breathing, his eyes faint as he gazes at me and mouths my name, my dagger driven through his throat.

I don't remember what happens next. There's screaming in the distance, and then I hear a voice filtering through, calling my name.

". . . Àn'yīng! Àn'yīng!"

Pressure on my wrists. Hands at my shoulders. A face swims into my vision, beautiful and made even more so in the rain. Wide, dark eyes, long lashes, full lips.

"Àn'yīng," Yù'chén repeats. He's holding my shoulders.

I react by instinct, my mind in overdrive, terrified that this is another illusion of nightmares from this hellscape of a forest. My blades flash. Yù'chén shouts, one hand coming up to block, but it's too late.

Blood sprays my face, flecks of it salting my tongue, hot and tasting of copper. It's this that jerks me from my state of frenzy.

I blink, and Yù'chén's kneeling before me, one hand clutching his cheek, face angled away from me. Streaks of crimson run in rivulets down his face where I cut him, mingling with the rain. There's a foul smell in the air, and it's coming from beneath me.

When I look down, I'm kneeling over a mound of rotting flesh: purpling, decaying skin; a swollen tongue; maggot-infested eyes; and pieces of exposed, pale skull. It's the huà'pí, stabbed beyond recognition.

My hands and blades are bloodied, my throat raw. The screaming I heard from earlier came from me.

"Àn'yīng," Yù'chén says again. He's breathing hard, but when I look into his face, all I can see is blood and the Higher One's smile as she gorged herself on my father's flesh.

I lean away from the dead creature and throw up the contents of my stomach. When I'm done, I crouch over the forest floor. Tremors roll through my body.

Soft footfalls as Yù'chén approaches. He bends, lifting my face with one hand, his fingertips stained red. "It's all right now," he says. "It's dead."

"It wasn't . . . *her* . . . my father . . ." I'm incoherent, but I can't bring myself to speak the words. I clasp my hands to Yù'chén's, searching his eyes, forcing myself to focus on his face, on anything but the image seared into my mind like a white-hot brand. "It wasn't . . . Bà . . ."

His gaze flickers with an emotion I can't understand. "No," he says quietly. "That wasn't your father."

"Not . . . my Mā . . . Méi'zi . . ."

"No. That was a huà'pí. It's dead now, Àn'yīng. It's over." His thumb strokes my face. "Your family's safe. You're safe."

I stare at him, willing his words to sink in. Then, with shaking hands, I grasp his collar and slowly, slowly lean my forehead on his chest. I feel him stiffen, then feel his arms encircle my back as he draws me against him. His skin is warm in the rain, and against my cheek, I feel the steady *thud-thud-thud* of his heart, the brush of his breaths against my ear, stirring my hair.

In this moment, I need to be held, even if it is by half a monster.

Gradually, my body stops shaking. My breathing evens out. And my senses return.

I draw back. The rain has soaked through my dress and washed all the blood from my hands and blades. I'm aware of how close Yù'chén and I are, how his touch on my skin trails heat across my lower back. He's watching me, rain dripping down his hair and lashes and chin. The cut on his cheek is already healing, the bleeding stopped.

I touch a finger to the skin, observing the way it knits itself back together like it was never broken in the first place. "I'm sorry," I say.

"Sorry you cut me?" he asks. "Or sorry you thought me a monster of nightmares?"

I'm not sure what I'm apologizing for. He's silent, droplets of rain clinging to his lashes, and I realize he's actually waiting for an answer. I frown and pull my hand away from his cheek as another thought occurs to me. My voice is still unsteady as I ask instead, "How did you find me?"

He draws a sharp breath, eyes darting between mine. "I . . ."

"Were you looking for me?"

He swallows and turns his gaze away from me.

"Why?" I press. I'm barely holding myself together, and I need him to say that he's doing all this for some sort of reason, a trade, a game . . . anything to tell me that the kindness he is showing me isn't real.

Yù'chén's lips part—then his eyes catch on something behind me, something that drains the color from his face. His hands tighten on my waist and he goes still.

I glance back.

At first, I see nothing. But then, through the trees, I make out a pale smudge: a prone, lifeless body, bare legs and pale silks just visible from here.

I'm about to turn for a closer look when Yù'chén's hand comes to my cheek, turning me sharply back to him. He is pale, and there is a wild, frenetic look to his gaze.

"Another huà'pí," he says, and his other hand grips my waist so tightly, it hurts. "Go, before it targets you."

If it isn't targeting me, that means . . . "Is it targeting you?" I ask.

He doesn't reply, only lets me go and stands. His sword flashes silver as he unsheathes it. "Go," Yù'chén repeats.

I push to my feet, my blades in my hands. I try to get a glimpse of the creature in the trees, of what form Yù'chén's worst fears might take, but he moves to stand between me and the monster. His mouth is tight, his face shuttered, his knuckles white.

It's the first time I have seen him look . . . afraid.

I want to know what in these realms can elicit this kind of a reaction in him. I hesitate, shifting my crescent blades between my fingers.

"Go, before I make you." His tone takes on a rough edge.

I search his face for a trace of the vulnerability I saw just moments ago. It's gone.

I turn and run into the night.

16

I don't know how much time passed in those moments I blanked out, but I estimate that I have about half an hour left to find my bracelet and get off this island. The rain is slowing, and a faint gray light lines the clouds, but every shadow I see I expect to be another monster.

I follow the direction in which Heart points, counting my steps and the seconds that pass. I'm ten more minutes into the forest when Heart shifts suddenly.

I turn as something pale streaks through the trees.

A small gray wolf gallops toward me. I raise my blades, but there is something familiar about its bright-green eyes, how its shaggy fur is speckled with white . . .

"Fán'xuān?" I exclaim.

The little wolf slows to a trot and bares his teeth in what looks like a cheeky grin. Between his fangs, I catch a glimmer of gold.

My heart leaps into my throat. "Is that . . . ? Did you . . . ?"

Fán'xuān wags his tail at me as I kneel and extricate a rather wet but otherwise unharmed golden butterfly. It flutters its wings weakly when I smooth them out to read the number engraved on its back:

44.

I have qualified for the Third Trial.

My eyes prick as I stare at my friend. "Thank you," I whisper. Fán'xuān thumps his tail and looks rather pleased with himself. "Any idea where Lì'líng and Tán'mù are?"

Fán'xuān cocks his head. Suddenly, his ears flatten and he emits a growl.

I raise my blades. A figure steps out from between the trees, but it's not anyone I recognize. A man, dressed in the brocade raiment of the north. He holds a whip, and his eyes gleam as they focus on my friend.

"Fán'xuān," he calls.

Fán'xuān shrinks back. His tail is tucked between his legs, and he lets out a sound between a bark and a whine.

"It's his former master," comes a voice to my left. When I look over, Tán'mù is striding toward me. She comes to a stop by my side, her two-pronged spear gripped tightly in her hand. She's staring at the silhouette between the trees with a tightness to her eyes. "They were raised in show pens."

She says this without emotion, but I suddenly understand. I have heard of these show pens: where yāo'jīng are captured and shipped to serve as entertainment or sold to mortal masters. I have heard of them only as horrible stories in passing: how the yāo'jīng are tortured into subservience.

As Fán'xuān whines again, something coils tight inside me. I palm Fleet and Striker; this time, I don't even hesitate. I charge the huà'pí at a run, propelled by Fleet's talisman so that it doesn't even see me coming. The pen master turns

to me just as Striker meets his forehead. He screams as I dig
into the monster's core, and then the illusion flickers and the
huà'pí thumps to the ground, a collection of bones and de-
composing skins.

I turn and walk back to Fán'xuān. The shaggy wolf glances
up at me, blinking. I reach out and wrap my arms around the
halfling shapeshifter, burying my face in his soft fur. When
I draw back, fur has turned to a shock of messy white hair,
snout and claws have turned into human face and limbs,
and the boy with those bright-green eyes sits by my side. He
blinks at me and looks down at my arms, as though he isn't
sure what to do.

Then he snuggles his face against my shoulder.

The rain has stopped. Some moonlight spills out from the
edges of the rain clouds, filtering through the canopy of the
forest.

A yip sounds through the trees. From between two pa-
goda bushes, a small white fox appears, looking at us expectantly. Lì'líng.

"She's saying we all have our golden butterflies, and we
have to go." Tán'mù gives me a long-suffering look that sug-
gests this isn't the first time she's had to translate for Lì'líng.
"She prefers to stay in her fox form until we're out—it makes
her feel safer."

The tightness in my chest eases as we fall into step next to
one another. Fán'xuān is back in his wolf form; Lì'líng trots
delicately by my side, nose in the air.

"Those huà'pí were something, huh," Tán'mù muses.
"They're saying the Second Trial is the test of courage.
Whether we can overcome our greatest fears."

I'm not ready to talk about my parents yet, but I tell her

how the huà'pí took Méi'zi's form. Tán'mù listens without a
sound. When I finish, we lapse into a companionable silence.

"Tán'mù," I say.

"Mm?"

I count my steps, measuring my words. "We must be careful. Number One's killer is still on the loose."

Her dark eyes go to Lì'líng and Fán'xuān, trotting a ways
ahead of us, tails in the air. "I'm always careful," Tán'mù replies, and I feel it when her gaze slides to me. She's silent for
a few heartbeats, then between the sound of our footfalls, her
voice drifts to me. "There's something you're not telling me."

I inhale deeply and give her the one thing I *can* tell her. "I was
the one who found her body. The wounds she sustained . . .
I don't think a candidate would have inflicted them." I finally
lift my eyes to meet hers. "Her chest was torn open, Tán'mù.
Her heart and organs were eaten."

Tán'mù's mouth tightens. "They're going to come after
us, you know."

By *us*, she means the halflings. The immortals know that
halflings participate in their trials.

What they don't know about is the presence of a fourth
halfling on their temple grounds, who's half-demon, half-
mortal—a creature whose very existence is unheard of across
the realms.

"Whatever killed Number One is dangerous," I say in a
low voice. "Xiù'chūn was the strongest among us, and she
couldn't beat it. Promise me you'll watch Lì'líng and Fán'xuān
while the immortals hunt down the culprit."

"I will." Tán'mù tips her head. "And I'll be watching you,
too. Like it or not, you're with us now."

Her words warm me as much as they weigh on me. I am

the only person who knows of Yù'chén's existence—and of the gate we created in the Kingdom of Sky's wards.

My stomach tightens. Tonight, I'll go investigate the gate—the one Yù'chén said he closed—and try to determine whether something got through from the outside . . . and is now hunting down the Temple of Dawn candidates.

The charm on my golden butterfly has not yet faded; its wings flutter gently as I brush my thumb along it time and time again, feeling the grooves of my number:

44.

There is something oddly comforting about it now, I think, as I cross the marble bridge with my friends. Here and there, we spot candidates trickling back into the Kingdom of Sky. Some limp; a few are wounded.

The disembodied gong clangs across the Temple of Dawn just as Lì'líng, Tán'mù, Fán'xuān, and I enter the Hall of Radiant Sun. I glance behind me as we step into the warm glow of lanterns. The marble bridge melts away into the night, shattering like ashes of stars. For a split second, I think I see the hulking shadow of a great landmass drifting in the darkened sky . . . before the fog swallows it whole.

Yù'chén is not back.

Twenty-six of us have made it. With each face that I scan that isn't his, my chest tightens a bit more. I remember the look on his face as he gazed at the pale, lifeless form between the trees, the way his voice changed when he told me to leave.

He pulled me out of the depths of my most vulnerable moment yet. And I left him there to face his greatest fear alone.

Immortal guards move to stand in front of the entrance to

the temple, declaring the end to the trial. I look for Hào'yáng, but I don't find him, either.

"Welcome back, candidates." Dòng'bīn's voice is a low rumble that fills the Hall of Radiant Sun. "And congratulations on passing the Second Trial.

"The Temple of Dawn is the first front in finding those worthy of joining the Kingdom of Sky." There's a shuffle of suppressed excitement around us. Up until now, the immortals have given us information in dribs and drabs, but Dòng'bīn is gearing up for a speech. "First and foremost, we value physical prowess with the mortal martial arts and practitioning arts, as well as the natural state of one's body. That was the First Trial: testing your ability to reach our temple. Yet we also value what lies beneath the strength of one's body—and that is the strength of one's heart. That is why the Second Trial was a test of the fortitude of your mind: a trial of courage, and your ability to withstand the depths of your own fears. Each of the remaining trials will test other aspects of what we value in our bravest and our best—qualities that, I am certain, these trials will reveal within a handful of you here."

The candidates' excited air takes an uneasy turn at his reminder: only a few of us will earn the elusive pill to the Kingdom of Sky.

"While we reward those who show desirable traits, we also punish those who break the rules we have set forth for this sacred temple." Dòng'bīn's gaze narrows. "This world was established according to the unbreakable laws of the Heavenly Order. Just as the realms must follow the Order, so, too, must all beings within the realms adhere to the laws set forth by their kingdoms, their temples, their households. And those who disrupt must be punished."

By his side, Shī'yǎ tilts her head. Nearly imperceptibly.

"Guards, bring out the perpetrator."

Footsteps sound from behind us. The entire hall turns to look—and I feel a crash of relief followed by dread.

A pair of immortal guards hold Yù'chén by his arms, marching him forward. His golden bracelet flashes on his left wrist; he passed the Second Trial.

Perpetrator. My breathing grows uneven; the hall seems to fade, blending into the memory of candidate Number One lying amidst the peonies and orchids and chrysanthemums with her heart and guts torn out.

And you've come to ask me if I killed her, ate her heart, and drank her soul like the wicked demon I am? As I sift through our conversation in my mind, I realize he's never outright denied that he killed her. And I, fool that I am, believed him innocent.

My skin is cold, my blood turned to ice. I cannot reconcile the possibility of Yù'chén as a killer with the man who held me in the forest earlier.

I don't look away as he passes me. Murmurs rise from the candidates around me: whispers of "murderer" and "killer." Yù'chén keeps his eyes straight ahead, unblinking, unflinching, as the guards lead him before the dais. They force him to kneel.

Dòng'bīn takes a seat; Jǐng'xiù stands, his bamboo scepter unfurling into a scroll. "Candidate, you are to receive divine punishment for breaking rule seventeen of the Temple of Dawn's Precepts. For the crime of theft, you are to receive ten lashes from the Thrasher of the Gods."

Theft? Is Yù'chén not being tried for murder?

One of the guards steps forward. A whip uncoils from his

palm, crackling with divine energy. I know of this whip from the legends: it's said the Jade Emperor once used it to punish his enemies, and that one of its lashes is equal to a hundred by the hands of a mortal. Ten is nearly unthinkable. What could he have stolen to deserve this?

Yù'chén stares stoically at a spot above all our heads.

"Begin."

The whip streaks through the air like lightning, and the first lash echoes in the temple. Yù'chén pitches forward slightly from the impact; a muscle feathers in his jaw, but after several beats, he straightens his shoulders and resumes his stony stare at the back wall.

The second lash prompts a sharp exhale of breath from him. By the fifth, his clothing has peeled from his back. By the seventh, blood spots the marble floors of the Hall of Radiant Sun.

When they finish with him, Yù'chén's eyes are closed. A lock of his hair falls in his face, pale and sweat-slicked. Blood darkens his back, dripping from his ruined clothes and blooming on the floor like red petals. When the guards step away from him, he falls, catching himself on his hands and knees. He's too exhausted to lift his head, but his hands twitch, as though reaching out for something, anything to hold on to— but there is nothing near him, no one there to help him stand.

I find my own hands fisted so tightly my nails dig crescents into my palms.

"Let this be a reminder," Jǐng'xiù says gravely, looking up at the crowd of candidates gathered before the dais in silence, "of the consequences of disrupting order."

★   ★   ★

Back in my chambers, I scrub my skin with my washcloth until it is raw, until the images of the huà'pí as Méi'zi and Mā and Bà fade. I focus on my true memories of my sister instead.

I wonder if she has received my gloves. I miss her so much it hurts. And there is only one person who can tell me if my message has gotten through to her.

An image flits in my mind's eye: Yù'chén kneeling alone at the front of the Hall of Radiant Sun, blood puddling on the floor from his back, too tired to lift his head. The twitch of his hands as he searched for something to hold on to.

I swallow and splash my bathwater, as though that will disperse the image. He'll be fine. He's a mó, and I've seen how quickly he heals. And even if he isn't fine, it's none of my business.

I turn my thoughts away, but the one image I cannot shake is the huà'pí's illusion as Méi'zi. Irrational as it is, I am set on edge by the possibility that anything has happened to my baby sister.

I look out at the courtyard through the slits of my shutters. There's a subdued air to this place tonight. Half the dorms' lanterns are extinguished. I register the numbers engraved on their doors, and I try not to think of the faces I learned to associate with those numbers. I wasn't close to any of them, but we still lived together, passed each other in the long walkways beneath the willows, ate at the same banquet terrace. We were human, together.

Now seventeen of us are gone. Seventeen mortal practitioners who might have had families to feed and villages to protect, just like me.

Suddenly, I think of the immortals lounging on their

thrones, surrounded by guards and plum wines served in porcelain cups and food brought out on silver platters. My heart clenches. I'm not here to disrupt the order; I've just witnessed with my own eyes what happens to those who do. I'm only here to win that pill of immortality for my mother, so things can go back to how they were. So Méi'zi can be happy.

I fasten my white dress, brushing my fingers along the new seams of seasilk. I strap on my crescent blades. Armed to the teeth, I set out.

I need to find Yù'chén—to ask him if my gloves reached Méi'zi. And then I'm going to check on the gate with my own eyes. None of this, I tell myself, am I doing because I want reassurance that he's healing himself with his dark magic—or because I'm curious what was so important for him to steal that he'd risk his life.

The rain and mist of Péng'lái Island seem to have crept into the Temple of Dawn. Candidates are clustered in small groups by the water and by their doorsteps, their quiet murmurs drifting through the night. Across the water from my chambers, the lanterns in Yù'chén's are extinguished, the shutters dark.

A few high-ranking candidates I recognize but who have never paid attention to me are seated at a pavilion overlooking the pond. I catch drifts of their conversation as I pass by.

". . . must have gone to the Spring of Healing Essence," a girl is saying. I recognize her as one of the girls who hung around Yù'chén during training. She's Number Five and has the classic beauty the poets and painters of old would have rendered in song and ink. I find myself wondering if Yù'chén is close to her.

I quickly stomp the thought down. As I turn away from them, one of the other girls' voices rings out: "Say, Xī'xī, do you know what he stole, anyway?"

"You'll never believe it." Number Five—Xī'xī—lowers her voice. "I heard it from one of the guards." She pauses, and the words drift to me through the sound of rain. "He stole a sewing kit."

17

Blood roars in my ears. The rain, the willows, the soft conversation of the girls, all peel away from me.

A sewing kit.

The information strings everything together: fragments of memories I have not paid heed to until this very moment.

A seamstress. His cajoling tone as he tried to tease out my past life. *Did I guess true?*

No. I just like to sew.

I thought it was part of the magic of this realm that gifted me a sewing kit. But I remember the night we went out to the sea, how I felt his gaze on the gloves I'd sewn for Méi'zi, the way he guided me to walk on water. *Can you think of it as sewing? Each current of energy is a thread being stitched, and you simply have to stitch the opposite way, in tune.*

This is the part of me that I haven't even shown to Méi'zi or Mā or Bà after our kingdom fell, for fear of disappointing them—that they would think for a moment I was unhappy in giving up my needles and threads to learn to protect them.

Somehow, in a few short weeks, Yù'chén has glimpsed the girl who once wished to sew oceans.

For the crime of theft. Jǐng'xiù's voice echoes in my mind. The crack of each lash against Yù'chén's back, the silence in which he bore them. The slight movement to his hands as he searched for something to hold on to afterward.

The Spring of Healing Essence is in the remotest corner of the gardens. The downpour of rain roars in my ears as I run, but I don't care. I know where I'm going.

I round an outcrop of jagged rocks, and the hot spring comes into view, its waters steaming gently despite the rain and the cold. Red petals are strewn across its surface, gilded by the lambent light of lanterns in a nearby pavilion.

Beneath a cluster of willows and flowering cherry trees, Yù'chén leans against a boulder, his eyes closed. Steam curls his hair, and he has shed his crimson cloak and black shirt to bare his skin. My mouth goes dry at the sight of his back. Between his corded muscles, the flesh is shredded and red. The lash wounds are already closing, perhaps from the healing energy of the spring and the demonic magic that runs in Yù'chén's veins.

He opens his eyes as I approach, but he doesn't look at me. His expression is walled off as it was back in the Hall of Radiant Sun. "Come to tell me I deserved it?"

A hundred questions and words tumble through my mind, yet I know that if I speak them aloud, everything between us will come crashing down.

"I came to ask if your crane reached Méi'zi," I say. My voice is tight, my fists clenched.

His lashes flutter. He looks exhausted.

"What do I get if I tell you?" His voice is low, harsh, and he tips his head back, closing his eyes with a sigh. "What can you offer me, little scorpion?"

I swallow, thinking of the first time he spoke those words to me. What could he want that I wouldn't give? I would give my flesh and blood to ensure Méi'zi's safety. I would give my soul to save hers.

But I realize that this isn't just about Méi'zi anymore.

I owe him. I owe him more than I can imagine.

"I'll give you whatever you want," I whisper.

Yù'chén's eyes crack open a sliver. They flash red as he assesses me. Through the steam, I can make out traces of darkness threading his skin: his demon's ichor, running through his veins, likely helping him heal.

Abruptly, he says, "Your life energy. I'll take some of your life energy to help me heal faster."

I swallow. "Fine," I say. "First, show me."

He reaches for his cloak, laid out on the bank, and pulls out a feather that seems to shimmer between silver and shadow. He blows on it.

The feather dissolves into light and darkness, swirling together to become an orb. Within, a scene forms, and I bite down a gasp. It's my house! Everything is slightly stretched and fuzzy, and I realize I am looking through the crane's eye as we soar down to the front door. My breath catches, and I actually reach forward, as though I can step into the feather's magic and transport myself back home.

The shadowcrane lands. In the predawn light, I see the gleam of the wards that I've put up around the house. The bird cocks its head, then turns to the old plum tree. Carefully, it places my gloves next to its trunk.

Then it flies behind the tree and settles in to wait.

The sun's glow lights up the sky. The front door opens, and Méi'zi steps out, rubbing her eyes and yawning. She's in the pajamas I gifted her, the ones with the pink plum blossoms in my unrefined stitching. I notice Shield strapped to her hip.

She glances around; then her eyes go to the gloves at the base of the tree. Tentatively, as though not daring to believe it, she creeps over and picks up the gloves. She stares at them, studying them as she runs her fingers over the stitches, discerning the signature to the patterns and weaves.

Suddenly, she breaks into a smile and her eyes fill with tears. *"Jiě'jie,"* she whispers and hugs the gloves to her chest.

"Méi'zi," I gasp, but she's turning around and going back into our house, and she can't hear me—"Méi'zi! *Chūn'méi*—" My voice cracks.

The magic of the feather is spent, and the memory dissolves, and I'm left looking into Yù'chén's face. He's watching me now, his eyes burning deep crimson.

My cheeks are wet as I whisper, "Tell me it's real. Tell me that wasn't a lie you made up."

"It's real," he says.

The rain is a deluge, roaring down through the canopy of flowers and willow leaves. I'm completely drenched, kneeling on the muddied banks of the hot spring, just an arm's length from him. Steam wafts between us, coiling through the red petals drifting in the bloodied water. Something has shaken loose inside me; my walls are breaking, and it's too late to salvage.

I lift my gaze and break through the last of it. "Why did you steal the sewing kit?"

He stares at me; his lips part in a breath. I see it, that momentary slip to his expression before it locks up again.

"To gain your trust," he replies. "To get close to you."

I stare at him. "Why?"

He lifts a hand and crooks a finger at me. My muscles lock. He's going to take some of my life energy.

I am afraid, but I refuse to run. The only path to him is through the water.

I slip into the spring. The water is hot, but I'm trembling, cold sluicing through my veins. With each step I take toward him, a memory grows clearer inside me: the image of that beautiful red-lipped woman, drinking my father's life energy, lips pressed to his as though in a lover's kiss.

I feel sick. I draw to a stop before Yù'chén, breathing hard, my crescent blades in my hands. He's splayed against the bank in the water, watching me with narrowed eyes. Slowly, he stands, water sluicing from him as he leans over me.

"Why?" he repeats. "So you can be indebted to me. So you can willingly proffer your flesh and blood to me, wicked demon that I am."

My heart's pounding wildly, but I force my hands to be steady as I raise Shadow to my palm. "If you're going to take it," I say, "then just do it."

Yù'chén catches my wrist just as my blade arcs toward my flesh. He brushes my hand aside. His eyes are as dark as pools of blood as he trails a finger up my neck. I feel my life energy stirring in my chest, following the stroke of his finger, welling up in my throat.

When Yù'chén's hand comes to grip my jaw, it takes every ounce of my willpower to hold still.

He is not going to consume my life energy through my blood. He is going to drink my life energy the way the Higher One drank my mother's soul nine years ago.

His finger trails to the soft curve of my throat. He pauses, eyes flashing as he meets mine. His thumb presses against the flutter of my pulse.

"Do you fear me?" he murmurs.

"No," I lie. "I *hate* you."

"Good," he says, and then he lowers his lips to mine.

We don't touch. Instead, I feel the soft caress of his breath against my cheek, the cold of his inhale. My life energy wells up from my throat and pours from my lips to his, faintly golden like scattered sunlight. I'm shaking, but whatever I'm waiting for—pain, helplessness, the feeling of my soul slowly being drained from me—doesn't come. Around us, the rain continues to fall, steam billows from the hot spring, and Yù'chén merely draws in another breath.

His grip has loosened, and his eyes have fallen shut, eyelashes sweeping dark crescents against his cheekbones. His fingers cup my jaw, his thumb tracing strokes against the crook of my neck. Like this, he looks as though he might be asleep; like this, he looks exhausted. Blood from his wounds darkens the water around us.

Why did you steal the sewing kit?

He's stopped drinking my life energy, I realize. He stands in place, swaying slightly, his thumb caressing my throat in slow, circular motions as he coaxes my life energy up. As our breaths tangle, he cracks his eyes open. His pupils are dark, dilated, and I'm transfixed by the golden glow of my life energy reflected within them. They roam up my face before trailing back down to my lips.

Yù'chén doesn't take another sip. Instead, his other hand comes up to hold the small of my back. Slowly, he dips his head. His gaze flicks up, meeting mine. Holding it.

When I don't move, he finally brushes his lip against mine.

His touch is electric, a spark that roars into a fire surging through my veins. Before I know it, I'm kissing him back, my hand reaching for his cheek, twining into his hair. I hold him, the way I wished to and the way I should have back in the Hall of Radiant Sun. His mouth is hot, near feverish, and he tastes like salt and blood and a hint of midnight sweetness.

Yù'chén exhales, as though finally surrendering himself. His fingers tighten around my waist, and he pulls me closer. Asking for permission.

I give it.

He pulls me against him with a splash. I gasp—the water is hot, the rain cold against my skin, and with his fingers digging into my waist and his mouth against mine, my body is a tumult of sensations. That all settles into an intense focus as he leans against the jagged rock and draws me so I'm positioned over him.

I hook my legs around his waist and give a shaky exhale at the hard fit of his body against mine, his head lifted to gaze up at me as though in supplication. His eyes are dark, endless pools, and I feel as if I'm falling into an eternal night as I lower my face and kiss him again.

He's slow, soft this time, his lips moving down my jawline and my neck as his fingers move up the bare skin of my leg. My dress drifts around my waist in the water, exposing the crescent blades strapped to my thighs and the thin sheet of undergarment between my legs. The rain and water have made my dress translucent, and I close my eyes as his mouth moves down my collarbone, then lower. I clench my fingers against his chest and he makes a noise low in his throat.

"Never without your blades, little scorpion?" he murmurs, his hand playing on one of my straps.

I slide Poison into my palm and hold it to his throat. "Never," I whisper.

He pushes against the blade, testing, as he takes my lips again, and I do nothing to stop him. His throat is at my knife-point, my blade digging into the corded muscles of his neck, but he leans forward and I yield, yield, until I feel my dagger's hilt against my own chest, my frantic, pounding heart. His hands trace up my bodice, caressing circles against my breasts and igniting a desire low in my belly. His breath hitches as he shifts his hips, the rough scratch of his pants pressing deeper between my legs. The ache inside me builds, and I inhale sharply, gripping the back of his neck and burying my fingers in his hair.

"Àn'yīng," he murmurs against my mouth, and I dig my nails into his skin. He makes another noise in his chest, then suddenly, he flips us so that I'm splayed against the edge of the spring and he is pinning me to the banks with his body. I gaze up, and between the sparks of pleasure misting my senses comes a bone-deep, instinctive stab of fear. I have been in this position before, trapped and helpless as prey.

Yù'chén blinks slowly, studying me. In the next breath, he pulls me up, straightening us so we are face to face, my crescent blade curving between our chests. He is gentle again, his hand around my wrist, placing my blade to the soft curve of his throat. Putting me back in control.

"Àn'yīng," he repeats, my name like a supplication on

his lips. Through the flutter of my lashes, I see that his eyes are on me, dark, heated, and hazy. There is a frantic edge to the way he kisses me now, cupping my face in his palms as though he's afraid I'll vanish. As his fingers brush my cheeks, my jaw, the nape of my neck, I can't help but think of how he held me back on that island of nightmares.

Of that prone, lifeless body the huà'pí showed him as his worst fear.

"Yù'chén," I whisper against his mouth. "What did you see in the forest?"

He draws a swift breath; his eyes fly open.

And then he pushes away.

I blink, frustrated, desire still pulsing through every nerve of my body. He's breathing hard, his hair in tangles over his chest. The water between us is red with blood and dotted with petals.

"No," Yù'chén says, his voice ragged. There is a wild, haunted look to the way he gazes at me, as if I am a ghost. The moment of terror passes, and his expression steels.

I stare at him, my heart pounding. "What did you see in the forest?" I repeat.

Yù'chén's eyes darken. Then he's gone, walled up and shuttered with that same stony expression he had back at the Hall of Radiant Sun tonight. "You should go," he replies, turning his face away.

"What did you see, Yù'chén?"

He looks at me again. "Nothing that concerns you."

I curl my hands into fists by my side, humiliation stinging my cheeks. "You saved me. You were there because of me. And then you told me to leave. You gifted me that sewing

kit, and you bore the punishment for it without telling me."
We've been dancing the same dance all along: drawing closer
to each other before pushing away. I'm tired of it. "Why?"

Yù'chén tilts his head away from me. His jaw is tight.
" 'Why?' " he echoes, and when he looks at me again, I can't
make out the expression he wears. "Àn'yīng, you told me I
disgusted you. That you didn't want to think of me as anything more than a monster. I would be remiss to force you to
spend any more time with me than necessary."

In the past, I might have convinced myself this was all a
ruse: helping me, showing me qīng'gōng, even stealing the
sewing kit . . . but tonight, back in the Forest of Nightmares,
something between us changed irrevocably. The way he held
me at my most vulnerable moment has broken through the
last of my defenses.

"I'm sorry, Yù'chén." My voice is soft, because I owe him
those three words. And then, because tonight, in that forest, he protected the softest, deepest part of me, I give him a
truth. "I want to know you. Who you are."

His lips part; I cannot read the expression on his face, but
it's gone the next moment. He grips the ledge of the pool,
locks of his hair hanging over his face. "No, you don't," he says
at last. "Don't forget, little scorpion, that this is all a game."

The cold steals in between us with the rain. My dress clings
to my bare skin, and I think of how his hands on me earlier
did not feel like the touch of someone who didn't desire me.

Worse, I think of how I crave it.

I hoist myself out of the water and wrap my arms around
myself. I'm exhausted, physically and emotionally; the illu-
sions from the Forest of Nightmares have drained me entirely, so there is no fight in my voice when I reply. "I'm not

playing your games, Yù'chén. The trials are enough as it is."
I cast a glance back at him. He's still standing at the edge of
the spring, rigid, as though locked in place. His eyes are dark
as he gazes at me.

I touch my hand to my lip. "With all the life energy I gave
you, I'll consider my debts paid."

Then I turn away and walk through the Celestial Gardens,
the rain cold against my skin.

18

The sun breaks bright in blue skies the next morning, as though determined to clear away all traces of the storm from the night past. Yet there is a palpable tension in the Candidates' Courtyard today. The remaining candidates are gathered in clusters, their faces serious as they register the missing or the dead. Within just a week, almost half of us have been eliminated from the trials.

Whispers of Number One's murder drift through every conversation, and along with it, Yù'chén's lashing from the night past.

"He killed her," I hear someone say from a group seated at the water's edge. "He was ranked second, so he wanted to eliminate his most powerful competition. Why else would the immortals have lashed him for something as petty as theft?"

"I heard her body was found in a bad state," a second candidate adds. "He always struck me as the violent type."

I pick up my pace and round the walkway to the moongates. In the daylight, the Celestial Gardens look nothing like they do at night. The flowers are in bloom, chrysanthemums and orchids and peonies and jasmine filling the air with their fragrance and brightening the gardens like gemstones. Guards are stationed on the main walkways, but Hào'yáng is not among their ranks again today.

The Temple of Dawn kept its word about increasing security. All the major training grounds have the presence of guards; seeing the glint of their white-and-gold armor and the flash of their white robes everywhere feels suffocating—especially considering where I'm going.

I slip out Shadow and Fleet and vanish between the trees.

The back of the Celestial Gardens is empty and quiet as I make for the section of the wards where Yù'chén made his gate just two nights ago. It's difficult to retrace my steps today—we came down a different path directly from the Hall of Radiant Sun—but when the sound of a burbling stream breaks through the morning's silence, I know I'm close.

Between two willows, the wards appear as an iridescent shimmer in the air like the mist of a waterfall in sunlight. Even here, the hum of their spirit energies reaches me.

I square my shoulders and step toward the stream that plunges off the edge of this realm. If I close my eyes, I remember the way Yù'chén held me as we stood knee-deep in the water. The way the skies opened to me in the realm beyond.

I open my eyes, willing any other traitorous thoughts away as I focus on the translucent wards. Yes, right here, Yù'chén lifted his hands and flowers bloomed from his magic, growing into a door in the wards. They opened into an archway, and everything from the mortal realm grew sharper and clearer, like lifting a veil: the salt-laced wind, the pearl dust stars.

Now the gate is gone—as Yù'chén said it would be.

I let out a shaky exhale.

Yù'chén told the truth. And I don't know how to feel about that.

Instead, I kneel in the grass before the ward. Since Bà died, I've had to learn to hunt for my family's survival. If a mó or one of the hellbeasts entered from the outside, I should be able to find some form of tracks.

A flash of crimson between the tall grasses catches my eye. I draw my blades out as I lean closer to look.

It's a red scorpion lily. In the daylight, it has lost its soft, alluring glow, but it rests between the grasses, a thing both beautiful and deadly. As I study it, I realize it's rooted in the soil and the stream just within the wards, its dew-kissed petals glistening like blood.

I'm about to reach for it when I hear footfalls behind me.

I whirl around, my blades already slicing through the air— and my heart leaps into my throat when I catch sight of the newcomer. White silks, gold lamellar armor.

My blade glances off a metal wrist guard with a *plink* as Hào'yáng easily blocks my swipe.

"Oh," I gasp. "S-Sorry."

A gentle wind plays with his hair, and the sunlight haloes him as he studies me. I can't help but stare back, recalling each sweep of his features as though I am underwater again, surrounded by the shifting tides.

Hào'yáng's gaze flicks down at my hand, curled instinctively on my collarbone where my jade pendant is tucked beneath my clothes. Somehow, the silence between us feels as taut as a drawn breath.

Then he says, "Don't be. I was looking for you."

My lips part, and as a wind picks up, sending petals dancing in the sunlit clearing, I can't help but wonder if this is a
moment carved in the wheels of fate, brought about by the
threads my father has carefully woven into my life throughout all these years, culminating here.

"Why?" I ask. My voice is almost carried away in the
breeze.

"Lady Shī'yǎ has asked me to train you in preparation for
the Third Trial."

Hào'yáng is indifferent, almost cold, as he leads me toward
a part of the Celestial Gardens I have never seen. I trail after
him, questions burning inside me.

"Can I ask—" I begin, but he shoots me a sharp look over
his shoulder.

"No," he says, and then amends, "not here."

We walk in silence through the gardens until the grass
and mud beneath our feet turn to sand. Ahead, the flowering
trees open up to an endless stretch of water that vanishes into
the horizon and the Sea of Clouds.

The Mirror Lake. I imagine all the candidates past and present have gathered here, at the edge of the Temple of Dawn
grounds, and gazed into the distance, at the looming mountains and lands and the promise of a life away from death and
danger.

The morning sun shining on the lake casts everything in
warm gold. Impossibly, cherry blossoms ranging from blush
pink to moon white grow from the surface of the water. I've
seen more of my namesake in this realm than I have in my
own, and I wonder if my father named me for his time here.

I glance at Hào'yáng. "Can I ask where we're going now?"

"Someplace we can train," he replies, scanning the lake with a narrow gaze. "Away from here."

"Candidates can't leave the premises," I remind him.

"Not by yourselves," he replies, then lifts his fingers to his lips and gives a short whistle.

In the distance, the slightest ripple dapples the surface of the lake. Then something shoots out from it into the sky: a serpentine shape wrought of a pale gleam of scales. As it twists toward us, it transforms. The mane of seawater and mist remains, but scales shift to hair, claws lengthen to legs and hooves.

It's a white dragonhorse. Legends say the first of these rare creatures was born of a noble mare who gave its life to bear its rider through the Golden Desert all the way to the Four Seas. Touched by the courage and loyalty of the animal, the dragons took its soul and reincarnated it into one of them, giving it the freedom to roam the skies and the earth in two forms.

The dragonhorse comes to a stop before us. As I study its intelligent brown eyes and mane that ripples like it holds oceans, a jolt of recognition courses through me.

The dragonhorse casts me an amused look and snorts.

Hào'yáng slides onto the dragonhorse's back and holds out his hand to me.

It's a tight squeeze to fit both of us on its back.

As the dragonhorse gallops into the waters of the lake, I end up awkwardly digging my fingers into the belt at Hào'yáng's waist. He is warm, and he smells of sunlight and incense, reminiscent of spring. Water splashes in my face, clean and cool against the sun's heat. Soon, we're climbing into the skies, the ground and the temples and the water falling away from us in a thrilling, dizzying way.

The immortal realm is *achingly* beautiful. The clouds, the distant mountains and lands, the blossoms and willows sweeping the waters—all of it seems to exude a radiant, golden haze, a perfection that the most talented mortal artists might dream of capturing in their art. I hold on to Hào'yáng, and I wonder whether the mortal realm might have had an ounce of the immortal realm's beauty before it fell. I wonder if I might have traveled the kingdom with Mā, seamstresses seeking to weave our world's wonders into thread and fabric.

Landmasses and mountains float lazily in the Sea of Clouds. Curved temple rooftops peek out from between folds of valleys, surrounded by beautiful blossoms and weaving waterways. I spot towns perched completely on lakes that drift between clouds, ending in waterfalls that spill over the edges. Larger cities of somber reds and rosewood, connected by stone walkways and arched bridges and flourishing with food stalls, flower fairs, and immortals arriving or departing by the wings of great snowy cranes. The wind carries the sound of distant laughter and music.

We alight on the shore of a lake. Its waters are turquoise in the sunlight and beautifully transparent, lapping against white sands. Gently sloping mountains rise behind us, covered in an array of hibiscus, camellias, lilacs, and violet cresses, which sway in a soft breeze.

I trail my fingers in the water, marveling at how it's nearly warm, how the currents sparkle as if they hide threads of gold. Deeper in, the colorful scales of darting carp flash like jewels.

Hào'yáng stands in the shade of a great camphor tree that overhangs a tide pool. Wild meadowsweet carpets the sands beneath him, and there's a hint of a smile to his eyes as he watches his dragonhorse graze. It's the first time I've seen him look relaxed, as though he has stepped out from the weight of his duty to the Temple of Dawn.

"Those are her favorite flowers," he says, and I nearly jump out of my skin. I didn't realize he saw me watching him. "She's nicknamed after them. Meadowsweet."

Hào'yáng turns to me. The calculation and intensity of his gaze is gone, replaced by an expression bordering playfulness that I haven't witnessed within temple grounds. He tucks his hands behind his back and tilts his head. "My mother set me to the task of training you," he begins.

"Your mother?" I repeat.

"Lady Shī'yǎ is my mother."

"I—oh." I assumed them to be husband and wife, but now, thinking back, it makes sense. There is an air of deference to how he treats her, and he somehow *feels* younger than her.

"I should say, my adopted mother." Hào'yáng's tone is light. "If you're worried about this impacting your standing in the trials, don't. She wouldn't have gone through all the effort of saving you and keeping you alive just to set you up for failure."

"But why?" I demand.

"You'll have to ask her," Hào'yáng repeats. He's walking toward me, and for some reason, each step closer he comes sets a strange fluttering in my stomach. My hand goes to my chest, fingers curling over my jade pendant beneath my layers of clothing. "There is no formal training offered prior to the trials anymore. But there is no Precept forbidding it, either."

"The Precepts forbid any type of relationship between the candidates and the immortals."

"You're right," he says, unfazed. He undoes the buckles of his lamellar armor. "But that rule doesn't apply to me." The pieces of his armor fall to the ground, and he steps out in a plain white shift. It's tight-fitting, and this close, I'm struck by how strong he is, muscles sculpted from what I assume to be an eternity of training and using spirit energy to cultivate his physical form into immortal perfection.

"Why not?" I ask.

"Because," he says with a wry smile, "I'm mortal."

Mortal. He's *mortal*.

I think back to all the details I picked up about him, and how this makes perfect sense. The way his complexion lacks the ethereal radiance and perfection of all immortals—how gazing at him feels like looking at the quiet steadiness of the earth instead of the brilliant, blazing beauty of the sun. How his skin is rougher and he carries traces of small scars our mortal bodies cannot heal as the immortals' can. How he couldn't fly or summon a cloud but had to call upon Meadowsweet.

Mortal sympathizer, the immortal with the fan called Shī'yǎ, and now I understand.

Hào'yáng watches the shock and epiphany play out on my face. "Don't believe me? If you hit me, I'll bruise just like you." Then he smiles, and it's like seeing the sun come out from behind clouds. "Your first task: get one hit on me. I'm going to assess your skills."

I tilt my head, considering. "One hit, one answer to a question," I negotiate.

"To a question that I *can* answer," he shoots back. "One

that doesn't involve the realm's security or political interests or other people's secrets."

I smile innocently at him and clasp my hands behind my back. With a flick of my wrist, Fleet is in one hand, Shadow in the other. "Deal," I say, and tap my spirit energy into them.

I charge. Hào'yáng swerves back, but Shadow's talisman is strong enough to bypass mortal eyes. Another pivot and my palm is pressed to his chest, daggers back in the hidden straps within my sleeves.

"Hit," I say, and release Shadow's talisman.

The edges of his eyes curve as I reappear in front of him, and he gives me a long, assessing look. "No magical daggers next round."

"They're crescent blades," I correct, but I'm also grinning as I draw my hand back. My grin fades slightly when I ask, "Did they find the killer?"

"No," he says, and I can see him weighing his response carefully. "But you were right. The immortals believe candidate Number One was killed by a mó."

A mó. I was right.

My mind inevitably flits to the only part-mó I know that has access to this place: Yù'chén. "You don't think it could have been another candidate, given the nature of the trials?" I say carefully. "If I were the immortals, I'd begin by investigating the top candidates."

"They are," he replies. "They've confirmed that the other top five candidates were all in the training temple at the time. We'll continue tracking everyone, but rest assured, there is heavier guard presence around the Candidates' Courtyard now."

A crash of waves roars in my ears. "Numbers Two through Five were in the training temple?" I croak.

"Yes." Hào'yáng pauses and gives me a narrow smile. "I think that was more than one question."

I nod and raise my fists, but my mind is elsewhere. *Why don't we survive this trial first, and then you can go back to accusing me of the monstrous things you think I do.*

Suddenly, Yù'chén's anger at me feels insufficient.

Without my blades, I'm no match for Hào'yáng, and my focus slips as my mind wanders to Yù'chén, to all the horrible things I've said to him and accused him of. When a missed jab throws me off balance, Hào'yáng catches me by my forearm to stop me from face-planting into the sand.

"Àn'yīng," he says. "*Focus.* The trials will only become more competitive; the Third could start any day. You almost died during the First, and I don't want to have to watch you—"

"How do you know I almost died?" That day, everyone knows I came last—but not that I nearly drowned in the sea. We are close, our chests rising and falling quickly, and it's through the tangle of our breaths that I catch Hào'yáng's slight inhale. His hand tightens on my wrist, and just like that, I see the walls go back up, the coolness return to his eyes as he considers his response.

I save him from answering by tapping my fingers to his chest. Unexpectedly, I feel the groove of something sharp beneath his clothes—a dagger, or perhaps another layer of armor.

"Hit," I say softly.

His eyes dart between mine. Then he gives a slow nod. Yields. "Hit," he echoes.

I hold his gaze and make my true strike. "Does any of this have to do with my father?"

I see it then, that one unguarded moment, in which his face blanches with shock. Turbulence ripples through his deep brown eyes like a storm breaking against rocks.

Find the One of the Vast Sea.

I was right.

It was him, that day in the ocean, so achingly beautiful that I'd believed him a water spirit; it was his dragonhorse I saw through the tides.

He is the one my father sent me to find in this realm.

Hào'yáng exhales. He still holds my wrist in his hand, as though he has forgotten about it. I find that I do not want him to remember.

"I did not know your father," he says quietly. "But I owe him my life."

The waves lap at the white-sand shores, the wind weaves through the great camphor tree leaves, but nothing in this world can steal the weight of his words from me.

My chest hurts. "Hào'yáng—"

"Ān'yīng. Please. Don't ask what I can't tell you."

There's a sting in my eyes and a lump in my throat. For the first time in nine long years, it feels as though my father and all the secrets he left behind are within reach—yet still so far away.

"Can I ask you one more question?" I whisper.

He lets my wrist go and steps back. The skin on my arm where his fingers were now feels cold. "If it is mine to answer."

"Why haven't you taken a pill of immortality?" It's the question I have always wondered about my father, and I don't know if it is foolish to look for an answer in Hào'yáng. After all, isn't the pill what most of us are here for? A ticket into paradise, away from all the suffering and pain of our short mortal lives. I would assume that the adopted son of one of the Eight Immortals would be offered one, if all it takes is a drop of their golden blood.

Hào'yáng looks into my eyes, straight and true. "I didn't want to forget what it meant to be human."

19

My joints groan as I slam into the sand for what feels like the ten thousandth time.

"Back on your feet."

I squeeze my eyes shut. Every single limb is on fire. "Hào'yáng, you're going to kill me before the trials do."

For the past few days, Hào'yáng has been relentless. From sunrise to almost midnight, we train on the beach beneath the camphor tree. I return to my chambers each night bruised and exhausted, managing only to scrub myself with soap powder and a washcloth before collapsing on my bed.

A shadow falls over me. I open my eyes to see Hào'yáng backlit against the sunset sky. Instead of frowning at me with the strict trainer's demeanor he's taken on, he sits by my side and crosses his legs. His armor is off. As a breeze pulls in from the water, he lifts his face to greet it, and I'm struck by how much younger and more mortal he looks.

He exhales. "The Third Trial could start at any moment. There are candidates stronger than you out for your blood. This place will swallow you whole. Believe me; I've been through it."

Dusk sweeps an aching, fiery haze across the grounds. Shadows begin to set in, velvet beneath the bright colors of blossoms and trees on the landscape; the remainder of the realm is aflame, the waters as red as molten lava, the clouds like swirls of fire. Hào'yáng's profile is carved in the last glow of sunlight, his shoulders drawn tight. With each passing day, the possibility of the Third Trial starting soon seems to weigh heavier on him, and I wonder if it's because he's afraid of failing to repay the debt he claims he owes my father or of failing the task his mother set to him—or both.

I blow a strand of hair from my face and change the subject. "How did you come to the immortal realm?" It's a question I've been mulling over. From the bits and pieces Hào'yáng has told me through our trainings, I understand he came here as a child—long before he could compete in the Immortality Trials and earn a spot in the Kingdom of Sky.

He glances over. Locks of his hair have come undone from their bindings, falling over his cheeks. "Your father brought me here," he says, and my world shifts.

I sit up. We face each other, the tides of the Mirror Lake rising and falling just beyond us, the winds murmuring. I could lift a hand and touch him, and this time, he doesn't move away. "Please tell me why," I say.

"Àn'yīng. I can't—"

"*Why not?*" I've burned through my patience. I've had enough of elusive responses, of questions he won't answer.

I reach into the folds of my dress. My half-sewn handkerchief is wrinkled and sandy, but the note wrapped within—because of its protective talisman—is as new as the day I found it.

I shove it at Hào'yáng. "The only legacy my father left me is on that piece of paper." It's hard to keep the tremor from my voice. "And all of it points to *you*."

Hào'yáng keeps his expression carefully blank as he reads the note. When he finishes, he looks up at me and sighs. "To tell you the truth," he says quietly, "I'm here because I need you, Àn'yīng."

I hold very still. "Why?"

"The answer is dangerous," Hào'yáng says quietly. "Many seek it, and would kill for it. My—and Lady Shǐ'yǎ's—protection can extend only so far within the rules of these trials. I know you need to win the pill of immortality for your mother first, and that's why I'm here now."

I don't recall mentioning Mā to him. "That's my business," I reply. "You don't have to protect me, Hào'yáng."

"I know how it feels to be hunted; I know how it feels to be prey. And I don't want you to have to go through that."

I realize I'm gripping my jade pendant so tightly, my knuckles are white. "Well, it's too late," I say in a low voice. "I already have." *For the past nine years.*

His gaze is searing in its intensity. "I don't want you to anymore."

"Who are you to lecture me about being hunted?" Anger rises in me like flames. "You met me weeks ago, Hào'yáng. You know *nothing* about me, about what I've been through."

I snatch my father's note back and shove it into my sleeve.

"I'm leaving," I say, and I turn and run toward Meadowsweet, ignoring Hào'yáng's calls.

Surprisingly, the dragonhorse flies me back to our usual drop-off spot in the Celestial Gardens. "Thank you," I whisper, petting her snout. She nudges me once and gives me a gentle look with her large brown eyes before taking off again.

The last rays of light are seeping out of the sky. The shadows have set in. The gardens are utterly silent as I walk; I am alone. In this moment, there is only one person I wish to speak with.

I lift my jade pendant from where it rests beneath my clothes. "Talk to me," I whisper.

The stone remains cold, the surface blank.

And suddenly, I wonder if any of it was ever real. Whether my guardian was merely an enchantment my father created, one of the talismans he drew on a stone, just like the blades he gifted me. Whether, now that I have found my way to the Kingdom of Sky, my jade pendant has lost its purpose.

The thought hurts so much, I stumble. That's when I hear movement behind me.

I turn, Shadow and Fleet in my fists, as a moan rises from the bushes. In the dim light, I catch sight of the hand first. It's a slender, pale hand with long fingers, protruding from a camellia bush. Then I see the blood, and the hulking, monstrous shape between two willows that moves rhythmically. A strange slurping sound breaks the silence.

A choked sob; unmistakably feminine. And then a voice—one I recognize—moans. "*Help . . .*"

It's Xī'xī. Number Five, the girl who was gossiping about Yù'chén.

I must have made a noise, for the thing in the shadows pauses. As it lifts its head toward me, I already know, with the bone-deep sense of having been hunted for half my life, what I'll see.

Two eyes, blazing like embers. Staring directly at me. Eyes as red as blood.

A being of the Kingdom of Night.

Cold grips me even as I heft my blades, shifting into a defensive stance. I should run. I should get to the Hall of Radiant Sun, find Hào'yáng, have the immortals hunt down the demonic beast loose within their borders.

Number Five lets out another small sob, and something unmoors inside me. It's the same impulse I had watching Áo'yīn hunt down Lì'líng; the same impulse that makes me want to protect Méi'zi and Mā and all those who are weak and vulnerable and hunted.

If I leave that girl to die here, I will never be able to live with myself.

My breathing quickens. I've done this before. Fought mó. Killed them, even. I can do it again.

I raise my blades.

The beast snarls at me and lifts a great, clawed paw, angling it toward Number Five's prone body for a killing blow.

I charge, obscured from view and faster than the hellbeast can anticipate with my two magic blades. I swipe with Fleet— but the beast is quick. It dodges and all I can see is the shadow it cuts across the growing darkness, blacker than black; the crimson of its hellfire eyes . . . and the glint of its claws in the moonlight as it swipes at me.

Pain explodes in my side. I know as I slam into the ground

that I've broken something inside me. A metallic warmth coats my tongue. White spots bloom in my vision.

But there's a fire in my veins, a light dancing beneath my skin. I'm filled with a euphoric rush of life energy, the knowledge that I have survived this long and I will survive again.

I will not be prey.

I spit out a mouthful of blood, hoist Healer into my palms, and push myself onto my feet. My sight has sharpened, and the sounds of the forest roar in my ears. Everything looks brighter, the leaves of the willows, the tips of the grasses, the roots of the trees all threaded through with gold.

I raise Fleet and turn to face the beast.

Except . . . there's nothing there. Just a patch of empty shadows between the trees . . . and Number Five's pale hand, limp on the ground.

The rush of adrenaline wanes. My vision and hearing dull. My crescent blades slip from my grasp, and my knees hit the ground.

That's when a long, sonorous note reverberates across the temple grounds.

The gong.

The Third Trial is about to start.

"*Candidates.*" Jǐng'xiù's voice rings across the grounds, carried by magic. It filters through my pain, reining my consciousness in to focus. "*Welcome to the Third Trial, and by the dragons, do we have a show for you tonight.*"

As he speaks, each star in the sky begins to glow. Light pours from them, streaming to coalesce like silver threads.

"*The Temple of Dawn has been transformed: twelve battle-grounds, each denoted by a zodiac sign.*"

My hand shakes as I take out Healer and activate the talisman with my spirit energy. Warmth rushes through me, and my pain begins to dull. I crane my head up and watch the starlight form distinct lines: a circle divided into twelve quadrants. Within each, the outline of an animal begins to take form.

"*In a few moments, your golden bracelet will morph into a waist pendant showing a symbol that corresponds with one other candidate. Your task is to meet that candidate at your assigned battleground and steal their pendant. Once you win, your pendant will direct you to your next battleground. Your aim is to collect as many pendants as you can by the end of the trial.*"

Healer's talisman has cleared my mind to the point where I can think through the instructions. Bà used to keep a celestial sphere in his room, a way of timekeeping from the gods. I can see it now, the dusty old thing, with a dial whose shadow shifted with the course of the sun. Each animal of the zodiac represented a certain hour . . . as well as a direction.

Tonight, I see the celestial sphere carved into the stars.

My wrist warms as my golden bracelet unfurls and wraps around my waist like a ribbon. It solidifies, and a pendant hangs from my hip. I raise it to see a rat engraved on the surface.

Midnight Rat, I think, *of True North.*

That means my battleground should be deep within the Celestial Gardens. And I have an inkling of where exactly it's going to lead. Straight north through to the back of the gardens is a set of cliffs overlooking the Silver Sea: a narrow and unpredictable body of water within the immortal realm, prone to great storms and whirlpools and said to be inhabited by mythological beings—dragon carp, sea serpents, and merfolk.

Pain lances through my ribs as I haul myself to my feet. I grip Healer harder, but the talisman on the blade borrows from my own spirit energy.

I'm in no state to fight, or even run.

But if I don't try, I will be disqualified from the trials.

And I will lose Mā forever.

I grit my teeth. The starlight overhead dusts the Celestial Gardens in a ghostly sheen as I begin to hobble north. Each step is agony; several times, I pause to catch my breath. Even with Healer's talisman dulling my pain, I can feel the full extent of it beginning to seep through the cracks. In the silence, I hear screams from the other battlegrounds.

The trees around me start to lighten. Between the leaves of the canopy, I make out the form of a rat in this quadrant of the celestial sphere. And beyond is the open night and the rush of ocean waves.

I've arrived.

I scope out my surroundings. No sight of my opponent, but in my current state, the only way I'll stand a chance against them is to fight with stealth.

I draw a deep breath. Then, clamping my teeth together, I sheathe Healer and palm Shadow and Heart.

White-hot pain streaks through my ribs. I bite down against a whimper and steady myself against a tree, gathering all my thoughts into a single, dagger-sharp desire: to beat my opponent and take their pendant. To win a spot in the trials and earn a pill of immortality. To see Mā open her eyes and recognize me again, sunlight in her gaze and her smile.

I want to sever my opponent's pendant.

I tap Heart with my spirit energy and throw it. It curves through the air, a silver flash, and then vanishes through the trees.

Moments later, there's a shout. I take off in its direction just as a throwing star whisks through the night. With a dull thud, it lodges in the trunk of the tree I was just leaning against—but I'm already halfway through the trees, Shadow obscuring my movements.

My opponent doesn't see me coming. At the last second, he hears my footsteps; he twists and aims a kick. I swerve, then dodge another throwing star before aiming my own jab. He blocks awkwardly; in the moment he's thrown off balance, I catch a glint of gold on the ground.

His pendant. Heart's aim was true, severing it from the belt on his waist.

I switch Shadow for Fleet, and in the instant I become visible to him, my attacker lets out a shout.

It's too late. I snatch his pendant from the ground and stumble back into the shadows of the trees. I don't want him to see how badly wounded I am.

But my opponent does something strange. Instead of trying to stop me, he raises his hand to the skies.

The air ripples with spirit energy as the acrid stench of smoke reaches me. There's a whistling sound and a spark, and moments later, fire powder explodes far above our heads. It shimmers in the air, red and in the shape of a crescent.

Its light illuminates my opponent, and I realize why he was fighting so awkwardly. Where his right hand should be is a stub, the hand cut off at the wrist.

My breath catches. It's Yán'lù's crony—the one who helped

abduct me that night in the Celestial Gardens. The one whose hand Yù'chén sliced off.

He glares at me, teeth bared. "Recognize me now?" he growls.

I lift his pendant. "I won," I croak.

He spits in the grass. "You think I care about that? Ever since your lover cut off my hand, you think I still care about these trials?" Above us, the fading glow of the crescent from his firework paints his grin red. "I've found a new way in this life. Someone who'll protect me, no matter what."

My pendant glimmers; the engraving on it has changed to a new constellation of the zodiac, but I don't take my eyes off my opponent for more than a split second. "I won," I repeat. Blood soaks the fabric of my clothing at my midriff; I have to lean against the tree to stay on my feet.

He notices, too. His eyes roam down my bodice, and his expression turns malicious. "You don't look so good."

"That's none of your business." My voice sounds breathy even to my ears, but I jerk my chin up at his firework and snap, "Extinguish your weapon and leave."

His grin widens. "Oh, that's not a weapon," he whispers, and I suddenly feel as though I haven't won after all. It was easy, too easy . . . the way he barely fought me, the way he didn't even try to take back his pendant. Instead, he sent . . .

A signal.

I sense them before I see them, shadows moving in the thicket.

"My flower," croons a voice, and my entire body goes cold as Yán'lù steps out. He's flanked by half a dozen cronies; the whites of their eyes and teeth flash as they close in from all directions. Herding me so that the only place left to go is the cliff—and the fall into an abyss and a deep, dark sea.

Slowly, I back away from them. The wind rises, laced with a cold, sharp tang of salt.

"What do you want?" I'm gripping my blades so tightly, their hilts dig into my skin. My muscles are frozen with the memory of being pinned down, helpless, and drowning.

Yán'lù smirks. "I want to see who's watching over you," he replies.

I'm visibly shaking as I palm Fleet and Healer. The world sways, and the pain from my wound sends shocks of cold through my limbs. There is no way out: in front of me, fanning out in all directions, are Yán'lù and his cronies. Behind me, a jutting cliff that plunges into the depths of the Silver Sea.

Something whistles through the air, followed by a stinging sensation in my shoulder. When I look down, a sharp black spike the length of a finger protrudes from my arm, glistening in my blood and another viscous liquid.

A slow, numbing sensation spreads through my skin, and I realize what the spike was coated in: *poison.*

I stagger. My movements slow.

"You won't be able to stand within half a minute," Yán'lù says. He takes another step toward me and his two remaining cronies close in from the other sides, their silhouettes blurred in my vision. "Then I'll be able to do whatever I want with you."

I back away one more step and hear rocks skid off the edge behind me.

"Tell me, my flower," Yán'lù croons. "Tell me who your guardian is."

My guardian. My guardian in the jade. Hào'yáng. Yù'chén. Their names blur in my head as the poison in my body spreads. I remember the last time Yán'lù had me cornered, the horrors my body still cannot forget.

As my legs begin to numb, I do the only thing I can think of. I turn and leap off the edge of the cliff into the darkness below.

My body yields to the poison, and I have no hope of controlling my fall. Clouds swallow me, and the world turns to swirling gray and blurred silhouettes, terrifyingly disorientating. Flashes of lightning illuminate shadows everywhere, followed by deafening thunder.

But the harsh impact of hitting the surface of the ocean never comes. Instead, the waters envelop me in a gentle caress. Everything goes quiet, and as I sink, I have the feeling I'm floating instead.

My chest burns. I turn my gaze up again, to the disappearing surface of the ocean, and I think of Mā and Méi'zi and all whom I have failed. I'm paralyzed by poison, drowning a realm away from them, and I can only pray that the gods will watch over them.

A tug around my throat: my jade pendant has freed itself from my collar. It rises, as though it, too, yearns for the surface, perhaps for the guardian within its other half that I will never meet.

In the darkness, something sparks. A tiny glow, approaching quickly, like a falling star. My vision is blurred, but I can make out a silhouette now, gold glinting off what looks like scales . . .

Not scales. *Lamellar armor.*

Hào'yáng.

He dives after me, cutting through the water with unnatural speed, the pale silk of his shift flying, armor glimmering— but here, in the water, he is haloed by *light*. He is as beautiful as the gods I imagined as a little girl in a world of nightmares. As beautiful as the first time I saw him in the depths of a different sea.

Water rushes into my mouth. I feel his arms wrap around me, drawing me to him, and then the warmth of his palm on the back of my head.

Gently, as naturally as though it was always meant to be, Hào'yáng lowers his face to mine.

He exhales.

Golden life energy pours from his lips to mine, driving the cold from my limbs and dulling my pain. The ocean water is pulled from my lungs. Fresh air floods them, and I inhale deeply. I can't move from the poison in my system, but I see him through my lashes, illuminated by the light of his life energy: his eyes closed, his hair flowing around him like currents of the ocean.

Most of all, I see the glow radiating from the object around his neck. I see the jade pendant rising from his shirt as bright as a star, drifting between us with the pull of the tides . . . and perhaps the pull of its other half around my own neck.

Time seems to slow as the broken piece of jade around Hào'yáng's throat meets mine. Every one of my pendant's jagged edges fits perfectly against his, until the pendant is at last made whole.

The world shifts. The ocean surges. Numb shock fills me,

followed by relief and joy so profound it is as though my soul weeps.

My guardian in the jade.

Hào'yáng draws back. There is a terrible grief in his eyes as he presses a palm to my cheek, searching my face. He speaks my name into the silence of the sea, and I understand why it has always sounded so natural coming from him. As he holds me tightly to him and touches his lips to mine again, breathing life and air into me, I know that I have finally come full circle with the destiny I have searched for throughout half my life.

"*Àn'yīng, stay with me.*" His voice echoes into the deep, the last thing I hear as I sink into the darkness closing in on my mind. "*I'm here now.*"

20

When I wake, it is night. I am on a bed of soft silks, in a chamber lit with a silvery glow. The wooden shutters are open, letting in a warm, fragrant breeze and yielding a perfect view of the night sky between the branches of a great osmanthus tree. Moonlight spills in, pooling on the rosewood floors.

I am alive.

I flex my fingers and wriggle my toes. The pain in my side is gone . . . from the life energy Hào'yáng breathed into me beneath the ocean.

I turn my head, and he is there by my bedside. He's asleep, cheek resting against the golden cuffs on his wrists, lashes fluttering as he dreams. Like this, he looks so young.

My guardian in the jade.

Suddenly, I can barely breathe. He's in his golden armor and white robes again, the stiff embroidered collar hiding any trace of the pendant around his neck.

My throat tightens as I recall the years between us, how

my broken piece of jade has carried me through some of the hardest moments of my life. How it lent me comfort during the earliest years after the invasion, how it taught me to hunt, which berries to forage, the best ways to grow cabbage . . . how it told me of the light lotuses, how to harvest them and boil them to sustain my mother's half a soul . . . and then, how it told me of the Temple of Dawn and the Immortality Trials as a way to save Mā's life.

In the days after Bà died and Mā became a hollow husk, I nearly broke. I remember the hope I felt when this pendant began to speak to me. How I held it in order to sleep, and how, in the darkest of times, I knew there was someone there, watching over me.

All along . . . it was Hào'yáng.

I take in his long, straight brows, the strong, smooth curves of his cheeks. My chest is tight in a way that I cannot describe, a heartache that feels, for the first time, good. Was he always this handsome? Was there ever a time when his ears were too big for his face, his teeth misaligned, his nose crooked?

His eyes open, and before I can do anything, he's looking back at me, his gaze clear and steady. "Ăn'yīng," he says, straightening, the sleep vanishing from his expression and shifting into alarm. "Why are you crying?"

I press a finger to my cheeks. They're wet. *He doesn't know I know,* I realize. He thought I was unconscious in the water; he's hidden his pendant from me again.

I swallow the words at the tip of my tongue. I feel as if my heart will crack open. "I . . ."

Hào'yáng reaches out a hand. He's holding a handkerchief— *my* silk handkerchief, I realize, with my half-finished embroidery of dragons on a sunlit sea. "May I?" he asks, and when I nod, he leans forward and dabs my cheeks. His movements are so gentle, I cry harder.

"Àn'yīng." He gives me a helpless look. He's cupping my face through the silk, his fingers warm and steady. "Forgive me that I wasn't there—"

"N-no." I inhale deeply to try to collect myself. "I'm sorry, Hào'yáng. I'm sorry about all those things I said to you. I'm sorry I'm not strong enough to survive here on my own—"

"Àn'yīng." His thumb brushes an involuntary stroke against my cheek as he holds my gaze. "You are the strongest person I know."

I know it's not true, that it *can't* be true—I'm the weakest of the candidates here—but he speaks as though he means it.

I smile back. "I must have an excellent trainer, then."

His eyes crinkle, and I want to catch this moment between us, store it in my memories like a piece of treasure. Hào'yáng clears his throat, and then he's drawing back, returning to the formal demeanor of a Temple of Dawn guard. He begins to fold my handkerchief, but something gives him pause. I shiver when he runs a careful finger over the stitchings. The motion feels intimate, and the way he's studying the half-finished piece stirs heat beneath my skin.

His gaze flicks up. "You never finished this."

"I'd like to, someday," I reply. He hands it back to me, the warmth of his palm lingering on the silk. I can't tear my gaze away from his face, from wanting to collect every detail: the way a few strands of his hair have escaped his cinch and frame his face, the way the lantern light catches against his lashes, the way his guarded, observant eyes can yield to hints of a smile when he thinks no one is watching. I want to know everything about him, all that I have missed in the past nine years.

Hào'yáng finishes arranging his sleeve and looks back up expectantly at me. He touches a finger to his cheek and raises an eyebrow. "Something on my face?"

"No," I say quickly, averting my eyes and grasping at anything to say. "How long have I been asleep?"

"Nearly one day."

I gape at him. "What happened? The trials—I fell—"

"The Eight Immortals granted you a win," he replies. "It was on the basis that you were already grievously injured by a demonic beast before the trial began. I saw—the claw marks on your side."

It suddenly makes sense. I lost. I almost died. Hào'yáng broke the rules by interfering in the trial and saving my life.

"The Eight Immortals are investigating the death of Number Five," he continues. "They are debating alerting the Jade Emperor's High Court. Everyone else—your friends included—is safe but confined to the Candidates' Courtyard until the culprit is caught." He hesitates. "Forgive me for bringing you to my chambers. Given how you've been targeted, I didn't think . . ." He clears his throat and gestures toward my body. "Lady Shī'yǎ changed your clothes."

I'm suddenly aware that I'm sitting in his bed, dressed in a fresh nightgown, my wounds cleaned and bandaged. My face heats, and I'm glad for the cover of darkness. "Please thank your mother for me," I stammer.

Hào'yáng nods, then reaches toward a set of rosewood drawers by the bed. He takes out a bundle and sets it next to me. My heart leaps as I hold up my white silk dress, perfectly mended from the gashes the demonic beast made in the fabric. Hào'yáng has also collected all my crescent blades; I run my fingers over each of them and the familiar talismans engraved into the metal. Last of all is a familiar note, sitting atop the pile.

I hold up my father's words. They glimmer in the starlight.

"I owe you an explanation," Hào'yáng says, and I look up to see him watching me. He holds out a hand. "How about some tea, and a private showing to one of my favorite views of this realm?"

Stepping out onto the open wooden pavilion outside his chambers, I'm met with a breathtaking sight.

The guards' houses are built into the cliffs overlooking a river that reflects the stars. Its waters glitter as though threaded with silver, and lotuses drift on its surface, white and pure, illuminated every so often by the darting glow of fireflies. Clouds coil around the mountains, plumes drifting over houses with curving tiled roofs and gardens of osmanthus, willows, and waterfalls.

"That's the River of Serene Starlight." Hào'yáng comes to lean against the railing next to me. He hands me a cup of chrysanthemum tea. "And there's the Hall of Radiant Sun. Beautiful, isn't it, from a distance?"

Sure enough, through the clouds rise the familiar golden roofs and marble columns. A marble bridge extends from it toward us, mirroring the bridge that leads to the Candidates' Courtyard. This one, though, is inlaid with golden engravings of sun and clouds, phoenixes and dragons . . . and the gods.

While we mortals might worship the immortals, the immortals pray to the gods: forces of nature that rule the realms, above even the immortal Jade Emperor himself. They are so ancient that they have long dissipated into the spirit energy of our world, into the myth that is the Heavens, taking form as wind and thunder, rain and oceans, sun and moon and stars.

I ask, "How was it? Growing up in the Kingdom of Sky as a mortal?"

Hào'yáng considers my question, his eyes reflecting the River of Serene Starlight. "It was lonely," he says at last. "I was educated with the immortal children, but they never saw me as one of them. So I trained harder and longer because I knew I couldn't be as good as them—I had to be better."

I study his profile in the moonlight, imagining him as a boy, thoughtful and solemn, brush poised as he writes back to the girl in the jade. Did he think of me as often as I thought of him?

"Did you ever go back to the Kingdom of Rivers?" I ask.

"I couldn't," he says quietly. "The immortals would not have allowed me back into their realm had I left. It killed me inside every day, knowing I was safe and comfortable here while others like me suffered."

I think back to his apologies, to the guilt and pain in his eyes when he saw me hurt. I think I understand a little, now, of why he wished to protect me.

"Àn'yīng." Hào'yáng is looking at me, his gaze suddenly as sharp as steel. "What if I told you there is a way to fight for it?"

I search his eyes. "What do you mean?"

"When the Kingdom of Night defied the Heavenly Order and began the war against the Kingdom of Rivers, the Kingdom of Sky turned its back rather than interfere and risk its own safety. What if I told you there is a small group of immortals who wish to join the fight?"

A memory surfaces: Fú'yí's face, fiery in the sunset. *You let them know we are still alive. You show them how strong you are. And when you have learned the arts, just as your father did, you come back and win this war against the Kingdom of Night.*

Bà's note is pressed to my bodice. I feel his words as though they're seared into my flesh. *I chose to train you for a reason.*

The jade pendant he gifted me . . . leading me here, to Hào'yáng. To this moment.

"Does this have to do with my father?" I ask.

"It has everything to do with your father," Hào'yáng replies. "He left a path for us to fight back. He was the seed of our rebellion."

"Yes." The answer falls from my lips before I can think. My heart has known it all along, even if my mind has not until this very moment. "Yes, if there's a way . . . of course I'll fight, Hào'yáng. *Yes.*"

He looses a breath. There is something of relief, of gratitude, on his face as he leans forward, his mouth curving in a smile that makes me want to hold on to this moment forever. "Then I'll arrange a meeting with Lady Shī'yǎ. She'll fill you in on the rebellion we've been planning, our next steps." It's the first time I've seen him so passionate, as if, piece by piece, the cool, restrained warrior's armor is falling away. "She taught me everything I know, Àn'yīng. You'll like her."

"Who else is involved?" I ask.

"Immortals from all positions and factions, including two members of the Jade Emperor's High Court. We have three members, Lady Shī'yǎ included, who are highly ranked and command their own armies." Hào'yáng meets my gaze. "Forgive me, that I've had to be elusive. This rebellion is a secret those of us involved must guard more carefully than our own lives. There are spies everywhere, eyes sent by other political factions across the Kingdom of Sky. By those who wish to stop us."

"Hào'yáng," I say. "I think Yán'lù might be one of them." Quickly, I explain how he has asked me twice who was watching over me.

Hào'yáng nods. "This is why I didn't want to tell you, so I wouldn't have to put you in danger. I can't break any more rules without the rest of the Eight suspecting something. Àn'yīng, promise me you'll be careful. Focus on the trials for now."

Hào'yáng escorts me back to the Candidates' Courtyard. The change that has occurred within a single day is startling: we run into several immortal patrols in the vicinity, and guards line the moongates leading inside.

"She was with the Eight for questioning related to the trials," Hào'yáng tells the immortals as we draw up to the entrance. I glance at him, thrown by how smooth the lie sounds, but his face betrays nothing. His usual cool, distant demeanor has returned, his hands drawn behind his waist, his shoulders thrown back.

"Captain," the guards say, inclining their heads to let us pass.

I glance up sharply at Hào'yáng, surprise widening my
eyes. *Captain?* I want to ask, and as though he hears my
thought, he flicks a glance at me, the corners of his eyes curving up, a hint of warmth and cunning in them. *How does a
mortal become a captain of immortal guards?*

Hào'yáng keeps a courteous distance as he inclines his
head to me—but I don't miss the way his lips curl when he
meets my gaze again, as though we share a private joke.

"Rest well, candidate," he says.

I try not to look back at him as I pass through the moongates.

It's nearing the middle of the night. The courtyard is deserted; most of the candidates have turned in for an early
night, likely still recovering from yesterday's trial. I fiddle
with my jade pendant as I make my way up to my dorm, past
the willows and water that are utterly silent at this hour.

"I didn't take you for the type to romance your way up the
ranks, little scorpion."

The voice shatters my joy. I freeze and look up.

Yù'chén leans against the willow across from my dorm.
I've been so busy training that I've barely seen him in weeks,
not since that night in the hot spring. As he straightens and
steps out of the shadows, I go very still.

The injured, pale version of him in the hot spring is gone;
he stands straight, sculpted shoulders and chest stretching the
black fabric of his shift, arms folded, full lips curled in a smirk.
His hair is half tied back, though it still has the wild, mussed
look. He wears his crimson cloak today, and I can't help but
stare at the way it accents the sharpness to his features, the
darkness to his gaze.

I tuck my pendant back into my collar. "I don't know what you mean. I've been busy training."

My words lack bite, and I can't stop thinking back to what Hào'yáng told me: that Yù'chén had an alibi at the time of Number One's death. That he was in the training temple, seen by a number of immortals.

That, all this time, he didn't deserve the horrid things I thought about him.

"Training," Yù'chén repeats, arching a brow. He narrows his eyes. "From sunrise to past sunset, in an unknown location, with a captain of the immortal guards."

As always, his words and the sight of him manage to rouse my temper. "Exactly, and I am *very* tired, so fuck off," I snap, stomping up the wooden steps to my room.

"Oh, I'd fuck right off," he replies easily, "if I weren't here to bring you news of your sister."

His words are lightning that jolts through every one of my nerves. My hand freezes, palm on the rosewood of my sliding doors.

"But it seems you're not interested. So I'll—"

I whirl around. "Wait."

He has already turned to leave. He pauses between the swaying branches of the willow, tossing me a glance over his shoulder. "Yes?"

"Tell me." My voice comes out tight, but I can't help it. No matter how strong I become, no matter how powerful, with one mention of Méi'zi, he has me in the palm of his hand.

Yù'chén turns to me. With slow, languid steps, he approaches. I retreat until my back is pressed to my door, but he closes in. I suck in a breath, my heartbeat elevating as my fight-or-flight instinct kicks in. I can feel the heat of his body, smell his scent of spice and roses, blood and night, as he leans toward me.

"I heard he almost killed you," he says softly. "Yán'lù. Tell me if that's true, Àn'yīng."

I stare at him. "What's it to you?"

He says nothing. Only watches me, expression unreadable.

"I just want to know the news of my sister," I continue when he's been silent for several heartbeats. "Tell me and we're done here."

Yù'chén's jaw tenses, but he draws out a familiar-looking crane feather. It seems to flit between white and black, like two sides of the moon, as he twirls it. He tilts his head. "What do I get in return for releasing the memory in this feather, Àn'yīng?"

I swallow. I can't believe I almost felt sorry for him. I *hate* him, yet I know in this moment that I'm powerless against his demands. I'd overturn kingdoms for my sister. "What do you want?"

"There are many things I *want*, little scorpion." Yù'chén's gaze flicks to my lips for a moment, and his eyes darken before he pulls them back to focus on mine. "But it would be most unchivalrous of me to demand them when you're in this position. So"—his lips curl into a smile—"I'll settle for you asking me nicely."

My relief comes with surprise. I have come to expect the worst of Yù'chén. I suppose when your expectations are in the Tenth Circle of Hell, anything can seem like a nice gesture.

With every ounce of self-restraint I have, I force a cordial tone and pinch my lips into a smile. "Could you please, oh please, be so kind as to show me the memory of my sister?"

Yǔ'chén's eyes gleam. He draws back. "There," he says. "Was that so hard?"

I roll my eyes, and he laughs. With one flick of his wrist, the feather dissipates into ash and memory. It settles into a scene: the window of our house, the one that looks into the bedroom I share with Méi'zi. It's daytime, but the skies are cloudy and a dim gray light filters into the room.

Méi'zi lies on the bed. Even from here, I can make out the unnatural flush to her cheeks, the sweat glistening on her face, the way she's curled in the fetal position, clutching her belly. She's trembling, and as I watch, her body convulses with a cough.

She's sick—dangerously so.

The world tilts around me. I turn, but I'm shaking, this one scene undoing all the walls I have built up within me.

"I have to help her." The words break from my lips as I try to focus my thoughts. There has to be some medicine here, in this realm bursting with magic, that I can take back to her.

But I can't do it alone.

Hào'yáng. My hand flies to my jade pendant. Hào'yáng will help me—I know he will.

Yet as I consider, I realize what I would be asking of him. *The immortals would not have allowed me back into their realm had I left.* More disastrously, he is one of the organizers of a potential rebellion—and he is Shī'yǎ's son, as well as a captain of the immortal guard. If he's caught sneaking into the mortal realm . . . I don't want to think of the consequences. He has already broken too many rules for me.

"Àn'yīng."

I blink, pulled from my frantic trail of thoughts. Yù'chén is watching me. His eyes are dim, the slightest crease to his brows. He's no longer smiling.

"Ask me," he says quietly.

I stare at him, my heart pounding. "Why would I do that?"

"Because I can."

There it is again, that raw sincerity to his voice, the quietly spoken words so at odds with his usual smirking nonchalance. At this point, I do not know which is real and which is the lie—or whether both are simply masks.

"Why do you do this?" I snap. "You help me, and then you push me away. Is this . . . Do you derive some sick pleasure out of it? Is it funny to you, watching me beg you to help me save my sister's life?"

He closes his eyes briefly. "No," he says.

I'm silent for a moment, trying to understand if this is another of his games.

So what if it is? a voice whispers inside me. Two can play at it. From the very start, our alliance has been transactional; I simply need to view this as another trade.

I need to save Méi'zi. I need to protect Hào'yáng. Yù'chén is my only choice.

I exhale sharply. "Can you help her?" I ask.

Slowly, he nods.

"How? With your dark magic?"

He says nothing, but his mouth tightens slightly.

"What do you want this time? More of my life energy?"

"No."

"Well, then, what?"

Yù'chén pushes off the door and turns away, running a hand through his hair. "Nothing that you can give me."

Again, I'm unsure how to respond. "I don't have the time or energy to play games with you over my sister's life," I say.

"I'm not." His jaw clenches. "My shadowcrane alerted me to her illness. I came to tell you as soon as I found out."

I arch an eyebrow. "So you're doing this out of the goodness of your heart?"

He looks away. "Is that so hard to believe?"

I sigh. "Just tell me what you want in exchange for your help."

He tips his face to the moonlight. His eyes and lips are as red as his cloak. "All right." Yù'chén exhales, and his throat moves as he swallows. "I want you to stop looking at me as if you're afraid, or suspicious, or disgusted. As if you're thinking of what I am instead of who I am." His voice turns raw as he faces me. "I want you to look at me and see *me*. Can you do that, Àn'yīng?"

"I . . ." I want to say *Yes, I can,* anything to get him to take me to Méi'zi and get the infection out of her body as soon as possible.

But the truth is, I will never see him the way I see Hào'yáng, or Lì'líng or my other friends, or the rest of the candidates and immortals here. Yù'chén holds, within him, half of the type of being that has ravaged my realm and brought the Ten Hells upon my people. They have destroyed my family and my life.

And yet. He has defied my expectations in every way. Despite the front of cruelty he puts up, he has never hurt me, only helped me.

I try to think of the Yù'chén who showed me the midnight sea. Who taught me to walk on water and dance on waves beneath the moon.

So I swallow and give him what I can. Half of a promise: "I can try."

An ordinary candidate may have had trouble with the guards posted around our quarters, but Yù'chén makes it look nearly effortless. He wraps us in a charm of his dark magic, and I hold Shadow tightly as we make for the moongates. None of the guards even blink as we pass by.

I loose a breath only when we're deep enough into the Celestial Gardens for the patrols to have thinned out. *"Now* will you tell me what your grand plan is?" I hiss. He's been irritably elusive.

I make out the flash of his red cloak in the night. "Patience, little scorpion."

At the sound of rushing water, I realize we're making for the waterfall at the edge of the Celestial Gardens again. "Are you going to open another gate in the ward?" He's silent. "Because if you are, I need you to close it as soon as we're out, then open it for us when we're back." More silence. "Yù'chén, answer me—"

"Do you know how much effort it takes to create a gate in the immortals' wards?" he replies.

"Then how do you plan to help my sister?"

We've reached the stream. Just beyond the willows, the wards shimmer into the night, iridescent, powerful, and impenetrable. Yù'chén turns and holds his hand out to me.

I don't take it. "Tell me what you plan to do, Yù'chén."

He hesitates, and then sighs. "I closed the gate, Àn'yīng, but . . . I can reopen it."

Ice cracks through my veins. "You just said you couldn't create another gate."

"Not create. Reopen," he says, and walks to the edge of the wards. By the waterfall, growing in the grass, is the scorpion lily I saw last time. Yù'chén kneels and touches a hand to it . . . and it begins to glow. "Dark magic leaves signs behind. Unnatural growths of flowers, birds and animals that don't belong, strangely shaped terrain." His voice is amplified, beautiful, and his eyes flash red as he turns to look at me. Behind him, the scorpion lilies are blooming in the glimmering ward, once again forming the shape of an archway. The gate—the one he told me he closed.

The one that might have let in whatever demonic beast attacked me and killed the other two candidates.

"Creating a gate and reopening a gate are two different things. In this case, I left behind a door that I could open and close at will." The scorpion lilies unfurl their long red petals, and the archway through the wards gleams, growing more and more transparent by the second.

But my teeth are chattering, and I'm backing away from him. "You told me you closed the gate last time."

"I *did*—"

"But it's still there!" My voice rises in panic. "Could something have gotten through? Two candidates have *died*, Yù'chén—I was almost killed by the same beast that murdered them—"

"You were attacked?" Yù'chén's expression is tight, inscrutable, but he suddenly moves toward me. I take the equivalent steps back and he stops himself, though his eyes dart over my face, my chin, my shoulders, my body, as though looking for my wounds.

"By a creature of the Kingdom of Night," I confirm. His gaze follows my hand as I instinctively touch my side, where my bandages cover the claw marks. "I saw it."

"Whatever killed those candidates didn't come through my gate, Àn'yīng. This I know."

The ice has spread to my heart, freezing my limbs, making my teeth chatter. "But you kept it," I whisper. "You lied to me."

He cuts me a cold look. "Shall I destroy my gate, then? I have no problem returning to my chambers and sleeping well tonight, Àn'yīng. It isn't *my* sister dying one realm away."

I flinch.

Something like regret crosses Yù'chén's expression. He holds out a hand again, and his tone is soft when he speaks. "I could destroy this gate with a single word from you. I could also save your sister and be back before the sun rises. The choice is yours, Àn'yīng."

Again, that damned sincerity to his tone, the way he looks at me as if he means it—I don't know what to believe.

But I look at his palm, the light of the scorpion lilies casting it in red. I know my choice. That has never changed.

I reach out and place my hand in his. "Help me save my sister."

He draws me to him, close, until we are facing each other at the edge of this realm, our clothes brushing, all but touching. His hands settle around my hips, and suddenly, my heart's in my throat and I find I can't breathe, can't focus on anything but the heat of his fingers on me.

"I did lie to you," he whispers in my ear, and I tense as a shiver rolls through me. "I have to use dark magic one more time tonight to get us to your sister." He laces his fingers through mine. "The mó have the ability to create passages between destinations in each realm, folding distances and traveling faster that way. Is that all right with you?" He leans back, his eyes roving my face, lips curling in a humorless smile. "One more lie from a wicked demon . . . to save your sister?"

No, I want to say. *None of this is right.* None of this *should* be right—I'm knowingly endangering the Kingdom of Sky by creating a breach in their wards and hiding the secret from them. I am just as culpable as Yù'chén, if not more.

But I would trade kingdoms to save my family.

"Yes," I say.

Yù'chén holds out a scorpion lily to me. This time, I take it. A tingle rushes up my fingers as soon as I touch its stem: the sensation of a velvet darkness brushing against my skin. The gate of flowers in the wards pulses gently, as though reacting to my touch. Beyond, as clear as glass, is the night sky of the mortal realm, bright with stars.

"Focus on the destination you want," Yù'chén says. "I'll do the rest."

I close my eyes and imagine my broken little house with its flowering plum tree and winding dirt path. Xī'lín, with its gray terra-cotta roofs gleaming like dragon scales in the sunset, the old pái'fāng of faded gold characters reminding us that better times once existed. A yearning rises inside me, so bone-deep that an ache grips my heart.

Power surges through the scorpion lily in my hands—dark, passionate, tumultuous—brushing against my thoughts. *Dark magic.* It twines through the images I've conjured of home . . . and in my mind, flowers bloom.

"Àn'yīng, open your eyes."

I do.

The gate of scorpion lilies before me no longer opens to a midnight sea. Two blooms of purple wisteria have appeared beyond it, their branches reaching for each other like lovers' hands. They extend into a tunnel of softly glowing flowers bedded on walls of shadow. It is at once beautiful and terrifying, and I cannot decide which way I feel.

"This . . . leads us to my home?" I ask.

Yù'chén nods. "The passage is temporary, in case that brings you comfort. It'll vanish as soon as we use it."

"And you'll destroy the *gate* once we return," I press.

His eyes are downcast, his shoulders tense, as though he is fighting something I cannot see. Then he exhales, and something like helplessness seeps into his face. He nods. "If you ask."

I hand the flower back to him and take out my blades. The heft of Fleet and Striker in my palms feels good, like landing on solid ground after treading water. "Then let's go," I say.

Yù'chén reaches for my hand again, but he does not remove my crescent blade. Instead, his fingers curl around my wrist. The tip of Striker skims the skin of his forearm with the motion.

"I'll lead you through," he says. "Just . . . remember,

everything will look exquisitely beautiful. These passages spun of our magic are . . . compelling to mortals. None of what you might see or feel is real. And don't touch the flowers."

I tighten my grip around my blades and nod. *Not real.* Skies, everything about the mó's magic is designed to enchant and ensnare us.

"Follow me, Àn'yīng," Yù'chén says, and turns. *"Just follow me."* His voice is impossible to ignore as his magic flares. My feet move of their own accord, tracing Yù'chén's steps through the wisteria trees into the pocket of darkness.

The hum of magic immediately cloaks us. We're in a tunnel of flowers, their fragrance sublimely sweet, their petals a soft blush against the dark. Between their branches, the night sky has come alive with stars. Light limns the petals, and I realize the wisteria has shifted. We walk beneath a canopy of cherry blossoms, their outlines rendered nearly silver by the moon that hangs low and bright, its surface fractured by the interwoven branches. My head feels light, as if I've drunk too much of the peach wine at the Banquet Hall.

"Àn'yīng." My breath catches at Yù'chén's voice. It was always beautiful, but here, it seems to echo, amplified by the magic. *"Àn'yīng, do not let the flowers distract you."*

It's too late, and they have. Magic falls from them like pollen, tangling in my hair and on my lips and in my senses. I have seen the rows and rows of cherry blossoms at the Temple of Dawn, radiant and sparkling in the sun. But I never expected that the sight of them in the darkness would take my breath away. And with each step, no matter how much I try to resist, their glow becomes brighter, and the real world falls away from me a little more.

Cherry blossoms in the dark, I think. *My namesake.*

I feel as if I'm dreaming. Yù'chén's grip is at once firm and gentle on my wrist, and he leads me forward with an urgency I do not feel. I reach out a hand and graze a finger against the petals of a familiar red flower.

"*Àn'yīng!*" Yù'chén's voice is sharp. He draws me to him and lifts my finger. It isn't until he touches it that I realize I'm bleeding. The blossom cut me.

A muscle twitches in Yù'chén's jaw. "Àn'yīng, I told you not to touch the flowers." His voice is still like music to my ears. He's talking about how these flowers are poisonous, how they will send mortals into a state of delirium that they won't even remember, but I barely hear his words. A delicious, hot feeling is tingling through my arm. I smile as I tilt my head up at Yù'chén. I'm not sure why he looks so angry, but for some reason, it pleases me.

"It was another red scorpion lily," I tell him. "You tried to gift one to me the first day we met, remember? Such a horrid gift."

He makes an exasperated sound between his teeth as he studies my bleeding hand. "I remember."

"Why would you wish me a fate of loss and tragedy?" I swipe a hand at his neck, but I can't remember why I ever wanted to cut it open. My crescent blade rests against his skin, and I lean forward, my fingers pressing against the cords of his muscles, admiring how warm he is.

"I don't wish such a fate upon you."

"Then why are you so wicked?" I barely know what I'm saying anymore, but the words float out like puffs of cloud, drifting between us. "You help me, and then you push me away. Why?"

Yù'chén's throat moves; his chest rises and falls with his

breaths. "Because I can't have you," he says quietly, "but I can't stop wanting you."

The air between us shifts as I lift my gaze to his, the words running circles in my head. My thoughts won't pull together, so I stop trying and let instinct take over, trailing my fingers down to his chest. "I can feel it," I say. "The beat of your heart. That's how you tricked me at first."

He lowers his gaze to my wrist, his lashes casting impossibly long, beautiful shadows on his cheekbones. His jaw clenches. He swallows again and gently pushes me back. The distance between us feels cold. "Enough," he says, but the world around me is sliding in and out of focus and I barely understand his next words. I vaguely make out that he needs to extract the poison. I'm about to ask how when he lowers his lips to my finger.

The touch is the spark that sets my body ablaze. I sway, shivers running up my arm as he sucks on the cut the flower made, taking my blood in his mouth and swallowing. I blink. The heat is beginning to drain from my body, but I don't want it to end. When Yù'chén straightens, frowning, I close the gap between us and press my lips to his with a sigh.

His mouth is sweet and tinted with a metallic tang, and I curl my fingers into his hair as I have dreamt of doing for so many nights. He tastes like bitter sugar, and a part of me wonders if this is the poison of the flower. A delicious, intoxicating poison I would gladly drink into oblivion.

He leans forward, and then he is kissing me back. It is nothing like the desperate, fumbling kiss of the hot spring. His mouth moves softly against mine, and his hand comes to cup my chin. Gently, gingerly, as though he holds something breakable in his palm. With his other hand, he skims his fingers along my hair, down to the sensitive spot behind my ear and my neck. He is tender. Cautious. No one, I think, my eyes fluttering shut, has ever held me like this.

"I want you," he whispers against my lips. "So much."

Gently, he pulls me against the wall of night blossoms, their pollen swirling around us, lighting his face and settling in his hair and clothes. The way he touches me, fingers tracing my jaw and thumb caressing circles on my neck, feels like more than just desire.

I suddenly realize I'm cold. That my head is no longer pounding or hazy, that my surroundings have filtered back into sharp delineation. That I'm in control of myself again, and I'm kissing Yù'chén. *It's not real,* I think as the discordant shock that registers in my mind wars against the hazy desire driving my heart. *It's not real.*

I wrench away, turning my face to swipe the back of my hand against my mouth.

He's a mó, a voice inside me screams. *What are you doing?*

What am I doing?

I squeeze my eyes shut, my fingers trembling against my lips. When I open them again, I find Yù'chén watching me. His lips are flushed, and he's breathing hard.

He quickly looks away.

For several moments, neither of us speaks. As the last of the poison cools from my body, I realize what he said.

Because I can't have you, but I can't stop wanting you.

"The poison should be gone from your system," Yù'chén says quietly. "You should feel like yourself again."

I can't bring myself to look at him.

"Follow," he says, turning and beginning to walk more briskly.

We are nearing the end of the passage. There is a light, a scene that looks like a faded portrait compared to the visceral beauty and colors of this passage—but it is one that I find more beautiful than anything else in this world.

Home.

My chest swells at the sight of my village's old pái'fāng, the faded words *Xī'lín* looking exactly the same as on the day I left it. We step out from between two cathayas, and I stumble toward my home at a full run. I could hug the pillars of the pái'fāng; I could kiss the dirt road at my feet.

When I glance back, the passage of flowers has vanished, as Yù'chén promised. Yù'chén himself is still standing just outside the pái'fāng. He presses a hand to the wood and winces, pulling it back as if he's been burned.

Of course—our wards, designed to stop mó from entering. In that moment, a part of me is glad to see him struggle, for it means our wards are still strong enough.

Yù'chén sees me watching him. His expression settles as he inhales deeply, then passes through the pái'fāng at a run. When he comes to a stop before me, his face is pale. His knuckles whiten as he grips the fence to steady himself.

"How does it feel?" I'm aware of the cruelty of my question, but I need to gauge how effective the wards are.

He turns his face away from me. His jaw clenches. "Like I'm burning from the inside." Despite how hard he tries to keep it even, his voice shakes.

"Does it hurt more for the pure mó?"

"A lot more, I'm certain, to the point where they can't get through or won't even try. But the most powerful mó have the magic to break through."

The Higher Ones, I think, my stomach twisting.

It's the middle of the night, so the streets are completely empty. As we walk, I notice how dusty and crumbling the houses are, some with broken shutters or crooked fences. The trees are growing bare in the face of autumn, the dry rattle of their leaves crunching beneath my boots. Everything looks rough and unfinished compared to the dazzling perfection of the immortal realm.

But it's mine.

My heart lifts at the sight of Fú'yí's house. The shutters are dark, but I spot the small pot of chrysanthemums she keeps outside her front door, the flowers she and her husband both loved. The soil within is wet, the flowers healthy and alive, and I find myself smiling.

I begin to run when I see my house, sitting in the same corner with the plum blossom tree. The bamboo door is bolted shut, as are the shutters. When I near, a shadow stirs in the darkened alley across the way, taking on the form of a large bird. Yù'chén's shadowcrane.

I pause to incline my head at the beast. No matter what it is, it has watched over my sister all this time, and I owe it gratitude, if not respect. It only blinks back at me with those unsettling red eyes.

I reach for my front door, but Yù'chén grabs my hand. "Wait," he says. He won't meet my eyes, and I catch something like shame on his face. "I need you to remove the wards around your house. I . . . I don't think I could get through a second set of wards."

I bite my lip. The thought of taking down the wards around my house makes me anxious, but I need him with me.

It'll only be for an hour or two, I tell myself. Besides, I still have the wards around the town borders as a first layer of protection.

I set to work. This is the first time I've removed the wards around my house in nine years, and it's dismaying how easily they come off. A swipe of fresh blood through the old talismans I've drawn, and I feel the spirit energies dissipate. The defensive ring around my house fades like a linked fence coming down, and within minutes, it's done.

I'm uneasy as I round to the front, but Yù'chén stands at the door, waiting for me. He looks so proper, like a guest in a clean crimson travel cloak, waiting to be invited in.

I square my shoulders, then open the doors to my home to let a mó through.

22

I feel like I've stepped through a passage in time, where everything and nothing has changed. My house remains the same: shabby, dark, with simple, cracked furniture and walls in need of repair. The shutters are closed so that only slivers of moonlight illuminate the living room, and my gaze immediately goes to the figure on the wooden bed.

"Mā," I whisper, rushing to her side. She's turned to the wall, her blankets drawn over her. Sucking in a breath, I place a hand on her shoulder and tense. I do not know whether to expect screaming or nothing at all.

I get the latter. My mother's eyes are glassy, fixed on the wall in front of her. She's dressed in a fresh gown, her hair smells like soap, and there's a cup of water on the small cabinet by her cot. I lean in and catch a familiar bitter herbal scent. *Fú'yí*. An ache rises in the back of my throat as I run a hand over my mother's thinning hair. My neighbor has kept true to her word; she has looked after my family.

But that doesn't mean she has the ability to save Méi'zi.

I turn to the bedroom, my hands beginning to shake. I'm aware of Yù'chén's gaze on my mother, but my mind is empty of anything and everything but my little sister.

When I push open the door, I can immediately tell something is off. The room smells of sweat and urine. A vase of chrysanthemums on the bedside cabinet has been knocked over, water dripping onto the floor. Fú'yí must have dropped by within the last day. My sister's sickness must have worsened after our neighbor's last visit.

My watering eyes immediately settle on the figure curled up on the mattress in the corner of the room.

"*Méi'zi,*" I choke as I stumble to her side. My little sister's eyes are pinched shut, a dribble of vomit on her cheek. Her breathing is faint, her face deathly pale.

I have not felt this helpless in a long time. My blades and my spirit energy, all the preparations I have made these past nine years and the training I have gone through at the Temple of Dawn . . . I have worked hard for each, layering them on one by one like pieces of armor. I thought I would become powerful enough to protect those I love.

Yet again, fate has proved me wrong.

I spin and stagger to Yù'chén, grasping fistfuls of his shift with both hands. "Help her," I say, and finally, I know how it feels to beg. "Please. Please save her. I'll do anything."

Yù'chén turns his gaze from Méi'zi to me. Something hardens in his face. He grabs hold of my wrists and yanks my hands away from him. "No," he says.

"I'm begging you—"

"You'll do it."

"I can't!"

"I'll teach you." His grip softens as he leads me toward the bed. Fear rises in my chest as I kneel by my sister. She looks so small, so frail—in so much pain, and all I want is to end it quickly.

"Yù'chén," I whisper. "Don't play games with me. Not about this."

"Àn'yīng," he replies, and his eyes flash red as he turns to look at me. "If I were playing games with you, I would be so much crueler. I would make you beg. I'm teaching you now so you don't have to beg anyone ever again. Including me."

I stare at him. Again, the strange feeling that we are dancing at the edge of something, that one wrong move and the walls between us will crumble.

Yù'chén takes my hand. I rein in my fear and focus on his voice, on the strokes of his fingers as he presses acupuncture points across Méi'zi's body, guiding me to find the pools of her life energy, to identify the shadows that seep between them as the corruption of life energy: death energy.

There is so much of it. My thoughts jumble, and I think of asking Yù'chén to take over. I could never live with myself if my sister died at my hands.

"Focus, Àn'yīng." His voice wraps around me in the darkness. "Think of them as tangled threads. You are the guiding needle. Unravel them."

Again, that metaphor   it works as no other. The world re arranges itself in my mind, the energies becoming live, interweaving threads. Sweat drips down my forehead, but I hold on to my consciousness of Méi'zi's energies, drawing out the death energies from her blood and bones and guiding them up her throat. I am sewing, that's what I'm doing: I'm sewing for my sister's life.

At some point, I feel Yù'chén's hands lift from mine. He

must be watching me, but I am in a trance, the life and death energies running beneath my fingers like silks responding to my touch.

"Good." Yù'chén's voice startles me; his fingers wrap around mine, stopping me. I'm focused on her throat; the death energies have pooled there, lodging as bile. "Very good. Normally, one would puncture the place where the death energies have gathered and bleed them out. But in your sister's state, she cannot stand to lose too much blood."

I realize I'm shaking from exertion. "Then what do I do?"

His hands tighten momentarily around my fingers, then he shifts mine away and presses his own to her throat. "This part, I'll do."

I shift back, leaning against the bed. It's all I can do to breathe, to still the fatigue that has settled deep into my bones. I'm drenched in sweat.

But I have learned to draw out sickness.

Yù'chén hunches over the bed, his body blocking my view of Méi'zi. I don't know what he's doing; I only feel his magic heating the small room, hear Méi'zi make little noises in her sickness. Finally, he rises and turns to me with a nod. I straighten.

"She'll be fine," Yù'chén says. His voice is low. "I've put her in a deep sleep. Her body needs to heal."

I hurry forward. My little sister is asleep, but her coloring has changed and her breathing comes easily. I wipe the sweat from her face and smooth her hair. Her cheeks are flushed and her lips red, but it's no longer the feverish hue I saw in the memory. I don't understand how the death energies of her sickness could simply have vanished.

I glance at Yù'chén. He's leaning against the doorframe,

eyes shut, one hand gripping the wall as though it pains him to stand. I can't tell whether it's the colorless moonlight filtering through our shutters or he's turned very pale. "What did you do?" I ask.

"I drew out the death energies of the illness and replenished her with some of my life energy." He doesn't wait for an answer before continuing: "I'll wait for you outside."

I clean the room and change the sheets and blankets. Then I wash Méi'zi's hair and wipe her down with cool water from our well. When the room is aired out and filled with the crisp scent of night, I sit next to my little sister, smoothing out the fresh nightgown I've dressed her in. The enchanted sleep Yù'chén put her in is strong; she doesn't stir.

I give myself another minute to sit in quiet contentment, stroking her face and combing her hair. I found the gloves I gifted her tucked beneath her pillows when I changed the covers; I lay them out by her side and press her fingers to the stitching. "Jiě'jie was here," I whisper, pressing a kiss to her forehead. "I'll always be here."

Then I force myself to rise, because I have my mother to take care of before I leave.

Yù'chén is not in the living room when I exit, but the front door is open a crack.

I find him sitting outside, leaning against the house, his eyes closed. A cold autumn wind stirs plum blossom petals from the tree, encircling him in a flurry of deep red and dancing shadows. As I draw closer, I make out dark circles under his eyes that I've never seen before, not even when he received the lashings back at the Temple of Dawn. His lips, normally flushed, are nearly white.

I drew out the death energies of the illness and replenished her with some of my life energy. I suddenly wonder if this means he had to absorb them with his own body.

An ache forms deep in my throat, near my heart.

He stirs only when I tap him on the shoulder. His eyes flare crimson, and I have never seen them this unfocused.

"Why are you out here?" I ask. "You'll catch cold."

His lips part; he glances at the door, then back at me. His voice is hoarse when he speaks. "I didn't think you'd want me inside."

He thought I wouldn't want a mó in my house.

Even after he saved my sister's life.

I want you to look at me and see me.

Wordlessly, I extend a hand to him.

Wordlessly, he takes it and follows me back into my house.

I suddenly feel self-conscious as we stand in my living room. Yù'chén is tall, and his head nearly scrapes the ceiling as he walks. Nothing about him looks as though it belongs in my small, earthly house, cracked and breaking at the seams, paint peeling and furniture chipped.

He looks around with a cautious curiosity and . . . a semblance of wonder.

"You can wait in the kitchen," I tell him. "I need a few minutes to take care of Mā." Fú'yí has taken good care of my family in my absence: my mother's nails are trimmed, her hair is freshly washed, and her nightgown still smells of soap. But I won't leave without caring for my mother. I don't know the next time I'll get to do this.

Yù'chén folds himself into a tiny kitchen chair and leans on the counter; even this doesn't rob him of his unnatural grace. I don't miss how his eyes roam our house, taking in the details, the spiderwebs in the corner, the shutters that have broken in storms and I've attempted to mend with oiled paper of my own making.

"It's nothing like the Kingdom of Sky," I say as I set a bucket of fresh well water next to my mother's bed. I'm curt, if only because I'm trying to preserve my dignity. "Not much to see."

"No," he says. "It's . . . real."

Real. I try to decide how I feel about that word as I dip an old towel into the bucket to wet it.

"I've not been in many mortal homes," he continues.

I wring out the towel and look sharply at him. "Were you raised in the Kingdom of Night?" There they are again, those threads of caution tugging at me, tightening. Being with him is like walking a never-ending cliff's edge. I never know when I will fall.

"No," Yù'chén says. "I was born in this kingdom. My father was mortal."

Was.

He's picked up a little teacup I made out of the clay mud I found down at the stream. I etched oceans and dragons into it with my needle. "My mother wished for me to be raised in the ways of the mortals, so I spent time with him," he continues, studying the little engravings. "Not a lot, and always in secret, stolen moments, because my mother was his mistress. When he found out what she was—and what I was—he tried to have us killed. My mother fought him off, and we escaped."

I process this as I gently guide Mā into a seated position. She leans against the wall, staring at a blank space somewhere between the front door and the window shutter. It's better this way. I don't want her to see me, or Yù'chén, in case she starts screaming again. Her cheeks are hollowing, I notice as I wipe sweat from her skin. Her bones are brittle.

She is dying.

"Àn'yīng," Yù'chén says quietly. "I'm sorry about your mother."

I focus on cleaning her face, her arms, each of her long, slender fingers, which are now swollen from lying on her back all day. I remember how nimble and clever they once were; how they embroidered chrysanthemums and orchids, mountains and rivers and oceans that made up my world when I was small. I remember her quick smile, the warmth of her eyes and the ring of her laughter, all of which she passed on to Méi'zi.

My eyes sting, and I reach for my mother's other arm. I try to keep my voice steady as I reply, "There's nothing for you to be sorry for. It's not like you drank half her soul and killed my father."

He's silent for a moment. His tone is low when he says, "I can understand why you hate me."

"I don't hate you." I pause, tasting the words on my tongue, then I reconsider, moving to wipe down my mother's legs and feet. "I don't hate . . . all of you. I hate half of what you are. But . . ." I draw a short breath. "I don't hate who you are."

A heavy pause stretches between us, and I feel Yù'chén's gaze burning into my back. I don't know what the point of all this is—whatever we have between us is a madness that will lead nowhere. And because the certainty of that settles like an anchor in my heart, I speak. One confession for one of his.

"My mother is the reason I'm doing the trials." I drop the

washcloth into the bucket of water, then pick up the wooden comb to tend to my mother's hair. It's her favorite, one her mother handed down to her, which she used to comb my sister's and my hair. I take my mother's thinning white locks and run the comb down them. "I learned a few years ago that the pill of immortality could heal her soul. *When* I win"— I emphasize the word *when*—"I don't plan to take it. I plan to give it to her."

I set the comb aside and press my hand to Mā's neck as I guide her back into her nest of pillows and blankets. She doesn't move; only the rise and fall of her chest indicates that she is alive at all.

I press a kiss to her cheek. Her skin is papery, as if it will tear at the slightest touch.

Then I rise and turn to my guest.

Yù'chén hasn't shifted his gaze. Something tightens in my chest at the way he looks at me: his face is drawn and tired, but his eyes are as dark as obsidian. He sits in a straight, nearly meditative pose, hands on his knees. I don't miss the red glow to his irises as he draws on his demonic magic to heal himself.

I look away as I rinse out the dirty towel and bring in a bucket of fresh spring water.

"Forgive my manners," I say. "You must be tired from helping my sister. Let me make you a cup of tea."

"I'm fine."

"I insist," I reply firmly and set the kettle to boil. I busy myself with scooping out the dried dandelion leaves we always keep in excess. They were once beloved tea leaves, but now they grow in clumps of weeds all around our village. Not much use for tea when you can barely fill your belly.

I look around for a decent mug, and I realize Yù'chén is still holding on to the little clay cup I made. His thumb traces circles over the childish engravings of dragons and ocean waves I carved a lifetime ago. For some reason, my neck warms at the way he's looking at it, a faint smile playing about his lips.

I clear my throat and extend a hand. "Pass me the cup."

Yù'chén stands, the scrape of his chair loud in the silence. He approaches, but instead of giving me the cup, he takes my hand and pulls me up. He takes the towel I've set to dry by my cracked old kitchen cabinet. Without a word, he lowers it to my cheek.

I close my eyes and suppress a shudder as he traces it across my skin, one cheek at a time, down to my chin and then the dip of my bottom lip. I think of that day after I fought Áo'yīn, of how gentle Yù'chén's hands were as he placed his cloak over my shoulders. I also remember how ruthless those same hands were as he fought Yán'lù. How those hands have the power to tear my heart from my chest.

But I don't move as his fingers dab at my throat, the curves of my neck leading to my collarbone and my chest.

I open my eyes. The moonlight limns his lashes and his hair, cuts his face into shadows and light. It brings out the red hue of his irises, like blood pooled in ink. It illuminates his darkened veins, coursing with his ichor and zigzagging through his skin. It's a sight I might flinch at, only now I focus on the familiar lines of his face. He looks exhausted, and it is as though any semblance of pretense has gone. The expression on his face, the way he looks at me, threatens to crack the shield over my own heart.

I shrink back slightly. "You look tired from the death energy you took from my sister."

"Mm." His voice is a low rumble.

"Take some of my life energy," I say. He pauses and cuts me a look, his hand with the towel on the back of my neck. The way he stares at me makes me add, "I don't want to owe you."

Yù'chén is silent for several heartbeats. Then, slowly, he presses a hand to my cheek and lifts my face. He searches my eyes. "I don't want your life energy," he says before he lowers his face to mine. Pauses, just before our lips touch. For some reason, I remember his words about my house. *Real,* he called it. *It's . . . real.*

I lean forward.

Yù'chén's gaze flickers up, to the open door behind us. He stiffens. "Àn'yīng—"

That's when my mother starts screaming.

23

A woman stands at our doorway, peering in. She wears a dirty purple robe that looks as if it were made for a child. In the darkness, her stance is predatory, shoulders hitched and arms spread, with that unnatural stillness not seen in mortals. Shadows wreathe her face, yet as she steps forward, a sliver of moonlight catches her ethereal beauty. Lips too full; eyes too large; hair that spills like ink onto a firm, willowy body. There is a detached curiosity to her face, one that instantly gives her away—if the other signs hadn't.

Mó.

She's absolutely still but for her head, moving as she takes in the room. Her tongue snakes out, and she licks her lips when she spots me. "Delicious," she murmurs, and her voice shifts to song: *"Come to me!"*

I grit my teeth as my feet move of their own accord, responding to the magic in her command. I reach for my crescent blades, and Yù'chén steps in front of me. He doesn't use his power to command me to stop, only advances with me, step by step, as I raise my weapons.

"Leave." His voice is a low snarl.

The mó pauses, her gaze pulling to him. She sniffs the air. "Mortal . . . *and* mó," she rasps, cocking her head. "I've never met one like you." Her eyes flash. "Which side do you take after, hmm? Do you desire the mortal girl, you poor thing? Do you want her—body, heart, and soul?"

Yù'chén's jaw tenses.

"Come. You can share, lovely."

"Get out," he growls.

Her expression twists at last, turning her into something feral and otherworldly. Demonic. "I've traveled far, and I'm *starving,*" the mó snarls, "and lest you wish me to eat you, too, *halfling,* then get out of my way."

My blades are out, ready to fight, but it's Yù'chén who moves first. Faster than I can blink, faster than humanly possible, he leaps at the mó.

She's even quicker. With a shriek of laughter, she dances around him, then she's close, too close, to my mother. "Oh, this one's spoilt," she simpers, then that simper turns to a scream as one of my blades finds her. Yù'chén's attack has thrown off the magic of the original command she gave me; her compulsion slips from me, and I'm free to move.

I barely scratch her. She's too quick for me, and as I pull away, positioning myself between her and Mā, a cloud of ichor spills from her side like smoke, hissing against my blade.

With the few mó I have encountered in my life, I have used tricks to fight them. Get them to underestimate me,

think me a defenseless mortal, and strike when they're most
vulnerable.

I don't have that advantage here, which means I have no
advantage at all. And this one isn't new to the mortal realm;
she's experienced. She doesn't strike me as refined enough to be
a Higher One—though I don't know anything about rankings
and status in the realm of mó, nor how they classify themselves.

A burning pain pierces my neck. I cry out as the world
tilts and my back slams into the floor with the mó's weight
on me. She is a tangle of hair and purple dress, hands and legs
pinning me down—

Then she's lifted bodily into the air, my blood dripping
down her chin, her teeth sharpened to terrifying points, her
eyes large and ravenous. Yù'chén's arms are around her waist;
he drags her back toward the door, and I hear him shouting
something at me, but there's a ringing in my ears and sharp
pains shooting up my head—

Wards, he's saying. *Put the wards up again.*

I push myself onto my elbows, shaking my head to clear
it. My mother's whimpers filter through the white noise, and
the awareness that real harm is just several steps away from
her and Méi'zi is what spurs me into motion again.

I crawl forward and trace a protective talisman on our
floorboards. Spirit energy shimmers to life, pulling from my
blood and knitting into a ward against the mó. Yù'chén is
wrestling with her at the door; I crawl forward as close as I
can to the two of them and trace another talisman.

The mó hisses as the ward flares up and comes into con-
tact with one of her elbows. She staggers back, out the door,
where she and Yù'chén slam into the grass beneath our plum
blossom tree.

I drag myself to the threshold of my sliding doors. I lift trembling fingers and draw the final talisman. There's a ripple in the air as the ward springs up, whole and complete, and my house is protected once again.

I turn to Mā. She's shivering, her eyes staring blankly at the wall again, her body twitching every once in a while. A part of her, I realize, remembers. Even if she is not conscious, her body and—I want to believe, *need* to believe—part of her soul knows when there is danger.

Swiftly, I close her eyes and lay her back in her blankets, where she continues to tremble. Then I run into Méi'zi's room and scrawl talismans on every wall. My little sister is still asleep, her breathing steady, though I see her eyes rolling in unquiet dreams.

That's when I hear Yù'chén cry out.

I turn and sprint toward the front of the house, Fleet and Shadow in my hands. What I see through the door sends a fresh wave of horror through me.

The mó has Yù'chén pinned to the ground. She straddles him, her face bent to his neck in what appears to be an intimate pose—but when he jerks against her, I see dark, glistening liquid drip down her chin and his neck.

She's drinking his blood.

For a moment I'm frozen, shock coursing through me at the incongruence of this scene. I have always thought of Yù'chén as the demon, the predator, the one who would be drinking the blood of mortals from their bodies . . . yet to see him in a position I had attributed only to myself, the prey, robs me of my reality and reverses my world.

Halfling. To me, he is predator and power, beauty and infallibility.

To them, he is prey. Weakness and imperfection, an abomination never meant for these realms.

He fights her with every ounce of his strength, but she easily overpowers him. With a sickening smile, she plunges knife-sharp nails into his stomach and then rips her hand from his torso.

Yù'chén makes a sound I never want to hear again. The mó's smile grows. As she trails her tongue up her forearm and her palm, licking off Yù'chén's blood.

Then she opens her mouth so that it splits her lovely face in half and plunges too many rows of razor-sharp teeth into his stomach.

Yù'chén screams; the mó laughs, and this is what gives me my opening.

I kick off in a burst of spirit energy that propels me so high, I'm somersaulting directly over her back.

This time, when I bring my arm down, Fleet finds its target. I feel the sickening crunch of bones and sinew and soft tissue, hear the mó gurgle from where she gorges on Yù'chén's blood and flesh. Smoky ichor leaks from her skin, but I'm not done. I pull out Striker and ram it into her chest.

The creature screams as her core shatters with the force of my blow. Her lovely face is no longer lovely but contorted, her mouth cutting from ear to ear to reveal pointed teeth, reddened with blood, and a tongue forked like a reptile's. I jerk back to avoid the ichor streaming from her, but I don't look away as she melts into smoke and shadows. The last to go are those teeth and her red, furious eyes.

Then there's nothing but the night breeze, the moonlight, and the whisper of trees and grass all around us.

My mind hasn't stopped spinning. A mó broke through

our borders. I need to stay, need to fix the wards around our village and around my house. But that'll take more time than I have.

There's a soft noise next to me. Yù'chén.

I turn to him, heart in my throat. "Yù'chén—"

But he's on the ground, holding his face in his hands, and twists away from me. "Don't," he rasps. "Don't come near me—"

"What are you talking about?" I reach for him. "You're injured—let me help you—"

"Don't look at me!" he yells, and I start back, because I think I see the reason why.

Between his fingers comes the glint of teeth sharpened to points. Where his skin should be, red-and-black scales bloom on his cheek. He's crouched over, hands grown over with the same scales. His shoulders shake.

"Please," he says, more quietly, his voice muffled by his hands. "Don't come near me."

I know that all mó wear the faces of mortals over their true, monstrous forms and that their beauty takes energy to maintain. I've seen the darkened veins over Yù'chén's skin when he has overexerted himself. But this—this is new.

I stare at the red-and-black scales covering the skin of his hand. "Is this"—I can't hide the tremor in my voice—"is this your true form?"

His silence is confirmation enough.

The seconds pass. Blood drips from the wound in his stomach. It pools on the ground with his cloak, fanning out like the petals of a crimson flower around him. His chest hitches with each labored breath.

If I don't do something, he'll die.

I take out Heart. A single slice, and blood flows from my wrist. I hoist myself behind Yù'chén and, careful not to turn his way, hold my arm out to him. "Drink, or my life energies will bleed out anyway."

For a few heartbeats, he doesn't move. But then I hear him shift and come up behind me, feel the rough scales of his hands clasp around my forearm, the heat of his lips as he presses them to my skin. I squeeze my eyes shut and try not to think of what I'm doing, of how I'm giving myself and my life energy to the very kind of being I've sworn I will kill.

Half of one.

Too mortal for the mó. Too demonic for the mortals. It's then that I understand, *fully* understand, Yù'chén's plea: *I want you to stop looking at me as if you're afraid, or suspicious, or disgusted. As if you're thinking of what I am instead of who I am.*

I look at him and see a demon, an enemy pretending to be human. But when the mó looked at him, she saw him as something beneath, something frail and breakable and mortal. Something to be used. He's unbelievably powerful in my eyes, but to the mó, he is no more than a plaything. Prey, just like me. His entire life, he has never been enough for either side.

At some point, he's stopped drinking. His fingers are warm, smooth, soft as they stroke over the wound on my wrist . . . and when I look down, I see skin instead of scales. I follow the line of his arm up to his bare neck and then the sharp edge of his jaw, and when he doesn't protest, I lift my gaze to his face.

He's breathing hard, veins still carving dark streaks across his face, a trace of my blood on his lips. Sweat glistens along his brow and jaw; his hair, wild and mussed, hangs over his downcast eyes.

I press my palm to his cheek. "It's all right," I say softly. "I'm still here."

He says nothing as he reaches out and draws me tightly against him. Only holds me, as if he never intends to let go. His hand comes up to cradle the back of my head. His chest rises and falls against mine, and I'm acutely aware of how my heart pounds against my chest, drumming out the confusion of feelings stirring inside me. Of how he must feel it, too.

"I . . ." He swallows and I feel the movement of his throat. "I didn't want you to see me like this." And then, quieter: "I don't want to disgust you."

I remember, so well, the cruel words I've cast at him.

I want to take them back. I want to apologize for every hurtful thing I've said to him. I owe him that and so much more, after how he saved my life and the lives of my family.

"You don't," I say. "You don't disgust me."

He tenses. His muscles are so tight, I can almost feel him shaking.

"Yù'chén," I whisper, "we should go."

He's silent for so long that at first I think he hasn't heard me. Then he says, a breath against my cheek, "I know." But his fingers thread through my hair and my long white ribbon, cradling the back of my head. Holding me closer.

The stars wink overhead. A breeze stirs the trees. And on the horizon, a seam of light appears.

There's a rustle of feathers next to us, and I look up to see his crane alight.

Yù'chén draws back. His shirt is shredded, revealing the black veins carrying his dark magic to his wound. It still looks terrible, but the bleeding has stopped.

"My crane will take us back," he says. He can barely stand, so I sling his arm over my shoulders and hoist him onto the shadowcrane. I climb on behind him. The shadowcrane's wings extend until they shroud half the starlit night. They wrap around me, and feathers smoother than silk, airy and liquid at once, slide beneath my fingers.

I glance back at my house one last time.

I hold on to Yù'chén tightly as we are borne into the skies on the wingbeat of a great, demonic crane. There must be enchantments at play, for the wind has taken on the scent of flowers and the moon brightens to a silver coin overhead. The landscape of my realm that we pass over takes on an impossibly beautiful sheen, the mountains and pines dusted with starlight and the rivers flowing like white gold.

Yù'chén has fallen asleep, leaning against me. I brush my fingers against his red cloak, noticing the tear in its bottom-left corner. The rest of it has escaped the mó's attack, but I can't take my eyes away from that corner.

I retrieve the rosewood box—the sewing kit he gifted me—from my storage pouch, where I've taken to carrying it.

I thread the needle and begin to sew. The tightness in my chest calms as I lose myself in the familiar motions. When I straighten, a red scorpion lily covers the bottom-left corner of the cloak.

I put my sewing box back into my pouch just as we break

through the clouds. In the distance ahead are the white stone and golden roofs, resplendent in the early morning light, of the Temple of Dawn. Wards, shimmering like sunlight on water, rise into the skies.

The shadowcrane circles, and it isn't long before I spot Yù'chén's gate amidst the clouds: an archway where the flowers and trees of the immortal realm look clearer and sharper. The red scorpion lilies are in full bloom; the gate yawns open at our approach.

We plunge through. The shadowcrane lands, and I help Yù'chén off. He touches her beak gently. With a bow of her head, the shadowcrane takes wing back through the gate.

Yù'chén sinks down against a tree. His breathing is labored; dark veins still pulse beneath his skin. "Leave me," he manages with a wince. "I have to . . . destroy the gate."

The sun has risen, and with it, reality comes rushing back. Given the ongoing murder investigation, I wonder if the other candidates are still allowed to train. Whether Hào'yáng will look for me this morning.

My stomach tightens as I bring my hand to my jade pendant. Here, in the clear morning light, whatever Yù'chén and I had between us—all that we shared in Xī'lín—will fade like shadows.

"Àn'yīng," I hear him call, as though he, too, has come to the same realization. "Àn'yīng—"

A scream cuts through the forest.

I palm Fleet and Shadow. "I'll be right back," I say, and I take off, ignoring him as he calls after me.

The Celestial Gardens are silent as I tread through the brush in the direction of the Mirror Lake, where the scream came from. I wonder if I misheard—if it was the cry of an injured bird or animal. The willows and blossoms are quiet, swaying in the breeze. Sunlight sparkles on the water. It's too beautiful a day for death.

That's when I stumble upon the body.

24

Even in death, Fán'xuān wears a hint of a smile. On the white sands of the Mirror Lake, his hair and robes fanning around him like snow, the first spots of color I see are his vibrant green eyes. They were once the color of willow leaves, of spring shoots; now they are as cold and still as jade. But as my gaze roams down his body, a violent shudder rips through me. He has been torn open. His heart and organs have been devoured, so there is nothing left in his chest but bones and the glistening red of his blood.

My mind blanks. A high-pitched ringing fills my ears as my world narrows to my friend, staring unseeing into skies he will never fly through again.

The sound of footfalls filters through my shock. I turn, blades raised.

It's Yù'chén. Slowly, he raises a finger to his lips. Points.

Above the beach, within the line of green willows and flowering trees, something moves beneath the canopy. Over the sound of waves, I make out a slurping, tearing noise.

"That," Yù'chén says quietly, "is the culprit you're looking for."

I stare at the hulking shape in the shadows, the sounds of its feasting growing more and more apparent. Its back is turned to us, and it's too dim for me to make out what it is, but my gut knows; I recognize the movements, the sounds.

It's the being from the Kingdom of Night that attacked me, killed Number Five, and likely Number One. And now . . . My throat tightens unbearably as I catch sight of Fán'xuān's pale hair ruffling in the breeze steps away from me.

Whatever that thing is, I'm going to tear it to pieces.

I raise my blades, but Yù'chén's hand catches my wrist.

"Àn'yīng, listen to me." His voice is barely audible. "In our current state, the two of us combined could not defeat that creature."

I thrust Yù'chén's arms away from me. "That creature didn't kill your friend," I reply, and then I'm staggering forward on the sand, toward the tree line. The Àn'yīng who started these trials would call me a fool to risk everything in this moment. Yet I think of Fán'xuān, lying behind me on the beach, alone and hollowed out. I think of the way he carried my golden butterfly to me during the Third Trial; the way he loved soaring on an errant breeze and dipping into the ocean. I think of his easy grin, of the excited glint to his jade-colored eyes and how they will never see again. I think of the short, bitter life he had in the halfling show pen and how he deserved so much more.

Yù'chén's right. We're in no state to fight this beast.

But I'm not going to do it alone.

Crescent blades gripped in my hand, I raise my jade pendant to my lips. "Hào'yáng," I whisper into it. "I know you can hear me." I pause. There will be time to explain later, to confess how I know who he is and sort out this confused mess I have made of my pendant and my guardian behind it. "I have the culprit behind the murders. I need help."

With that, I let the pendant dangle outside my dress as I approach the murderer.

The slurping sounds it makes grow louder as I near. In the shadows of the canopy, I see its hulking silhouette, the way its back is hunched as it bends over another victim. I can just make out the face of the candidate—a man I recognize—his eyes glassy, his expression blank. I think he is dead.

I hope he is.

Fleet and Shadow are in my hands. I'm pressed against the trunk of a great willow, as silent as a wraith. I have the advantage of stealth and surprise; I won't be fighting it full-on, as I did the mó back in Xī'lín.

The monster shifts its position, and for a moment, a sliver of sunlight through the trees lances across its face.

My blood goes cold.

I recognize it.

It's Yán'lù.

I must have made some noise, or perhaps drawn too swift a breath. Yán'lù—the monster that is Yán'lù—freezes mid-bite. Slowly, he—it—lifts its head and looks in my direction.

It's him; there's no mistaking it, except it's a horribly grotesque, twisted version of Yán'lù. His face is bloated; in his mouth are row upon row of razor-sharp fangs stained with gore. The whites of his eyes have disappeared, replaced by black that's tinted a crimson hue. Dark veins spiderweb across his face and down his neck, then encircle his arms—the demon's ichor that coexists with his mortal blood.

Yán'lù . . . is part-mó. The realization robs me of breath. Number One, Number Five . . . that male candidate . . . Fán'xuān and now another . . . It was all Yán'lù's doing. All along.

His eyes lock on me, and his lips widen into that sneer. I step out, but it's too late; I've lost the element of surprise.

Yán'lù's bloodied mouth curves in triumph. His gaze is cruel and utterly foreign. "I told you," he rasps, and his voice seems to hold multitudes—sharp and high-pitched while at the same time low and deep—"I never forget. I'm going to ravage your body. I'm going to drink your blood." His teeth flash. "But I won't kill you, as I did the others. No, you're going to suffer until you give me what I want."

I raise my blades. "I'm going to *destroy* you," I say in a low voice.

He throws his head back and roars with laughter. That's when a shadow falls by my side.

I see Yù'chén against the trunk of the nearest tree. He winces slightly as he draws his blade. Sweat drips from his chin, and he is still pale, his lips without the flush I'm used to. He lowers into a fighting stance.

Yán'lù's eyes flash as they settle on Yù'chén. "Going to turn against your own kind?" he crows. "Don't tell me you've truly fallen for one of them."

Yù'chén's face is broken by the dappled shadows of the canopy. Disgust is etched in his features, mingled with a deep anger. He steadies his sword and bares his teeth, eyes glinting red.

Yán'lù lunges forward. As he does, strands of his hair shoot out, forming sharp bristles aimed at our hearts. I recognize them: it was one of these that numbed my body in the Third Trial.

I dodge one and catch two, but the third swipes against my left shoulder. I feel bursts of excruciating pain where it punctures my skin, followed by the familiar prickling numbness that begins to wind its way down my arm. My blade falls into the grass with a dull *thump* as I lose control of the muscles in my hand. The poison on Yán'lù's bristles must paralyze his victims so he can kill them more easily.

I think of Fán'xuān and wonder whether his last moments were like this: frozen and helpless and alone, unable to move or scream as he was devoured.

I may have lost the use of one arm, but I still have another—and I'll be damned if I don't get this bastard.

Yù'chén is fighting, but he's slower than I've ever seen him. The wound in his stomach has torn open again, and fresh blood sprays the grass as he moves. His balance is off, each swing heavy as he fends off blow after blow from Yán'lù. The veins in his skin are pronounced, and when he snarls, I catch a flash of sharpened teeth and red-and-black scales beginning to form on his chin.

Yán'lù seems to sense his opponent's exhaustion. With another triumphant roar, he swipes his hands—which have shifted to claws with talons made to shred flesh—across Yù'chén's chest. A long lash of his spiked tail catches Yù'chén square in the stomach.

Yù'chén slams into the nearest tree with a horrifying *crack*. Blood drips down his chin as he drops to his hands and knees. His fingernails have lengthened to claws; scales bloom up the back of his hands.

Yán'lù lifts his hands for the killing blow, and I leap out from behind, Fleet clenched between my teeth, Striker in my right hand. I focus all my spirit energy, all my strength, and all my fury over Fán'xuān into my blow.

But after all this, I am still mortal. And I come up short.

Yán'lù twists. I feel the slice of flesh and crunch of bone and sinew as I bury Striker's blade in his chest—a hand's breadth below his heart.

Pain erupts in my midriff. When I look down, one of Yán'lù's bristles protrudes from it. Already, my chest is going numb with the prickling heat of his poison.

I look up through a blur of tears and twist Striker.

Blood spills from Yán'lù's lips. He gives a snarl of fury and slams me into the sand. For a moment, a high-pitched ringing fills my ears and my vision pops with sparks of black. When I come to again, Yán'lù stands over me, his spiked tail raised.

That's when my jade pendant heats against my skin. Its glow reflects in Yán'lù's eyes as he looks down at it.

I am here, the golden words on its surface declare.

Yán'lù stares at it a moment longer. Slowly, understanding seeps into his features, followed by a vicious delight.

"I've found it," he whispers, and lifts a claw. *"I've found it!"*

I press a hand over the pendant. But Yán'lù laughs even as blood seeps from the wound I've inflicted in his chest. Dark magic swirls on his palm, coalescing into a black bristle. It ripples in a sudden wind, then vanishes.

Something whistles through the trees behind Yán'lù. A golden arrow buries itself in his heart. The brute stops laughing. He looks down at his chest, at the protruding arrowhead, as though he can't quite process what he's seeing. A dark liquid drips from the gold: blood mixed with ichor that begins to drift up like smoke.

Yán'lù collapses to the ground. His chest stops moving and he falls still, his mouth still open, features frozen in the last of his laughter.

He doesn't dissipate like the other full mó I've killed; rather, his mortal body seems to shrink slightly in size, his muscles deflating until he loses that unnatural bulk. I look away from his pointed teeth, still coated in shreds of flesh.

Five immortals step out from the trees, bowstrings taut, arrows aimed at Yán'lù's motionless body.

"Dead, Captain," one of them calls, while another exclaims, "Impossible—it's a *mó* halfling!" And a third: "Mó can't have halflings."

Warm hands envelop my shoulders, turning me so that I'm looking into a familiar face. Brown eyes as steady as the earth, strong brows currently creased in worry.

"Hào'yáng," I mumble.

"Àn'yīng." His grip tightens on me, and his eyes rake over my wounds. "What did he do to you?"

"Paralyzed," I mumble. "His poison . . ."

Hào'yáng turns to the others. More guards are emerging from the trees or landing on the beach from their wisps of cloud, weapons drawn. Their attention immediately goes to him as he speaks. "I'll take the candidate to the healing temple," he begins, and then he catches sight of Yù'chén.

My heart staggers.

Yù'chén is crumpled on the ground beneath a tree. His chest is torn open in four long gashes, his shirt shredded, exposing the veined flesh beneath. Red-and-black scales are rapidly blossoming along his collarbone, shoulders, and arms. Veins spiderweb up his face, and his eyes . . . they have grown black, with glowing red pupils.

I must make a sound, for Yù'chén's gaze snaps to me. Taking in how I lean against Hào'yáng's shoulders and how his arms wrap around me.

Quickly, Yù'chén turns his face away, his hand flying to his neck and clamping down on the scales growing there. His body arcs in a gasp, I feel a dampening of his dark magic . . . and then the scales slow as they reach his chin.

"What—" One of the immortal guards nearby catches sight of Yù'chén. He takes a startled step back. "Another one here, Captain!"

With his free hand, Hào'yáng draws his weapon. Metal sings as he turns to face Yù'chén and raises his sword over his head—

"No!" The cry tears from me. With the last of my strength, I wrap my arm around Hào'yáng's waist, holding him back.

Hào'yáng hesitates. "Àn'yīng," he says, "this man—this *half-ling*—is part-mó. He was likely in league with the other one—"

"He wasn't," I whisper. "He saved my life."

Yù'chén watches me from where he lies, one step away from us. His chest rises and falls faintly beneath the shadow of Hào'yáng's sword. The scales have stopped growing; his face, apart from his eyes, is still human.

He gives me a nearly imperceptible shake of his head. "Don't," he says, quietly enough so that only Hào'yáng and I can hear. "I'm not worth it."

I cling tighter to Hào'yáng, tipping my head so he's forced

to meet my eyes. "Please believe me. It was Yán'lù; he confessed to the other murders right before you came. You saw him eating the candidate's heart; you saw him hurt me and Yù'chén fight him."

"Until now, we didn't believe mó halflings existed, Àn'yīng." Hào'yáng turns an assessing gaze to Yù'chén. "Yet two of them have managed to enter our trials, deceiving our wards with their mortal blood. This cannot be a coincidence."

I swallow, breathing hard. "Hào'yáng, please. Believe me."

Hào'yáng hesitates, his gaze searching mine. Then his mouth tightens and he lowers his sword. There is ice in his eyes as he turns to the other guards gathered around us and raises his voice. "At the very least, the Precepts of this temple demand an interrogation in the face of crime. This mó's life is not mine to take, just as his fate is not mine to decide."

"Forgive me, Captain, but our duty is to slay any mó we come across," another guard says.

"He is half-mortal," Hào'yáng replies. "Our Precepts list no precedent for the children of mó and mortals. This isn't a matter we can take lightly." He casts Yù'chén a look. "Take him to the healing temple. Chain him and ensure that he lives. We will take him for interrogation to understand how he is alive, how the demon's ichor inside him hasn't killed his mortal flesh, and how he and the other one bypassed our wards. And if he is indeed an enemy, we will torture him for information before executing him."

"Àn'yīng," Yù'chén begins, but two immortals grab his arms and begin dragging him. He strains toward me against their grip. "Àn'yīng—" His voice is cut off as a third guard makes a sharp gesture and silences him with magic.

Hào'yáng steps in front of me. His expression is cold, guarded, but sorrow tinges his eyes, and he is achingly gentle as he picks me up. He is displeased with me, and as I let him carry me away, I cannot help but feel that I have made yet another mistake.

25

I wake to sunset, soft silks, and plush pillows. A warm wind stirs the gauze drapes that hang between the rosewood pillars. I recognize this as the Temple of Tranquil Longevity, the healing wing.

"You are awake."

The voice is not one I recognize: it is soft, feminine, and beautiful—as is the figure that steps out from the shadows of the chamber. She walks into the light, and it is as though the sun worships her, kissing the soft honeyed tones of her cheeks, the perfect bow of her lips, shimmering down the blush of her dress, gold silks woven through, and the lotus flower she holds. She smiles, and all the realm's blossoms might turn to her in this moment.

"Honorable Immortal Shī'yǎ," I whisper, feeling as though I have stepped into the world's most beautiful dream. I shift into a sitting position on the bed, leaning against its frame.

I have yet to see an immortal this closely, and this personally; the proximity convinces me she is real and that she is something otherworldly. There is an absolute grace to her movements, a divine radiance and beauty that spills from her. Yet beneath the cool exterior with which immortals seem to view the world, there is a semblance of warmth to her gaze as she regards me.

"I am sorry it has taken so long for me to see you," she continues. "The rules are strict here, but Hào'yáng has created this opportunity for us to meet."

Hào'yáng. I remember the disappointment in his features as he carried me away earlier. "Where is he?" I ask.

"Making a report to the rest of the Eight Immortals." Shī'yǎ smiles, and her eyes seem to drink me in. "You do resemble your father."

I draw in a tight breath. In the bodice of my dress, my handkerchief seems to pulse. "How did you know my father?" I ask.

Shī'yǎ gestures with one hand. A steaming porcelain cup appears on the cabinet by my bed. "You must be thirsty, and it is a long story," she says.

The tea is camellia and mint—my father's favorite, I realize as I sip.

"Your father arrived at the Temple of Dawn just thirty years ago," Shī'yǎ begins, and something settles in her expression, as if she recounts a faraway dream. There is a hint of sadness to her lips and the slant of her brows. "Back then, mortal practitioners registered at our temple to train under the discipleship of immortals. The goal was to cultivate their practitioning arts and their power, not simply to achieve immortality. The borders between our realms were open, and those who gained immortality could still return to the Kingdom of Rivers to share their knowledge. They could lead a life between the realms." She looks at me, and her lips curl.

"Certainly, your father wished to. You see, he was my disciple for ten years."

"Oh," I say softly. No wonder his journals recounted a very different experience to the Immortality Trials and the Temple of Dawn. "Why did the trials . . . change?"

Shī'yǎ's expression shifts: the shadow of a cloud, racing briefly over sunlit waters. "They changed when the Kingdom of Night defied the Heavenly Order. The Kingdom of Sky sealed its borders. But our High Court knew the Kingdom of Night would not stop at the mortal realm; they decided we needed more warriors to defend ourselves against the mó. And so they turned the trials into an opportunity to re-cruit mortals. To turn the best of you, the most worthy war-riors . . . into *ours*."

That's why the discipleship my father mentioned in his journals is gone. They don't care to train us, and they don't want to share their knowledge for us to bring back into our realm. No, they want to recruit the strongest of us into their ranks. To protect *them*.

"You disagree with this," I state carefully, observing the small crease in her brow.

"Yes."

"Why?"

"In large part, because of your father. Most immortals view mortals as . . . fleeting. At best, mortals resemble cherry blossoms: beautiful when they bloom, yet ephemeral—there one season, gone the next. Why bother caring or fighting for anything when your lives are so short, when at the end of everything, all falls to dust and ashes for you?"

"It is *because* our lives are so fleeting that we have to fight," I reply. A stinging ache has arisen in my throat, and a flame resembling anger curls in my belly. "We have only this short life, this one life. If there is something we want, something we desire, we must fight for it."

Shī'yǎ is watching me with bright eyes. "That is almost exactly what Zhàn'fēi said to me," she says softly, and for some reason, my breath hitches at the way she says my father's name. "Eternity makes us cruel, does it not? Why care when you have all the time in the realms?" Shī'yǎ's lips part, then curl at the corners. "I digress. I came to speak with you on a topic Hào'yáng tells me he broached with you."

"The revolution," I whisper.

Shī'yǎ nods.

"Why me?" I ask. It is the question that has been burning inside me since I arrived, since the day she vouched for me. "Is it because of my father? Is that why you saved me?"

"So much has to do with your father, Àn'yīng," Shī'yǎ says quietly. "When he won the trials and rejected our pill of immortality, he set a great wheel in motion. He asked us to save his place in this kingdom should he one day have need. A place that almost went to you. A place that, instead, went to Hào'yáng."

Everything in me falls very still. The jade pendant is warm against my collarbone. Throughout these long years, I have always wondered at the reason my guardian in the jade—Hào'yáng—has watched over me.

Now I know.

It is because my father gave him a life of safety, of shelter, of security, away from our own dying realm. A life that should have gone to me. Or Méi'zi. Or Mā.

I did not know your father, Hào'yáng told me. *But I owe him.*

"Why?" I whisper. I would not wish for a place in the Kingdom of Sky should it be handed to me, for I need to be home to protect my family. But the place could have gone to Méi'zi, then barely a child of five. Or Mā, whose soul might have been healed here. I'm breathing hard as I think of Hào'yáng, strong and healthy and radiant and everything that my mother or my sister might have been.

"Because," Shī'yǎ says, "Hào'yáng is the sole surviving heir to the emperor of the Kingdom of Rivers."

My breath catches.

"Your father and I corresponded when the Kingdom of Night first invaded. I begged him to bring you and your sister here; I told him I would face any ramifications and break any rules to help. He agreed—until the day he showed up with a young boy instead."

All the pieces are now falling into place. How my father was away at war, leading the army from the Southern Province during the initial resistance the emperor led. How he returned months later, somehow changed, and began to focus on fortifying our town.

So he had gone to the Imperial Palace and he had found the emperor's last child and brought him to safety here.

He had planted the seeds of a future resistance against the Kingdom of Night, long before anyone had thought past the first war.

All this time, my father was thinking of the greater cause, yet now, a small, selfish voice inside me can't help but cry, *What about me? What about Mā and Méi'zi?*

"Over the years, Hào'yáng and I have been forming alliances with those who believe in fighting back against the Kingdom of Night," Shī'yǎ continues. "The pieces are nearly in place, Àn'yīng. All we needed was someone familiar with the mortal realm to join us, and to help him once he decides to return to the Kingdom of Rivers and gather an army. I wished to . . . place that burden on you, on account of the work your father did to make this possible in the first place.

"I know it is a heavy weight to carry, and I would ask for your forgiveness and preface my request with this: I understand that you have obligations, to win the trials and to heal your mother's soul. My respect for you and Hào'yáng's affections for you will not change should you decline; you will not lose our support for the remainder of the trials. And I need no answer today. I simply thought it was time you knew the truth."

She turns to leave, and I have the acute feeling, in that moment, that my fate, my destiny, everything my life has been building up to, will slip away with her if I do not seize it.

I am tired. I am *exhausted*. Deeply, down to my bones, I do not wish to fight any longer. Nine years I have been alone, taking care of my mother and my sister, dedicating my life to protecting theirs, ensuring our survival. I close my eyes briefly and lean back against the rosewood frame. A memory finds me: Méi'zi, four years old, running to me in a blooming courtyard of spring, her laughter piercing through the bleating of goats and the squawking of chickens. I recall the flashes of her hair, warmed by the sun, as she ran through the ripe fruit trees in our village. I think back further, to Mā sitting on the small, creaky wooden stool in our yard, beneath the shade of the flowering plum tree, Méi'zi curled on her knees and watching as she sewed.

Winning the trials might cure Mā, but the mortal realm will continue to sink into the Kingdom of Night, mó will continue to threaten our village, and we will continue to die out.

How could I live with myself if I had the chance to turn that all around and let I it go? How could I knowingly walk away from the chance to fight for that sunlit afternoon beneath plum blossoms for Mā and Méi'zi?

I settle on the image of sunset, red and blazing against Fú'yí's weathered face. *You let those bastards in the Kingdom of Sky know. You let them know we are still here. You let them know we are still alive. You show them how strong you are. And when you have learned the arts, just as your father did, you come back and win this war against the Kingdom of Night.*

My eyes fly open. My tea trembles in my hand, once.

"I'll do it," I say. "Please tell Hào'yáng I'll do it."

Shī'yǎ half turns to me as she opens the fretwork doors. The sun haloes her, outlining her side profile and the smile that lights her lips. "You may wish to tell him yourself," she replies, and then she is gone, as though she has simply vanished into the wind and the flurry of blossom petals outside.

In her stead, a different shadow falls on the gauze drapes: tall and armored and familiar.

Hào'yáng steps in, and suddenly, everything and nothing has changed between us. I take him in—the cool beauty of his face, the strength of his shoulders, the commanding air of his stance—with the knowledge of who he is.

The child of our emperor. The heir to the Kingdom of Rivers.

We are both mortal, but it suddenly feels that we are a realm apart.

"Àn'yīng," he says. He stops by the door and does not try to come any closer. We face each other, and I feel it again, the threads of destiny that have brought us to this moment. My guardian in the jade, rendered real in flesh and blood and standing just ten paces from me. All the secrets that were once barriers between us are gone.

Yet with that knowledge, it is as though I have lost the friend I have made in Hào'yáng these past few weeks. Before me stands the stranger I know most intimately in this world.

My hands curl around where my jade pendant rests at my collarbone. "All along, it was you."

His gaze flickers. "You must despise me."

I hear the unspoken words in his question. *You must despise me for taking the place your father earned in the Kingdom of Sky. For living a life most dream of while you were mired in a world of nightmares.*

"How could I?" I whisper. Hating him would be like hating a part of my own heart.

His eyes soften. "It must be strange, that you have known me for just a few short weeks yet I feel I have known you for nine years."

The sun dapples him; an errant breeze stirs petals into the blue skies behind him. Again, I have the feeling that I am in a dream.

I slide off my bed and stand. Step by careful step, I approach him, my heartbeat easing as though pulled by an invisible string. He does nothing, only watches me, his eyes never leaving my face. I peer up at him, trying to reconcile the quiet, steady hand that wrote to me through the jade . . . with this man before me.

"I know you," I say softly. "I wouldn't be here without you."

He gives me a look I can't decipher. His eyes trail every edge and curve of my face as if he is allowing himself to gaze at me, truly gaze at me, for the first time in his life. His hands are folded behind his back, his shoulders tight. *He's nervous,* I realize. Hào'yáng, captain of the guard and heir to the Kingdom of Rivers, is nervous meeting me like this.

He clears his throat. "I've imagined this moment a thousand times and prepared a hundred different things to say to you, yet I find that I cannot remember a single one of them," he confesses with a rueful smile.

I remember what he told me of growing up as a mortal in the Kingdom of Sky, and I imagine him as a young boy, perched by a smooth piece of stone, imagining meeting the girl inside.

Only, he doesn't know that on the other side of that jade was a lonely girl, holding on to that piece of rock as if it was her life.

"Then I'll consider it a debt," I jest, and I'm surprised at my own audacity. "We'll have plenty of time for you to remember the hundred different speeches you prepared."

Hào'yáng's smile widens, and it's the loveliest thing I've ever seen: like the sun coming out from behind clouds, shining upon me. It's a smile, I realize, reserved only for me.

"I wish you'd been there all along." It is only after the words fall from my lips that I realize I have spoken aloud.

He studies my face. "Àn'yīng, you're safe now," he replies, and I marvel at how he reads the words I don't say instead of the ones I do. "The culprits behind the murders have been caught. I will coach you through the remainder of the trials, and together, we will return to the mortal realm to cure your mother and spread the word that we are fighting back against the mó."

The culprits have been caught.

Cold pierces my heart. "Yù'chén," I whisper. Hào'yáng—and the rest of the guards—must still believe him to be guilty. "Where is Yù'chén?"

The warmth leaves Hào'yáng's expression, as though he has slid on a mask: that of the cool, efficient captain of the guard I first knew him to be. "He is being held in a solitary chamber in this temple. We must heal him before we subject him to interrogation, then execution."

Interrogation. Execution.

"No." The room spins a little. "Hào'yáng, listen to me—Yù'chén is innocent—he was *fighting* Yán'lù—"

"He is a mó, Àn'yīng. The Temple of Dawn has seen demonic murders committed on its grounds, which has heavier implications: that the Kingdom of Sky could have been infiltrated by the Kingdom of Night."

"He's a halfling—"

"—who could be here in the employ of the Kingdom of Night," Hào'yáng interrupts. His hand is back on the hilt of his sword. "We won't know until we interrogate him. You must understand how serious this is. Until now, the Heavenly Order declared the child of a mortal and a mó an impossibility; demonic ichor cannot run in the same veins as mortal blood. We must find out how he is alive, whether there are more of his kind, who his parents are, and how a mó came to produce a child with a mortal even before the Kingdom of Night broke through the Kingdom of River's wards. His existence changes much of what we know about the war."

"He isn't responsible for the murders," I say desperately. "He had an alibi for the first murder—you told me yourself. And he has protected me from other mó. You saw him fighting Yán'lù."

Hào'yáng looks away, toward the open window. "Àn'yīng,

even if I wished, I could not save him. The Eight Immortals are aware, and the High Court will be here in the morning. His interrogation begins at sunrise. Even if he is found innocent of any affiliation with the Kingdom of Night . . ." He exhales. "There is no precedent to a half-mó. The High Court made the Kingdom of Night their enemy. I don't know that they have it in them to let even a half-mó live."

I suddenly feel sick to my stomach. I remember Yù'chén's ask of me: *I want you to stop looking at me as if you're afraid, or suspicious, or disgusted. As if you're thinking of what I am instead of who I am.*

Now he is going to die precisely because of what he is—and because he helped me.

It's all my fault.

"Hào'yáng. I have to help him." My voice is low. "Please, tell me what I can do. I'll . . . I'll speak to the Eight Immortals, surely there must be a way—"

"The Eight are powerless against the High Court," he replies. When he lifts his gaze to me, the sorrow on his features is clear. "And if you testify for him, you would jeopardize not only your standing in your trials but also your *life*, Àn'yīng. The brewing war against the Kingdom of Night is a long-feared subject among the immortals in this realm. Now that they know two demons have gotten past our wards—even if he is a half ling, there will be no mercy. The High Court is ruthless; they will make an example of him . . . and any associates they find out about."

It is all I can do not to sink to the ground with the enormity of what I have done—the consequences of my failures. I have sentenced a man to death for helping me break the rules to save my sister's life, and for saving my life. But if I do anything against the wishes of the High Court, I could jeopardize the standings of the Eight Immortals; of Shī'yǎ and Hào'yáng and the entire resistance they have worked toward. And I could risk my own life if I try to help Yù'chén.

If I am dead, it is as good as sentencing Mā and Méi'zi to death, too.

"Àn'yīng." Hào'yáng doesn't move his eyes from me. His brows are creased, and there is something akin to sorrow in the way he watches me. "Don't throw away your life and your family for him."

"I owe him so much, Hào'yáng," I whisper.

He is silent for a few moments. Beneath the calmness of his expression, I can feel him thinking, deliberating. Then he says, "There is nothing I can do to save him. But if you wish to see him one more time, I can help."

My head snaps up. "I wish to see him," I say. "Please."

Hào'yáng gives a single, slow nod. "He is in the last chamber of the healing wing. At nightfall, I will arrange for the guards to momentarily retreat and for the wards to temporarily allow entry to his confinement chamber. Then, when the moon is highest in the sky, I will lower the wards, allowing you—and only you—to leave the chamber. You must look for the sign; you will have only a moment to slip out."

He turns to leave; for some reason, at the sight of him, my chest knots.

"Hào'yáng," I say quietly. "Thank you."

He pauses at the door to glance back at me in the light of dusk. I can't make out his expression.

Without speaking, he bows his head. Then he is gone.

26

The night is starlit when I leave my healing chamber. In the distance, I can hear the sounds of revelry. Hào'yáng told me there would be a banquet to honor the murdered candidates and celebrate that the culprits have been caught. Music and laughter drift from the direction of the Banquet Hall, which is lit in the faint glow of lanterns.

The Temple of Tranquil Longevity is silent and dark, its long, open-air hallways connecting the individual empty chambers. Chrysanthemums sway in my wake, their fragrance filling the air with hope of the health and longevity they symbolize. A wind has picked up, masking my footsteps as I approach the last chamber of the temple.

I've left my jade pendant back in my chamber. This is the first time I've taken it off since my father gifted it to me. Its meaning has changed now that Hào'yáng holds the other half. Its weight against my heart has begun to feel more significant, and it took me a while to realize that what I felt earlier, when I begged Hào'yáng to let me see Yù'chén, was guilt.

I don't know what to make of it, other than that my path in life was always meant to lead to Hào'yáng just as a river flows to the sea—yet tonight, I went against his warnings.

But seeing Yù'chén again, perhaps for the last time, is a moment I wish to keep to myself. A moment I wish to experience alone for the first time, without the presence of my guardian in the jade.

My neck feels bare and too light without it, but I remind myself it is only until the moon rises to its highest point in the sky. Just a few hours.

Hào'yáng is true to his promise. There are no guards in sight as I draw up to the chamber where Yù'chén is being kept. When I press a hand to the door, testing for wards that may ensnare me, nothing happens.

I suck in a breath, slide it open, and slip in.

There are no lanterns in this chamber. Moonlight spills through a fretwork window, granting some degree of light. I feel the wards pulsing against the walls and closing over the doorway as soon as I enter. There will be no escaping from within.

Standing beyond a set of sheer drapes, gazing out the window at the moon, is Yù'chén. I catch the crimson of his cloak first, shimmering like blood. Yù'chén's fingers absentmindedly caress the bottom-left corner.

He stirs now, as though from a trance. His eyes find mine across the room; shock ripples across his face. "Àn'yīng?" He speaks my name in disbelief.

I don't know what to say or do. I don't even know why I'm here. I have no plan to save him, and I can't—I can't risk anyone finding out that Hào'yáng helped me get in here against the rules. I can't tell the Eight or the High Court of my involvement with Yù'chén and jeopardize my standing in the trials and my mother's only chance to have her soul back.

I have wished to be powerful my entire life, yet in the end, in the face of the most important moments, I am still powerless to change anything.

Yù'chén turns to me. He looks healthy again, his skin smooth and free of scales and dark veins. Beneath his cloak, he wears a fresh set of black robes.

He walks toward me and lifts the gauze curtain with one hand. The way he looks at me fills me with emotions I'm not meant to feel.

"Tell me this is real," he says.

There are no words I can offer to make up for the wrongs I have done him. I have despised him on the basis of his birth, suspected him and doubted him time after time even when his every action was to help me, to protect me. I have accepted his help without consideration of the consequences for him as a half-mó—and I have sentenced him to death.

My vision blurs, and because my chest aches with all the empty apologies I can't offer him, I speak his name: "Yù'chén."

He crosses over to me in several brisk strides and reaches for me—then hesitates. We stand there for several heartbeats, his fingers lingering by my cheeks, and I realize I'm waiting for him to touch me.

Yù'chén swallows and slowly, very slowly, retracts his hand. He draws a deep breath and shifts his gaze to a spot behind me. "You shouldn't be here." His voice is hard.

"It's my fault," I choke out. "I asked you to help my sister—then the mó—and Yán'lù—"

"It's all right," he says. "I'll be all right."

"It's not. You won't. They're not going to give you a fair trial, Yù'chén."

Something settles on his expression: a resignation I have seen before. The same expression he wore when I confronted him about being a half-mó. When he asked me to see him as anything but. Finally, he looks at me again, his eyes as dark and as deep as the night.

"Àn'yīng," he says, and his voice is steady. "When we are born, we are set on a path to walk. One drawn by our birthright, our status, our blood. Some are born with golden crowns on their heads, beloved and made for a life of glory and dreams; others are less fortunate. That is fate, drawn and allotted by the Heavenly Order. I have known since the start what mine was meant to be. And if it should end here, I have no regrets."

I clench my teeth, and this time, I cannot stop the tear that carves its way down my cheek. "I don't know why you don't hate me," I whisper.

His expression softens. "You," he says slowly, "are the first person who has treated me as if I'm . . . human. As if I am deserving of anything other than revulsion and disgust."

I flinch. *You* disgust *me,* I once told him.

I steel the storm in my heart and meet his gaze. "Yù'chén, do you remember what you asked of me before we left to see my sister?"

He stills. "Yes."

I reach out and press my palm to his chest, where his heart beats. "I see you."

It is too little too late after all that he has done for me, where he is now, and what will happen to him tomorrow. But it is all that I can give him.

Yù'chén closes his eyes; a shiver passes through him, nearly imperceptible. When he opens them again, they are raw. They catch mine and they *burn,* and it's as though they ignite something in my heart and in my very soul: a fire that has been there all along and that roars to life at his gaze.

"Àn'yīng." He says my name as if it is the most important thing in this world. His expression is careful as he beholds me. Slowly, ever so slowly, he lifts his hand from where it rests on the bottom-left corner of his cloak. Lifts it toward my cheek. He pauses. A question.

I don't look away from him. An answer.

His eyes heat, and his fingers finally fall, coming to rest on my cheeks. His touch sends shivers of pleasure through my body. Yù'chén doesn't move, just holds me, barely, his palm cupping the edge of my jaw. His gaze, though, roams my face, as if he is studying the map of my features, committing every line and shadow to memory.

Slowly, ever so slowly, I reach up to touch his jaw. My breaths quicken as I trace the sharp lines of him, all made for devastating beauty and destruction. There is something different to the way we interact with each other tonight. It is nothing like the clumsy, passion-fueled embraces of the hot spring or the hazy stupor of the flowers' poison back in his passage. This time, we are both awake, our breaths taut, so carefully and painfully aware of what we are doing, of this new level of intimacy between us as we explore each other beneath the fragile light of the moon.

And perhaps it is the awareness of our time running out

that makes me bolder, or perhaps it is the certainty of the feeling that has possessed me all along finally coming to light.

"Yù'chén," I whisper. I ask the question that has been haunting me for weeks since that night at the hot spring. "What did you see in the forest?"

He hesitates, but he does not close off. No, there is only a weary grief to the way he pauses. His fingers are on the edges of my jaw now, sweeping over the sensitive crook to the back of my neck.

"I saw you," he replies, and I shiver at his voice, at his touch, at the meaning in his words. "I saw you, dying, a demon drinking your soul."

The Forest of Nightmares. I remember now, the way he froze at the sight of that blurred figure between the trees, the body lying within its clutches. The painted skins had manifested our worst fears. To Yù'chén, it had manifested my death.

He retracts his hand. The space it leaves behind is cold. "That was when I knew," he finishes, "that if I continued down this path, there was only one way it would end."

"So you pushed me away." My voice is a whisper.

"I tried."

"Yù'chén." I move my fingers to his lips, soft and full and wide, remembering how easily he smiled in the days when we first came to know each other. And because I know I cannot, can never, and will never choose him, I say instead: "I see you. I'm sorry it took me so long."

He draws a swift breath. "Àn'yīng, you should leave," he says, and his voice breaks. "Please. If you don't leave now, I don't know that I have it in me to let you go again."

I can't. I have known how our story would end since the very beginning. I have resisted, but I no longer wish to.

I press my other palm to his cheek. His hand comes up, his fingers lacing gently in mine, splaying my palm against his mouth. He presses a kiss there. I shiver. Slowly, he trails his mouth to my wrist, where he moves his lips into another kiss. He pulls up the silk of my sleeve, and the cold rushes in against my bare skin, but his mouth is hot as he traces up my arm. It is on his third kiss, at the crook of my elbow, that I realize I've stopped breathing.

He pauses at the straps that house my crescent blades on my upper arm, normally hidden beneath my sleeves. I feel his mouth curve into a smile against my skin. "Little scorpion." He chuckles. "Never without your blades."

I hold his gaze. Slowly, I draw out Poison. The talisman gleams, and the blade catches an arc of moonlight as I hold it out.

I drop it. The crescent blade falls to the floor in a clatter. Yù'chén's eyes flick to it, then to me.

"Disarm me," I whisper, and I pull him down to me in a kiss.

He inhales sharply, then his hands are on my cheeks and tangled in my hair, and he's kissing me with barely restrained desire. We stagger back until I'm pressed against the wall and his body is hard against mine.

"Disarm me," I repeat against his mouth.

He bends to press a kiss to my neck, and I shiver, feeling the heat of his hands as they trace up my other arm. Striker falls to the floor, and Yù'chén's lips trace up my jaw to the outside of my ear. His hands pause on my left thigh, where

Fleet rests. I feel the graze of his fingers against the silk of my dress, his desire clear in the darkness of his gaze, the way his body presses against mine.

I lace my fingers through his. Slowly, I guide his hands to the slit on the side of my dress. His eyes never leave mine as he pushes up my skirt, his palm sliding along the bare skin of my thigh. He unstraps Fleet, then his hand moves to my right thigh. Shadow is next.

He hesitates, breathing hard as he looks at my bodice, where my last two blades rest on either side of my ribs. "Àn'yīng," he says. Our heartbeats pulse in the air between us. "I can't do this. I . . ." He swallows and draws back, his hands curling into fists at his side. "I will not live past tomorrow. I would ruin you."

The earnestness, the honesty, in his voice and words crack me.

I catch his wrists, stopping his retreat. Then I push him backward. One, two, three steps . . . more, until he bumps against the end of the bed. I push him down, and he obeys, his eyes on me as though he is held by some unknown spell that I have cast over him. He could snap my neck in the blink of an eye, but instead, he yields to my touch as if I have all the power in the world.

I find that I love it.

He falls back on the silk sheets, his eyes widening as I slide onto his lap, parting my knees so I'm straddling him. My hair has come undone; still wound through with my white ribbon, locks of it curl against his throat, the collar of his black shift, as he looks up at me. His hands fall onto my hips, and I feel him strain against me as he sits, facing me, our faces inches apart, our breaths tangling.

I press my hand to his cheek. "Do you want me?" I ask.

Yù'chén tips his face up to me, baring the elegant curve of his throat. He swallows hard. "I've wanted you so much for so long, Àn'yīng," he says softly. "You have poisoned me, little scorpion, and I would gladly let you do it over and over and over again."

I shift against him, and his grip tightens on me, his eyes darkening. "Then I want you to ruin me," I say, and crush our lips together.

He pulls me onto the bed with him, and this time he kisses me with abandon, with a hunger and desperate desire that unravel something inside me.

"Disarm me," I command again, and he complies, his hands traveling up my thighs and farther up, into the bodice of my dress. I feel his fingers against my ribs, feel cool metal as Healer falls onto the silks and, at last, Heart. My hands work at the buttons of his shirt, then the samite belt at his waist, just as he loosens my undergarments. His hands settle on my hips again, and I don't break his gaze as I move over him.

He pauses, his kisses turning gentle and slow as he eases me onto him.

I squeeze my eyes shut as he holds me. His touch is agonizing, at once lighting a fire inside me and creating a thirst I can't quench, too much and not enough. Yù'chén kisses me again with a tenderness that makes me shiver. When I open my eyes, he is looking at me, and I find my reflection in the dark of his eyes. My dress pools at my waist, silver in the moonlight as it connects us, as beautiful as a blossom in the night.

I remember what he told me in the passage of flowers, and my silence after, and I nod as I finally give him my response. "I want you," I whisper—and that's when I realize it's not true. After all we have been through together, I am not certain *want* is the word that describes how I feel toward him, and that frightens me most of all.

His hands cup my cheeks. "Àn'yīng," he whispers, his voice raw. "I want you, more than anything in my life. More than anything I have ever felt. I . . . want you."

And I wonder, too, if *want* is the word he means to use.

His hands grip my waist, pressing me tightly to him as he turns us around and sets me gently against the bed of silks without breaking us apart. His body covers mine, but he suspends his weight on his elbows so he does not hurt me. I tighten my legs around his hips and wrap my arms around his back, burying my face in the crook of his neck. I have the feeling I am falling into an endless night of stars with him holding me.

I find that I am no longer afraid. I capture his lips with mine and arch into him, running my hands down the contours of his back and feeling the ridges where he bore lashes to gift me my sewing box. I touch the hard planes of his stomach, the wound there healed from his fight with the mó outside my house and then with Yán'lù—all for me. An ache builds inside me as I think of all he has gone through for me, and all the times I have pushed him away because of what he is. The way he touches me now, the way his lips trail my skin and he holds me like I am his end, leaves me no doubt as to how he feels, as to why he did all that he did for me. And the least I can do is give him one last truth.

I dig my fingers into his hair and press into him, the closest I can be to him. "Yù'chén," I gasp, and then I lose myself in him.

He shudders against me, a noise breaking from his throat, and I cling to him as I give myself over to him, to the knowing that from the very start, there was only one way this could end.

Yù'chén shifts to lie down beside me and draws me against him, pressing butterfly kisses to my cheeks, my jaw, my neck. But my gaze is drawn to the window behind him, the way the moon has climbed halfway into the starlit sky. Its light spills on Yù'chén, frosting him in a beauty that is impossible and impossibly cruel, because I know the moon worships him, and I know the moment it rises to its highest and I will have to leave.

"You're thinking."

I blink, pulled back to the present by Yù'chén's voice. He watches me through those long lashes, like strokes of ink, his fingers absently tracing the curves of my lips. My throat knots at the way he looks at me, his eyes bright with joy.

"Tell me what you're thinking," he says.

I brush my hands against his cheeks. "I'm thinking about you."

His lips pull up in that grin, the one I remember from the very first day we met in that clearing in the mortal realm. He takes my hand, threads his fingers through mine, and brings it to his mouth. His lashes flutter as he kisses my palm, his touch sending shivers up my spine.

"Àn'yīng," he murmurs, his lips grazing my skin, his breaths hot on my hand. He hesitates, then lifts his eyes to mine. He is no longer smiling. "In any other life . . . if I weren't mó . . ." He swallows. "Is there a chance that you would choose me?"

I tip my head back and search his eyes. No more masks, I realize; no more charm and flirting, cruel smirks and teasing.

Beneath it all is a yearning that I know with my own heart, that all humans share.

Why is it in our natures to want that which we cannot have?

I know my answer. I've known since he risked his own life to protect me from that stray mó, or perhaps when he saved my sister from death by trading his own health . . . or perhaps even earlier. The debts I owe him run through my mind in an endless tally, and for a moment I can't breathe against the waves of guilt threatening to drown me.

I want you to look at me and see me.

I touch a finger to the corner of his mouth, recalling the easy way it stretched into a grin. Trace my hand over the sharp curve of his cheeks, the long lashes and dark brows, and think of the charming young practitioner draped in red I met in the forest.

"Yes." The word unfurls from me in the softest whisper, barely a sigh. He freezes, shock blanching across his face, and I sit up, unable to meet his eyes, because it is breaking me. "I have to go."

"Àn'yīng—wait—" He catches my wrist and pulls me against him, wrapping his arms around me so tightly that I feel the gallop of his heart against mine, hear its rhythm beat out all the words unsaid between us. He buries his face in the crook of my neck, and I feel his muscles coiled so tensely he's shaking.

"I'm sorry," he whispers hoarsely. "I'm sorry. I—I just . . . I just want to hold you for a few more moments."

My eyes burn. *I can't,* I think. *I can't.* The fates have granted us a crossroads on the two paths we walk, paths that were never meant to meet. Maybe, under different circumstances, in a different lifetime, the stars would have been kinder. Maybe I could have loved him without knowing it would burn down the world.

But meeting the right person at the wrong time, the right love in the wrong life, is a tragedy written from the start.

Yù'chén exhales. He seems to be fighting something, fighting himself, and it seeps through the cracks as he untangles himself from me. "Go." He smooths my hair and fixes my dress, button by button. He dresses himself, then picks up my two blades on the bed and hands them to me. "Go, and be happy, Àn'yīng. Promise me you'll be happy."

In that moment, I'm not sure I can feel joy again without tasting this sorrow.

Yù'chén slides us off the bed. He picks up two more crescent blades. Kneels at my feet and slides them back into their sheaths at my thighs, then presses two light kisses on me there. When he reaches the final two blades, he slips them into the sheaths on my arms and draws back. We stand like this, gazing at each other, the distance between us an abyss as we race toward the end.

"Forget me, Àn'yīng," he says at last.

The words taste like ashes against my tongue. "I'm sorry."

"Don't. I'm not worth it." His eyes search mine, and something like shame, like resignation, crosses them. "Àn'yīng, I want you to know . . . I'm so sorry for what the Kingdom of Night has done to your realm."

I give him my last truth. "We're going to fight back, Yù'chén," I whisper. "There is a resistance brewing against the Kingdom of Night. Hào'yáng and Shī'yǎ have planned it and gathered allies in the Kingdom of Sky. We will return to the mortal realm to declare war, and Hào'yáng will fight to take the throne." I press my hand to his heart. "I'm going to make a safer world, for mortals and for halflings alike. For you."

So that, in your next life, you can have the right to fall in love with whomever you wish.

So that, in his next life, Fán'xuān can roam the realms as free as a bird.

So that, in their next lives, Lì'líng and Tán'mù won't spend half their lives in a halfling show pen.

Yù'chén swallows. He reaches out to brush a strand of my hair behind my ears. His fingers linger on my cheek.

"Forget about me, Àn'yīng," he repeats gently, and that is when the moon shifts, and everything in the room glows as though there is magic spinning in the air.

It's a sign, for me: that it's time to go.

I press my palm to his hand, leaning into his touch for the last time. Then I turn around and slide open the doors to exit.

The problem is, there is someone on the other side.

27

I am frozen in time, fallen back into an old, familiar night-mare. The woman standing in front of me is a ghost in the moonlight, shadows parting around her to reveal black hair and white skin and . . . red. Red lips, curved in that same smile; gleaming red eyes and that red, red garnet at her throat. The world blurs around me, and I see her face from nine years ago, looking up from my father's open chest, his blood stain-ing her chin and her teeth as she beams at me.

An illusion, I think. *The same one you've seen for nine years.*

But this is nothing like the blurred hallucinations. She stands before me, clear in the moonlight, larger than life. The raw fear coursing through my veins tells me that this time, it's real.

I should scream, I should attack with all the fury and grief of the past nine years, I should drive my crescent blades into that chest of hers where her demon's core sits. But somehow, at the sight of her, I cannot move, my years of training and fighter's instincts dissipating like ashes. Before her, I am, once again, the helpless child of nine years past, kneeling on my kitchen floor and watching as she eats my father's heart and drinks my mother's soul.

It lasts only one moment. In the next, I am moving to palm Striker and Fleet, my arm lashing out in a slicing cut—

—which she easily sidesteps. I turn, but she is gone again, and that's when I feel her arms wrap around me from behind, the soft purr of her laughter as she drags me against her.

"Be still, little flower," she murmurs, and the power in her voice is unlike any I have experienced. All the other mó's magic feels like rivers, whereas hers is an ocean, crashing down upon me and wiping out any possibility of resistance. I instantly go limp. My blades clatter to the floor. She holds me, caressing a hand across my face and neck. "There's a good girl."

Terror claws its way into a scream that's trapped inside me, but there is nothing I can do.

The Higher One who killed my parents is here.

She is in the Kingdom of Sky.

Yù'chén has gone completely motionless, in that unnatural way of his that comes from his mó essence. A muscle pulses in his jaw. "Let her go," he growls, and I have never heard such a voice coming from him: feral and unrestrained, dangerous enough to remind me of what he is, what powers live inside him.

"Why?" The Higher One's voice is as melodic as I remember it. I can imagine the curves of her beautiful lips, the twisted sparkle in eyes that enchant so wholly and absolutely. "Do you plan to bring her along, too? As your plaything?"

My body is frozen, but now it is as if my mind locks up as

well at her words. I don't understand. I can't. But I'm looking at Yù'chén's face as he stands directly across from me, his entire body tensed as though about to fight.

"Don't," he snarls at her.

"I would gladly give you all that you desire, Yù'chén," the Higher One continues. "You know that." The hands lift from my throat, and her voice commands in my ear, *"Go to him."*

My limbs obey; I haven't a choice not to. I straighten and begin walking to Yù'chén. He stands across from us, frozen; the wrath on his face shifts as another emotion penetrates it.

Fear.

His eyes flicker between me and the Higher One behind me, darkening with fury. When I reach him, he pulls me against him, but his muscles are taut, and I feel his heart pounding in his chest.

"Let her go," he says, and his voice hitches, his defenses breaking. "Please."

"But I already have," the Higher One replies, the false confusion in her voice perfectly pitched to be mocking. "You want her, don't you? I know you do; I saw what you saw in the forest, Yù'chén. After all, I was the one who led you to her when the huà'pí cornered her."

The Forest of Nightmares, where Yù'chén confessed he had seen me dying in the arms of a mó. I recall now that I saw *her,* too, standing between the parasol trees, watching me through that gap between the realms. I thought her a ghost come to haunt me in the spike of my fear.

I was the one who led you to her.

Had she truly been there?

I'm suddenly shaking, nausea churning inside me. Was

the vision I dismissed as a hallucination real? If so, how many others were, too?

Yù'chén's fingers tighten against me, but he can summon no response.

"You want her, and you know exactly who she is," the female purrs. "But the question is, Yù'chén, have you told her who *you* are?"

"Stop," he begs.

"Does she know why you approached her in the first place? Why you've protected her all along?" She speaks faster, and I can tell she delights in this. "Why you helped her through the First Trial, why you did everything in your power to gain her trust, stole that sewing box and helped her send those gloves to her sister, all just to win her poor, gullible little mortal heart?"

I'm reeling from her words. Because those are memories that should be private, that should be mine, and mine alone. It is as if I am listening to a story told from another's perspective, the truth between the lines now irrevocably written out. The moment I ran into Yù'chén in that clearing; when he saved me from Yán'lù and his cronies and accepted my ask of alliance; the cliff at Heavens' Gates, when I thought I hallucinated her between the trees, and Yù'chén called out to me in fear and desperation as he used his magic to command me for the first time.

The sewing box. The gloves, the dance on the ocean, the journey to my home to save Méi'zi . . . I recall it all now, but differently. I see the hands holding the strings.

"If I let her go, would she still come running to you, Yù'chén?" The Higher One utters something, and the magic binding me in place, holding me against Yù'chén, loosens its grasp. I stumble back, ripping my hands from him, steadying my legs and my shaking breaths.

"Have you told her why you're here and who you are," the Higher One drawls, relishing her words, "my son?"

Whatever hope was left on Yù'chén's face flickers out; his expression goes blank. I'm shaking so hard, I need to hold on to the wall to stop myself from falling down. As I look at him, I suddenly see everything that I have missed—the shadow of *her* on his face: the impossibly sharp angles to their jaws and cheekbones, the full red curves to their lips, her delicate arched brows rendered stronger and more masculine on him. I see it so clearly I do not know how I could have missed it in the first place.

Yù'chén is her son.

He is the son of the Higher One who killed my father. Who maimed my mother. The monster who has shaped my life and who is the reason I am here, in these trials, fighting to regain some semblance of it back.

It is a twisted circle, a sick hand of fate.

"Àn'yīng," he begins.

"Don't," I spit out, *"say my name."*

The Higher One is watching with that same smile. "What a beautifully tragic ending to this love story," she murmurs, stepping forward. The moon has shifted, I suddenly realize; the wards on this chamber are back up again, and I am trapped in here with them.

Good. Because I'm going to fucking kill them both.

The Higher One's eyes flick toward me, almost lazily, as a cat might watch a sparrow. *"Don't move,"* she says, and I'm frozen again, my blades halfway to my palms. She's looking at Yù'chén, dark triumph on her face. "I think it's time we finished this tale and began our new one, don't you, my son? The one we've been waiting for your entire life?"

Yù'chén stares back at her coldly. "What if I told you I've changed my mind?"

The Higher One's smile widens. I feel a sudden lash of magic directed at Yù'chén, and the next moment, he's doubling over, his veins bulging from his forehead and his neck, his breaths heavy. He groans and bares his teeth, but the mó's hand twitches, and he falls to his knees, his muscles locked and twitching against his will. She's inflicting some sort of pain on him; a lot, from the way he's shaking.

She watches him a few moments longer, and then I sense the magic fade. Yù'chén gasps and slumps over, barely holding himself up with his hands. His breaths grow ragged.

When I was small, the first time I saw this female, I'd had no experience with the mó. To me, they were all the same: beings with power so far beyond my imagination. As I learned about them throughout the years, I began to realize that there were different levels even within the mó. I understood why some were newborn, some were ordinary, and some the practitioners of my town named the Higher Ones.

This female is the most powerful mó I have ever seen.

She glances over at me as though sensing my thoughts. Her smile is heartbreakingly beautiful as she speaks: "I ought to introduce myself properly, as I have been waiting nine years for this moment, Àn'yīng. My name is Sansiran."

The name is like lightning in the tight space of this chamber. *Sansiran.* I know that name, spoken in hushed whispers by the greatest practitioners of the mortal realms. I know it for the fear that has haunted me day and night for the past nine years, sometimes distant and sometimes near, that the queen of the demon realm will come for us all.

Sansiran, the Demon Queen. Sansiran, the Empress of Fallen Darkness.

Sansiran, the Ruler of the Kingdom of Night.

"Thank you, my son, for creating gates through the immortals' wards for our army to enter," Sansiran continues, and I feel ice cracking in my veins, freezing me until my teeth chatter. The gate he lied to me about; the one he hadn't destroyed the first time I asked him. The one we left open after returning this morning. And from what she said, it sounds like he made more.

The Kingdom of Night's army is coming—through those gates.

"I was going to destroy them," Yù'chén says. He's looking at me as he speaks. "After tonight, once I was strong enough. But I never had the chance."

"After tonight?" Sansiran repeats, amused. "When your head hangs from the front gates of the Kingdom of Sky, an example they like to make of us?"

Yù'chén draws a sharp breath, and I think of what he told me earlier, in this very chamber. *When we are born, we are set on a path to walk. One drawn by our birthright, our status, our blood. I have known since the start what mine was meant to be.*

I should have known there was only one path a demon could walk.

"Don't do this," Yù'chén rasps. "They don't deserve it."

" 'They don't deserve it'?" Sansiran echoes. Her features grow sad for a moment before turning cold with fury. "Did I deserve it, Yù'chén? Did I, a *queen*, deserve for the mortal emperor to use me for his pleasure as a bedthing, only to be discarded when he found out what I was?" She stalks toward him, and he doesn't move, only flinches slightly as she presses a hand to his cheek. Her voice is softer when she continues: "Did you deserve it, my son? Did you deserve for your father to raise you in the shadows, scorning you for being a bastard of *his* creation? Did you deserve to be sentenced to death when he found out what I was, and what you were?" Her grip tightens; her nails, long, sharp, and crimson, dig into his skin. Yù'chén is still on his knees; he looks up at his mother in powerless supplication. "Never forget that this life you have right now is the one *I* gave you, twice over. One that *I* fought for and pulled from the clutches of the mortal emperor and his sword."

My mind is struggling to keep pace with all that is being shared. *Mortal emperor. Bastard.*

The story fits with what Yù'chén told me of his life—that he was born in the Kingdom of Rivers, that his father was mortal. He had simply never mentioned *who* his father was. *Who* his mother was.

My mother was his mistress.

When he found out what she was—and what I was . . . he tried to have us killed.

My head spins; the world seems to slow to a stop.

Yù'chén is the son of the late mortal emperor. A halfling son, heir to the throne of the Kingdom of Night . . . and the Kingdom of Rivers, by blood. Half brother to Hào'yáng . . . with a claim to the mortal realm.

"So tell her, my son," Sansiran finishes, her tone sharpened by cold rage and pure spite. She pulls her nails from his face and thrusts him away so that he is facing me. "Tell her what you have been here to do all along. Tell her how you have manipulated her mortal heart into trusting you. Tell her what you truly are, and see if she still claims to love you. *Tell her.*" Her voice amplifies, and I feel her tremendous magic shudder in the air as it wraps around Yù'chén.

He struggles for a moment as though with an invisible force; unlike me, he can fight off her magic, if only temporarily. I see it as it takes hold and he falls still, his eyes dulled, his tone hoarse and resigned. "My mother wished the mortal emperor to take her as his empress, and for me to be his heir. When he refused, she began the war." He swallows. "She killed him, but the mortal heir fled that night—saved by a man with ties to the immortals. Your father."

The mortal heir—Hào'yáng. My father escaped the capital with Hào'yáng . . . and gave him over to Shī'yǎ in the Kingdom of Sky, where he would remain safe and hidden from the war.

"She tracked down your father and learned that he had given the mortal heir into the protection of the Kingdom of Sky," Yù'chén continues.

"Oh, it was so difficult to wring that from him," Sansiran says. "He watched me drink his wife's soul rather than tell me. Then he proffered his own body." Her eyes flick to me. "It was only when I threatened his darling girls that he admitted I would never find the emperor's son, because he had put him in the one place I could not reach.

"Looking back, I should not have killed him out of anger," she sighs. "I had no choice but to bide my time and wait. I was certain that a mortal with ties to the Kingdom of Sky would have left a path for his offspring, too." She smiles sweetly at me. "I watched over you all these years, Àn'yīng.

I made sure you did not die. Not before you led us to the secret your father had kept."

I can't breathe. All those times I glimpsed her beneath the
plum blossom tree, that shadow waiting in the night, I dismissed as figments of my imagination. As hallucinations from
my trauma.

But the monster outside my window was real all along.

"I went through your father's journals," she continued,
"and I learned of a way into the Kingdom of Sky." She bares
her teeth. "The Immortality Trials: the only time the immortals would allow mortals to cross into their lands. I made sure
you found his journals and learned of the trials, too. By the
time you were old enough to attend them, so was my darling
son. When you finally left for the Kingdom of Sky, I sent him
after you; I told him to earn your trust, to capture your heart,
to do whatever he needed to do to find the emperor's son hiding among these immortals, and to break the wards that kept
us out. Wards that are impenetrable from the outside, yes . . .
but not so much from the inside."

I stare at Yù'chén. From the start, this was all a show. Everything he did was to deceive me into giving up Hào'yáng's
identity.

And he succeeded.

"I don't have what you want," Yù'chén says quietly. He
won't look at me, but his jaw locks as he looks up at his
mother. "I don't have the identity of the mortal heir."

Is he lying, or did he simply not realize what I spoke of
when I told him of the revolution Hào'yáng was planning?

Sansiran studies her son with a small smile. "You don't
have it, or you won't tell me? Answer me, my son."

In his silence, she moves so fast that I don't catch it. A

resounding *crack* echoes in the chamber as she brings her hand across his cheek. Tremors of dark magic emanate from her, forcing Yù'chén to fold in on himself. He hisses a breath as he rolls over on the floor. Blood darkens his lips.

Sansiran glances at me. "Fortunately, I knew my own son all too well. He is a fool, drawn to the weaknesses of his mortal heart. So I sent another to watch over him, in case he failed."

Realization dawns on me. "Yán'lù," I whisper.

"Unpredictable and violent," Sansiran says, her lips curling in disdain. "Greedy, too, for he believed he would be rewarded if he was the one to hand me the name of the heir. My second-in-command fathered him and warned me of his beastlike tendencies." She brushes at an invisible speck of dust on her sleeve, her fingers extended like claws, dark magic pouring from her in torrents. Sansiran barely looks at her son, writhing on the ground from the pain she inflicts on him, as she muses, "Better that he is dead, or I would have killed him myself. Perhaps there is reason to the Heavenly Order after all. Halflings *are* aberrations; there is no telling what monstrous traits they might harbor.

"But the halfling Yán'lù served his purpose," Sansiran continues. "From the start, unknown to my son, Yán'lù watched him and reported progress to me. He threatened you and tried to find out the identity of the mortal heir from you. He failed, but he gave me one crucial piece of information before his death."

I recall Yán'lù's last moments. The fight on the shore, the way my jade pendant lit up. The black bristle he conjured with his dark magic.

Who's watching over you? he'd asked from the very

beginning . . . and I had inadvertently given him the clue: my pendant.

Sansiran watches me with a small smile, as if she sees the thoughts running through my head. "Thank you for leading us to our victory," she says softly, and begins to cross the chamber to me. She is illuminated by the moon, so I catch the gleam of the jade pendant she pulls out of her sleeve. *My* jade pendant, the one secret I still hold that allows me to reach Hào'yáng.

The one I left behind in my chamber when I came to find Yù'chén.

"No," I whisper.

The demon queen bends to me. "Call to him," she says, and her smile is sweet as she slips the jade pendant back over my neck.

"No," I snarl. *"Never."*

She tips her head at me, eyebrows lifted. "No? I see. Well . . . what if my darling son asks?" she says, waving a hand toward where Yù'chén lies on the floor. The chamber fills with the hum of dark magic, trembling through the walls and rippling through the air, so powerful that the air echoes with the *cracks* of floorboards as they splinter.

Yù'chén tenses; his nails dig into the floor, and he squeezes his eyes shut.

"Go on, my son," Sansiran croons. "Beg her. Let her prove how much she cares for you."

She flexes her hand. Yù'chén's body arches, and finally, a sound breaks from him. It might have been a sob or a gasp. Blood drips in a steady stream from his lips as he chokes out, *"Please."*

I don't know whether he addresses this to me or to his mother. I'm shaking, too, but I clench my teeth against the plea at the tip of my tongue. He deserves this—I *know* he does—but it doesn't stop the ache in my heart as his voice rises to a scream.

Veins begin to darken his skin. His teeth sharpen into points, a forked tongue darting out between them. The whites to his eyes yield to black, leaving only a red, glowing pupil. Red-and-black scales bloom on his face as a horn twists from his forehead.

Sansiran flicks her wrist, and Yù'chén rises to his knees. She crooks her fingers, and her magic pulls his head up to face me, and I'm seeing him for the first time, his full demonic form that he has hidden from me for so long. His eyes—in their horrifying demonic form—are dull. His hair hangs before his face, from which a pair of red, pointed ears protrude. His teeth extend over his lips. His entire body is covered in red-and-black scales, his fingers grown thick and clawed.

There is nothing of his ethereal beauty left in his face. Like this, he is terrifying. Like this, he is the very image of the mó that have haunted my nightmares for nine years.

I know I must have flinched. And I know he must have seen it.

Yù'chén's gaze is fixed on a spot on the floor.

"Look at her, at the disgust on her face, my son," Sansiran purrs. "See how she would gladly watch you die for no reason other than what you are. She could never love a creature like you. You would do well to remember where your loyalties should lie."

With that, she flings him back down, relinquishing her

grasp on him. Slowly, Yù'chén's ragged pants steady; slowly, the claws retract and the scales vanish and the horns and ears shrink as he morphs back into the form of a human.

Yù'chén is very still. Moonlight glistens, wet, on his cheeks.

I hear every *clack* of Sansiran's silk slippers hitting the floor as she approaches. Feel the sting of her nails as she grips my face with her hands—the very hands that killed my father.

"Fine," she says, meeting my eyes. "*I'll ask.*" Her voice hardens, amplifies. "*Call him. Call the heir to the Kingdom of Rivers.*"

The air trembles with the magic of her command. It wraps around me, plunging through my veins and my mind. And I am determined to fight it with every ounce of my being.

Easily, her magic twines around my jaw and pries open my clenched teeth. It unlocks my throat, and I make a choked sound as it forces itself through my chest.

The magic tears me open. The words fall from my lips.

"Hào'yáng," I whisper to my jade pendant. "Help . . . me."

28

In the silence that follows, I feel my heartbeat pulsing inside me. The enormity of what I have done, of the consequences of my failure, presses down on me from all sides in the surrounding darkness.

I have courted the enemy. I have unconsciously *helped* a spy from the Kingdom of Night penetrate the Kingdom of Sky, meant to be a safe frontier from the mó invasion. And I have just summoned the surviving heir to the Kingdom of Rivers into the waiting claws of the enemy.

The jade pendant warms against my neck, for it has never failed—*he* has never failed. For nine years, the pendant and the boy inside it have been my salvation, the only piece of this world that has not abandoned me. Now, steadfastly and expectedly, it heats against my heart, confirming to me again what has become my very worst fear. I can still see Hào'yáng from earlier this afternoon, limned in the light against a backdrop of sunset skies and dancing petals. *I'm here now,* he told me.

Sansiran lifts the pendant from my neck. "Yù'chén," she

says, and with a flick of her fingers, he stirs. "Take her as you so wish. Keep her out of the way while I deal with the mortal heir."

"No," I whisper. "Please. You already have the mortal realm."

"Oh, but I don't," she replies. "I can only truly have it once I kill the mortal heir."

I think of the rumors of how, nine years after our kingdom fell, the mó have kept solely to the Imperial City. A rumor that Yù'chén himself confirmed to me.

Fú'yí's words come back to me in this moment: *It is because there is old magic in the bones of our land—magic as old as the Heavenly Order itself. It safeguards this kingdom for mortals. And it remembers who the true rulers of this realm are.*

I dismissed her ramblings as confusion, as the desperation of one who had begun to believe in fairy tales.

But what if there was truth to those words? The legends, after all, must come from somewhere.

When the gods created the realms, the dragons gave the first mortal emperor a drop of their blood. That power runs within us still, centuries later.

"No," I beg, but Sansiran is already turning away.

From across the room, Yù'chén glances at me. The blood on his face and whatever other wounds his mother inflicted on him are all gone, wiped clean with her dark magic. He is beautiful again, but the sight of his flushed cheeks and lips stirs my disgust. His face has closed off in that way it used to, so that I see only the hard, shadowed planes of his features, the dark red of his irises.

"Àn'yīng," he says harshly. "Come here."

His command flows through me, a familiar caress of

darkness I know intimately. I rise to my feet and approach him, yet with each step, I test the limits of his power. I can feel the difference now between the magic of a halfling and the magic of a demon queen. Sansiran's power bore the weight of mountains, useless for me to resist.

Yù'chén's is softer. Gentler. Almost as though . . . he doesn't mean it. I think of the past few times he compelled me, how I was distracted and not focused on resisting. But if I steel myself now . . .

I gather every ounce of my willpower and dig my heels in.

My next step falters. I glance down, then quickly up at him, and I see his gaze mirroring mine, darting from my feet to my face. He says nothing; only his arm snaps out, pulling me against him and flipping me around so my back is pressed to him and I'm watching the scene before us.

"*Be still,*" he says to me, and this time, his power is absolute, twining around my limbs, my ribs, my core, binding me to him. I have no choice but to remain frozen as his hand sweeps to my waist, his other to my arms, pinning me in place. His heartbeat thuds against his chest.

Halfling, it seems to remind me, and I find courage in that. Yù'chén is a half-mó; his power was not even enough to defeat a regular, full mó. If I resisted just now, I can do it again.

I wait for Sansiran to face the sliding doors before I try. Every muscle in my body strains. Then one finger twitches. My other hand gives a shake. Once more, and it might be enough to bend my wrist enough to flick out a crescent blade.

I hear Yù'chén swallow behind me; feel his fingers come to lace themselves with mine.

He twists my arm so hard that I cry out. His other hand pulls me tighter against him. He is rough, cruel, and nothing like the man who trailed kisses up my skin, who cradled my chin in his hands as if I were something breakable.

I know now how deep deception can go. And I will never make the same mistake of trusting him again.

"I *hate* you," I whisper, tears warming my eyes.

His voice is low, a rumble in his chest. "I know."

From beyond the doors of this chamber comes a burst of spirit energy in the night. It is an energy I am familiar with, one that conjures blue skies and white clouds, the radiance of the sun.

Hào'yáng is here. The heir to the Kingdom of Rivers, the child my father gave his life to protect, and my guardian in the jade who has in turn protected *me* all these years, is walking into a trap. Because of me.

Yù'chén has forbidden me to move, but he has not forbidden me to speak.

"*Hào'yáng!*" I scream. "Hào'yáng, don't come in! It's a trap—"

A palm clamps over my mouth, muffling my cries. "*Be silent,*" Yù'chén commands me, and I obey—but not before I sink my teeth into his flesh. I hear him curse, taste copper in my mouth, but I continue to bite down, and he does not move his hand away. His blood fills my mouth, drips down his wrist.

Another pulse of spirit energy, and the doors slam open.

Hào'yáng stands in the doorframe, his hair and uniform whipping in the wind. Spirit energy rolls through the chamber like thunder. His gaze immediately snaps to me across the room, then locks on Sansiran.

"You have summoned me," he says, his voice crackling like ice. "The rest of the Heavenly Army is not far behind. Unhand her."

Sansiran's smile stretches wide and red. Cold fear pierces my heart. I have seen that smile before—in the moments before she drank my mother's soul.

"That is quite all right," Sansiran says softly. "I'll be finished with you by the time they're here."

She strikes.

A flare of light arcs like the edge of a curved blade, so bright that I squeeze my eyes shut. When I look again, Hào'yáng's sword is out. A glow pulses from it, driving back the darkness of this chamber, the darkness emanating from Sansiran. An ancient power, strange and foreign and containing unimaginable depths, vibrates from Hào'yáng and his weapon. A rippling turquoise light fills the chamber, undulating against the walls as though we have fallen into the sea.

Sansiran hisses and throws up her arm. Behind me, Yù'chén staggers slightly from the sheer force of Hào'yáng's spirit energy. His magic wavers; his grip almost slips, but I go careening backward with him. We crash into the wall. He makes a pained noise and lifts his hands, and I notice his fingers and palms blistering beneath the light emanating from Hào'yáng's blade.

I take my chance. I ram my elbow into his ribs and hear him grunt; I manage to shift my legs just slightly, almost enough to swipe my feet at his ankles.

"Such a neat toy the immortals have gifted you," Sansiran snarls at Hào'yáng. A pulse of her power thrums across the chamber. His light—his sword's light—flickers.

"Wrong," Hào'yáng replies, but I hear the strain in his voice. "This isn't from the immortals."

"No matter who it's from," the demon queen purrs, "you're *finished*."

I shout as a coil of dark magic whips out from behind Hào'yáng. He hears my cry and pivots, lifting his sword just in time. The shadows ram into him, driving him to his knees.

When Sansiran raises her hand again, Hào'yáng is vulnerable.

This time, her darkness meets a light brighter than the sun.

Warmth fills me, seeping through my veins into my core. At the same time, the chamber reverberates with the sheer magnitude of the new magic. Sansiran screams; Yù'chén moans in pain. The mó, I realize, are affected by immortals' magic in a way that I am not. His hands slide from me as he falls to his knees; I go down with him, our limbs tangled and his arms heavy against my shoulders. His magic falters and dissipates, releasing me from its hold.

The light in the chamber dims to reveal a silhouette within.

Shī'yǎ stands before Hào'yáng. Instead of her lotus flower, she now holds a sword that glimmers petal-pink, the hilt a deep leaf green. Power radiates from it in waves, as inexorable as the heat of the sun, flooding the room. Shī'yǎ's expression is calm, her eyes belying nothing but still waters.

"Demon Queen Sansiran," she says gently, but somehow, her voice seems to echo. "Your reputation precedes you."

Sansiran's lips curl. "As does yours," she replies coldly, "Yī'lín Shī'yǎ, the mortal-lover."

Shī'yǎ only blinks slowly. "The Heavenly Army will arrive at any minute. The High Court has been alerted. Take your army and retreat now, Sansiran, before it's too late."

"Not until I have what's mine, Yī'lín Shī'yǎ," the demon queen growls. "For so long, the immortals have taken the glory and respect across the realms, dictating the Heavenly Order and the laws across the kingdoms. The mó have been vilified, so much so that even a mere mortal emperor refuses to show respect to his own son and rightful heir!"

"There is much to the Heavenly Order that should be changed," Shī'yǎ says steadily, "but waging war against an entire realm is not the way, Sansiran."

"Do not stand there with your holier-than-thou attitude and preach to me when you have benefited from the very structure that gives you and your kind the most privilege!" Sansiran's voice rises with the static in the room, the frenzied way the shadows shift. As the demon queen's magic explodes, Shī'yǎ counters with a shield of her own. The sheer power in the chamber rams into me, choking me. I can't breathe. I can't see.

The room shifts; I feel the wall against my back, and suddenly, a shadow falls over me. The unbearable pain and power dim.

Yù'chén stands between me and the battle. His entire face is contorted in pain, but he props himself up, hands splayed against the wall on either side of my head. Shielding me from the painful, overwhelming clash of magic. Blood drips down his nose, and ichor darkens his veins.

For a moment, I only stare at him, confusion giving me pause. *Why?*

Then his gaze meets mine, shaking me from my stupor, and I know what I must do.

When I reach for my blades, Heart slides into my hand. I remember now that it is Yù'chén who placed my crescent blades back in their sheaths one by one.

I angle the dagger, and I thrust.

I mean to pierce his chest, to where his heart beats. I mean to kill him.

But I made a fatal mistake in selecting Heart, and in allowing my own heart to take charge.

Halfway through my strike, the blade changes direction. It is subtle, just a slight shift in the angle, but it makes all the difference in the world.

The tip of my blade meets Yù'chén's skin, an inch away from his heart. And it slows, pulled back by my own traitorous will.

Yù'chén's hand snaps out. His fingers wrap around mine, around the hilt of my crescent blade.

There is a split second, a half breath, between when he grips my hands tightly in his and when my blade pierces his flesh. A fraction of a moment when he could have stopped me.

I feel resistance—but only in the form of metal slicing through flesh, sliding between bone, and coming to pierce the soft, slick texture of his lungs.

Yù'chén exhales, his breath wet. Blood dribbles down his chin, splattering onto our joined hands; onto his fingers, wrapped around mine; onto mine, wrapped around the hilt of the crescent blade. His body pitches forward and his head slumps, thudding against the wall. I feel his body against mine, the heat of his blood, the shallow hitches to his breathing. His hands tremble as he draws shuddering breaths.

And I think . . . I think I hear him whisper a word:

"*Go.*"

Behind us, Sansiran screams.

Shadows wrap around me, and the next moment, I'm dangling in the air. Sansiran's magic tightens over me, rushing up my nose and my lips, suffocating me. The pain is the worst I have ever felt: as though my skin is peeling from me and my bones are melting from within, as though ten thousand daggers pierce my flesh. I hear my own scream reverberating inside my skull, and another voice echoes in my ears.

"*You dare threaten the life of my heir,*" Sansiran snarls at me. "*I will destroy you so that your bones burn and scatter as ashes.*"

"*No!*"

This time, though, the cry comes from a familiar figure: Shī'yǎ.

Warmth envelops me. The pain lessens, and the darkness retreats, yielding to a lambent light. I feel I am drifting, but the surroundings of the chamber are gradually returning to me. When I look up, it is as though the world has cleaved into night and day.

Sansiran's darkness, which shackled me, has broken. A shield of light shimmers between me and the dark magic, emanating from Shī'yǎ. Her teeth are clenched, her expression is tight—and her magic wavers. Sparks fall like ashes as her shield begins to dissolve, swallowed bit by bit by Sansiran's encroaching darkness.

Hands wrap around my shoulders. Hào'yáng crouches next to me, his sword pulsing that blue light of ocean waves I saw earlier. As he draws me under the cover of its magic, the pain recedes and my head clears.

"Hold on to me," he says, and with one hand around my waist, he lifts me, supporting me as I find my footing.

Somehow, we make it to the doors. I glance back one more time. Beneath Shī'yǎ's fading light and Sansiran's growing darkness, Yù'chén is slumped against the wall where I left him. His chest rises and falls in shallow breaths, and veins spiderweb across his skin as his dark magic counters the wound I gave him. His hand is on the hilt of Heart. His gaze never leaves me.

I turn away and hold on to Hào'yáng as we stumble outside, into the gardens of rock and water and chrysanthemums. The clear night air fills my lungs—but instead of silence and stillness, the courtyard *writhes* with movement. Beings that are not immortal guards or candidates stalk through the trees and between the pillars of the open-air pavilions.

The mó army is here, in the Kingdom of Sky.

Hào'yáng lets go of me. "Defend us," he tells me. His spirit energy stirs as he begins to conjure a talisman.

A demon appears at his side, lunging at us.

I greet it with my blades. The tip of Poison tears a gash across the mó's chest. As he stumbles back, stunned, I follow through by driving Striker into his core. His cry of pain is disturbingly human, and I can't help but think of Yù'chén and his hands around mine as I cut my blade through him. The sound he made, the way his body twitched against me.

I rip Striker through the mó's chest. He—*it*—dissolves into shadows and smoke. The last to go are its red eyes.

The next one is on me before I can draw a breath. I spin, my body in overdrive, adrenaline fueling my every slash, every duck, every move.

There's a trilling sound behind me. A spark shoots into the skies and blooms like a firework, showering the courtyard with gold illumination. Hào'yáng's talisman flares brightly in the night, strands of light weaving into a sun over clouds: the symbol of the Kingdom of Sky.

A distress signal.

Hào'yáng places two fingers in his mouth and whistles.

Then he turns and he's moving, his sword flashing, a deep blue light in the darkness. I have trained with him, but I have never truly seen him in action. He is *incredible*. I didn't think a mortal could fight as he does, as though not only his body but his entire soul as well moves to the rhythm of his sword. Spirit energy sings from him, so powerful that it creates flashes of gold in the night as he clashes with demons.

I place myself behind him. We are in this together, our bodies in tune with each other's movements, as if we are melodies of the same song, threads of the same tapestry, two souls with the same fate, winding together.

But Sansiran's spell has weakened me. My legs shake, and my slashes slow in spite of everything I throw into the fight. And the mó—they keep coming, all emerging from the direction of the Celestial Gardens. From the gates Yù'chén created.

The next mó ducks my blade and rams me into the ground. Its face, in the form of a young man's, is frenzied with blood-lust as it sinks its teeth into my shoulder.

Striker finds the mó's stomach just as Hào'yáng drives his sword through its core. He rips the mó off me and holds out his hand. I take it, and he pulls me up, his hand steady on my waist as he supports me.

Behind him, something shimmers in the night. Small at first, but growing larger as it weaves through the stars and plunges down toward us.

A snowy dragon lands right in front of us, scales glimmering white. Ancient, powerful magic clings to its body like frost, sending the mó around us scattering. As the dragon turns its large brown eyes to us and gives a shake of its ocean-colored mane, I realize I know her.

It's Meadowsweet—in her dragon form.

Hào'yáng pulls me to her. "Hold on to me," he says, throwing his legs over the dragonhorse. "I need to get Shī'yǎ."

I settle over the dragonhorse's back and grab onto Hào'yáng's waist. Despite the scales and the heaving muscles of the serpentine body beneath us, this is familiar: me holding on to Hào'yáng as Meadowsweet takes us through the skies.

"Shī'yǎ is still inside," Hào'yáng tells the dragonhorse.

She huffs, steam curling from her nostrils as she bares her teeth. Then she plunges forward.

The world rushes by, night and ichor and stars, until we burst through the doors of the healing chamber.

The darkness is overwhelming. It roils from Sansiran as though she is an endless well, an abyss. She is aglow, as though moonlight spills from her, outlining the red of her eyes and lips, that garnet at her neck and her imperial robes.

Shī'yǎ's hands are thrown up before her. The circle of light has shrunk to envelop just her body. There is a crease between her brows, which I have never seen before.

Sansiran fists her hands. Her magic shifts, the darkness sharpening into a blade.

Hào'yáng shouts, but it's too late. Sansiran's magic strikes, piercing what is left of Shī'yǎ's shield. The immortal lets out a cry that tears through the night.

Watching her fall is like watching a blossom fall from a tree. Time seems to slow as Shī'yǎ's body arcs, graceful even in her pain. That ethereal glow haloing immortals flickers for a moment, and then begins to drift from her like ashes.

Sansiran's face is alight in triumph even as Meadowsweet circles behind Shī'yǎ, even as Hào'yáng catches her in his arms. The demon queen whirls, aiming a bolt of her lethal power at Hào'yáng—but Meadowsweet deftly ducks it as she pivots for the door.

"*This is the end.*" Sansiran's voice echoes behind us, amplifying, her darkness seeming to wrap claws into us as we soar toward the light. "*My army has arrived. The wards to the Kingdom of Sky are falling. We will hunt you to the ends of the realms.*"

We burst free into the night, the white dragonhorse's back rippling as she canters for the Hall of Radiant Sun. I hold on tightly to her, to Hào'yáng.

In his arms, Shī'yǎ's light dims, sparks of it trailing off like a dying star.

29

The grounds near the Hall of Radiant Sun are a flurry of movement. The night skies are filled with streaks of light—immortal guards and warriors astride clouds, descending upon the mó on the ground. Already, sounds of sword-fights and battle ring out.

We circle around to the back of the hall, where the bridge splits off to the immortals' residences in the clouds. As we plunge through the layers, our vision becomes a blur of fog and shadows. I reach for my blades, waiting for monsters with teeth and red eyes to appear—but the dragon seems to know where she's going.

The clouds clear. An island appears, adrift among the stars, large enough for a single courtyard house. The first thing that strikes me is the great cherry tree that spirals from its center, flowering branches reaching for the moon. A stone bridge arcs over a pond, and the curved eaves of tiled roofs appear as we circle lower. Flowing drapes ripple gently in the

wind, stirred by our presence when we alight on the rosewood patio.

Hào'yáng carries Shī'yǎ into the house. I can't help paus-
ing at the sight of the peaceful courtyard, at the cherry tree
whose flowers fractal into the sky, petals brushing against
stars. Something stirs in me—a strange feeling of destiny, of
foreboding, of a secret tangled between its roots that I am
about to unearth.

I hurry after Hào'yáng into a room. Besides a cherrywood
bed, on which he has laid his mother, and bookcases filled
with tomes, the chambers are simple. A waterway trickles
in from the outside, pooling into a small pond at the center.
Blush lotuses drift on its surface, and I realize this must be
Shī'yǎ's house.

"Niáng'qīn." Hào'yáng's voice is gentle. It is the first time
I have heard him address her as "Honorable Mother," and
there is something so profoundly tender to the gesture. He
kneels by her bed, one hand on the hilt of his sword, the other
clasping the immortal's. "Rest. I am here."

Shī'yǎ murmurs something, and Hào'yáng turns to me.
"Àn'yīng," he says, "she would like to see you."

As I approach, my alarm grows. The immortal bears a gash
across the center of her chest. From within spills a glow from
a core so bright that to look at it is like attempting to look
into the sun. *An immortal's core*, I think, my stomach tightening. The light that bleeds from it scatters into this realm and
dissolves even as I watch.

I know immortals cannot die, at least not in the mortal
sense. If fatally wounded, they reincarnate without any of the
memories or powers they once held. Their experiences and

lives may differ, but their souls are one and the same: permanent in the endless churn of realms and time.

Shī'yǎ's gaze is dim, but it brightens as I kneel by her side. I bow my head. "Honorable Immortal, you asked for me."

"Àn'yīng," she murmurs, and I startle at the tender way she says my name. "Look at me."

I obey. One look at her face from this close and I understand the stories of lovesick mortals spending their lives searching for their immortal lovers. She is more radiant than words can describe. Yet the golden glow that thrums within her skin flickers as her brows crease in pain.

She holds out a hand. Her core glows brighter, and strands of light begin to interweave on her palm, condensing into a shimmering, pearl-like object.

The immortal meets my gaze. "For your mother," she whispers.

The world falls away as my gaze homes in on that small, sparkling speck on her palm, no larger than my pinkie nail. It pulses with spirit energy, with magic, and I know instinctively what it is.

A pill of immortality. The cure for Mā I have sought for nine years.

"Honorable Immortal." My voice shakes. "I cannot—"

"Take it," Shī'yǎ breathes.

"Niáng'qīn," Hào'yáng says quietly, "what are you doing?"

Shī'yǎ turns her gaze to him. "My spirit energy has withdrawn from my blood to my core in order to heal the wound there. In my current state, only a piece of my core will be strong enough to serve as a pill of immortality."

Hào'yáng's brows pull together in confusion. "If you give away a part of your core, you may not reincarnate."

"Hào'yáng, my son," she murmurs, and his eyes soften at this. The immortal takes her sword, which has transformed back into a pink lotus flower, and holds it out to him. "You know what this is. You know what to do."

"Niáng'qīn. I need you, for the rebellion." Hào'yáng's hands close around his adopted mother's, but he does not take the lotus.

Shī'yǎ smiles faintly. "Son of my heart," she says gently, "I have lived many lifetimes—too many to count, for one who began her life in these realms as a mortal. Mortals desire the eternal life that we immortals are blessed with, yet they never know how much we envy the one lifetime they have. Immortality is long, my son, and it is lonely and cold in these skies. We gaze upon the mortal world, aching for the warmth of a fire and food on the table, for the laughter of a family huddled together, for the burning love of a lifetime that never fades."

My throat knots, and I recall Yù'chén's words: *Why is it in our natures to want that which we cannot have?*

Shī'yǎ turns to look at me. "I have known one great love in my long life," she murmurs, and I am suddenly frozen, a slow and impossible realization beginning to grip me. "I am fortunate to have those I care for by my side in these moments. Son of my heart, daughter of my blood, know that my love for you is greater than anything else in these realms. Treasure each other."

Hào'yáng's gaze snaps to me, and I see the open shock on his face. His lips part, and he says something, but I can't hear it.

All of a sudden, the fragmented, broken pieces of my life fall into place. My father's secrets, the writing on the handkerchief, the reason he chose me, and the reason I am alive today. How I survived that fall into the ocean during the First

Trial; how my body carried me through the trauma of the Second and Third. My name, Àn'yīng, the cherry blossom in the dark, and the very tree that sits in Shī'yǎ's courtyard.

Shī'yǎ presses the gleaming pill of immortality into my hand and closes her fingers around mine. "Know that you have the love of more than one mother: the one who gave birth to you and the one who raised you." She squeezes my hand. "You can still save her."

I hold her fingers in my trembling ones as I search for traces of my face in hers. Mā always told me I took after my father when I was growing up, yet now I find in Shī'yǎ's countenance the curve of my nose, the shape of my cheeks, the taper to my jaw. My face is less refined, a shadow of hers, the way pond water might wish to capture the full beauty of the stars.

"Àn'yīng," she says softly, my name like song on her lips. Her gaze turns to the cherry tree outside her window, radiant in the darkness, in the moonlight. "The cherry blossom in the dark. You were named for both your mothers, did you know?" She heaves a breath, and when she speaks again, the weight of the past twenty years seems to unspool from her. A story half-forgotten, the missing parts now pieced together. "When your father returned with you to the mortal realm, it was in the thick of winter. It began to snow heavily as he sought shelter from the endless forest."

As she speaks, it is as though a memory plays in my mind— one Bà and Mā have told me countless times over. *It was in the thick of a blizzard, and your father thought he was lost.*

"The blizzard was worsening, and the temperature plummeting. Your father was afraid he would lose not only his life but that of his newborn daughter as well."

Then he saw, in the snow, the bright blossoms.

"That was when he spotted a blossoming tree in the blinding snow. He staggered up to it and found a house. The woman who opened the door was kind. She asked no questions about him, only wrapped his newborn in swathes of beautifully embroidered blankets and fed her warm goat's milk." Shī'yǎ smiles faintly. "What your father thought would be a short stay . . . turned into a lifetime."

The answer to my name; the mistake behind the plum tree standing before our house and my name, the cherry blossom.

My eyes heat, because I now understand the sacrifice both women have made for me. Mā, who took me and raised me and loved me as though I were her own. And my birth mother, who has quietly watched over me all these years.

"Why did he leave you?" I whisper. *Why did you let me go?*

Shī'yǎ's lashes flutter. "The Heavenly Order forbade us from remaining together. Your father was given a choice: take the pill of immortality and remain in the Kingdom of Sky forever . . . or leave, never to return. He was the most honorable man I knew, Àn'yīng, and he had come through the trials in order to share his knowledge with practitioners of the mortal realm. He chose his kingdom." She pauses to draw a labored breath. "Your father and I did not wish you to grow up here, facing a life of ostracism and hostility, so we made the decision that you would be raised far away, in the mortal realm." A single tear shimmers at the corner of her eye, pooling like a pearl. Slowly, it slides down her cheek. "Know that it was not for a lack of love. I loved your father and you more than I have loved anything else in this long life I have lived."

There is so much I need to say, yet nothing comes to mind as Shī'yǎ—my birth mother—moves Hào'yáng's hand to mine. She presses them together. The glow coming from the open wound in her chest is dimming; the sparks grow sparser.

"Ǎn'yīng carries my title," she whispers. "No matter how tenuous it is . . . she holds that right to the High Court. Hào'yáng, you understand . . . you must finish this." She looks at both of us, at our joined hands. "The key to taking back the Kingdom of Rivers . . . is with the two of you. *Together.*"

"Niáng'qīn." Hào'yáng is so tense, I realize, his knuckles white against mine. "I will search for you across the realms. I will not stop looking for you—I will *never* stop."

"Promise me," Shī'yǎ breathes. Her core is embers and ashes now. "Promise me you'll stay with each other."

And because I have nothing else to give, I give my word. "I promise."

"I promise," Hào'yáng echoes.

Shī'yǎ closes her eyes. The last light of her core flickers and dies, and as the radiance begins to drain from her skin, she starts to fade. Hào'yáng holds very still, both of us gripping her hands until they dissolve from between our fingers.

"Niáng'qīn, wait for me," he says, his voice breaking. "I will find you. *Niáng!*"

But she is gone. On the silks of her bed, there is nothing but a faint warmth and the fragrance of lotuses, carried away by the wind. Hào'yáng's and my hands remain clasped together, palm to palm, fingers interlaced now that Shī'yǎ's are no longer here.

Between our hands sit the last items our mother left us. Her magic lotus, pulsing gently with enchantment and power . . . and, in my palm, as round as a bead, is the pill of immortality she gifted me. The one that will save Mā's life.

Outside, from beyond the cover of clouds, come flashes of bright light and sounds of battle, dulled by the wards around Shī'yǎ's courtyard house.

Hào'yáng and I sit very still in the now-empty chambers. And though I have the answers to the questions I have been asking my entire life, I have never felt more lost. I am daughter to an immortal and a mortal: a halfling that should not be in existence, according to the Heavenly Order.

And my birth mother, on her deathbed, has asked the impossible of me. *I* have agreed to the impossible: to enlist in a rebellion against one of the most powerful realms in existence, against a demon queen who was able to slay one of the Eight Immortals.

When I first began this journey, I was just a mortal girl, fighting for a way to save my mother's life. Now . . . the enormity of the truth threatens to crush me.

"Àn'yīng."

I blink. Hào'yáng's voice pulls me back, grounds me in the present. He kneels by my side, one hand still outstretched on the cooling silks. As he lifts his gaze to mine, the unguarded grief in them hits me harder than any of my own fears. He has always been the infallible warrior, the captain of the guard, the heir to our kingdom—cool and collected and unbreakable. But now . . . now, he looks just as lost as I am.

I wonder if this was how he felt nine years ago, when his father died and his kingdom fell. I had my family, at least; I had Méi'zi and the hope of rescuing Mā all these long years. But Hào'yáng has had only Shī'yǎ. And now she is gone, too.

He seems to gather himself in the span of a few heartbeats. The grief in his eyes vanishes, the walls go up, and his features settle into that practiced blankness I have seen him wear like a shield.

"You should take the pill home to your mother," Hào'yáng says, and he pulls his hands back from mine. My fingers are cold where his once were. "That is why you were competing in the Immortality Trials in the first place. I know how much your family means to you. I know you committed to fighting with us to restore the Kingdom of Rivers . . . but now that we've lost Lady Shī'yǎ, things will change. It will be much, much harder. So . . ." He exhales. "I understand if you need to reconsider."

He looks away. His expression is indecipherable, his stance neutral, but I have since learned to look beyond them. I observe the tightness of his shoulders, the way he clasps his hands together so that his knuckles are white. And I recognize all too well the pain he quietly hides under an armor of steel. I know the signs, because they are a mirror to my life over the past nine years, hiding my pain beneath the armor I've built to survive.

Promise me you'll stay with each other.

I know the answer—I know what it has always been, since I was a child clinging to the broken piece of jade in the aftermath of Sansiran's destruction of my realm and my family. I know where I am meant to be and what I am meant to do.

The path I was born to walk.

I pull Hào'yáng to me and wrap my arms around him, breathing in his scent, of sunlight on river water, of meadowsweet on the beach. My guardian in the jade.

"I'm here now," I whisper to him. "Every step of the way, Hào'yáng."

He stiffens, as if he does not know how to react to someone else's touch. But as I hold on to him, our heartbeats whiling away the seconds, something shifts. His arms fall against my back, his cheek comes to rest on my shoulder, and he holds me, truly holds me, for the first time since we met.

I close my eyes. I am ten years old again, small and frightened and alone, left to fend for myself in this world with a voice that spoke to me through the jade. I have imagined this moment for so long. In my arms, I hold my boy in the jade.

Hào'yáng draws back. There is something unrestrained to the way he gazes at me now. His hand comes to touch my temple, just a feather's brush, before his expression closes off and he straightens. "We need to get back to the Hall of Radiant Sun," he says, his tone steeling as he shifts back into the warrior. The heir.

"The candidates," I say. "I have to go help them." I know that in the chaos, no one will be looking out for them; I know they will be as trapped as fish in a net, waiting for their deaths. Lì'líng, Tán'mù—I haven't seen them since before the Second Trial, which was just several days ago, but it feels like an eternity. An ache blooms in my throat as I think of the memorial banquet the immortals held, of my friends finding out about the loss of Fán'xuān in that manner.

"Go," I tell Hào'yáng. "You're needed at the Hall of Radiant Sun, with the immortals."

Carefully, he tucks Shī'yǎ's lotus into the pouch at his belt and holds out his hand to me. Together, we stand. "I'm coming with you, Àn'yīng," he says. "I am not losing you again."

I count my blades as we stride from Shī'yǎ's chambers. I

am down three already: Heart, I realize, I have left behind with Yù'chén.

I grit my teeth and force my thoughts away from the fact that he is alive, away from the moment I could have killed him yet my blade and my traitorous heart spoke otherwise. Away from the moment when he could have stopped me . . . but he didn't.

Hào'yáng casts a last glance around Shī'yǎ's chambers, now achingly empty. A look of deep sorrow passes over his face before he turns away and strides out. I, too, linger before I follow him, wondering if there were any other clues to my father's first love that the immortal left behind in her chambers. Wondering if I'll ever know their full story.

Meadowsweet awaits us in the courtyard beneath the flowering cherry tree in her dragon form. The legends describe dragons as taller than mountains, as long as the great rivers that wind through our lands. Meadowsweet is the size of a large horse. The way Hào'yáng treats her, as if they are partners and equals, makes me wonder how they came to find each other.

Hào'yáng glances at me as though he can read my thoughts. "Her real name is She of the Moon-Frosted Sea," he tells me. "A mouthful, so she likes Meadowsweet."

I slide onto the dragonhorse's back and wrap my arms around Hào'yáng. As we soar into the clouds toward the Hall of Radiant Sun, the sounds of battle grow loud. Bright flashes of light penetrate the mist, and in the distance, I hear screams.

With a *whoosh*, the Sea of Clouds ends, and we are cantering above the Temple of Dawn, spiraling down toward the Candidates' Courtyard. As we draw closer, I make out figures locked in battle: candidates against the mó army that has slipped into our courtyard looking for easy prey.

As Meadowsweet lands, the mó draw back with hisses. The candidates nearby pause to gape at the dragonhorse in awe.

Hào'yáng grabs my hand. "We can't take all the candidates, Àn'yīng."

"We can clear a path to the mortal realm," I reply. "A path for them to live."

He hesitates, glancing toward the Hall of Radiant Sun. "I have to fight."

"No, you don't," I tell him.

"I'm the captain—"

"There are too many mó. The Heavenly Army is either here or on their way. One warrior in their ranks won't make a difference." I pause. "But you are the key to saving the Kingdom of Rivers."

He gives me a long look.

"This isn't your fight, Hào'yáng," I say softly. "Your path has always led back to the mortal realm."

The echo of his adopted mother's words seems to settle his decision. Hào'yáng cuts an assessing look at the battle around us. "The Immortals' Steps will be blocked," he muses. "The mó are attacking the wards at the front of the Temple of Dawn . . . there's no way we'll all get through."

My grip tightens on my blades, and I think of a moonlit walk, an ocean in the night. If the mó are congregating at the Hall of Radiant Sun . . . that might just leave us a path out.

"I know a way," I say quietly.

Hào'yáng doesn't question me. He only nods.

"*I will help,*" comes a voice like bells chiming. It's Meadow-sweet, watching us with her large brown eyes. She blows a puff of steam through her nose.

"Àn'yīng!" comes a cry. I turn and my heart soars. Tán'mù charges toward me; by her side is a familiar small white fox—Lì'líng.

I shout their names; we clasp hands, and for a moment, I feel as though things will be all right.

Almost.

We have always been four. Our friend's absence is conspicuous. I realize we will never again all be together; never again have one of those golden afternoons in the pavilion by the water, watching cherry blossoms dance in the breeze.

"Fán'xuān," I whisper, an ache deep in my chest.

In a blink, Lì'líng is back in her human form. The sorrow on her face is heartbreaking; her wide amber eyes fill with tears, which fall like raindrops. "He's in a better place," she whispers, moving to twine her fingers with Tán'mù's. "His next life will be one of joy. Of freedom, of endless blue skies and clear waters."

Tán'mù looks away sharply. "That bastard Yán'lù," she breathes. "I'm glad he's dead." Her eyes narrow. "The next time I see Yù'chén, I'll kill him myself."

I don't tell her that I almost did. That I had the chance and missed it.

"Help me round up the candidates," I say instead. "We'll follow the dragonhorse through a gate back to the mortal realm—I know a way. This is not our battle; at least, not one we can win."

They both nod at me and run off, corralling the fighting candidates. There are only a handful left who have survived the Kingdom of Night's attack. I turn away from the bodies littering the ground and focus on the path ahead.

"Everyone's here, Àn'yīng," Tán'mù pants. Lì'líng has returned to her fox form; she gives a little yip of approval.

My heart tightens as I scan the group. There are about twelve of us left, a fraction of the forty-four who came here seeking shelter, safety, and a better life.

Hào'yáng nods at me. His sword gleams as he angles it and turns to the candidates. "Stick together," he calls. "We'll follow Àn'yīng and Meadowsweet. Form a tight circle and fight any mó that try to attack."

"Everyone here can walk on water, right?" I ask, and receive nods from the candidates. "Good. You'll need to."

As the candidates cluster together into formation, I ready my blades and step up next to Hào'yáng. "Stay with me," I say.

"Lead the way," he replies, falling into step by my side.

We break into a run. Though the battle largely takes place near the Hall of Radiant Sun, the Temple of Dawn has become overrun with mó roaming its grounds. Several charge our group; together, with Meadowsweet, we fend them off.

The Celestial Gardens are dark tonight. Branches cast shadows like claws, scratching the fabric of my clothes as we pass. I know I'm going the right way when clouds begin to seep into the grass as we near the edge of the island. The sound of running water emerges between the trees, and when we round a great willow, I see the waterfall . . . and the open gate.

I remember the last time I was here, with Yù'chén. How his hands wrapped around me, how he led me in a dance across a midnight sea.

How everything was a lie.

It's deserted here; my guess was true. The demon army is

closing in on the Hall of Radiant Sun, leaving the perimeters of the Temple of Dawn deserted.

The candidates gather between the willows. The rippling, iridescent wards rise into the skies ahead; before us, glowing and too bright, are the scorpion lilies that form an open archway leading to an entire other realm.

"What is that?" Hào'yáng asks quietly. The blossoms reflect a harsh red light on his face.

I swallow. "Dark magic." My voice is barely a whisper.

He looks at me but doesn't question me. If he knows that I have betrayed his trust with this secret, he says nothing.

"That gate opens into the ocean below, to the mortal realm," I tell everyone. "It isn't far from land. You'll have to jump."

"*I will fly down first,*" Meadowsweet says, her voice echoing. "*I await you all below.*" She splashes into the river, her serpentine body rippling. Then, almost as though she is part of the water, she slithers forward and vanishes over the edge.

"Àn'yīng and I will go last," Hào'yáng tells the waiting candidates, "to make sure everyone gets through safely. Who is first?"

"We are," comes a crisp, sweet voice. From between the trees, Lǐ'líng steps forward, her hand tightly clasped in Tán'mù's. She glances at the other girl, and her eyes light up and soften at the same time. "Together."

Tán'mù nods. "Together. See you on the other side, Àn'yīng."

"May the winds be with you," I reply.

My heart is in my throat as I watch my friends wade to the edge of the waterfall. In the darkness, I imagine a third person by their side, his shock of white hair shifting into the feathers of a white heron or the scales of a carp. I think of his easy grin, how his green eyes never lost their light, even given his past. Perhaps it is those who have experienced darkness who can shine brightest.

Still holding hands, Lì'líng and Tán'mù cast one more glance back at me. An errant wind stirs their hair, Lì'líng's white dress, and Tán'mù's black robes.

Then they turn, leap—and vanish.

The rest of the candidates go, in pairs or threes, and soon, only Hào'yáng and I remain. He looks at me, then back at the embattled temple. There is a glint of grief at the edge of his lips that only the moonlight can draw out. He moves and it's gone, and he's sheathing his sword and turning to me.

Hào'yáng holds out his hands to me. "Together," he says softly.

I reach for him. Our fingers interlock, and as he pulls me toward him, I think of my jade pendant, of how my path has always led to him.

"Together," I echo.

We step to the edge of the waterfall—and that is when I sense the presence behind us.

I turn.

From beneath the shadows of a blossoming cherry tree, a familiar figure steps out. I'd have recognized his red cloak and his wild spill of hair anywhere.

Yù'chén's sword glimmers in his hand. The gash in his shift I made with my blade is still there, and I catch a sliver of his pale stomach underneath—healed. He does not move to hurt me or to stop me. He only stands, watching me with the unnatural stillness of a mó.

Steel rings out in the night as Hào'yáng draws his sword.

The motion jars me into action; I flick my crescent blades into my hands. This time, I will not miss.

Even from here, I can make out the red in Yù'chén's eyes and how, in the darkness, they suddenly ripple with an emotion I cannot decipher. His knuckles whiten against the hilt of his sword.

"Go," he says quietly to me. "Go with him."

For some reason, I can't bring myself to move.

"Go!" Yù'chén's voice cracks. *"Go, before I change my mind!"*

With a fluid stroke, Hào'yáng sheathes his sword and takes my arm, tipping us off the edge. The last I see of Yù'chén is his face split by shadows and moonlight, the black veins pulsing beneath his skin, and the crimson of his eyes, on me.

Hào'yáng and I fall through the night.

Back into the mortal realm.

30

We reach land sometime in the ghost hours of the night: rocky shores overgrown with pines and mulberry trees. I know in my bones we are back in the mortal realm; there is dirt and grime, the trees are imperfect and crooked, and the landscape lacks the ethereal perfection and soft radiance of the immortal realm. Here, everything is duller in color, solid and still and dusty.

Real, whispers a voice in my head.

I shake it off, the memory of Yù'chén dissolving into the darkness.

The candidates are exhausted. With Yán'lù gone, the remainder of the candidates are quiet and cooperative. There is an air of camaraderie, of mutual interest, between us, now that we are no longer competing in the trials—now that we are all equally prey.

Now that another realm might fall.

Deep in the forest, when we are certain we are far enough from the borders of the Kingdom of Sky, we stop. We agree on taking shifts so we can rest: Lì'líng and Tán'mù take first watch. Meadowsweet, back in her form as a white horse, settles down by Lì'líng's side, and the girl snuggles against the dragonhorse. Tán'mù leans against a tree. Her face is drawn with exhaustion, but she gazes at Lì'líng with tenderness.

I turn to Hào'yáng. His hand is on the hilt of his sword, and he faces the direction of the ocean, toward the night skies and the clouds beyond which sits his home of nearly ten years. He catches me watching him and says, "You should rest."

I'd like nothing more than to sleep, but my mind is buzzing from all that has happened. "I should," I agree.

"But you can't," he finishes for me.

I shake my head.

"Walk with me," he says.

I fall into step by his side. Out of habit, my hand strays to my collarbone to touch my jade pendant—and I realize it's gone.

Panic rises, sharp against my throat. Hào'yáng casts me a swift look.

I swallow. It's silly, since I know I will no longer need it, but I somehow feel unmoored without its familiar weight against my chest. "My jade pendant," I explain to Hào'yáng. "I left it back at the Temple of Dawn."

Hào'yáng's gaze flicks to the hollow of my throat. Then, wordlessly, he reaches up and slips off his own pendant and proffers it to me.

"I won't need it any longer," he says, reading my silence. "You're here now. Take mine if it lends you comfort."

His half of the jade pendant glimmers as I take it and tie it around my neck. It settles against my throat, still warm. I curl my fingers around it, rubbing a thumb against its unfamiliar edges—edges that are a perfect complement to my own pendant. "Thank you."

Slivers of the skies show through the canopy of fine willow leaves, and the salty tang of the ocean begins to weave in the breeze.

We break through the line of trees to the sound of waves crashing against the shore. This beach is nothing like the white sand beach where we trained in the sun. Here, the shore is rocky, gritty, and strewn with fallen leaves and twigs.

But the ocean is the same.

The sky is beginning to lighten to gray, hints of an imminent dawn seeping into this realm.

"Forgive me, Àn'yīng," Hào'yáng says, breaking the silence between us. "So much of the pain in your life was caused by my existence." His gaze is set straight ahead, his tone light, but I can tell from the way his fingers tighten around the hilt of his sword that this is important to him. "Had your father not pulled me from the wreckage of the Imperial City that day, he would still be alive. You would not have been involved in any of this."

I stop and turn to Hào'yáng, and he mirrors my movements. The ocean wind stirs our hair and clothes, the faint light of the impending day limning his broad shoulders and white-and-gold uniform. I find myself thinking of the legends of gods and dragons, of how they blessed the mortal emperor's lineage with their magic. And I find, as I gaze at Hào'yáng, that he is no stranger, no distant prince. That all along, I've seen the traces of my boy in the jade in this man.

I clasp one hand to the pendant at my throat and reach

toward him with my other, daring myself to be bold. "May I?" I ask.

He says nothing. Instead, he simply leans forward slightly, dipping his face toward me. I close my eyes and let my fingers fall on his cheeks. I allow myself to slip back into the frightened, lonely girl of these nine years, hiding in the dark and dreaming of meeting her guardian in the jade. My hands graze Hào'yáng's jaw, feeling the warmth of his lips, the steadiness of his breath, the slight flutter of his lashes, and the sculpted edges of his features.

When I open my eyes again, he is still here. He has not vanished like a phantom in the night. He watches me calmly, haloed by the lightening sky and the sea.

I know him. I know him with the bone-deep awareness that our lives have been intertwined for years. That all along, he has been there by my side, watching over me unseen. That he has never abandoned me.

"In each life, we are born to walk a path," I say. "If this is the path the fates or my destiny has drawn for me in this life, then I will walk with you to the end."

Emotions ripple through Hào'yáng's eyes, like currents in the depths of an ocean. It's gone the next moment. "I think I have a story to finish telling you," he says. "It is the one Lady Shǐ'yǎ told me, of the reason I had to watch over the girl in the jade."

We sit atop an outcropping of rocks overlooking the sea, and Hào'yáng begins: "Long ago, an immortal fell in love with a mortal warrior. He was at the Temple of Dawn to train as a disciple and to compete in the Immortality Trials. Yet when he won them, he declined to take the pill of immortality and cross over into the Kingdom of Sky. He was needed back in the mortal realm, where his skills as a practitioner would serve the Kingdom of Rivers.

"The immortal bore him a child: a baby girl. The High Court was furious with her for defying the Heavenly Order—yet, by the laws of the Kingdom of Sky, her halfling daughter was entitled to a life in the immortal realm due to her immortal blood. Still, the mortal warrior left the Kingdom of Sky with his newborn daughter. In the Kingdom of Rivers, he married a woman he loved, who knew his secret and still loved him and his daughter, and who bore him a second child.

"All was at peace for years to come. Yet when the Kingdom of Night waged war, the mortal warrior enlisted to fight for the imperial army. By the time he reached the palace, it was too late: the emperor was dead, and all was destroyed. All except for one small life, buried in the rubble, one that the mó army had missed." Hào'yáng pauses here and looks directly at me. "You know this: that your father traded your spot in the Kingdom of Sky to save my life. He asked Lady Shī'yǎ to love me as she might their child. In turn, she broke a jade pendant she carried by her heart and gave half to him. Their destinies were written to be separated by sky and earth, but with the jade pendant, they would always carry a piece of the other with them.

"Lady Shī'yǎ handed me her half of the jade and told me that I owed my life to the little girl within. She told me that the jade would call out to me when she needed help, and that I had to protect the girl—because we were connected by threads of fate spun long before either of us were born."

The skies are aflame with pinks and corals and reds, setting this realm on fire. The night is receding; day is coming. It gilds Hào'yáng in a fierce, blazing light, as if the sun itself worships him.

"Ăn'yīng, I wish to show you something," he says, and rises, offering his hand.

I take it, lacing my fingers through his, and he draws me to him and gently places a palm on my back. Then he pulls us off the cliff.

My breath catches at the initial plunge. Yet beneath us, the ocean roars, rising to greet us. Waves entwine us, encircling us and lifting us into the sky. Droplets of foam arc through the air like crystals, catching the early sunlight.

"How . . . ?" I cannot find the words; I only know that ordinary practitioners cannot summon waves and water like this. At most, we may bend its energies to our use. But the sea wraps around Hào'yáng as if it is alive beneath his touch. A part of him.

"I never told you the story behind Meadowsweet," he says. "The truth is that she chose me at birth. You see, the mortal emperor's lineage carries a secret. There is a reason our symbol is the dragon; a reason the prophecies speak of our people as descendants of the dragons." He draws a deep breath, as though steeling himself for this confession. "The blood of dragons runs through us, Ăn'yīng, along with their power. Your father knew this, and Lady Shī'yă did, too."

The blood of dragons. I stare at Hào'yáng, at the ocean waves dancing behind him, as if he sits on a throne of water, and I think of the enormous spirit energy I've felt emanating from him—too strong for any mortal.

"So the legends are true," I say, and he nods. "Is it also true, then, that the dragons' old magic guards our realm?"

He nods again. "Our civilization was founded from the soul of the Azure Dragon, when she laid down her bones to gift us the Long River. Without the blood of the dragons, one cannot rule the Kingdom of Rivers. Though their magic runs strongest in my lineage, every mortal who has grown from these lands and drunk the waters of our kingdom is entitled to our realm. The mó do not belong here, and they never will."

But I remember something that makes me suddenly cold. "Hào'yáng," I whisper. "Yù'chén—he is the son of the demon queen Sansiran . . . and your father."

His grip tightens on me momentarily. Hào'yáng lifts his gaze, and his expression takes on the calculating look I have seen him wear when he thinks. "That explains how they were able to break through the wards of our realm and take down the Imperial City nine years ago," he muses.

"Does that make him eligible for the mortal throne?" I ask.

"I don't know," he admits. "There is no precedent to a halfling child of the demon queen and the mortal king. I imagine Sansiran has been using him to hold on to her tenuous grasp of the Imperial City. But until the Kingdom of Rivers completely sinks into the Kingdom of Night, our land will continue to reject them." Hào'yáng looks back at me. His gaze is calm but with the strength of steel and the power of oceans. "No matter what, Àn'yīng, I will win this war against the Kingdom of Night and take back the mortal throne from the mó.

"Lady Shǐ'yǎ recruited immortal allies who pledged themselves to our rebellion," he continues. "The next step is to rally what remains of mortals—of us—who wish to fight back against the mó. But first, I must seek the backing of a fourth realm."

"The realm of dragons," I murmur.

Hào'yáng nods. "The dragons are so ancient that they have almost faded into the canvas of our realms, just as the gods have. But the realm of dragons is very much real. It lies somewhere within the Four Seas. I will journey there."

"And I will go with you," I promise him, promise the skies beneath the sunrise, the spirit of our mother, who might be listening. "Every step of the way, I will fight with you, Hào'yáng. Until the Kingdom of Rivers is ours again."

His expression softens; the light of the rising sun dances across his features. "Àn'yīng, there is one last thing," he says, and hesitates for a breath. "You recall I told you that Lady Shī'yǎ, along with two other members of our rebellion, commanded a portion of the Heavenly Army? As one of the Eight Immortals, she held status in the Kingdom of Sky, and therefore a say and a stake in the politics of the realm. When I came of age and we began strategizing on taking back the mortal realm, she proposed a strategic alliance to secure the support of the High Court and the immortals in aiding me."

"A strategic alliance?" I frown. "I don't understand."

Hào'yáng turns his face to the horizon. "She proposed joining with me in marriage, so the alliance between the immortal realm and the heir of the mortal realm would be complete. It would only have been a marriage in name—I viewed her as my guardian and my mother—and it would only be for the duration of the war against the Kingdom of Night, so I could gain the pledge of support from the immortal troops."

An inkling of understanding dawns on me as Hào'yáng's

gaze returns to mine. His expression is tinged with regret. "Forgive me, again, for asking more of you," he continues. "You are her daughter by blood, and by the laws of the Kingdom of Sky, you are entitled to your status as her heir."

My heart is beating very fast. The world is suddenly lighter than I remember. "You are asking for my hand in marriage."

"Only if you would wish it. It would be a marriage in name only, to help me secure forces from the Kingdom of Sky to support the fight for our realm. You would be under no obligation to me in any way; you would be free to pursue your life as you wish, to love as you wish. And once the war is over, you would be free to annul the marriage." He pauses, his voice growing gentle. "If you would wish it at all . . . then, Àn'yīng, I would be honored to have your hand in marriage, and your support by my side in this fight."

The sky bleeds crimson, its light painting us red. I consider it, this moment of pure magic above a sunlit sea, hand in hand with my guardian in the jade, the mortal heir and son of dragons.

He catches my hesitation, and his eyes curve. "You do know you are free to reject my proposal?" he says with the hint of a smile, as if we share a secret between us. He draws back, straightening. "I would simply strategize my way into commanding a portion of the Heavenly Army by some other means. It would take longer, but—"

I step forward, I reach for his arms, and I pull his hands back to me. He falls silent, awaiting my response.

I have never disillusioned myself with the notion that I am destined for any great love. If I can be with my guardian in the jade in this way, if I can use my title as Shī'yǎ's heir to secure us forces in the Heavenly Army and win back our realm . . . wouldn't that be worth more than I have ever imagined for myself?

The ocean stirs, and it's as though the waters, the willows, the skies, whisper of destiny. The clouds shift, and for a moment, the sun spills clear and bright against the water, lancing off white-capped waves as if they are made of crystals and lapis.

I tilt my head, eyes narrowing slightly as I take in Hào'yáng's features, softened by the radiant glow of day. Briefly, I think of another face, one that the night worships and the shadows serve; one that remains in the shadows of my heart. One whose path was never fated to cross mine.

Perhaps I should never have danced on the ocean at night. Perhaps, all along, it was the sunlit sea that I yearned for.

"Yes," I say softly, pressing my palm to his chest. "If this is the path the gods or the fates have chosen for me, then I will walk it with you to the end."

Hào'yáng's hand moves to cover mine. His smile is radiant; the ocean reflects in his eyes as he beholds me. Around us, the waves dance under his command, rising higher and encircling us. Together, Hào'yáng and I turn to the horizon, where the sea meets the skies, where the clouds of the immortal realm linger. A battle wages, and we must play our part in the war that will engulf this world and all its realms.

I will return home. I will heal my mother's soul, I will see my little sister and hold her in my arms. There, I will marry the mortal heir and secure our political alliance. Together, we will command an army of immortals and mortals alike, and we will call upon the dragons of the Four Seas for their support.

And then we will take back the Kingdom of Rivers.

But first, in this moment, I stand in the arms of my guardian in the jade, surrounded by blue skies and clear waters, cradled by the glittering sea as we watch the sun rise over the realms.

Day breaks over the Kingdom of Rivers, warming the clouds and spilling over the land like honey. A journey that once took days takes mere hours flying on Meadowsweet's back. Autumn has swept over the mortal realm, deepening the foliage to a tapestry of gold and red, the rivers glinting like silver threads.

By the time we land before my village's pái'fāng, Meadowsweet is once again a horse the shade of moonlight. Hào'yáng's arms are warm and protective as he holds on to me, allowing me to steer. It is only the two of us. Of the rest of the candidates, a few will return to their own homes, but a surprising number agreed to fight with us against the Kingdom of Night. We have yet to reveal Hào'yáng's true identity to them. I gave them precise instructions to my village—but there is something I must do first, something that cannot wait.

We canter through the empty streets of Xī'lín. I don't stop until I see our plum tree.

Beneath its branches, a small figure straightens, and my heart flows out like a river to the sea. Before I know it, I've leapt off Meadowsweet and I'm running, my vision blurred by tears, and Méi'zi's sprinting toward me, calling my name. When we collide, I sweep her into my arms and hold her as if I never intend to let go. She's shaking, her bony little shoulders digging into mine. When she draws back, I wipe away

my tears long enough to take in the flush of her cheeks, the
shine to her eyes.

I don't forget the reason she is still alive. The person who
made this moment possible.

"Jiě'jie," she whispers. "You kept your promise."

I smooth out her hair. "Méi'zi," I say, and a laugh bubbles
up in my throat as I draw out the pill of immortality from my
storage pouch. "Everything will be all right."

My sister's eyes go wide as she beholds the pill, and then
even more so when she sees the heir and the dragonhorse
behind me. I only smile wider and take her hand, stepping
into our house. There will be plenty of time to explain after.

In the days since we came to cure her, Méi'zi has cleaned
the house. The living room smells like clean sheets and fresh
air, and a new bouquet of wildflowers sits on our table in a
cracked teacup. In the corner, perched against the couch and
staring out the open window, is my mother. She doesn't react
when Méi'zi and I approach.

Méi'zi casts me a frightened look, and I respond with a
tight nod. Our fingers are intertwined. Clasped between our
palms, gleaming like a pearl, is the pill of immortality we have
waited nine years for.

I swallow and give a firm nod. "Together," I whisper.

"Together," she echoes.

We slip the pill between my mother's parched lips, as easy
as popping in a tiny sunflower seed. Then we wait, counting
down each heartbeat, holding each other's hands like small
children.

Outside, a breeze rises, stirring the branches of the tree
and carrying its fragrance into the house. The sunlight shifts,
cracking over my mother's figure like yolk.

Mā blinks. She blinks again, then draws a deep, shuddering breath. Slowly, she turns her head to us, her gaze bleary yet growing clearer, as though she's waking from a long dream. When she speaks our names, her voice is like the sough of wind, but her eyes: they are radiant and warm, and they hold the sun within.

ACKNOWLEDGMENTS

I write this in the car on a trip to É'méi'shān, a mountain that sits between history and myths, and I would be remiss not to first thank the rich trove of Chinese stories and legends I grew up with that make appearances in this book. This book is my most self-indulgent yet, and it's for all the other kids who grew up with tales of immortals, magic pills, dragonhorses, and epic battles and love stories.

My gratitude, first, to my family, who raised me with such magic. Mama, who read me stories like 《宝莲灯》 and 《牛郎织女》 and countless others each night: I vividly remember your fingers—callused from chores—fluttering as you imitated those of the weaver girl making her tapestries. Lǎolǎo, whose sìhéyuàn served as inspiration for hidden magic in the corners and talismans on jade pendants, where I spent Sundays watching 《西游记》 and wished for a white dragonhorse of my own. Papa, whose boundless knowledge of history and geography I stitched into the tapestry of my own tales, who will entertain tales of gods and immortals flying through seas of clouds with me. And of course, Weetzy, who spent weekends and summers playing pretend with me that we were little warrior girls blessed with special powers to save the world, and who climbed mountains with me and braved rooms of rats to follow me through mystical temples. I know our family will have many more years of these magical travels walking the "rivers and lakes."

In the publication of this novel, I continue to be fortunate enough to work with the best team. My first thanks to Pete, who had been working with me on our flowery fairytale book until one night I sent him a dark, angsty, stabby sample I'd written in a fever dream—and who encouraged this drastic change of direction with his eternal verve and enthusiasm. (I promise I haven't given up on a flowery fairytale book. One day.) Thank you to Krista for loving my hot Chinese demon boys and putting up with the spice, for the wild travel stories, and of course, for always, always helping shape my stories to become the best they can be. Lydia, thank you for appreciating the spice; I am so honored to witness your incredible talent and to be publishing alongside you.

To the Park & Fine Literary Media team: Stuti Telidevara, thank you for being such a perfect partner to work with and never missing any details. Thank you to Abby Koons for being the best champion of my stories across the world; Danielle Barthel, Emily Sweet, and Andrea Mai for the tremendous support throughout the creative, marketing, and publication process.

Thank you to the team at Random House Children's Books: Colleen Fellingham and Candice Gianetti, for your incredible eyes over all the details and grammar I'm not smart enough to catch. Josh Redlich and Cynthia Lliguichuzhca, publicists extraordinaire, who have opened so many new doors for me this past year. And to Liz Drezner and Danzhu Hu for the stunning cover.

My gratitude to Claire Wilson and Ajebowale Roberts, as

well as the HarperVoyager team, who continue to champion my stories across the pond—I am so blessed to be working with the A-Team in the UK. Thank you to to Dong Qiu again for the incredible cover illustration that brings my darkly opulent Chinese world to life, and HarperVoyager UK for another breathtaking design.

My thanks to Daphne and Anissa, as well as the incredible teams at Illumicrate and FairyLoot, for bringing my stories into so many more hands—and in such ethereal, beautiful editions.

Thank you to my incredible, talented colleagues for taking the time to read this book in rough form, and for the kind blurbs you've offered. Rachel Gillig, Adalyn Grace, Danielle L. Jensen, Brigid Kemmerer, Vanessa Len, Nicki Pau Preto, Allison Saft, and Nisha J. Tuli—as a huge fan of all of your work, I am deeply humbled and eternally grateful for your support.

Thank you to my C-drama girls, in particular Jennifer Zhang, for the professional guidance on the Chinese title for this novel—as well as for the professional guidance on the best Chinese shows to watch. Thank you to my cousin, 赵小小哥哥, for all your knowledge on xianxia and wuxia novels and webnovels and the guidance on the Chinese title for this book. Thank you to Crystal, my most avid fan, who has been my first reader across all of my novels and is somehow still enthused about my writing career; I'm so grateful for the day we crossed paths at the NYU Transfer Orientation and you thought me mad for leaving SoCal. Thank you, Betty, for hosting me at your place as I finish this deadline—work trip mad sprint, and Kathlene, for putting up with my shenaniganery over the years. Rattata ftw, and let's congregate at the

H. Hub again soon. Thank you to all my friends, from Beijing to the U.S., for being alongside me all these years, and for bringing joy and positive energy into my life; the ski trips and future Japan writing retreats, the fantastic chats about publishing and life and the incredible stories I'm lucky enough to read over the years; the good food and good drinks and good vibes.

Thank you to Mom and Dad Sin, and Ryan and Sherry and Queen Olive for all the SoCal days, the yummy homemade food, the mahjong and laughter.

Finally, thank you to my pewp, Clement, for being there in all facets of life; for the morning and evening LTs, taking care of our adulting things and our house-searching when I was struggling with the job and deadlines, the Blob days and the anti-Blob days. Thank you for leaving space on the bed for GTSS. I can't think of any greater joy than sharing this ordinary life with you.

ABOUT THE AUTHOR

Amélie Wen Zhao was born in Paris and grew up in Beijing, where she spent her days reenacting tales of legendary heroes, ancient kingdoms, and lost magic at her grandmother's courtyard house. She attended college in the United States and now resides in New York City, working as a finance professional by day and fantasy author by night. In her spare time, she loves to travel and spend time with her family in China, where she's determined to walk the rivers and lakes of old just like the practitioners in her novels do. Amélie is is the *Sunday Times* and internationally bestselling author of the Song of the Last Kingdom duology and the Blood Heir trilogy.

ameliezhao.com